SECOND CHANCE MATES

FATED SOULS SERIES
BOOK 1

SAVANNA ROSE

Copyright © 2024 by Savanna Rose

All rights reserved.

No part of this book may be reproduced or transmitted in any form or by any means, electronic or mechanical, including photocopying, or by any information storage and retrieval system without the author's written permission, except for the use of brief quotations in a book review.

This book is a work of fiction. All characters and places in this book are fictitious. Any resemblance to actual persons, living or dead, events, or locales is entirely coincidental.

Cover design by Trinah Kei

Editing by Kirsty McQuarrie

This book is intended for an 18+ audience.

This book is written in British English.

*To anyone healing from invisible scars.
You are seen, heard, and loved.*

TRIGGER AND CONTENT WARNINGS

- Sexual abuse (not on page and not between MMC and FMC)
- Physical and emotional abuse (not between MMC and FMC)
- Self-harm
- Suicide ideation
- Panic attacks
- Anxiety and PTSD
- Nightmares
- Amnesia
- Grief
- Descriptions of violence, gore and torture

1

JAXON

*P*ain.

Sometimes, *pain* is all I feel. The heart-wrenching, soul-destroying kind. It's like a void in your heart that can never be fixed.

Happiness is nothing but a distant memory. Half my soul is missing, and I'll never be able to fill the emptiness that suffocates my chest. It's been nine months since I watched my beautiful mate be brutally murdered. Everyone tells me there was nothing I could have done to prevent it, but that's not true. There is always something.

I blame myself every damn day.

All I remember is the screaming...the *endless* screaming. From her. From me. It haunts my dreams in the middle of the night and occupies my mind when I'm wide awake. I will never be able to escape it.

My other half is gone. *My* mate is gone. I will never see her face again. The heartache is unbearable—even today. Being an Alpha doesn't make it any better; it only makes things worse. The pack are relying on me, and I've done nothing but mourn for her in sheltered silence.

I've been hard on my pack since she passed, but I'm not entirely sure what they expect of me. I don't even know what I expect of myself. My life and future are gone, and now, I'll live the remainder of my life mateless.

Everyone has heard the horror stories of mateless wolves. They eventually go insane from loneliness and depression. The days don't get better. The pain gradually worsens, and eventually, our wolves give up from their broken hearts.

A knock at my office door stirs me away from my desk, although I was hardly paying attention to my work. I struggle to stay focused for extended periods of time. My mind seems to wander, and I'm left in this spiralling rut.

"Come in," I shout as the door cracks open.

My eyes focus on my Beta, Kayden, as he stands in the doorway to my office. "Alpha," he greets me.

"Do you need something?" I clear my throat and glance back down to the papers on my desk. I can't even remember where I left off. My eyes flitter across the words.

Did I even start?

Kayden walks across my office and stands directly in front of me, crossing his thick arms over his chest. "I wanted to know if you'd have dinner with us tonight. It's been a long time sinc–"

My hand raises. I don't even want to hear it. I know I haven't been the best Alpha. I don't need him to state the obvious. "I'm busy. Another time."

When he doesn't move or dismiss himself, I look up. His dark eyes are watching me carefully. I sigh, leaning back into my chair. "I know you're going through a tough time, Jaxon. But we rarely see you as it is. The pack needs you. They can support you."

My jaw tenses, bones cracking in the process. "I can't."

"Why?"

I run a hand down my face. This isn't the conversation I want to have right now. I need to finish this work, and this is another unnecessary distraction.

"Because I can't bear the thought of seeing other people happy, alright?" I snap, instantly regretting the words. Kayden's brows soften, and he drops his hands to his sides. "Is that what you wanted to hear? That I'm selfish as fuck? Since I lost Julia, I can't find it in me to look at Lucy and Sebastian together, or anyone, for that matter. It fucking kills me."

Kayden's mouth parts, and I brace myself for his bullshit, but it never comes. Instead, he consoles me, and I hate that even more. "It's not selfish, Jaxon. You lost a part of your soul; we all understand that's something that won't heal overnight. But we're here for you. We want to show you what a pack's love can do. We're family, and all of us want to help. But come on, Jaxon. Give us a chance."

Love.

I silently scoff at the word. The only love I want is from my soulmate.

But she's gone.

When I hear my Beta sigh and take a step away from my desk, I sink further into my seat. "You know where we are if you want to join us. I can't imagine how hard this is for you, but we don't want to see you deteriorate. I'm running out of things to suggest, and I hate seeing you like this."

"Me, too," I murmur as I numbingly stare at a spot on my desk.

Moments later, my office door shuts with a soft click. "Fuck," I mutter under my breath and swipe a bunch of papers onto the floor out of frustration and self-hatred.

A concoction of emotions crawls through my body like

trapped poison in my veins. The ones that paralyse me every day and take control of every thought.

Sadness.

Guilt.

Regret.

My airways begin to tighten. I ball my hand into a fist and shoot up from my chair. My back hunches over my desk as I try to control my breathing. Fuck. I need air. I need to get the hell out of here.

I storm across my office, throwing open the door. It crashes into the wall loudly as I rush down the stairs before my lungs constrict from all the tightness consuming me.

"Jaxon!" I hear my sister, Lucy, call out to me.

But I ignore her, my vision tunnelling. I set my eyes on the front door, and then I'm outside before I can even blink. I need to get as far away from here as possible.

My entire pack has taken the hit of my grief far too many times. I despise myself for the pain I've caused them, but they will never understand the agony I experience daily. The only way I know how to deal with it is to isolate myself. Grieving is not easy; anyone who says it gets better is a liar.

As soon as I step outside, the crisp air whips against the back of my neck. The heat that radiates from my body is alarming, but it's the least of my worries. I rip open the door to my car, start the engine, and drive away. My mind is occupied with a thousand different thoughts, making my fingers wrap around the leather steering wheel tightly.

I wish I could run out into the woods and shift, spend the evening with nature. That would calm me. But I can't even do that.

When Julia died, my wolf went into hiding. I haven't seen him for nine months. I haven't felt him—haven't felt his instincts or feelings. It's like he's dead inside me. The only reason I know he's still there is because I'm alive.

If I lost him, too, I wouldn't be here right now.

He's weak and heartbroken—we both are—but he doesn't want to be seen. I'm envious of him in that sense. I would do anything to be wholly alone.

What is the point of living without your mate, the only person that could ever make you feel truly complete? The bond never lies. The bond is eternal. The bond that I will never get to experience again.

I suddenly snap out of my trance and realise I've been driving for minutes on end without thinking.

Shit.

My mind needs the distraction and a change of scenery, but it's hard when it wanders without permission.

My fists continue to grip the steering wheel as I turn down a long, empty road. The night is pitch-black, the sky full of clouds and not a single star in sight. That doesn't make me feel any better. Sometimes, I like to think she's watching over me. My own angel looking from the sky above, yet I cannot see one star that wants to peek out behind the clouds of pure darkness.

The road starts to narrow, and the trees grow taller over me, but it's an illusion. I drag a hand through my hair and focus on the road ahead. Not Julia. *Anything* but Julia.

Why is nothing ever simple? I wish I could switch off my overactive brain for even a minute. That would be true peace.

My nose tingles as a soft scent swarms me. All my senses become unbearably sensitive. I glance down at my arms to find my skin rising in goosebumps. I straighten in my seat, squinting my eyes at the dimly lit road. I have exceptional vision, but something is off.

The smell is faint, but it's undeniably beautiful—a subtle scent of vanilla mixed with a heavy dose of chestnut. Where is it coming from? It's becoming stronger by the second. Pins and needles develop in my hand, and I take my fingers off the steering wheel to give them a quick stretch.

The darkness of the trees reflects down onto the road. It looks a lot more sinister than it actually is. They blow aggressively in the wind as if the atmosphere has taken a turn for the worst. My foot presses on the brakes, slowing down. I'm on edge from twitching at every movement I see.

My eyes snap to the left side of the road as the bushes rustle. The scent is even more intense now. It's suffocating my lungs to the point I'm struggling to breathe.

Within a second, I slam my foot down on the brakes full force when I see a young girl emerge from the wooded area. She dashes across the road with a slight limp, her clothes shredded.

She attempts to make it to the other end of the road without looking. I almost hit her. I do my best to swerve, but there is nowhere else to go on this narrow road. My tyres screech to a halt as her hand presses on the hood of my car, and her body wobbles, her feet now out of sequence.

Her terrified eyes peer at me through my windscreen, her chest heaving with every breath she takes. Her entire body is trembling, with cuts and bruises painting her skin.

The scent is so intense that my heart begins to race rapidly. I capture her dark, willow eyes with mine. For a moment, it's like time stands still, and nothing else matters.

My wolf howls inside me, bringing everything back to life I thought I had lost. I part my lips in complete and utter shock, unable to move from my frozen stance and the new waves of emotions I forgot existed.

Mate.

2

JAXON

The girl's eyes are wide and alert with pure terror. I watch as she rips her hands off the hood and darts into the woods.

I hook my fingers into the door handle. "Wait!"

Her knobbly knees attempt to carry her as fast as she can move. The smell of fear drips off her with every step she takes. It mixes with her scent and leaves a sour taste in my mouth. *Fuck*. The last thing I want is to scare her further, but it's clear she needs medical attention.

It doesn't take long to catch up to her with my long legs. She's weak, but she's obviously pumped full of adrenaline and is likely using every last drop of energy. Her brunette hair is a matted mess as it cascades down her back and over her shoulders.

"Please, stop," I say gently. "I want to help you."

Her breathing hitches at the sound of my voice echoing across the trees. Somehow, her legs pick up speed, her feet dodging the roots that have overgrown and are protruding out of the ground.

I manage to catch up with her, but I know better than to

touch her right now. I have no idea what she's been through or where she's come from. Her wide eyes look up at me in shock as she stops in her tracks. The loudness of her lungs is all I can hear, along with the heavy thumping of my heart.

Now that I can finally get a good look at her, she's severely malnourished. The clothes she's wearing are hanging off her bones, dirt marks smearing across what's left of the fabric. There is a large gash that covers her abdomen, along with other bruises and wounds that look infected.

As I take one cautious step forward, she takes a small, shaky one back. Her bare foot crunches on a fallen branch, and it cracks under her weight. I blink, and her whole body loses balance. She falls down onto her backside, a quiet hiss escaping her mouth.

My hands hold up in defence, somehow trying to prove that I'm not going to harm her, but something tells me it's not going to be easy. She scurries backwards on her hands until her spine hits the stump of a tree with a thud.

Those petrified eyes glisten with tears which soon fall down her cheeks, rolling over her pale skin. "P-please don't hurt me," her quiet voice begs.

I lower down to her level, attempting not to seem intimidating, but she flinches anyway. Her body curls into a ball as if she's trying to protect herself by hiding behind her knees.

"I'm not going to hurt you," I whisper as I drop my tone.

The girl's breathing becomes harsher. Her gaze hesitantly wanders over my face and studies my body language.

"It's okay," I say. "I'm not going to hurt you."

I glance over my shoulder for a split second to gauge how far we've moved from my parked car. Out of the corner of my eye, I see her scramble and run off with a strangled cry.

"Please, stop." I stand and follow after her. "I want to help you. You're hurt."

Before she can get too far, I lean forward and wrap my hand around her wrist to stop her. I know I shouldn't have touched her. It's the last thing I should have done, but I can't let her go—not after my wolf's discovery.

As soon as our skin touches, tingles race through my arm. It paralyses my body for a moment, and I resist the urge to close my eyes at the new sensation—a feeling that is all too familiar yet completely different.

"I'm sorry," I say, my heart straining. I release her. "I'm sorry. I shouldn't have touched you."

"Please," she whimpers, her body trembling with panic. "Please, just let me go."

Her bottom lip quivers as tears continuously fall from her red eyes.

"You're hurt and clearly in danger. Please let me help you. I'm not going to hurt you," I plead, but I realise how hard it must be for her to trust a stranger.

My wolf is clawing at me to do more, but I don't know what else I can do. I refuse to force her and bruise her trust further. It's the last thing she needs. I can't let her run off into the night, not knowing if she's safe or if she'll make it.

She shakes her head vigorously. "I'm not going anywhere with you."

I sigh. *Lucy. I need your help. Right now.* I demand through our mindlink.

My eyes remain focused on the girl my wolf screams is our mate. I'd be a liar if I said my mind wasn't a mess right now, but I can figure everything else out later. Her well-being is a priority, not my newfound emotions. Mate or not, she needs help.

"I'm not going to hurt you," I say again. I could say it a

million times, but I know she's not going to believe me. I dread to think what awful events she's been through. "I would *never* hurt you. I won't touch you again. I promise."

She scrunches her eyebrows together, her head pulling back slowly. "I don't believe you."

What's wrong? Are you okay? Lucy's voice echoes around my head.

I quickly take in my surroundings and tell my sister where I am. She'll see my car on the edge of the road. Despite my wolf screaming at me, I ignore the lightbulb flickering in my head.

Okay. I'll be five minutes.

"You don't have to believe me right now," I say gently, even though she continues to tremble with what must be uncontrollable fear. "But I promise you can trust me."

Her expression twists into a look of horror. I curse in my mind.

"You don't know me!"

The words she screams are pure distress. It makes my wolf wince to even imagine what she's endured. I choose to push it to the back of my mind for the sake of not losing control.

"I know I don't know you, and you don't know me, but I can get you to safety. I can get you the help that you need. I know it's a lot for you to trust me right now. I'm a total stranger, I get it. But please, I won't hurt you," I try again, but it's like I'm at a dead-end. "I only want to help."

"Please, I don't want this," she sobs. "I just want to get away. Please. *Please.*"

I open my mouth to speak, but the sound of Lucy's voice floats through my head. *Jaxon, we're here. Is it safe?*

Yes.

My eyes stay trained on the terrified girl when I hear

footsteps behind me. The hairs on the back of my neck stand as I sense Lucy and Sebastian's scents. "What's going on?" my sister demands.

I twist my body slightly to face her, and Lucy immediately looks past me to see the girl sitting against the tree, crying her heart out. "Oh my Goddess," she gasps quietly. "Are you okay?"

She pushes herself further into the tree, digging her heels into the dirt. I watch her mouth, but she says nothing. She flicks her eyes between Lucy and Sebastian hesitantly.

"Are you hurt?" Lucy tries again. It's obvious she's injured, but making small talk is better than nothing. The presence of a woman might help her trust us.

The girl shivers against the tree from the crisp night and lack of clothes on her body. "I-I just want to get away," she murmurs again.

"Then, let us help you," Lucy says softly. "We can get you all the help you need. You're safe with us. You're injured. We can help get you cleaned up, and then we can get you to wherever you need to go."

For a moment, I see her guard drop. It's clear she's battling with herself whether she should believe us or not. I get it; trauma doesn't go away in seconds. But I fear she's about to make herself incredibly ill if she's not seen to soon.

The sound of a branch cracks behind us, and I spot Sebastian inching closer. I tense my shoulders to find her trembling from the unexpected noise. Lucy shoots him a look, and Sebastian moves away. "Please, please, please," she begs desperately.

"Hey," Lucy's hand moves forward, but she doesn't touch her. The girl eyes her fingers. "Hey, easy. It's okay. It's–"

I watch as her eyes roll into the back of her head, and

she slumps against the tree. "Shit," I curse. Her exhaustion must have forced her body to shut down.

"What should we do?" Sebastian asks.

"Take her home," I state.

Lucy looks at me like I'm crazy. Maybe I am. But she doesn't know the main reason I want her to come home with us. "We can't take her home. That's literally kidnapping, Jaxon. We weren't brought up to be those kinds of wolves."

"What do you expect us to do?" I hiss under my breath. "Drop her off at the police station? Goddess knows who or what is after her, and I don't trust those shitty cops. She's already in an emotional state and clearly vulnerable. The safest place for her is our house."

Lucy's blue eyes flick between mine rapidly. "Or the damn hospital, Jaxon. She's a human."

"And?"

"She doesn't belong."

My jaw grinds. "And she's about to die if we don't get her seen to as soon as possible."

Sebastian sighs from behind us, and Lucy glances at him. "And when she wakes up?"

I shrug because I haven't thought that far ahead. I want her safe first. "We'll figure it out. Please, just trust me. I need to do this."

Lucy's eyes are weary, but she nods after a few moments. "Fine," she huffs. "But only because her injury looks severely infected, and even I can't heal something that serious, especially on a human."

"Can you keep her in a deep sleep until we get home?" I ask. "Use your powers to keep her safe for the time being. The last thing we want is her waking up mid-drive and trying to throw herself onto the road."

"I don't like this, Jaxon," she grumbles but moves closer.

"I want her healed, and I want her to find her family, friends, or whoever can help her after whatever she's been through."

I bite down on my tongue before I say the wrong thing. "Agreed."

Lucy gently casts a hand over the girl's face. A wave of energy emits into her body which will keep her asleep for a little while longer. Once she's in a comfortable, deep sleep, I scoop her up into my arms and carry her to my car.

I choose to ignore all the sensations running through my body. Now is not the time to be having a revelation when she's fighting for her life. I might be desperate to know more, but her health comes first.

"The infirmary?" Lucy suggests.

I nod. "Then we can get her settled in one of the spare rooms for privacy."

Once we get back to the house, I carry her towards the infirmary. A pack doctor inches closer to see the injured human in my arms. "Alpha?"

"She needs her own room."

"Right this way."

I step into the private room and let her down onto the soft bed, her frail body dropping as she rests against the pillows.

"Jaxon?" Lucy grasps my attention, but her voice is too loud for my liking. "Are you going to tell me what on earth is going on?"

I press a finger to my lips and shake my head once.

She's still sleeping. I shoot through our mindlink.

One of Lucy's brows flexes, and she places her hands on her hips, waiting for an answer. I love my sister to death, but it's annoying that she always figures out when something is wrong, even when I feel like I'm good at hiding it.

I hold her stare. *She's my mate.*

She doesn't move. She doesn't say a word; she just stares at me.

What do you mean?

She's my mate. My wolf felt it. I felt it. Something is there between us, and I know that sounds crazy, but I can't explain it. I just know.

Lucy looks dumbfounded. I am, too. *Jaxon, are you su–*

Yes. Yes. I'm sure. I'm not going crazy. I know what I feel.

How? Second-chance mates are a myth.

Evidently not. I know what I feel. Just trust me on this.

Her eyes wander over my mate as she sleeps against the white bedsheets. *What's her name?*

I don't know. We didn't get that far. A deep sigh escapes my lips. I study her chest as she breathes, every movement rigid and harsh. *But I know whatever she's gone through has been hell.*

My fists tense, and I grit my teeth in anger at the state I found her in.

I turn back to Lucy. *When she wakes up, can you please be here to help? She's petrified, and maybe seeing another woman will help her calm down. I'll have the doctors on standby.*

Of course. She nods and she reaches out to take my hand, giving it a quick squeeze. *I can't believe this, Jaxon.*

I can't believe it either.

3

JAXON

Lucy leaves the room to locate my leading pack doctors whilst the other doctor begins to check her temperature. "Her abdomen," I point. "She's wounded, and it looks infected."

The doctor glances at the large gash and studies it for a moment. "Gemma and Alyssa will need to heal this. I fear my powers won't be strong enough for a human body."

When he leaves, I find myself studying the fragile girl lying against the soft sheets. From an outsider's perspective, I realise how odd this situation may look, but I couldn't have left her. I want answers. I need to know who did this to her. I need to know how it's possible that I have a second-chance mate.

She begins to stir from her sleep as soon as Lucy is gone. The second she sees me standing at the end of her bed, her back twists in fear, and she pushes herself into the bed.

"Hey, hey," I murmur softly. "It's okay."

She shakes her head at me as she takes in her unknown surroundings. She passed out in the woods and magically wakes up in a random house she doesn't recognise. This is a recipe for disaster.

She's awake. I say desperately to Lucy.

On my way. Gemma is coming now.

"I'm not going to harm you," I raise my arms in defence. "We want to help you heal and get better. That's all. We're not here to hurt you or to make you do anything you don't want to."

Those big brown eyes are swimming with tears again, and I can't fathom how tired she must be. I want nothing more than for her to see the pack doctor, have a hot meal and a bath. It won't solve everything, but it'll be a start.

Lucy emerges from the hall, and my mate jumps, her gaze flicking between us with quick intensity. "Hi," Lucy says gently, smiling towards her as she pauses by my side. "What's your name?"

Those saddened eyes cloud with terror. She clamps down on her lip so hard it almost draws blood. I don't like the sight of it; it's like she's trying to harm herself, and it sets my wolf off into a murderous frenzy. My lungs take down as much air as possible to calm these waves of fury.

"I'm Lucy," my sister introduces herself as she presses a hand to the centre of her chest. "And this is Jaxon, my brother."

The fear that radiates from her makes my stomach churn in agony. Bile rises in my throat. "What's your name?" she asks again.

When she doesn't reply, Lucy takes a step forward. The girl shields herself with her arms. "It's Ava," she answers, her voice croaky. "Just p-please don't hurt me."

"We would never hurt you, Ava."

Ava's eyes soften a fraction at her voice.

"We want to help you," she tries again.

"I don't want your help!" Ava's voice trembles. "I don't know you."

I shift between my feet. "No," I admit. "You don't. But if you don't get that wound checked out, it could make you really sick."

Ava glances down at the gash in her stomach. It's bloody and gooey. I have no idea how long it's been like that, but I can already see the infection spreading. With her human genes, it won't take long for it to dive into her bloodstream and end her life.

"Please let the doctors check you over," I say again. "Then you can have something to eat, a soak in the bath, and fresh clothes."

Ava's eyes glisten at me, and she releases a quiet sob. "I'm so tired."

I glance at Lucy and she flashes me the same heartbreaking look. This is fucking destroying me. "Then, let us help you," I take one step towards the bed. "It'll only be a quick check-up with the doctor. We can go at your pace; you can stop for as many breaks as you want. You don't need to fear us."

Lucy offers me a supportive smile. Thank the Goddess I've said the right thing rather than letting my possessive side get the better of me.

"Okay," she whimpers, but the word is a struggle. "I don't want a man touching me. I don't want men anywhere near me."

I nod in understanding. I'm definitely the problem right now. "Of course."

My leading doctors arrive seconds later. They're sisters who have been training as healers for the majority of their lives and are wise beyond their years. I greet Gemma and Alyssa at the door and welcome them inside the room.

"Good evening, Jaxon," Alyssa bows and then her sister —using my name instead of my title in front of a human. "It would be best if you left the room so we can examine her within her own boundaries."

I meet Ava's eyes. Her back is still firmly against the wall. "Sure." I nod and focus on the pair of them. "Look after her, please, and do everything you can to heal that wound."

"Of course, Jaxon." Gemma offers me a smile.

A few moments later, I leave the room with Lucy. I begin to pace the hall, a tight sensation clenching around my windpipe. "I don't know how I can earn her trust."

"Patience," Lucy states immediately. "This isn't something that can be solved within hours or days. I see the way you've been looking at her, and I can tell you now, the last thing she needs is to be manhandled by you."

My jaw grits at her words. "I didn't manhandle her."

"No, but I can see the thought racing through your mind. You need to gauge that self-control because this isn't about you right now, Jaxon." She huffs and throws her arms over her chest.

I pin her with a stare. "I am using every ounce of self-control not to try and comfort her because I know that isn't what she needs."

"Maybe we should head to the kitchen, and give Gemma and Alyssa some time," Lucy suggests.

I shake my head. "No. I want to be here to hear what they say."

She sighs and leans against the wall. "Fine."

"Thank you for what you did in the woods," I say after a few moments.

"Well, I'd be stupid not to use the powers I was blessed with, hmm?"

I nod once. "Of course you're the one who was blessed by our witch ancestors, while I was left with nothing."

The corner of Lucy's lip tilts. "You were given the Alpha title. I think that's good enough."

Lucy's abilities to heal are only half of what my pack doctors can achieve, but she possesses greater power elsewhere. The selfless things she has done for this pack, I'll be forever thankful for.

Thirty minutes later, Gemma and Alyssa emerge.

"Alpha," Alyssa directs towards me. "We have healed the wound on her abdomen. It's clear of any infection. It will be sore for a while, but with rest and good nourishment, she'll be healed in no time."

I step forward. "Thank you, both," I say heavily. "I'm extremely grateful."

Gemma gives me a soft smile. "We know you are."

"She's asleep at the moment because we needed her to be still and calm when we cleaned the injury. But she should wake soon, and we recommend water and a small portion of food," Alyssa says while straightening out her white shirt.

"Of course." I nod and glance back at Lucy. "I'll have someone bring food over from the kitchen. Are there any other serious injuries we need to be aware of?"

"We've checked her over for broken bones and internal bleeding. One of her ribs is cracked, and she has sprained ankles. When she has enough strength, we'll be able to heal the rest of her, but we need to take our time and not overwhelm her human body." Gemma offers me a smile.

When Gemma and Alyssa dismiss themselves, I step back into the room with Lucy by my side. I don't loom over the bed to study her injury; I trust they've done the best they can.

"I think we need to give her some time to adjust," Lucy comments.

"Yeah." I glance at my sister, but her focus is on Ava. "What is it?"

Lucy's eyes start to water, and her mouth opens, but nothing comes out. *Oh, Goddess.* Her voice echoes into my head.

"What's happening?"

"H-her body, her mind is dragging me in." She pauses to take a strangled breath. "I-I can't stop it. It's going to make me see her past."

My eyes widen in surprise. Lucy usually has a strong grasp on how her powers are used, and it's rare she can't control them. She's always had the ability to look into someone's past, but sometimes, it takes her by surprise, and she has no choice but to accept it. It's a blessing and a curse.

"Oh, Goddess," she cries out again, but this time, her eyes have clouded over, and the blueness of them fades. "I'm going to see everything. Fuck. Jaxon, I can't stop it."

"It's okay," I plead with her. "Relax, Lucy. Breathe. Just breathe through it."

Lucy's body slumps forward, and her knees hit the floor. I lower down beside her and clutch the back of her neck. Her eyes are misty, and she's non-responsive.

"Shit," I curse.

She trembles over and over. I glance up at Ava, but she's sleeping peacefully on the bed. I close my eyes and pray whatever happens in the next ten minutes isn't going to have consequences for Ava or Lucy—especially since my sister's powers are unpredictable.

4

AVA

When the lunchtime school bell rings, we all stand up from the bench we've made our home for the last forty-five minutes. "Are you coming to study hall?" Kayleigh asks.

I shake my head as I slide my bag over my shoulder. "Not yet. I'm going to meet Danny in the car park quickly—he said he wanted to see me. Stall Miss Lowe for me, please?"

Kayleigh rolls her eyes, but she can't fight the smile that creeps onto her lips. "Alright, lover girl. You owe me."

"Thank you," I exhale gratefully before giving her a half-hearted hug. I don't have long to see Danny. He's always busy playing football at lunch.

I dart off to the sports block and approach the car park. My eyes scan the area, hoping I'm not caught by a teacher for being out of class.

My legs carry me to the other end of the car park, where I spot Danny's car, but he's nowhere to be seen. I check my phone, and surprisingly, I have no messages either. I huff out a breath and slump against the side of his door when a van pulls up with blacked-out windows.

The hairs on the back of my neck stand immediately, and I push off the car. I grab my bag tighter and stare at the man as he peers out of the window, looking at me like I'm an animal at the zoo.

"Hey, darlin'." His voice is rough as he chews on a toothpick.

I furrow my brows at him before walking away. Do they not have better security at this school? Either that or one of the maintenance men is being extra creepy today.

The van slowly pulls away and begins to follow me as I walk towards the exit of the car park. I keep my head down. It's best not to engage.

"Aren't you a pretty little thing?"

When I look at him with disgust, he drops me a sleazy wink which makes my stomach roll with discomfort. My feet burst into a run, but I hear the van door open and slam behind me.

"Grab her," another voice demands loudly. "She's the one. She's *mine*."

Blood pounds in my ears as I run to the path, but I'm too slow. A sweaty hand clamps over my mouth to muffle my scream, as forceful hands latch onto my arms, tugging me backwards. I kick and wriggle, but I'm outnumbered. The back door of the van opens, and I'm shoved inside. Darkness swarms me as they slam the doors shut and laugh.

~

My face burns from the punch that leaves me whimpering. Blood swims in my mouth, making me nauseous. I'm sick of the taste. I'm sick of swallowing back copper that burns my throat.

"Now, tell me again, where did you used to live?"

I partially open my swollen eyes to look at my kidnapper, Lucien.

"I-I don't remember," I croak between heavy breaths. Blood drips down my chin as I speak and splashes onto the stone-cold floor.

Lucien flashes me a smile of triumph. "Good pet. And your parents?"

"My foste–"

The next hit is more painful than the last. My entire face stings beyond words. Flinching, I release a groan of agony. My body almost touches the floor. But before I hit the ground, Lucien takes a fist full of my hair and tugs me towards his face.

I stare back into his lifeless mossy eyes that I have despised since the moment I came here. My jaw clenches, and I am hit by another wave of tangy blood that makes me gag. "Who are your parents?" he asks again.

My lips tremble, and I know better than to act smart or tell the truth. "I-I don't remember," I whisper as I flick my eyes between his.

Lucien finally releases my head and throws me to the floor. "Good," he grumbles as he stands up and dusts his hands on his trousers. "We'll come back to this again tomorrow. The quicker you forget, the quicker we can get on with everything we have in store for you."

My entire body shakes against the wet floor. I close my eyes as they fight to stay open. I've never felt so defeated and useless. My only wish is that this is all over soon. Yet, I know barely anyone will be looking for me.

∼

"There's my beautiful girl." Lucien flashes his evil smile at me as he enters the room I'm chained up in.

I stare up at him through my damp lashes. "Fuck you." My voice is a weak whisper.

His dark, cackling laugh echoes around the freezing room as he takes a few steps closer. I flick my eyes to his hand as he slaps my cheek hard. The corner of my lip splits open within seconds. Blood bursts across my tongue, but I'm used to it now.

My head rises as I look up at him. His chest heaves with fuelled disgust at my profanity. I gather the blood in my mouth and spit down onto the ground next to his feet. Before I know it, he's grabbing my face painfully between his fingers and lining his nose up against mine. "Oh...you stupid little mate. Everything would have turned out alright if you were an actual wolf and not a human."

I refuse to let my eyes water. He's been going on about werewolves and mates since I was brought here against my will. I didn't believe him at first, but he showed me the transformation, which I thought was impossible. A part of me was convinced that I had died, but the reality soon hit.

I'm living in hell on Earth instead.

My gaze zeros on him. "Do you know how embarrassing it would be to bring out a pathetic, weak, human Luna like you?"

"Just let me go," I say through gritted teeth.

Lucien pouts and twists his head, his evil eyes flashing at me without an ounce of remorse. "Oh, sweetheart, but that's no fun!"

His fingers dig into the flesh on my cheeks, which makes me wince, but I refuse to make a sound. I don't want to give him that satisfaction. I want to fight. "You still owe my Beta and my male wolves a show."

Immediately, my skin runs cold, goosebumps invade my arms. I clench my throat to stop the bile from rising, but the mention of his pack has my body triggering its fight-or-flight instinct. Except I have nowhere to go, and the only choice I have is to play by their despicable, unfair rules.

~

"You even think about showing me up, and I swear I'll make you wish you were never born." Lucien's eyes are lifeless as always, but today they seem deadlier, and by the tone of his words, I don't want to play games.

His voice echoes around my head. *I'll make you wish you were never born.* Little does he know, I already do. I know I'm never getting out of here, and now, I'm nothing but a dead soul inside a shell.

"It's showtime," he sings in my ear, and I grimace at the heat of his breath on my skin. I study his hand as it raises before he gives my cheek a light tap.

He pulls me up roughly by the strands of my matted hair, making me cry out in agony. He drags me into the hall and down to the room of nightmares. Terror doesn't even do it justice. This room makes me wish I was dead.

As I enter, I can't ignore the jeers, misogynistic comments, and wolf whistles that are directed my way. The testosterone in this room is lethal, and I wouldn't wish this on my worst enemy—unless it's Lucien, then I'd make him go through this a thousand times over.

My head remains down as I step inside, refusing to make eye contact with any of these hormonal wolves who clearly haven't seen a female in a long time. "Remember what I said," Lucien demands quietly in my ear. "You don't want to let me down today, sweetheart."

Nothing could prepare me for what is about to happen, even though I know the process. I wish I could say it gets easier, but it doesn't. Every time, I wish someone would put me out of my misery—bludgeon me to death, quick and easy.

Lucien throws me down onto the floor in the middle of his wolves. My knees scrape against the uneven concrete. I grit my teeth, but I don't make a noise. My shoulder hits the ground as silhouettes surround me.

"Get on your knees, bitch." I hear Lucien's Beta, Damon, as he grips the back of my head and yanks me up onto my knees, which crack against the hard ground.

I look straight ahead and despise the sight. Tears roll down my cheeks endlessly. All I can do is wonder what I ever did to deserve this.

∼

My body has been attempting to give up for a long time now. There is barely anything left of me. I can't remember the last time I had a decent meal.

I cannot tell you how happy I am to die.

The door to my chambers opens. I don't usually expect Lucien at this time. Except it isn't Lucien; it's his little brother, Evan. He's the only kind soul in this place. His youthful face is like seeing flowers after a rain shower.

"Ava," he says softly as he approaches me on the floor. A cold hand presses to my cheek, forcing my eyes to look at him, but I'm weaker than I've ever been before. "Ava, look at me."

My body trembles. "Evan," I whimper hoarsely. He starts to undo my shackles with a bunch of keys. "W-what are you doing?"

"They are going to kill you, Ava. You need to go now before they get back!"

My head shakes from confusion. Is this real? I must be dreaming. I haven't had a drop of water in forever. I'm going out of my mind.

"I-I don't understand," I murmur, attempting to lick my cracked lips but my tongue is equally as dry.

"Ava," he shakes me again. "Don't you dare be stupid right now. Lucien rejected you. You have a whole life to live. Please just run and never look back. Get as far as possible and go seek help. I should have stood up for you sooner. I need you to go before they come back!"

Evan unbuckles my last shackle, and it hits the floor with a thud. "There is a door down at the end of the hall they never lock for easy access. It takes you out into the forest. Turn right and run. Find the road, it'll take you to the nearest town. You have an hour until they notice."

I blink at him in disbelief. "W-why are you doing this?"

He's risking his own life for me.

"Because you don't deserve this. I'm so sorry for everything that's happened. I've been silent for too long, and now I'm ready for the consequences. Just go!"

I stand on shaky legs and take a breath, even though my ribs ache. I don't know if I'm going to make it, but I have to try. I haven't gone through hell and back to give up now when I'm given my only chance.

With a few wobbly steps, I rush down the hall and out the back door. I blink rapidly from the brightness and shield my eyes for a moment before turning my head to the right. Then, I run for my life.

5

JAXON

For the past five minutes, I've been watching Lucy intently as she whimpers and grimaces. I know better than to snap her out of her trance. I've seen what it can do, and it's not a pleasant experience. I have to let her ride it out–even if she didn't want to dive into Ava's mind in the first place.

Her facial expressions twitch and change almost every second, her lips trembling with what looks like pure fear. My heart pounds in my throat as I wait. Patience is not my friend right now.

After what feels like an eternity, the white film casting over Lucy's eyes finally dissolves to restore her natural blue. Her lips part to take a huge gulp of air, but it's not just one breath, it's multiple. She's panicking. Never in my twenty-six years of life have I ever witnessed Lucy have a panic attack.

"Hey, hey," I say softly. I press my hands to her shoulder to remind her she's safe. "Lucy, slow down your breathing."

But she doesn't listen. I don't even recognise her right now.

Bash, Lucy needs you. I mindlink her mate because she needs their bond to soothe her. *Infirmary, now.*

"Lucy, you need to take slower breaths." I move in front of her as those terrified eyes glaze over mine. "You're hyperventilating. Try to focus on my breathing."

Nothing I say helps. My hand slips down her shoulder, and I give her arm a soft squeeze to let her know I'm here. "It's gonna be okay, Luce. I've got you, and Sebastian is coming. He's going to be here any second."

Tears stream down her face without her even blinking, staining her rosy cheeks. The door pushes open behind me, and I glance over my shoulder to find Sebastian. "What's going on?" he demands.

He wraps an arm around her protectively and caresses her hair. "It's okay, Luce. I'm here. Nothing is going to happen to you."

I watch them for a long moment. Lucy continues to breathe heavily, the sound erupting around the room. Then it suddenly dawns on me—whatever she's panicking about, is what Ava has been through. I struggle to swallow the lump in my throat as my body freezes.

Lucy's chest eventually slows, and she grips her mate for comfort and familiarity. "Are you okay?" I lean forward. Sebastian cups her head and brings it towards his chest so she can listen to the beat of his heart.

After a few moments, she nods, wiping stray tears from her cheeks with shaky hands. "What happened?" Sebastian asks, searching her face for answers. "Did you look into her past?"

"Yeah," she rasps. "I couldn't stop it. Her entire mind took over my body, and I tried so hard not to see the things I did. I'm sorry for scaring you. I didn't mean to panic, it just came over me all of a sudden. Ava must get panic attacks because you know how sometimes, people's memories can affect me afterwards."

"You're safe, sweetheart." Bash kisses the side of her head delicately.

Lucy sniffles. "I know," her voice cracks. "But I don't think she is."

Goosebumps graze my skin as she beckons her head over to Ava as she sleeps peacefully. "What do you mean?" I dip my head.

Her droopy, red eyes find mine. "S-she had a mate before, Jaxon." I ignore the pang of something in my chest that I have no right to claim. "And he was an Alpha."

My brows clench together at her statement. "What happened?"

"I shouldn't have seen the things I saw." She blinks harshly, and more tears erupt. "They were private. I tried so hard to control it, but I couldn't. It was impossible, and I feel *so* guilty."

Sebastian whispers something in her ear as he strokes back her hair. My fists tighten at the tremor in her voice. "They abused her?" I ask, but I already know the answer. I think we all do.

Lucy's eyes find mine again. "You're going to have to ask her what happened, Jaxon. It's not fair for us to invade her memories like that. I had no right to do that. She doesn't deserve this."

"It wasn't your fault," I remind her. "Don't blame yourself."

She swallows harshly. "But it's a pack of men. They don't care about women. They're disgusting, vile pigs and deserve nothing but a slow, painful death."

I close my eyes, trying not to imagine the horrors she's been through, but it's proving difficult. Sebastian's arm continues to run up and down Lucy's. "It was horrible. She must be scarred for life," she whispers. "I've never seen anything like it."

My heart aches at the pain Ava must be in. Not just physically but mentally. Now, I want nothing more than to slowly torture each and every person who ever touched her, hurt her, or even fucking spoke to her.

"Did you hear what the Alpha's name was?"

Lucy's eyes water, flicking between mine slowly. "Lucien."

My stare hardens. I don't directly recognise the name, but I sure as hell will find him and make him pay for what he's done.

"Let's just say we've got a mission to fucking plan."

⁓

WE GIVE AVA SOME PRIVACY, despite my wolf wanting to be in the room with her at all times. It's not going to help me earn her trust.

She wakes up in the early hours of the morning, and my wolf demands her attention. The hairs on my arm raise as I sit outside her door. I wouldn't be able to sleep. So instead, I wait until she's ready—but I soon realise I might be waiting a long time. Lucy joins me later and knocks on the infirmary door.

"Ava? It's Lucy. Can I come in?"

Silence.

I sigh. "Ava. We just want to check on you. Then we will leave. Just have some water and food. What do you think?"

A few long minutes later, the door cracks open, and Ava emerges. Lucy smiles at her softly. "Hi, how are you feeling? You must be so thirsty."

My gaze focuses on her as she stares at the bottle. Her thoughts are loud and clear in my head, it almost makes me lose my balance. She's sceptical of what's inside.

"It's not drugged," I offer, swiping the bottle out of Lucy's hands and taking a generous swig. "See?"

Those big brown eyes study me for a moment before her shaky hand reaches out. I extend my arm to pass it quickly. "Have it," I say with a soft smile.

Her nimble fingers latch onto the bottle before lifting it to her lips. She takes two big gulps before closing her eyes, droplets rolling down her chin.

"Do you want something to eat?" Lucy asks.

She doesn't answer straight away; instead, she lowers the bottle and glances down at her stomach. Her hands grip the material of clothing to expose the skin and find her wound mostly healed. I clear my throat gently to get her attention. "I had doctors come in to help with your wound. How does it feel now?"

Ava purses her lips and studies her stomach, brushing her fingers across the skin in amazement. "H-how?"

"That doesn't matter." I shake my head. "What matters is that you feel better."

She tilts her head to meet my gaze. The fear that was once there slowly washes away, but I feel her reservation. She's going to need a lot of time to truly heal.

"Let me go make you something to eat," Lucy says as she throws her thumb over her shoulder. "You must be so hungry."

Ava begins to violently shake her head, and I frown at her reaction.

"What's wrong?"

Her fist clenches the bottle, and the plastic cracks. "D-don't leave me with him."

"Ava," Lucy says, moving closer to her. "I promise you, no one here is going to hurt you. You're safe."

I nod at her answer. "She's right. I don't have to come into the room at all. I can stand out here and wait until Lucy gets back. Would that make you feel better?"

Ava stares at me cautiously, and I step back to make my point clear.

"I'll be back in ten minutes," Lucy promises. Ava looks to her for reassurance. "I know you find it hard to trust anyone right now, but we want to help."

After a few moments, Ava nods, and I move further back to give her space. If she wants to slam the door in my face, fine. I won't take it personally. But instead of doing so, she stares back at me, holding onto the door with shaky fingers.

"Once you've eaten, would you like to shower and get changed into some fresh clothes?" I ask as she fiddles with the hem of her dirty T-shirt.

She doesn't say anything. She just analyses me.

"I'm sure Lucy can lend you some clean clothes. Get you into something more comfortable and warm," I suggest.

I don't expect her to reply, but when I hear, "Please," I shatter.

Her voice is quiet like a mouse and drained of energy.

"How old are you, Ava?"

Her brows furrow as she thinks. The murderous thoughts in my head worsen. "I-I'm not sure," she admits through a whisper. "Twenty... maybe."

"You're safe here, okay? No one is going to hurt you again."

"D-do you know him?"

I tilt my head slowly. "Who?"

"*Him.*"

"I don't know who you're talking about, Ava."

Her glassy eyes flick between mine rapidly. "L-Lucien. His name is Lucien."

"No," I admit. "I don't know a Lucien."

Ava sways, and I lean forward to stabilise her. I shouldn't touch her, and I hate myself for doing it, but I don't want her hitting the floor. The electrifying bond shoots down my hand and into my body at the touch of her skin. Guilt rides me like a wave. Her lips part, and she slowly looks up at me with conflicting expressions.

"I'm sorry," I whisper and guide her to the bed before she hurts herself.

Her eyes search my own for a sense of meaning as her skin tingles against mine. Blood rushes to my ears as zaps of energy erupt around our gentle embrace. I remove my arms from her the next second.

"You could be bad like him." Her lips quiver. "You could be lying to me."

I grit my jaw and nod. "I want you to understand that, yes, there are bad people in the world. But not everyone is bad, and I know that's difficult for you to believe right now. All I want is to make sure that you're okay."

I don't know what rushes past her eyes, but it looks like she's trying to find hope in my words. "Why are you doing this?" Her voice sounds stronger than before.

Because you're our mate, my wolf whimpers inside my head.

But I refuse to add fuel to the fire. That should be saved for another day.

"Because you deserve better, and I want you to find your family, your friends."

She closes her eyes for a brief moment and says nothing more. I take a step back, respecting her space.

Lucy appears at the door with a tray of food. "I'm back,"

she declares, and I glance over my shoulder to find her looking at me with pinched brows.

She's okay, I say through the mindlink.

"Are you hungry, Ava?"

Ava nods timidly and eyes the food on the tray.

My wolf howls at knowing she's being cared for, although I'm a thousand steps away from earning her trust.

6

JAXON

It was a relief to watch Ava eat. Although it took her a while to get through half of the meal, I'm glad she managed to digest something. I know she probably doesn't have much of an appetite, so starting off small so she doesn't make herself sick is key.

After her meal, Lucy took her upstairs to one of the spare rooms. She showed her how to use the shower and let her borrow some clean clothes. We said we'd wait downstairs in the living room to give her some breathing space.

"She should see the doctor again," I say to Lucy as I pace the cream rug in front of the grand fireplace. "To double-check that everything is okay."

"I agree."

"I don't want to push her too far," I comment, running a hand along the stubble on my jaw. "But at the same time, I want to make sure she's okay."

My sister nods. "I don't think you should be pushing yourself too far either."

"What does that mean?"

She sighs and chews her bottom lip. "I know you're not

over Julia. You will never be over Julia. She was your first love. But Ava has been through horrific trauma, and she needs care and patience. I don't think you're in any frame of mind to give her that right now."

I flinch at her words. "What are you talking about?"

"You might end up hurting her further."

"How could you possibly think I'd hurt my own mate?" I shake my head in disbelief.

"Not physically, Jaxon; I mean emotionally. You are not ready for a new relationship. You were in love with Julia. You still love her, but Ava, she nee–"

My fists tighten beside me as I bark over her, "Stop."

The living room falls to silence.

"I know I'm not entirely ready to move on, Luce. But that doesn't mean I can't try and get to know Ava and build trust between us. I will never forget Julia. Do you not think this is hard for me?" I exhale as waves of shame hit my sternum. "The last thing I want is to jump into a relationship with her, but something is telling me to hold on. When we're both ready, we can have that conversation together—if at all. Right now, it's about protecting her and nothing else."

Lucy tilts her head back slowly. "Just–" she cuts herself off. "Be careful. I get she's your mate, and you're feeling one hundred and one new emotions, but there is no rush. I want you to be okay. I want her to be okay."

I nod as her words sink in. "How are you feeling now?" I ask, changing the subject.

"Better," she admits. "What I saw still haunts me, but I need to remember Ava is the one who experienced it. We need to focus on her now."

I wrap an arm around her and tug her into my chest. "Thank you, Luce. For all of this."

"We've missed you," she murmurs into my T-shirt. "So much."

My chest tightens at the thought of not seeing my family because of how badly I've been grieving. Yet, they will still drop everything to help me, even if I don't deserve it.

Guilt floods my heart intensely. I've barely thought about Julia since I left the house yesterday, and it makes me feel rotten.

I scratch my head as I pull away. Lucy must be able to sense what's on my mind. "It's okay to feel confused, Jaxon." She offers me a small smile. "This would be difficult for anyone. Julia will always be special to you."

"She'd hate this." I release a morbid laugh. "If she knew I had another mate."

Lucy's mouth twists into a sad smile. "Yeah, well, life goes on, Jaxon. I know you love her. And I know you miss her, but she's not here anymore. You still deserve to be happy. All I say is handle Ava with care, in all aspects."

"I will," I hum. "Always."

I become cautious of how long Ava is taking upstairs. Lucy agrees to check on her and make sure everything is okay. I wait as patiently as I can without my wolf eating my insides. The hairs on my arm begin to stand, and I immediately turn my attention to the glowing sensation tickling the back of my brain.

My gaze collides with Ava's dark brown eyes. Her hair is damp and drapes over her shoulders, and Lucy's jumper hangs off her small frame.

From the way she carries herself, I can tell she's ready to run if she needs to. Her legs are twitchy, and her head is low, but her eyes are bouncing around.

"Hey," I greet as her fingers entwine in front of her. "The doctor is ready to see you again if you would like. She won't do anything that makes you uncomfortable. It's all for your wellbeing. The ball is in your court."

Her dark brows crease in my direction. "Y-you said they healed me."

"Only the wound on your stomach," I say. "It's your choice. I'm not going to force you. If you need more time then I completely understand."

Ava blinks at me, droplets of water falling from the ends of her long hair. "I-I–" her voice trembles before pausing. "Okay."

I take her back to the infirmary wing, where Gemma greets us. Ava hangs back behind Lucy. Her fingers pick at the skin around her nails, and her eyes flick around her surroundings once again.

"Hi, Ava," Gemma says warmly. "How are you feeling?"

"Fine," she says hesitantly.

"How do you feel about letting me check you over? I am the senior doctor. But if anything makes you uncomfortable, let me know, and we can stop."

A warm sensation spreads throughout my chest, tapping at my ribcage. My pulse races at the unexpected wave of what was once far too familiar. But through our growing mate bond, I understand how apprehensive she is from the dread lacing through her.

I didn't expect the bond to be this strong—let alone for it to arise this early without any physical connection. It starts to pull on my heartstrings, and I resist the urge to rub my hand over my chest.

Eventually, Ava nods.

Gemma continues to smile as she holds out her hand, but she doesn't take her palm. Instead, she follows her further into the infirmary.

Lucy sighs from beside me. "I am exhausted, I have no idea how she feels."

My eyes ache with heaviness and all the foreign emotions weighing down my body. "I know."

When the minutes tick by, I'm strung with worry that Gemma has found something that puts Ava's health in danger. Overthinking is a bastard.

The door opens, and I stand from my seat in the hall. Gemma guides Ava back to us. "Everything okay?" I ask.

"I managed to get a better look at those cracked ribs and torn ligaments. But they're all healed now. Ava will be weak for a few weeks, so she needs a lot of rest. Hydration and nourishment are also going to be crucial in her recovery. Everything else between us is confidential." Gemma's brows raise towards me which means not to fight her.

"Thank you, Gemma," I say gratefully.

Ava's head is firmly down, and I frown at the action. "No problem, Alpha." She nods. "Ava, if you ever need to come and talk to me about anything, I'm always here, or you can call for me. Okay?"

"Okay," she whispers, not meeting her eyes.

Gemma flashes me a sympathetic smile before bowing to me.

We walk back to the living room. It reads past midday on the clock. I know she's been in and out of sleep all night, but I bet she's exhausted.

"Would you like to go back to your room so you can rest?"

"Yes, Alpha." She bows her head like Gemma did.

My face flinches at the title. I turn towards her until those big yet tired eyes meet mine. For a moment, she looks scared of the proximity between us. "You don't need to call me Alpha or bow to me, Ava." I tighten my fist beside my leg to stop myself from caressing her cheek. "You and I are equal. I am not higher than you. But you can call me Jaxon, Jax, or whatever you want to call me."

Ava's lashes brush her skin as she takes in my voice, realising I'm being serious. "Jax," she repeats, and the sound of my name rolling off her tongue has a shiver running down my spine.

∼

When I climbed into bed later that night, I knew I wouldn't be able to sleep. Ava was in the room down the hall from mine, and despite my wolf telling me to check in on her, I knew better than to push her boundaries. I need to respect her needs. It's the bare minimum.

She needs time to adjust and find her own trust in us. I roll onto my back and rub my hands over my face. I refuse to look at the time because then I'll have no hope of getting to sleep.

An unsettling feeling churns in my stomach. I clasp my abdomen and grunt at the sensations diving through me. The tightness of my chest becomes almost unbearable, and I'm tingling all over.

Stop. Stop. Stop. Stop. Stop. Stop. Stop. Stop.

Ava's thoughts. I can hear them loud and clear.

Immediately, I sit up in my bed and glance at the door.

Help me. Help me. Help me. Help me. Help me. Help me.

My first instinct is to jump out of bed and storm into her room, but after a moment, I realise she's having a nightmare. I close my eyes, hating the fact I can hear every word laced with pain and suffering. Her unconscious thoughts come flooding through my head over and over.

Stop. Help me. Stop. Help me. Stop. Help me.

When they become louder, I can't help but groan in frustration. I am helpless. Completely and utterly helpless.

I twist and shoot a mindlink to Lucy. *She's having a nightmare. A bad one. I can hear everything.*

Ugh, Jaxon. What time is it? She murmurs back after a few seconds. *Don't go in there. You'll scare her.*

I bury my head in my hands. *I don't know what to do. I don't know how to handle this, but I can't just sit here and listen to it. It is killing me, Luce.*

I know, Jaxon. I know it's hard. But you need to give her the space. Otherwise, you'll end up pushing her further away.

This is ruining me, I say weakly.

Lucy is silent for a moment. *Then attempt to use the bond to calm her without actually going into her room. Use everything you have to comfort her.*

I push my back into the headboard and nod. *You're right.*

It's been too long since I've experienced a mate bond that I forget the true power it possesses.

My eyes close, and I imagine the bond. My breathing slows, and I tell myself to push out her agony from my body and focus on pleasant thoughts instead.

Ava whimpers in my mind, and I clench my eyes tighter at the haunting sound. I continue exhaling through the bond, imagining pictures of sandy beaches and lavender fields. Places of peace. Places of tranquillity, all projected into her brain. Her thoughts slowly begin to fade away, and I push a little harder on the bond like a soft caress.

My mate's nightmare quietens down, and after a few minutes, it stops. I keep flashing images of beautiful sunrises and picturesque mountains, representing true freedom in my eyes.

A soft sigh of relief echoes down the bond, so quiet I almost miss it. There is so much pressure inside my head, but I don't stop. I don't want to risk her nightmare coming back before she manages to fall into a dreamless sleep.

When Ava's breathing aligns with mine through the bond, and I'm comfortable she's asleep, I let the images fizzle out, and my eyes open. If I have to do it every night, I will. It's the least I can do without crossing her boundaries.

7

JAXON

The past week has been tough to say the least. I've barely had a wink of sleep. Every night I stayed awake projecting images into Ava's mind to stop the nightmares until she was able to fall asleep peacefully.

It's agonising listening to her screams, knowing I can't comfort her instead. I've been visiting her once or twice a day, but I don't get a lot back. She hasn't left her room. She's barely said two words to me. But I don't push it. I take every day as it comes.

I hold a cup of coffee in my hand which has turned cold from staring endlessly at the wall. If I don't, I'll peer around my kitchen to find plates and cups dotted everywhere as no one bothered to clean up last night. It irks me that my private kitchen is treated like university accommodation.

"No sleep over Ava, huh?" Lucy's voice echoes around the kitchen as she walks by me. Sebastian follows and gives me a slow nod.

"I have every right to be worried about her," I grumble under my breath. "And were you guys born in a fucking barn? Every damn morning there are dirty mugs and plates everywhere. Put. Them. In. The. Dishwasher."

Sebastian and Lucy share a glance before laughing quietly. I don't even want to know what that means. "Oops." My sister continues to smile. "Our bad. I'll do it now."

"I've cut off this section of the house for family only," I state as I pause by the counter. "Until Ava feels comfortable. So if you see anyone around here, tell them to leave. The guards already know."

"Sounds fair," Sebastian comments. "It's your private annexe, anyway. I'm sure the pack will understand when everything is explained to them."

Lucy glances at someone behind me. I turn hoping that it's Ava, but deep down, I know she wouldn't show her face. Not without being coaxed out by Lucy, which has only happened once and never since.

"Good morning, Kayden," she greets brightly.

"Morning." He smiles at both of them and then cuts his brown eyes to me. "You good, Jaxon?"

His hand slaps my shoulder gently. It's rare that we call each other by our titles when we're together as a family, but if I'm with the pack, then I expect people to call me Alpha out of respect.

"What's been happening the last week?" he asks.

I glance at Lucy, and she shrugs back. "I'm surprised gossip hasn't spread around this pack like wildfire."

Kayden pauses by the fridge and tenses for a moment before glancing at me. "I mean," he starts. "Yeah…it has, but I wanted to hear it from you. Rumours are rumours. Right?"

"And the rumours are?"

"That you found a second-chance mate."

Lucy and Sebastian freeze. "Then, I guess the rumours are true."

Kayden's brows hit his hairline. "Wow–" He pulls his head back. "I...I don't even know what to say. I mean, it's a shock. Congratulations? That doesn't even sound right. Eh. How?"

"Trust me, I don't know what to say either." I hunch over the counter.

"You get two mates, and I can't even find one," Kayden murmurs under his breath and throws his arms in the air. "How the hell is that fair?"

Lucy grips his hand supportively. "She'll turn up soon. I guarantee it."

"Goddess. The fifth wheel really is a fun job." He shakes his head. "I'm happy for you, Jaxon, I am. But I'm ready for it to be my turn now. I'm starting to think I've done something to piss off the deities, and I'm being punished. The Moon Goddess hates me."

"She'll probably turn up when you least expect i–"

My voice is cut off when a burning sensation spreads across my back like I've been set on fire. I release a groan and press a hand to the centre of my spine as it grows in intensity.

"Jaxon?" Kayden is at my side. "What's happening?"

The pain eases up, and I take a shallow breath. "I'm fine."

My hand raises to wipe the sweat beading on my forehead, but this time, I flinch when the pain continues to spread over my back. It's ten times hotter than before. My eyes water at the pressure.

What the fuck is happening?

Then, realisation suddenly hits.

"Ava!"

My body moves faster than I can blink. I sprint out of the kitchen and up the stairs, unable to control the primal desire to protect my mate from whatever she's experiencing. I knew it was Ava's pain. She's hurting herself, and I'm experiencing it through the bond.

Kayden and Lucy instantly run after me, their footsteps echoing in my clouded head. The way my chest heaves has all of the blood in my veins vibrating.

Her scent lingers behind the bathroom door. I stop directly in front of it. My hand latches onto the handle, but it's locked from the inside. The burning on my back increases, and I bite down to stop the groan falling from my lips. I don't even hesitate to kick the door in until it snaps off its hinges. My arms throw the door to the side as huge puffs of steam waft towards me.

My eyes narrow as I step inside the misty room. I hear Ava's whimpers of distress in between deep, uneven breathing. The heat of the room clings to the fabric of my clothes.

As I step closer, I spot the showerhead on full blast, the scalding water pounding heavily against her reddening back. She's crouched down against the porcelain tub, sobbing over the loudness of the shower.

"Ava," I rasp pathetically. Before I even think of my next logical thought, I reach in to turn off the taps. The heat from the liquid burns my skin, but I don't flinch when it hits me.

Lucy stands over me and gasps quietly. "Put her on the floor. I should be able to heal her," she demands, but the panic is evident in her voice.

I don't have time to second-guess her abilities right now; instead, I lean into the tub and pull her body into my chest. I glance down at her face and watch as she falls into a lightheaded state. Her entire body is different shades of red and pink.

Lucy rushes from the room and grabs a dry towel before laying it out on the floor. I flick my gaze to Kayden standing in the doorway, his eyes upon my mate with great horror.

Give us some privacy, I snap.

His head bows, and he turns to leave. *Let us know if there is anything we can do.*

I place Ava down on the towel and sweep her dark hair away from her injured back. Lucy hisses, and I grit my jaw at the sight before me. "Fuck, Jaxon. This isn't good."

Blisters have already started to show. Parts of her skin are broken and weeping. How long was she up here doing this to herself? Heaviness clouds my eyes, and I try to calm myself down.

Lucy kneels beside Ava and places her hands gently on her back.

"If you can't do it, Gemma will be able to."

She dismisses the idea. "I can do this."

I study her every move as she closes her eyes and projects her power onto Ava's injuries. A minute passes, and nothing happens.

I groan silently. "Lucy," I warn.

"Shhh."

I bite down on my lip hard enough to draw blood. This is taking too much time. Knowing the severity of Ava's health, it could be fatal. My eyes close at the thought.

No. She'll be okay. Lucy knows what she's doing.

When I open my eyes and focus on Ava's back, I release a quiet breath of relief as the blisters and broken skin slowly begin to heal. Lucy's face is deep in concentration, and I tell myself not to make a sound. Another few minutes pass, and her skin is restored back to its original state. She removes her hands and slumps backwards, her powers instantly lowering her energy.

"Thank you," I say gratefully. I watch as she peels off her

cardigan and wraps it around Ava's naked body. "Trust me when I say, I'm going to murder those people who have made her do this to herself."

The bond makes my body tingle as I take her hand delicately between mine—a place where I know she's safe.

"I know, and you have every right," she says softly. "But instead of focusing on that, you need to focus on her and her needs."

As much as I want to rip out Lucien's throat and anyone else who has ever laid a finger on her, Lucy is right. My priority is building a slow companionship with her—one that is built on trust, safety, and comfort.

"You're right, Luce. She comes first."

～

Ava doesn't come down in the afternoon, and I need to know if she's okay without overwhelming her. Three hours has been far too long. My mind can't fathom the idea of her hurting herself on purpose. It lights a fire inside me that makes me want to tear this world apart.

I knock on the door gently. "Ava? It's Jaxon. Are you okay?"

For a long moment, I stand at her door. I contemplate knocking again, but I don't know if I'm doing too much—and yet, not enough. The sound of fumbling echoes loud in my ears until the door opens, and I stare back at Ava and her red-ringed eyes.

All the distress from her body floats into mine. "Hey," I say calmly. "How are you feeling?"

Those big brown eyes keep me in focus at all times—swimming with tears. She doesn't respond, and a part of me wonders if she heard me. She takes a step back and looks down at her feet.

"Are you okay?" I ask.

She nods, but we both know it's far from the truth.

"Lucy is a healer. She healed the burns on your back."

She gnaws at her lip, clenching her fingers together tightly.

"Hey," I whisper to catch her attention. I resist the urge to lean over and take her hand. As much as I am in desperate need to, it's not about what I want. "When you need some support, talk to me. Or Lucy. Or Gemma. Please. None of us want you going through it alone."

Her wobbly hand presses to her head, eyes closing. "I'm not meant to be here," she whispers.

"What do you mean?"

"I belong in the human world." She cups her hand over her mouth. "Not this fantasy world. I know who you are, and I'm not like you. I'm not from here. I want to go home. *Please*, let me go home."

My heart cracks like a porcelain doll. Her soft cries make my wolf claw my insides. He wants to tell her she is home—right by our side.

"Where is your home, Ava?"

This halts her crying. She sniffles and raises her head. Those pale lips open, but she doesn't say a word. Her eyes close as she tries to concentrate. "I-I don't know," she whimpers. "Why can't I remember?"

The haunting edge to her voice makes me want to wrap her up in my arms again and rock her until she knows she's going to be okay. But I don't. We're far from that kind of affection.

Ava's arms gather in goosebumps as she whips her head around the room. "Was someone else here?"

"What?"

"Who else has been here?"

My brows crease at her words. "Lucy and Kayden were here earlier."

"Kayden?"

"Yes, he's my Beta."

"Y-your Beta?"

"Yes." There is a slight hitch in her breathing, and I lean forward. "What's the matter?"

She shakes her head, avoiding eye contact. She shifts back into the shell she protects herself with. "Do you want to get some dinner?" I offer, changing the subject. "I bet you're super hungry. Lucy will be downstairs."

Those tears on her cheeks begin to dry, and she holds my stare. "I don't have an appetite," she admits.

"Well, what if you pick at some of the food?" I suggest.

She follows me with her eyes. "I can't go down there."

"Okay. Then I'll bring it up. Hmm?"

Ava doesn't nod; she just stares.

"Why don't you wait here, and I'll be back with something to eat?"

She doesn't protest, and I give her a gentle smile before leaving.

8

JAXON

I knew the weeks that came next wouldn't be easy for Ava. Some days, she'd continue to shut herself in her room and not come out to eat or show her face. On other days, she'd only want to talk to Lucy. At least she's found comfort in my sister. I barely had a chance to speak to her, but I know gaining her trust is something that will not happen overnight. I'm ready to persist.

She hasn't wanted to be in the same room as me without Lucy to make her feel at ease. I don't take it to heart. She deserves to be understood. As much as it hurts, I know she needs time and space.

Over the last two weeks, I've thought of Julia constantly. A part of me knows I shouldn't be diving into this new bond with Ava because my love for Julia won't magically disappear. She was my Luna. Now, I have been graced with another.

Some days, I grieve. But, some days, my wolf forces my attention towards Ava.

It alarms me how easily he has moved on. It's as if she never even existed in his world, and it makes my head ache.

It's a clusterfuck of emotions I can't seem to control. We are two separate entities with different perspectives.

I'm stuck between wanting to hold onto my non-existent bond with Julia and allowing myself to feel the new bond with Ava. I don't want Julia to think I've forgotten about her because I haven't. She was my life and soul.

Every day, I'm sick to my stomach with guilt.

In this time, I've been working closely with Kayden. He looked after the pack for nine gruelling months, and now, I'm ready to take the reins again. My pack deserves an Alpha that actually shows up for them, and I'm ashamed to admit I became someone I hated.

Today, I leave the house for the first time in a while. Lucy reassures me she'll look after Ava. My Alpha duties don't stop because of my past and present mate bonds. I still have to make an effort for my pack—I refuse to let them down after they were so patient with me.

I trust Lucy with Ava. She's made herself known to the other members of my pack, but her shyness has her hiding away in her room when she's overwhelmed. If she feels safe in her room, then I won't take that away from her.

When she officially met Kayden, I'd never seen a face pale as quick as hers. I don't know what she saw in my Beta, but whatever it was, she truly feared it. I can only imagine he reminds her of someone in the past, and until she feels comfortable around him, I won't force their company. Not when she's still healing.

Despite not spending much time with each other the last few weeks, the bond is growing stronger between us. I didn't think much of it until I left the house, and the tugging on my heartstrings was begging me to go back. I have no idea if she feels half of what I feel, but my wolf's desperation is destroying me internally.

After three long hours of meetings in the district amongst our allied packs, I gladly left with the information I came for. I've had my eyes set on hunting down Lucien and his wolves, but first, I needed some inside details.

The Stagborn Pack.

All men. All vile creatures.

I discovered his whereabouts, which is west of our district. I'm eager to hunt, invade, and attack until none of them are left. All we need now is to set a plan that will give us the greatest advantage.

When I finally get back to the pack house, I exhale in relief. I made it through the day without my heart ripping out of my chest—I've missed the warmth a bond can give you. It's chilling and beautiful at the same time.

The weather outside takes a dark turn, as the skies are covered in grey clouds. Heavy rain pours on the pebbled floor. It echoes loudly in my ears as I walk through the front door. I make my way to the kitchen, where I find Lucy and Phia, my sister's closest friend in the pack.

"Where's Ava?" I ask, interrupting their conversation.

Phia offers me a small smile. "Hi, Alpha Jaxon."

"She's outside," Lucy says before turning back to Phia.

I frown immediately. "What do you mean outside?"

Lucy glances up before extending her arm towards the window that overlooks a small patio. "Look for yourself."

I'm moving towards the window faster than I can blink. My gaze flicks towards my mate standing outside in the rain, barefoot on the wet grass and drenched to the bone. "What the–" I cut myself off. "Why is she outside?"

"She wanted to go outside. She said something about seeing the rain."

My eyes widen. Lucy must be out of her damn mind. "Are you stupid? What if she ran off? What if she got hurt?"

She rolls her eyes at me, and I clench my jaw. "And you're the one saying she needs to trust you."

"Lucy–" I clench the bridge of my nose and walk towards the back door.

"She promised she wouldn't run off; she just wanted to see the rain."

"And you believed her?"

My heart is pounding like an alarm clock in my chest. "Uhh, yeah," she huffs as if I'm the one who's overreacting. "She's been out there for five minutes, and she hasn't moved."

I grip onto the door handle. "Five minutes?"

Before she can respond, I hop down the patio stairs and pull up the collar of my jacket as the rain pours over my head. It's so loud I can barely hear myself think. It's bitter and cold, and I have no idea how she's out here with no shoes on.

"Hey," I say over the rain but quiet enough that I don't startle her.

Ava turns to me with an unexpected smile, one that covers half of her face. I can't even class it as a smile because she's beaming at me. My breath lodges in my throat, and I tell myself not to reach out and move the piece of brunette hair which has clung to her forehead. The raindrops have completely drenched her head and lashes. Her clothes cling to her rosy skin.

Her eyes light up with excitement, and I can't help but smile back at her. I can see it in her gaze; she knows she's free. My wolf howls at the sight because he wants nothing more than to see her happy.

"What are you doing out here?" I ask as I shrug off my jacket.

She doesn't flinch when I move it around her body, so I

lower it down onto her shoulders, attempting to keep her warm even though every part of her skin is wet.

"The rain." She grins, holding her palms flat to the sky so the droplets touch her fingers. "It's amazing."

Ava tilts her head and closes her eyes, inhaling deeply. My fingers itch to touch her precious cheek, but it's not right. "You've never seen rain before?"

A surprising laugh barks out of her. "Of course, I've seen rain. But it's been what feels like years since I've seen the rain, and it just...it just–"

"It what?"

"It makes me feel alive. It reminds me I am alive." She shudders but not with coldness, with vibrancy. "It's like I can actually feel something that is real. I can go outside. I can feel the rain. I can breathe all this air. It's real. It's not a dream. I'm really living this."

My lips spread into a bright smile. "Yeah. It's real. All of it is real. You're not a prisoner here, Ava. You are free to do whatever you want. Whatever makes you feel alive."

Her eyes glitter in my direction, and I suck in a breath. The way she's looking at me makes my chest glow with a tender warmth.

"You must be freezing," I say as I focus on her lips, which are losing colour by the second. "Let's get inside. You don't want to make yourself sick."

Ava steps around me, and we walk back towards the kitchen. I hold the door open for her as we step inside. She takes off my jacket and hands it to me.

"How was the rain?" Lucy asks.

I glance at Ava, who looks down to the floor where she's dripping rainwater. "I loved it. Thank you for letting me go outside."

"You don't need permission to do anything, Ava," Lucy

states slowly. "You're allowed to do whatever you want. Right, Jaxon?"

"Yeah," I agree, despite feeling bad for what I said to my sister earlier. "Like I said outside. You're not a prisoner. You're one of us."

The corner of her lip twitches, but it doesn't reach capacity. "Okay."

"Would you like to watch a movie in the lounge?" I suggest. "It's a quiet evening."

Ava chews on her lip. "Alone?"

"We don't have to be alone. I won't force you to sit with me if you don't want to. If you want Lucy to sit with us, I'm sure she'll join us."

She looks to Lucy who gives her a supportive smile. "Okay."

I nod with relief. "Why don't you get changed into something warm and dry, and I'll meet you in the lounge? We can agree on a movie together."

"Okay," she whispers once more before disappearing upstairs.

I move to the living room and light the fireplace to make the room cosy. Then, I collect as many blankets and cushions as I can find.

"You two getting along well then, huh?" I hear Lucy's voice behind me.

"This is the first time she's wanted to actively spend time with me. Especially something that doesn't involve mealtime. I'm not jinxing anything, but I want her to be comfortable," I say honestly. "Taking it one day at a time."

Lucy nods in appreciation. "Good. I'm glad."

Soon, Ava appears beside Lucy at the door to the living room. She's wearing a loose T-shirt and pyjama pants, her fingers closely entwined in front of her. "Do you want me to join you?" Lucy asks Ava.

"Uh," she hesitates and meets my eyes. "Please. I'd like that."

"Okay, sure. I'll be back in a second."

When my sister leaves, Ava watches her go. I perch on the end of the sofa and beckon with my head. "Come," I say softly. "I've got blankets and snacks."

She tugs at her fingers once more before walking towards me. But she doesn't sit next to me; instead, she keeps her distance. "What's your favourite movie?"

Ava is silent for a long moment, her bottom lip between her teeth as she thinks. "I-I don't know." She exhales. "I think I liked comedies or drama pieces. Nothing sad or scary."

I offer her a smile. "I don't like anything scary either."

Her eyes widen in surprise. "Really?"

"Hell, yeah." I nod without an ounce of shame. "Demons and poltergeists are terrifying."

Ava's throat releases the quietest laugh. "Yeah, they are."

"Let's pick something together, then." I beckon my head to the TV. "Nothing scary. Nothing sad."

Lucy returns and sits on the other side of Ava. When *Stepbrothers* starts playing, I hand over some blankets, which she snuggles into, wrapping herself up like a burrito. Her delicate scent wafts towards me as time ticks by, and I take shallow breaths to keep my eyes on the screen. It's more powerful now, intoxicating my lungs with how beautiful she smells.

Halfway through the movie, she lifts her head and looks at me. "W-where were you today?" Her voice is quiet as I shift my gaze towards her.

"Making sure no one ever hurts you again."

A confused frown falls on her face. "What do you mean?"

"You don't have to worry about anything right now, okay?"

She stares at me for a long moment and nods once.

"Can I ask you a question?" I whisper when she says nothing more.

She nibbles her lip in anticipation. "Yes."

"Do you remember who your parents are?"

Suddenly, she looks away from me and focuses on the bookshelves across the room. "I-I can't remember."

"Do you remember where you grew up?"

"No," she whispers heavily.

My jaw tightens at the sadness forming in her eyes. "It's okay. We can figure it out together as time goes on. I want you to be able to reunite with your family and friends."

Her lips begin to tremble. "Me, too. I just–" She strains. "I can't remember."

When her head lowers, I ache for her. I wish I could take away her pain without terrifying her through the bond. I've only done it when her nightmares occupy her mind at night. I take my sister's thoughts into consideration. I'm still grieving. I shouldn't be forcing myself into a new relationship when my head isn't in the right place either.

"Hey," I rasp, catching her attention. "Let's watch the rest of the movie. We don't have to think about it tonight."

"Yeah," she whispers back as her eyes return to the TV.

One day at a time.

9

AVA

Tonight, I couldn't sleep. I've barely managed a couple of hours each night for the past four weeks. Most start off with nightmares that torment my mind until the dream changes, and instead of being terrified, I am comforted. It's an odd sensation that I don't understand.

I hear the calmness of the waves and the gentle breeze over a mountaintop.

Every night, it's something different. A new place. A new safe haven. I don't fight them. I submerge in the images, and I'm grateful when I finally settle into a dreamless sleep.

But tonight, I toss and turn in the sheets until they make my legs itch. I have no idea what I'm still doing here. I should have left as soon as my injuries healed and attempted to find my home. Why can't I remember my home?

The thought makes my brows pinch together painfully. A deep ache makes me question the last few years. I huff out a dissatisfied breath and bury my head into the pillow.

Tears threaten my eyes once again. I don't belong here. Yet, I don't belong anywhere if I can't remember. My lips tremble at not knowing, not remembering. Are there people out there looking for me? *No.* How could I be so stupid? If they were, they would have found me. Instead, I endured years of abuse for a reason I'll never understand.

By the time I turn around and glance at the clock beside my bed, I sniffle. The fabric of the pillow beneath me is wet from my endless tears. I silently whimper as the numbers of the early morning stare back at me.

I throw the covers off my body before I overthink my next actions. My mind wanders endlessly. I need a distraction. The house is silent at this time—everyone's in bed. It gives me the perfect opportunity to explore when no one should cross me.

My hands close around my elbows as I step into the dark hall. The floorboards creak beneath my feet, and I cringe at the sound but carry on. I find myself walking further down the house until I pause outside a room with the door wide open.

I step in the doorway. This room smells like Jaxon—freshly cut wood and a hint of something spicy. My nose tingles, and I blink. How are my senses so strong? He's not even here.

Curiosity builds in my chest as I creep inside. My hand slides to the wall, and I flick the switch, lighting up the room. I'm met with what looks like Jaxon's office.

I know he's the Alpha of this pack. At first, I thought all Alphas were brutal beings who only wanted to cause pain and misery to others. But now, I'm starting to believe that might not be the case. Jaxon seems...different.

Every piece of furniture is built of dark wood with a large display of maps and ancient books on the walls and shelves. There is a circular rug in the middle that resembles a symbol I don't recognise. I nibble on my lip as my eyes sweep over his desk. I know better than to snoop, but it's already distracting my crowded mind. I can't stop myself. I'm being dragged in before I can think of the consequences.

I notice stacks of papers, a pen pot, and a closed laptop. But my eyes dart to a gold picture frame facing away from me. For a second, I hesitate, but then I pick it up and twist it towards me. As soon as I see the picture, I realise I shouldn't have started snooping.

It's a picture of Jaxon and a woman I don't recognise. She has dark blonde hair with piercing blue eyes, olive skin, and a killer smile. Jax is kissing her cheek as she beams at the camera, flashing off her pearly white teeth.

Who is she? I've never seen her around the house.

Jaxon never mentioned he had a girlfriend. But why would he? We haven't spent much time together in the last few weeks. Not that it's any of my business.

My head pounds with a thousand new thoughts. Maybe this wasn't a good idea at all. I study the picture for another long minute because I can't tear my eyes away, no matter how hard I try.

"Ava...what are you doing in here?"

A voice behind me snaps me back into reality. My entire body jolts at the same time my fingers loosen around the picture frame. It takes seconds for it to smash against the floor by my bare feet.

Panic chokes my throat. I'm in so much trouble. Crap. I attempt to catch my breath, but I've destroyed something of the Alpha's. A picture of him and his...lover? Bile rises in my throat.

My eyes widen when I find Kayden, Jaxon's Beta, at the door, watching me with a stunned gaze. Oh, God. Oh, God.

"I-I–" I stutter before lowering down onto the floor and

frantically picking up pieces of glass that scattered across Jaxon's office.

I grab as much as I can, as quickly as possible. I'm not thinking clearly because the tiny shards pierce my skin, and blood begins to rise to the surface.

Kayden inches closer, and I don't dare look at him. My stomach churns inside me at the thought of being alone with a Beta. I have no idea if they're all the same or if my emotions are playing tricks on me—I don't want to experience that pain again.

"What do you want with me?" I blurt out of nowhere.

Kayden twists his head. "Nothing. I'm on night duty."

My entire body trembles as I take in his face.

"Goddess," he hisses and lowers down to my level. "You're bleeding."

I stare up into his dark brown eyes and shiver. He looks genuinely concerned, but I shake at the proximity between us. "Please, get away from me," I murmur.

Nausea rips through my stomach. The waves of embedded anxiety through my bloodstream heighten, and I struggle to inhale.

Kayden pulls back slowly and raises his hands in defence. "I'm not going to touch you," he clarifies before looking down at my hands. "But you need to clean those wounds and make sure there is no glass in the cuts."

I stare at him long and hard, trying my best not to let my eyes leak tears, but it's nearly impossible. My entire body shivers at his presence. He might not have done anything to me personally, but I can't take chances. Not when I'm certain I'll break this time. I'm barely hanging on.

My blood drips against the floor, and I don't realise I'm clutching the shards of glass. I don't take my eyes off him. The air in the room grows thinner, and I can't inhale.

"Ava." Kayden's face turns to stone. "Drop the glass. You're hurting yourself."

When he reaches over, I'm convinced he's about to touch me. I open my mouth and release the loudest scream. It deafens me. It wrenches from my chest because my body jumps into fight mode. It's the last resort.

I close my eyes to try and block out all the crucifying emotions that clutter my head. Blood pounds in my ears, and everything slows down to the point I'm disorientated.

Voices start talking, but I don't hear what they're saying. My breaths become shorter, and I'm out of oxygen, yet at the same time, I can't get enough. My vision blurs when another silhouette settles in front of me.

"Ava." The sound is muffled. "Ava, you're hyperventilating."

Why do I sound like I'm in a bubble? I don't even know if I'm alive right now.

"Breathe, Ava." The voice softens. "There is so much air in this room. Okay? Don't let yourself think there is no air. You have it. Breathe. Nothing is going to happen to you."

It feels like it might. I'm going to die.

Just breathe, Ava. You can do this, I tell myself.

"Please, can I see your hands?"

I'm far too in my head to protest. I raise my shaky palms towards the soothing voice. A soft hand clasps the back of my wrist, and an instant rush of calmness takes over my body. It makes my skin rise in pimples like an electric shock.

"Okay, okay," he says. "Hear me. Listen to me. Take down as much oxygen as possible, and when you breathe out, hold it for as long as you can. Four counts, six counts, eight counts. Each time, you move higher and higher."

My eyes leak tears. Four counts? I attempt the technique because I literally have nothing else to lose. I don't succeed

SECOND CHANCE MATES

the first time. But on the third attempt, I manage to breathe out for four long beats before sucking in air like I'm suffocating again.

"There." The voice makes me relax. "You've got it. Now, for six. Ready? Let me count with you."

His thumb swipes across my knuckles gently, and I tell my lungs this is the one that will calm me down.

"One, two, three," he whispers through my exhale. "Four, five, six."

It takes me another few minutes to calm down to a pace that reminds me I'm alive. I sniffle at the exhaustion coursing through my veins.

"Open your eyes, Ava."

My sore eyes obey slowly. I'm met with Jaxon's dark sapphire eyes full of concern and care—I forgot what that looked like.

He got me out of a panic attack. No one has ever done that for me.

"It's okay," he tells me again. "I've got you."

I take in his face—light stubble on his jaw and dark hair messily placed from his sleep. A single tear rolls down my cheek in distress, and Jaxon's hand raises to wipe it away with his thumb. I don't flinch. I don't even move. I'm numb.

"I'm sorry," he replies under a harsh rasp directed at himself. I follow his eye-line to my hand. They're splattered with blood stains. "They're only shallow."

He reaches up to his desk and grabs a box of tissues before pressing them to my skin. It soaks up a few droplets, but most of it has dried or dripped onto the floor. "We'll get these cleaned up in a moment, hmm?"

"I'm sorry, I-I smashed y-your picture," I whimper pathetically. "It was an accident, I promise."

Jaxon's hands slip under my fingers again, holding the

tissue to them. A surge of warmth spreads up my arms, unlike anything I've ever felt before. It makes me cry harder because my head spins. "It doesn't matter, Ava. It's just a frame. It can be replaced."

I lower my head and attempt to control my breathing once more. I don't want to feel out of control. I despise that feeling. "You don't need to cry, Ava. I promise I'm not mad. No one is mad."

"I shouldn't have been in here." My lip quivers.

Jaxon frowns softly. "You can go wherever you want in the house. You are free to do whatever you want. No one is going to stop you."

"D-did I wake you?"

"I don't care about me."

My hands clench in Jaxon's hold, and I grit my teeth at the tiny pieces of glass still lodged between my cuts. I wince as he pulls the tissue away.

"Will you let me take you down to the infirmary? I can have Gemma pull out the glass and heal your hands," he suggests, angling his head so our eyes meet again.

I nod because the pain is beginning to throb. As soon as we reach the infirmary wing, I find comfort in being faced with Gemma. I recognise her. I trust her. She's helped me in more ways than one.

"Hi, Ava." She offers me a smile. "Let's go sit over here, and I can sort out your hands."

My gaze returns to Jaxon as he gives me an encouraging nod. "I'll wait out here for you," he says as he takes a seat in the hallway.

I follow Gemma to the room, where she disinfects my wound, removes the glass, and patches me up until my skin is repaired. My eyes feel swollen as I inspect her handy work.

"I'll never get used to that," I whisper.

Gemma smiles. "It is strange. But it's very practical for our lifestyle. Even though we heal faster than humans, we need to be able to patch ourselves up quickly. How are you feeling, Ava?"

"Tired," I admit far too easily.

"Are you sleeping well?"

"No."

"Are you having nightmares?"

"Yes."

Gemma gives me a supportive smile. "Ava, have you thought about talking to someone?"

"Talking?"

"I know you haven't been here long, and I can't imagine how overwhelming all of this has been. But have you considered talking with a therapist?"

My expression twists. "I-I–" I pause for a moment. "No. I don't know if I'm strong enough for it."

She nods in what I believe is understanding. "Of course. But it doesn't necessarily have to be digging up the past; it can help with coping mechanisms, positive affirmations, and healing today. Not talking about details you're not comfortable with."

"They have people for that...here?"

Gemma nods once. "Yes. We have lots of different therapists. All sessions are confidential, of course. We can't even report back to Alpha Jaxon as we believe in patient-doctor confidentiality. You'd be surprised how many people go to therapy."

"D-do you think I need it?"

"I'm not going to tell you what you need; that's up to you to decide. But talking about certain things, even if they seem small, can help more than you know. It might be worth considering." Gemma's eyes are peaceful. "You don't have to make any decisions right now. I thought I'd put the offer out there. This is a safe space. We want the best for everyone."

I chew on the inside of my cheek. "Thank you, Gemma. That's...kind of you."

"You're welcome, Ava. My door is always open."

I can't remember the last safe space I had, but Gemma opens up a door to a bunch of possibilities. I'm not there yet. Although I want to be.

10

AVA

The sun continues to dip in and out of the clouds as I perch on the patio steps. I prepare myself for rain—not that I'd mind. My eyes close as I wrap my arms around my knees and inhale the fresh air.

Last night was the best night's sleep I've had since being here. It wasn't great, but better than usual. Ever since the incident in Jaxon's office, I've been keeping to myself. I'm still mortified over waking the entire house.

The back door creaks open, and I glance over my shoulder to find Jaxon. He's in a black T-shirt that stretches over his broad chest and thick arms. "Hey," he greets. "May I sit with you?"

I stare at the spot beside me, and I brush my teeth across my lip. "Uh. Okay."

Jaxon nods and perches on the other end of the step. Enough space between us that I don't have to count my breaths. "How are you today?"

I shrug and look at the grass. "I'm okay, I think."

We fall into silence as I clutch my legs closer to my chest. Jaxon happily sits beside me. I don't hate his company—I'm just wary of it. I take a peek at him, but he's looking out to the trees.

"Can I ask you something?" I whisper, my curiosity getting the better of me.

He turns with those intense blue eyes. "Of course."

I swallow and take my time to find my words. "Why is it when I'm with you, I somehow manage to feel calmer? With my panic attack. I don't understand. It sounds stupid when I say it out loud, but I felt...something."

His gaze flicks between mine. For a moment, I think he's not going to say anything, and then he says, "Do you know what mates are?"

My eyes widen a fraction. I nod once.

How could I not know what mates are after Lucien threw that word around every damn day? *Worthless, pathetic human mate.* He made it known.

"Well, when two people are mates, they share a very special bond which is unique to every couple. Sometimes, they can feel emotions, thoughts, and each other's pain. Sometimes, they can tune into each other, give each other peace and calmness," he explains. "Mates keep each other safe."

My heart thrashes in my chest at his statement. My lashes tickle my cheekbone over and over as I try to digest his words. That sounds nothing like what I endured with Lucien. All I felt was suffering.

"But that can't be true."

"It is because the Moon Goddess believes mates have what the other needs. The power one might yield could help the other and vice-versa."

My forehead creases at his statement. *Does that mean I deserved all the abuse from Lucien?* A sinking sensation forms in my stomach.

"B-but I'm not a werewolf."

Jaxon's mouth curls in a half-smile. "I know."

"So, what are you saying?"

He takes down a long breath and holds my gaze. "I'm saying that you are my mate, Ava. I felt your pain. I felt your distress. I felt your panic. I knew something was wrong because the bond between us told me, and that's why I came up to make sure you were okay. It's the same as the other night. I used our bond for reassurance, but you are the one who stopped your panic attack."

Every part of my body turns rigid. Tears threaten my eyes, and I'm swamped with utter confusion. *How? Why?*

Lucien said I was his mate. Was that a lie? I release an internal groan of pure frustration. I hate this world. I hate trying to understand their reality. What does any of it truly mean?

"I know this is difficult for you to understand," he says gently.

I continue to stare at him. "A bond?"

"Yes." He nods confidently. "It's something that connects us."

For a moment, I pause and glance over at the trees swaying in the wind. "But I didn't have one with..." I whisper to myself. "Him."

His expression warps into what looks like deep sadness. "Because bonds only grow and work when both mates accept it."

"I haven't accepted anything with you," I murmur with cloudy vision.

"I know," he agrees. "But accepting my help with your panic attack definitely sparked something. You said you felt something. That's the bond."

My head shakes over and over. "This is crazy. This is–" I

cut myself off and stand, wiping my hands on my leggings. "None of this makes sense. So...what? Now I belong to you?"

Jaxon remains on the step. "No. You don't belong to me. You are your own person. I'd never take that away from you."

Tears spill over my eyes, and I wipe them away with a newfound anger. "I don't understand anything," I grumble. "I don't understand how any of this is real."

After a few moments, he stands, his height advancing on me. I wrap my arms around myself. My head pounds, and I wish I could play catch up, but I'm a thousand steps behind. "It's okay to take your time. I'm not pushing anything on you. You deserved to know the truth, and I was trying to find a good time to tell you, but then you mentioned feeling something between us."

How can I feel nothing but pure dread with Lucien, but with Jaxon, I feel like my sky-high walls could lower even an inch? That messes with my head.

"I'm sorry." I push my tears away. "I-I just need a moment."

Jaxon nods. "Of course. If you want to talk about it more, then I'm here to answer your questions and listen to your worries."

I spare him one more glance before I walk back into the house and let my lungs collapse.

~

THE LAST THING I want this morning is to be alone. Yet, I feel like I have no one to go to. Jaxon's pack floods in and out of the house on duty, training, or heading to travel through the district to complete missions. I don't know much about this pack, but it's different to Lucien's.

Jaxon is out on Alpha duties with his wolves and told me he'd be back later—if I need to contact him then I go straight to Gemma downstairs. I have the house to myself. That's probably why I feel so alone, yet the company of someone also makes my skin crawl.

Why can't my emotions make up their mind? It's like I'm on a rollercoaster, and I can't get off.

I find myself wandering down to the infirmary wing. I know why, and I don't stop myself. My arms wrap my cardigan tighter around my body as I step inside. A few of the pack doctors offer me a smile as they walk by.

My feet come to a halt in the middle of the corridor. I release a soft sigh and inhale the smell of disinfectant. I've never had an issue with hospitals which explains why the scent comforts me.

"Ava?"

I twist to find Gemma walking out of her office with a clipboard.

"Everything okay? Do I need to contact Alpha Jaxon?"

My head shakes. "No. Not at all."

She immediately relaxes, her shoulders drooping. Her eyes roam over my face slowly before she beckons her head to the room on her left. "Would you like to come in and talk?"

"Please," I whisper and grip my hands together.

Gemma flashes me a comforting smile. "After you."

I nod and drop my gaze, following my feet to the room she appeared out of moments ago. When I step inside, I glance at the walls that are painted white but have pretty pictures hanging against them. Most of nature, others of positive quotes.

"Would you like me to shut the door, Ava?"

My head whips over my shoulder. "Keep it open," I say quickly. "*Please*."

"Of course." She nods. "Whatever makes you the most comfortable."

I swallow around the ball of razor blades forming in my throat. My eyes tear away from Gemma's, and I look at pictures on the walls once more.

"*Showing up for yourself is the biggest step. Be proud of every achievement.*"

My head glances at the next quote.

"*It's okay not to be okay. But when we're not okay, we shouldn't put pressure on ourselves. We should treat ourselves with kindness. We should take it one day at a time. We're all human. We all feel the same emotions.*"

Gemma's presence pauses at my side. "I like that quote," she says quietly. "Although we could argue we're wolves, not humans."

"Does being a wolf feel different to being a human?" I ask curiously.

She hums softly. "Well, I know for a fact wolves definitely feel emotions harder because of the bonds given to us by the Moon Goddess. But that doesn't take anything away from how humans feel. We're all unique. We're all different. No one should tell us how we feel."

My tongue runs along my bottom lip as my mouth turns dry. "Sometimes, I don't know how I feel."

I clutch my elbows and tug my arms closer to my chest for some kind of self-comfort. "How do you think you feel?"

"Lost."

Gemma nods in understanding. I expect to see sympathy or pity, but nothing of the sort crosses her face. She looks at me like she sees me. She *really* sees me.

"I understand," she says, tucking a piece of hair behind

her ear. "Being here must be confusing and overwhelming for you. So many new faces, new feelings, new emotions."

My lips part, and I hesitate before I speak. "I guess I don't know who I can trust. I'm scared to get close to anyone to find out they're not who they say they are."

"Has that happened to you in the past?"

I shake my head. "No. I knew who the bad guys were immediately. But I don't think I'll survive it if I find out the people in this pack aren't good people, and I'm trapped."

"You aren't trapped, Ava. No one is stopping you from leaving. I understand Alpha Jaxon bringing you here might have triggered something for you, but he did it so we could treat your wounds. I fear you wouldn't have made it if he had let you go." Her voice softens, and I find myself believing her.

I move my head and walk to the next painting. The air in the room feels a little tighter than before. I didn't come here to talk about anything in particular. I came to get out of my own head and gather company in the doctor whom I am gradually learning to trust.

"Did you want to sit down?" she offers. "We can talk about whatever you want."

My throat clears. "No, thanks. I want to stand."

"Whatever you wish."

I roll my finger over my elbow slowly, playing with a piece of thread that has fallen out of sequence. "I guess–" I start and stop immediately.

Gemma doesn't push me to continue.

"I guess I'm feeling a bit lonely today."

"And you came here to seek company?

My head nods subtly. "I feel safe here. Is that stupid?"

"Not at all. If you want this to be your safe space, this can be your safe space. My office door is always open, unless I have another patient. But we have plenty of other rooms exactly like this."

I clutch my elbows tighter. "I want to remember... before."

Yet, my memory is clouded with all the bad things I've experienced instead.

"If you want, we can attempt to work through it together. Figure out things you remember without diving too deep into the parts that make you feel uncomfortable," Gemma says from across the room.

A sigh escapes my lips. "I told you before. I don't think I'm strong enough."

"I'll never push you to speak about things you don't want to."

I roll my lips together and stare at the picture of a rainbow in a daisy field.

"Jaxon says I'm his mate," I blurt out.

Gemma offers me a small smile.

"I don't know how I feel about it."

"Why's that?"

Tension builds in my chest, and I push it away before I start breathing too quickly. "Because Lucien said the same thing, and he–"

I pause, and Gemma remains silent.

The words almost form in my mouth, but they taste like poison. I squirm at the thought and bite down on my jaw in response. "H-he did things to me. He hurt me."

"And you're fearful Jaxon will be the same?"

All I can do is nod.

"Which is completely understandable, Ava. You've been a human your whole life, and being thrown into this new world is confusing. Even us wolves find things hard to digest."

I lower my head. "Is there anyone in the house except Jaxon you feel comfortable being around?"

My teeth clamp on my bottom lip. "Lucy," I exhale quietly. "I'm more comfortable being around women."

"Now, this is just a suggestion, and I'm not telling you what to do. But if you told Lucy you'd like to spend some more time with her, I know she'd drop everything in a heartbeat. That woman is wonderful." I glance over my shoulder to find Gemma beaming at me with honesty.

"Maybe."

Gemma slides her hands into her pockets casually. "The past of someone doesn't define them. I see you, Ava. I see a strong woman who is bound to shine. It's okay to do things at your own pace."

The corner of my lip twitches, but it doesn't quite make a full smile.

"Not sure about the strong part," I murmur.

"I beg to differ. You could set yourself a goal or a task; it doesn't have to have a timescale. Only when you feel comfortable. This pack treats everyone like family, and they will always have your back."

I stare at the blank wall and fill my lungs with oxygen. "I can try."

"And I'll be here if you wish to talk. Small progress is still progress. Don't let anyone tell you any different."

11

AVA

When some of the pack enter the house a few hours later, I timidly loiter by the stairs. My eyes focus on Lucy as she talks with Phia. I remember her from my day in the rain. Lucy spots me from across the hallway and approaches.

"Hey, Ava," she says warmly. "How are you?"

"I'm okay," I admit.

Lucy's smile is warm and makes my bones relax. "I'm just about to make some lunch in Jaxon's private kitchen. Would you like to join me?"

My head nods before I register I'm doing it. "Yes, please."

Her expression lights up, and I can tell she's trying her hardest not to overreact. It's been a while since I've spoken to her one-on-one. I think about what Gemma said, and this is progress, even if it seems tiny to some.

I follow her into the empty kitchen. I'm relieved Jaxon has private areas for his family. "Remind me to tidy up after lunch," Lucy murmurs. "Bash was almost banned from coming in here this morning."

"Why?"

Lucy glances at me. "Because Jaxon cannot stand mess. He likes everything tidy, the sides wiped down, and no plates lying around. He takes it pretty seriously, especially in his private kitchen."

"Doesn't everyone want that?"

She snorts. "Not in the way Jaxon does. He sees a crumb and loses his head."

"Where is he today?"

"He's still out," she says as she walks towards the fridge. "Did you need him?"

I shake my head. "Just curious."

"He'll be back soon."

"Okay," I whisper as I settle on the stool by the counter.

My eyes follow Lucy as she walks around the kitchen, preparing food for our lunch. "How are things?" she asks.

"They're okay," I admit. Nothing more or less than okay. I guess I'm just surviving right now.

After my episode in Jaxon's office, I haven't stopped thinking about the way he knew how to calm me down. I've never come around so quickly. It's like the sound of his voice was an antidote to all the fears that echoed in my head.

Then I remember the picture frame I smashed.

"Lucy," I breathe. "Can I ask you a question?"

"Mmm," she nods. "Sure can."

I let my mouth hang open as I find the words. The question is simple, and I'm not sure why I care—my curiosity is getting the better of me. "Who is the woman in the picture with Jaxon in his office?

She stops what she's doing immediately and looks at me. "I–" she starts. "Uh. I want to tell you, Ava, but it should come from Jaxon. He wants to tell you, and he will, but he wants the time to be right, for him and for you."

For him and for me?

"I haven't seen her around," I blurt.

"Because she's not," Lucy sighs. "I don't want to say any more. It's Jaxon's story to tell."

"Okay."

Lucy's head moves awkwardly, and she scratches the back of her head. "Actually, Ava, I have something I need to admit to you."

My eyes flick between hers as she moves closer. "You do?"

The heat across my body spikes. "I'm not just a werewolf." She runs her tongue across her lip. "I'm also a witch. I have the ability to see into people's pasts. I can usually control it, but other times, I can't."

I stay silent as guilt washes over her eyes. Tightness forms in my throat.

"The day we brought you here, I couldn't control my powers. I saw things I shouldn't have seen, and I'm sorry. I carry so much guilt with me." Her voice heaves, and tears sting my eyes. "I didn't tell anyone else what I saw. I only mentioned to Jaxon a name because we wanted you to be safe. I'm so sorry."

My entire body shakes. *She saw.* She saw what I went through.

Lucy steps closer, but she doesn't touch me or suffocate my space. "I know it was a complete invasion of privacy. If I could change it, I would."

"Y-you saw?"

She nods slowly. "Not everything. Parts."

My head pounds at the confession. What exactly did she see? A strange wave churns in my gut. "I'm sorry," I whisper.

"Why are you sorry? It's not your fault."

I shrug helplessly. My entire soul was on display.

Goddamn this world I don't understand.

"Why didn't you tell Jaxon?"

"Because it's not my story to tell." Her voice is gentle, but I can't meet her eyes. "And I understand why you don't trust us. But I'm proud of you. I'm proud of your strength."

I haven't heard those words in a long, *long* time.

The hairs on the back of my neck begin to stand, and I know we're amongst company right now. "Hey." Jaxon's voice is deep. "You guys okay?"

My head lifts to meet his gaze across the kitchen. I know tears are still resting in my lash line, but I don't have the ability to push them away. A breath fills my lungs, and instead of being filled with dread, it's replaced with a lighter emotion I didn't expect.

"Yeah." Lucy nods and places a hand on her hip. "We were just talking about my wedding."

The change of conversation is quick, and I'm relieved, but I still gawk at Lucy. "You're getting married?" I glance down at the beautiful sapphire and diamond ring on her finger.

"Yes," she hisses through a forced grin. "That's literally what we were just talking about."

Jaxon flicks his eyes between us suspiciously, and I realise I need to play along because I don't want to bring up our past conversation. "Yes." I nod in agreement. "When is it?"

"A few months yet." She busies herself with lunch again. "And, of course, you're invited, Ava. We could go into town and find you a dress."

I find myself blinking at her suggestion.

"Easy, Luce," Jaxon cuts in. "One day at a time, right?"

I'm thankful to hear him speak because he's right. I didn't think I'd be invited to her wedding. We barely know each other. My eyes focus on Jaxon as he folds his broad arms over his chest. Only now have I really noticed how tall he is, but his presence doesn't necessarily make the room smaller.

"How did he propose?" I ask genuinely.

Jaxon groans as he inches closer to the counter and rolls his eyes. "You did not want to ask that."

I study his playful features as his dark blue eyes settle on mine. He offers me a small smile, but I'm all for listening to the story. "This is my favourite story to tell." She grins back at me. "Basically–"

Jaxon shakes his head and flashes his large hands. "Alright, before you get into this story for the hundredth time, I'm going to take a shower."

"Fine." She waves him off. "Go."

I swallow and look back at him, then he gives me a simple nod and leaves.

"So, Sebastian had been so quiet to me the week he was planning on proposing, and I thought something was wrong. Turns out he was just nervous." She smiles, and I try to replicate a small one. "He took me to this beautiful little village near the seaside. The sun was shining, and the sand was golden. We took our shoes off and took a little dip. It was just us, and I didn't expect a thing."

I prop my hand on my fist to listen in. "He said he wanted to take some pictures of me against the sun as it started to set. The sky was lit up in the most beautiful colours of orange and red. Then, when I turned around, he was on one knee and asked me to marry him."

She presses a hand to her heart, remembering the moment. I'm pleased for her. I'm glad someone gets their happy ever after.

I can't remember the last time I was happy...

"I know it doesn't sound all flashy and whatnot, but it

was perfect. It was just us. We could hear the waves behind us. Oh, my. It is my favourite day ever." Lucy glances down at her stunning ring.

"That sounds lovely," I admit. "Peaceful."

She grins in my direction. "It was. I'm so excited to marry him."

"He's your mate?"

"Yes." She continues beaming. "Soulmate. Fated mate. My absolute everything."

My heart pounds for her. "How long ago did you meet?"

"Around five years ago."

"How long did it take for you to fall in love with him?" I ask before I can truly think it through.

Lucy's eyes glimmer in my direction. "Not long. Obviously, our wolves were inseparable, but we had an instant connection neither of us could deny. But I know it's about getting to know them as a person."

Her outburst of confessions makes my chest twinge. Is that how mates are truly meant to be? The kind of love you read about in books and see in movies—the kind where you genuinely cannot live without the other.

"I'm pleased for you," I say quietly. "I'm glad you're happy."

"And you, too, Ava. You will find your happiness soon."

12

JAXON

I sit in my office, staring down at my dark wooden desk. The picture inside the frame Ava smashed rests on the corner. I haven't had time to replace it. I lean over to take the photo between my fingers.

My heart thumps at Julia's face. The pair of us. All the grief I've endured over the past year. I notice that my face falls into a soft frown when I can't take my eyes off her. I despise myself for being in this situation, especially now I've been given a second mate who needs all the love one could possibly give her.

When my mind twitches to Ava, my wolf howls at the thought of her. I could never forget Julia, but he's got other ideas. Right now, Ava is the centre of his focus. I miss Julia more than anything, but Ava's presence has spun my world entirely.

There's a knock at my office door, and I lower the photo. "Come in."

Kayden emerges and offers me a nod. "Jaxon." He bows his head slowly. "Busy working?"

"All of the stuff I missed? Yeah. I'm trying to get everything back under control. I can't believe I left everything for this long. The pack would have fallen apart without you."

"Don't overwork yourself. You've been up here for hours."

I shrug. "It's not overworking when there's a pile-up."

"Then, let me help."

"No, you've done more than enough."

Kayden raises his brows, calling bullshit.

"What?" I slump back into my chair.

"I can see where this is going." He holds up his hands in defence. "I know you're a perfectionist, but not everything needs to get done within seconds. You're going to end up burning yourself out or messing up. That's the last thing we need from you."

My eyes roll. "Did you need something, Kayden? Other than bothering me."

"It's my job to bother you." He flashes me a lazy smile.

"Don't I know it," I mutter under my breath.

"Just checking how you are. How are things going with Ava? You seem like you're getting your spark back again."

My brows raise. "I do?"

"Yeah." He pauses by my desk and shoves his hands into his pockets. "I know you miss us. I know you miss stepping up as our Alpha. I can only imagine this has to do with Ava and the bond that's growing between you."

I lean back in my chair and sigh. "My head's a mess. I feel guilty for wanting to let the bond strengthen between us, and then I think about Julia. My heart hasn't been the same since she left us."

Kayden nods. "I get that. But don't you think she'd want you to be happy? You're not going to forget about her. She's always going to be a part of your life, but that doesn't mean you can't develop things with Ava. The Moon Goddess doesn't lie. She's blessed you with a second mate for a reason."

I bury my head in my hands. "Some days, I wake up excited to see Ava's face, and then I think about Julia and the way she looked when they–"

"Stop torturing yourself, Jaxon." Kayden's loud voice snaps me back into the room and away from my wandering thoughts. "I get it. She's gone. We all miss her. But Ava, she needs you. She needs us as a pack, even if she's human. Sometimes, I wanna kick your ass to make you see sense."

"Fucking dare." I point a finger at him.

Kayden's mouth stretches into a shit-eating grin. "When you need it, I'm going to deliver. Don't you worry."

I huff out a breath through my nose.

"I know things are hard, but when do you ever give up?"

My eyes harden. "Never."

"Then let all of these negative emotions go. You can grieve; I am not taking that away from you. But your family has been here the entire time. We're not the same when you're not with us. If anything, it's Ava who has allowed us to see you more over the past month. She's bringing you back slowly, even if you don't see it yourself."

Deep down, I know he's right. I've spent more time in the house than I have in my office, all because I want to make sure Ava is comfortable.

"I'm taking it one day at a time."

"And I'm proud of you, brother. But if you ever make me say that soppy shit again, I'll have to kill you."

The corner of my mouth tips in amusement. "I'll call a training session for today. It's been long overdue."

Kayden grins. "Thank the Goddess. I know work is important, but so is reconnecting with the pack. They'll be ready and waiting."

SECOND CHANCE MATES

∼

I DEFINITELY MISSED TAKING charge and being with my loyal pack members. How could I not? They've stuck by me, even when I've been an asshole and deserve nothing but silent treatment. I've been absent during the time I was grieving Julia, and I have a lot to make up for.

At least I can admit it's good for distractions, even when I didn't want to listen to their words of advice. I thought I knew best, and I thought wrong.

Alphas don't like being told what to do; I can vouch for that.

During our training session, I find my wolves are more than eager to please, and I appreciate every second of it. They respond to my orders, and together, we connect on a new level. Despite not being able to shift because my wolf refuses to show himself, I've used my human strength to push through instead.

By the end of the training session, I know I've worked them to the bone. I might be a pusher, but it's for the greater good. They need to move outside of their comfort zones to improve, and I'm making up for lost time.

I'm not going to let them down again. I'm not going to let myself down either.

I'm striving to be a better man—someone my dad would be proud of.

When we all prowl back to the pack house, I spot a figure in the window. I recognise Ava's long dark hair and piercing brown eyes. My lip curls at her curiosity. She's beginning to ask more questions, but it's mostly directed at Lucy because they spend more time together. A part of me is slightly envious, but at the same time, I know she needs her comfort first.

My time will come, when I've earned it. I'm sure of it.

I slip through the back door of my private kitchen where Ava is standing. Her eyes roam over my body, taking in my sweaty skin and dirty forearms before landing on my face.

"Hey." I smile at her. "You okay?"

Ava nods once. "Hey." Her voice is quiet. "Yeah. I was watching you guys."

Warmth spreads in my heart at her confession. "It's been a while since I've been out there."

"Why?"

"I've been isolating myself."

"I do that, too. It doesn't help anything," she admits, wrapping her hands around her elbows.

My head moves in agreement. "You're right; it doesn't."

Ava's mouth opens and then shuts. I frown as she reserves herself and steps away, turning her back on me to leave the kitchen.

"Did you want to ask me something?"

Her shoulders tense for a moment before she glances at me. "I have a thousand questions," she whispers. "But I'm not sure I'm ready for the answers."

My forehead pinches at her statement. "I don't want you worrying about being here. If you have concerns or questions, I want you to be able to ask them."

Ava glances over my body. "I guess you should shower first."

"Sorry, do I smell?" I say playfully.

Her nose twitches. "A little. Yeah."

A deep laugh rumbles from my chest, catching both of us by surprise. Her eyes widen slightly, but she doesn't look frightened. "I'll go shower, and then I'll meet you in the living room?"

"Sure."

I'm gone for no longer than fifteen minutes. Ava is sitting on the sofa in my segregated lounge. Here, we have all the peace and quiet she needs to ask her questions.

I perch on the other end of the sofa, reminding myself to give her space.

"Okay," I say, taking her in. "What did you want to ask?"

Ava twiddles with her fingers for a long moment before her lips part. "Are we on land where there are only wolves?"

"Yes." I nod. "For miles, this is werewolf territory. This area is called Wildemount, and that's the name of our pack. The human district is further north."

"Wildemount Pack?"

"Yes."

"And you're the Alpha?"

"Yes."

She hums softly, and I study her lips as she presses them together. "I don't understand much about the bond and what it means. Why us? Why me?"

"The Moon Goddess makes these choices for us. She pairs us with people she thinks are compatible," I explain.

Ava's face morphs into disgust. "So she mated me with Lucien because she thought we'd be a good match?"

I wince. "That's something I can't explain, and I'm sorry. I'm only grateful that she's led you into my path where you're safe. She's granted us both a second chance, which is unheard of in our realm."

She's startled. "Oh."

The room falls silent for a moment, and I let her digest my words.

"The woman in the picture," she blurts suddenly.

"Yeah."

"Who is she?"

"Julia. Her name was Julia. She was my fated mate before she was taken away from me."

"How?"

"She was killed."

Ava frowns. "I'm so sorry."

My eyes lower to the sofa. "It's been almost eleven months, but it's been hard. At first, it felt like half of my soul had been ripped from me. But since you came into my life, I've been fighting a thousand different emotions."

"How long were you together for?"

"Almost two years."

Ava's eyes glimmer with sadness. "I'm so sorry for your loss."

"It's okay."

Silence envelops us again for a long moment before she asks, "And what does that mean for us?" Her brows crease in confusion.

I clear my throat. "I'm as surprised as you are. Second-chance mates are known to be a myth. But something happened, and we've both been directed towards each other for a reason."

She swallows harshly and stares at me for a few seconds. "Everything is hard to grasp when Lucien kept a lot from me."

"I get that," I say slowly. "But nothing between us has to be forced or rushed. I'm happy to go at whatever pace. My heart is still grieving Julia, and it's not fair to put you through that. I want to be honest and transparent with you."

"She's not someone you can easily get over." Her expression softens. "You will probably love her for the rest of your life."

I slide my hands down my thighs. "Yeah, I probably will."

"Do we have to be together?"

"No," I state. "But being without each other will hurt us internally and our wo–" I cut myself off. "My wolf. But I won't force you into anything. I'm not that kind of man. I want what's best for you and nothing else."

Ava buries her head in her hands. "How can I be mated to two wolves but be human?"

"I don't know," I admit. "Human mates are extremely rare, but second-chance mates are unheard of. You must be one powerful anomaly."

She leans back into the sofa and shakes her head. "I can't believe this is happening to me. I can't believe *any* of this is happening to me. It's messing with my head."

"I know." I frown. "And I'm sorry."

I pray she starts to remember her past so she can have some kind of connection to the human world. I fear she's losing her sanity, being in our realm and adjusting to our way of life.

"Tell me more about the mate bond," she says suddenly. Her feet move to the floor, and she angles her body towards mine. "That day you found me in your office, the sound of your voice and the way you cradled my hands had me calm within minutes. H-how?"

I offer her a small smile and lean forward. "Because mate bonds are there to help one another. To ground them and remind them they are loved and cared for."

Ava blinks once. "It felt so warm like someone had wrapped me up in a blanket and gave me a hug. I-I've never felt anything like it in my life."

"Because it's unlike anything else in the world. It's indescribable."

She nods in agreement. "Panic attacks hurt me, and the pain was masked. It was like you absorbed some of it."

"The mate bond probably did. I used my power to take away your agony."

"That's incredible," she whispers, unable to take her pretty eyes off me. "I just don't understand how."

I stare down at her hands cupped in her lap. "It's a hard concept to grasp, I know. Over time, it'll only grow stronger as the connection builds. What you felt the other night is nothing in comparison to what it could be."

Ava's mouth falls open. "How do you build the connection?"

"By being around each other, talking, touching."

"Oh—"

"But we don't have to do any of that. Only what you're comfortable with."

Ava's eyes dart to my hands and she chews down on her lip as if she's in deep thought. "What if you held my hand again? Would it do it, then?"

I nod when she glances up. "It will."

Silence washes over us for a long moment until she meets my gaze and hesitates. "C-can we—"

"You want me to hold your hand?"

"Uh—"

"How about you hold my hand?" I suggest.

Ava's head moves, but she fixates on my palms. "Okay."

She doesn't move at first, but after a few minutes, she leans over and holds her fingers above the centre of my hand. We don't even need to touch to feel the electricity that courses through my veins. I glance up at Ava. She doesn't seem to feel it the same way I do, but I know my wolf's senses are heightened.

After another minute, she drops her finger to mine and loops them together. Relief and comfort crash over my body like a wave. I close my lids for a moment before snapping them open to watch. She fights her eyes to stay open as she squeezes her finger around mine.

But to my surprise, she stretches her other fingers out and laces them through my own. Fireworks explode in my mind at the small connection. It's intensified by a million because she's the one who initiated it—I have a very small portion of her trust.

A sharp breath escapes when she slides her hand against my palm. A shiver trails down my spine. Her cheeks begin to heat to a rosy pink, and her pouty lips part as she explores my hand with her own.

"Wow," she exhales. "This is..."

She can't even finish her sentence, but I know exactly what she means.

"Beautiful?"

"Refreshing."

My lips curl into a smile, and our eyes meet. Her fingers pause on my palm, and she reluctantly pulls away. I'm met with coldness, but my wolf is happy to be in her presence.

"Thank you," she whispers.

"For what?"

"For letting me do it on my own and reminding me that I can."

13

JAXON

I've had an early morning of sifting through piles of more work I've ignored over the last few months. This is the third morning in a row—which often drags into the afternoon. Kayden's thoughts buzz around my head. *You're going to overwork yourself.*

Maybe I'm heading that way, but I won't stop until it's done.

Once I've cleared my backlog, I'll be able to focus on calculating a plan to take down Lucien's pack. I don't want to make any mistakes. I want to wipe him and anyone who has ever touched Ava from this world. I don't care what their excuses are; I want them to pay for what they've done to her. I want her to be at peace, knowing they no longer exist in the world.

I head downstairs once I've completed as much work as I can before my head explodes. I need to call a meeting soon to pitch my ideas and see where the plan can lead us.

When I reach the kitchen, I'm surprised to see Lucy standing outside on the patio, trimming the plants she's been growing. I never took her for the type to have a green thumb, but she's done well not to kill them.

"Where's Ava?" I ask as I push open the back door.

"She's with Gemma." She offers me a small smile. "She's been having a lot of sessions with her."

My brows rise. "I know."

"Do you know how they're going?"

"No." I cup my elbows. "I don't want to push her. I'm letting her come to me."

Lucy nods and attends to her gardening again. "And how's that going for you?"

"She held my hand on her own accord the other day," I admit. "That was a big step for her."

"Good for her." She flicks her blonde hair over her shoulder, and I catch the smile she's sporting. "She's slowly finding her feet."

I hum softly before leaving her to the plants. I find myself wandering around the perimeter of our house, checking in on our security guards and those who are on territory watch. Everything seems in check.

Since I met Ava, I stepped up security within our land. I'm not taking any chances. I want this place to be her sanctuary.

When I return, I find Ava making herself a drink in the kitchen. I knock on the door so I don't startle her, but she turns unphased. "I knew you were there."

"You did?" I raise my brows and lean on the counter beside her.

She stirs her tea and nods. "Whenever you're around, the hairs on my arms stand without me even seeing you. I've got used to it now."

That proves the bond is strengthening—and not just on my part.

"How was your session with Gemma?" I ask curiously.

She turns towards me with cautious eyes. "Yeah, it was fine."

"Only fine?"

"As fine as therapy can be," Ava says quietly. "W-we're trying to figure out my past."

I pause for a moment and take her in. "Yeah?"

"Yeah."

"How was it?"

"Unsuccessful."

The frown that covers her face is adorable and hurts my heart at the same time. "It's okay," I reassure her. "There will be other chances for you guys to talk and figure things out in your own time."

Ava sighs softly and looks away, pulling her teaspoon out of her mug and leaving it on the side. The clean freak inside me tightens, but I don't want to disrupt this conversation. Instead, I take the spoon and silently place it in the dishwasher.

"I guess. It's frustrating because I want to remember, but everything's so blurry, and I can't concentrate on a single detail."

"You'll get there eventually. I know it," I say with a smile.

She nods but doesn't respond. Lucy and Sebastian enter the kitchen a few moments later. "Guys, I had the best idea ever!"

"What's that?" I ask over my shoulder.

"The sun is shining, and the weather is gorgeous. We should totally head down to the lake and take a swim, enjoy the sun, and eat some late lunch. What do you guys think?" Lucy's expression glows.

"Don't you have lessons with the witches today?" I quirk a brow.

SECOND CHANCE MATES

My sister shakes her head. "We got up early and did them this morning. But you wouldn't know because you're too busy working away in your office."

"For important reasons."

Lucy dismisses me. "But it will be good to get some fresh air and get away from the house."

I turn back to Ava, who is holding her scalding tea between her hands and raising it to her lips. "Do you want to?"

Those eyes cut to mine, and she pulls back. "I–Uhh–" She pauses. "I don't have anything to wear."

"You can have something of mine," Lucy interjects. "Might be good for you to get out of the house. What do you think?"

She flicks her gaze between the three of us. "Oh..." Her throat constricts.

"You don't have to. Don't feel pressured."

"No." Ava shakes her head. "I want to. Like you said, it'll be good to get out of the house. I think I could do with a change of scenery."

Lucy claps her hands together. "Amazing. We're just going to grab our things, and then we can leave in half an hour. I'll leave some clothes on your bed, Ava."

"Thanks," she says from behind me.

Soon, she leaves to pack her things together and get dressed. I do the same. I can't remember the last time I was at the lake. It's been a long few years since I enjoyed my free time.

I tell Kayden to take charge whilst I'm gone. It's rare I take time for myself—except for my dark days. Now, it's not just for me; it's for Ava, too. If getting her out of the house can help with her mental battle in any way, then I'm here to try it.

Lucy and Sebastian are waiting for me when I reach the bottom of the stairs. Ava tucks a piece of hair behind her ear as she watches me approach. To my surprise, she smiles, stretching those pretty pink lips.

We jump in my car and take the short journey to the lake. Luckily, it's on our property, meaning it's ours whenever we want to use it. It's one of the benefits of owning a lot of land within our district and guaranteeing privacy.

The car comes to a stop, and Ava glances out the window at the entrance to the lake. She pops the door open and steps out, leaving her hand on the edge of the window. "Wow," she whispers. "It's beautiful."

I step out after her and look across the lake that the sun is gleaming off. The tall trees crowd the rippling water, making the place look majestic. I've always loved coming here—it reminds me of where I grew up, and this feels like home from home.

"The water is so clear," Ava whispers under her breath.

My mouth forms a smile. "Did you think it was going to be murky and green?"

"Yeah. I guess I did. I don't know why."

"Ahhh, I love it here," Lucy squeals as she joins us. "Let's set up and get into the water. It's a hot one today."

As she rushes away with Sebastian, I glance back at Ava, who grabs her bag and takes timid steps towards the lakefront. "You okay?" I ask.

A soft hum vibrates through her lips. "Yeah. I'm just–" She pauses. "I'm grateful to be here."

Something weird happens to my heart. A pang almost sends me toppling over. I struggle to take my eyes off her as she takes in every last detail of the lake. She's counting her blessings for this freedom.

All I know is that revenge will be *sweet*.

Lucy and Sebastian are already swimming off towards the other side. "Do you want to get in?" I ask before grabbing the hem of my T-shirt from my neck and tugging it off my body.

Ava's eyes immediately focus on my bare chest, and then she blinks once, then twice. I clear my throat quietly as her cheeks bleed with a blush that makes her look incredibly innocent. My head tilts down to my abs and muscles, which are all packed together. If anything came from Julia's passing, I spent a lot of time exercising to get myself out of the darkest depths of hell.

"Yeah," she says after a long moment. I turn around when she takes off her leggings. "I feel more comfortable going in like this."

She's in one of Lucy's old T-shirts. I nod my understanding. "You don't have to explain yourself to me."

I know I shouldn't be looking, but I do. Her arms and legs are beginning to fill out from when she first came to the house. She's been eating her portions and even going in for seconds, which makes my heart sing with pride. I'm relieved she's treating her body with the care and love it needs. But when I look down to her ankles to find scars of where she's been shackled and cuts and marks across her thighs and arms from where she's endured pain over and over, I tell myself to take a breath.

My eyes close automatically. The thought has my wolf ready to turn back and run straight to Lucien to kill him right now. How could anyone do that to someone, let alone their mate?

The thought makes my stomach fold.

Ava pauses at the lakefront and dips her toes in before releasing a low shriek. "What's wrong?" I step towards her.

"Co-ld." She shudders, and I release a chuckle.

"I know it's cold this time of year, but surely, it can't be that bad."

Ava's brows rise to her hairline. "It's freezing!"

I take one step forward and let the water meet my bare feet. She's right. It's definitely not warm. "Pfft," I say teasingly. "*Baby.*"

Her mouth hangs open, and then she lowers down to scoop the clear water up between her palms and throws it in my direction. The water hits my body with a splat at the same time, a gust of wind ripples by and makes me groan internally. As werewolves, we have high internal body temperatures, but having it splashed at you still isn't enjoyable.

Then, the most beautiful sound falls from her lips. *She laughs.* It's like all the questions in my life have been answered in those few split seconds. I stare at the way her face lights up with joy and fuck–

I want her to laugh every day.

"You think that's funny, huh?" I flash her a grin.

"I had to prove a point." She covers her hand over her mouth, and I resist the urge to take her wrist so I can witness every second before it disappears.

I shoot her a playful look, but her eyes sparkle.

"Fine. Point proven."

14

AVA

The air tastes so fresh. That might sound like a silly thing to say, but it does. I lift my head up towards the sky and take down a large inhale of oxygen. The cold water of the lake laps around my ankles, and the gentle breeze brushes my skin. This is true freedom. It's like experiencing nature for the first time.

Jaxon walks ahead of me in the lake. I try not to stare at his impressive back muscles, but I can't help it—my eyes instinctively gravitate towards him. Before he can get past his knees, he turns back to me.

Those blue eyes sparkle with calmness, despite being splashed seconds ago. I don't know what came over me; it felt like a natural reaction. It certainly released a burst of amusement through my veins. I can't remember the last time I laughed. The sound was alien, but it felt good, it felt —*liberating*.

He holds out his hand gently, flashing his palm. "Come with me," he says. "You'll warm up once you're in."

I chew on my lip as I focus on the callouses across his fingers. Even though they look rough to touch, they were incredibly soft when I held his hand the other night. Now, I'm faced with the option again. I roll back my shoulders and delicately place my hand in his. He wraps his thumb across my fingers to keep them in place, and a shudder rushes through me.

If I thought I was cold before, I'm wrapped up in a blanket of warmth now.

I glance up to meet Jaxon's eyes, who gives me an encouraging smile. He doesn't clutch my hand in a death grip, but just enough to know he's there. My entire body vibrates at the sensation.

My feet take one step, and before I know it, my knees are under, then my thighs, then my hips. The water doesn't even phase me—not when he's holding my hand like it's the only thing in the world that matters right now.

The hem of my T-shirt dances in the lake as we venture deeper, and soon, I'm treading water. I almost release a whimper when all my limbs start floating like I'm weightless. Jaxon doesn't let go of my hand, and from where he's standing, he can still touch the bottom of the lake.

A ray of sunlight casts over his face, accentuating his tan skin and dark sapphire eyes. "Warmer now?" he asks.

"Yeah." I nod in agreement as the water laps my chin. "Much."

"How does it feel?"

"Incredible."

Jaxon's smile continues to grow. "I love this place. It's so peaceful."

"Do you come here much?"

He shakes his head. "Not as much as I should. It's good for finding your own peace of mind."

"Yeah," I exhale and swim a little further. Our hands leave each other, so I use my arms to keep myself afloat. It's been a while since I last swam, but my muscles are crying at the privilege. "Can I ask you a question?"

"Yes."

"About yourself."

He smiles. "Yes."

"How long have you been the Alpha of this pack?"

"Almost four years."

My brows hit my hairline. "Four years?"

"Yeah, it's flown by."

"How old are you?"

"Twenty-six."

My mouth falls open. "You became Alpha at twenty-two?"

"Yeah. I had to. It's a long story. I won't bore you with it."

I blink and shake my head. "I want to know. This world interests me. I don't really know much about it. I know barely anything."

"Okay." Jaxon nods. My feet continue to kick underneath the water, but I struggle to keep my chin above. "Take my hand."

I watch as his hand raises to the surface. I take it, and he gently tugs me to where I can stand comfortably in the water. The last thing we need is for me to start drowning while he's telling his story.

The corner of his lip twitches a second later. I tilt my head.

He didn't hear that, did he? Maybe I said it out loud.

"Around six years ago, there was a disease that started infecting the werewolf species. Wolves were dropping dead left, right, and centre. People who were infected were highly dangerous, and it was a crisis amongst our districts for a while," he explains, and I watch him intently. "My father was the Alpha of this pack, and my mother was by his side as our Luna. He was a powerful man, and you didn't want to get on the wrong side of him. But the district loved him because he was loyal."

I nod slowly and wait for him to continue. "The disease wasn't going away, and people started to panic. Then rumours started to spread that my father was keeping wolves down in our warehouse basement to torture them. But he wasn't; he was experimenting on the infected to try and find a cure. The district didn't want to believe the truth after wolves started going missing and then ended up dead."

"Oh my God," I exhale shakily.

Jaxon nods. "Yeah. People even started to believe he was the one who created the disease. All he wanted to do was help. I understand that taking wolves and doing your own medical experiments isn't seen as humane, but as a district, we were desperate. I didn't know about the experiments, but I believed him when he told me."

"But no one believed his true intentions?"

"No. Things got out of hand. They tried to push us out of the district. They wanted revenge. They wanted to hurt us." Jaxon's eyes harden. "My father tried to make a deal with the district, but they wanted him dead. They wanted his blood. We had no choice but to move the entire pack to a new district with vacant land before they slaughtered us for his revenge. It was a difficult time."

My mouth parts. "What...you had to move?"

"Yes. But news travelled fast, and my father and mother were ordered to leave our new district to keep the peace. None of us wanted them to go, but they left to guarantee us our safety and security. My father handed down the title of Alpha to me and said to start a new life as best as we can. I haven't seen them in years, and I have no idea if they're alive," he admits.

"I'm so sorry." My lips part, and I shake my head. "What about your safety?"

"The past four years have been hard. We've had a few security scares, and we've been training non-stop. I know they can find us, but a part of me thinks they're looking for my parents instead. They can kill us, but what's that going to do? My father might not even be around to witness it."

I tilt my head away from the sun. "And when your pack moved here, the district accepted you?"

He nods. "We got lucky. I have no idea how. But we've caused no issues in the last few years. We've helped out in the district where we can and have created good allies. I feared becoming an Alpha because I didn't know if I could do a good job of leading after moving from our home. I thought no one would trust us, and I didn't even know if I trusted myself to get us through that mess."

"And each of these districts..." I trail off. "They're big?"

"Huge," he clarifies. "We're talking over a hundred thousand people."

My mouth falls open. "And you know everyone in the district?"

"No. There's no way we'd be able to know everyone, but I try."

"Oh–" I pause, wondering if I'm asking too many questions. A few more can't hurt, hopefully. He seems to absent-mindedly nod at me, so I carry on. "Did it take you a long time to settle into becoming Alpha?"

"Yes," he says without hesitation. "It was hard. It took a good couple of years before I had a grasp on things. I didn't know how I was going to live up to my father. Everyone adored him. I was thrown into it and felt extremely out of my depth. But I had to push through. I had an entire pack behind me, and I refused to let them down. I was definitely a little too rough on them at the start, and I'm still finding my feet today. It's a continuous journey."

I frown softly. "Do you still struggle?"

"Yes," he admits easily. "Every day is a new learning curve. I'm not perfect, but I'm trying my best. I owe my pack a lot after their patience with me. The Goddess knows that I probably don't deserve it."

"I'm sure you do amazing." I smile at him. "So, what about the disease?"

The water around him ripples as he swipes a hand through his hair. "The disease came from a cursed territory. It started infecting rogues, and then it spread to districts, and it took years for it to stop. But then it became eradicated, thank the Goddess."

"Is that what happened to Julia?"

Jaxon's eyes flare with sadness, and I sink into the stones beneath my feet. I shouldn't have said anything. It's not my place to probe him when he hasn't done the same to me.

"I'm sorry." I scrunch up my face in frustration for myself. "I shouldn't have brought her up."

"Is what, what happened?"

I stare into his eyes, and his expression twists to a look of pain. My mouth opens, and I shut it again, rethinking my wording before I say something out of touch. "You said she was murdered; was it by them?"

His lashes brush his cheekbone as he looks down. "No," he whispers. "It was by rogues on our land. They caught us off-guard. I lost sense of everything, and I wasn't thinking logically. At first, I questioned if it was revenge, but there was no evidence to prove it."

"I'm sorry," I say gently. "I can't imagine how much you miss her."

He flashes me a smile that doesn't reach his eyes. "I do.

But I have a family I need to be there for, a pack to run, and now, you're a priority to me."

My heart beats out of time at his declaration. "You care about them a lot."

"I care about you, too, Ava."

An influx of heat spreads across my sternum as Jaxon's gaze moves over my face slowly, taking in every little detail. I release a breath that is clutching my chest. His entire expression softens. Even though we're not touching, I can feel the bond.

How?

"I want to try something, but I don't want to freak you out," he says.

"What do you mean?"

Jaxon closes his eyes and takes down a large gulp of air. A tingling sensation taps around the edge of my head, and I raise my hand to itch it away, except it doesn't go anywhere. The pressure increases, but it's not uncomfortable; it's light and reassuring in ways I don't understand.

Instead of pushing against the sensation, I let it in.

That's when I hear, *Hello. Can you hear my voice?*

I startle. What was that?

Jaxon's lips didn't move an inch, but I heard every rounded syllable of his voice. It wrapped around my brain like a scarf. My mouth opens to speak, but nothing comes out.

"Ava?"

"W-what the hell?" I blurt. "What was that?"

Jaxon's lips curl to the side. "So it did work."

"Did work, *what*?"

I think I'm going crazy. I'm definitely going crazy.

This. It did work.

There is his voice again. In. My. Head.

I shudder at the wave of fulfilment that rushes down my spine. I've heard his voice a bunch of times, but why does it sound so much clearer and intimate when it's in my mind?

No. This must be a joke. It's impossible.

"Are you playing some kind of trick on me?" I flash him a concerned look.

Jaxon releases a deep laugh. *No. It's called a mindlink. I wasn't sure if you'd be able to hear me because you're a human. It's something werewolves can do between mates, family members, and their pack. It's an efficient way of communication.*

I stare back at him, dumbfounded. "At least your phone bills will be low."

That smile spreads, flashing off all of his impressive white teeth. "You're taking this surprisingly well..." he trails off.

"I mean." I scratch my head again. "I don't entirely get it, but your world is full of surprises. It's just strange to hear you...up here."

"Try it on me," he says, giving me a look of encouragement.

My head tilts to the side in confusion. "How? I don't even know where to start."

Jaxon's large arms fold over his chest as he studies me for a long moment. "Just close your eyes," he starts. "Think of directing a message to my head. Think the words loudly and imagine them being sent off into the sphere between us. Aim straight for my mind—nowhere else."

I furrow my brows at his instructions. That sounds like a lot of work for a message. What if I send it to the wrong person?

"Okay," I murmur before closing my eyes.

At first, I imagine his mind, but that's because he's standing right in front of me. I know where he is and how far away he's standing. My eyes squeeze tighter, and I focus on him and nothing else.

"That's it," he praises. "I can feel you. But tell me something. Speak to me."

My teeth clamp down on my bottom lip. *Hello?*

God. This is stupid. Who am I kid–

Hello, Ava.

I snap my eyes open to meet his impressed gaze. "Y-you heard me?" I stutter. He nods with a smile that looks like it'll never disappear—pride shines in his eyes. I'm doing a basic skill they probably use every day. Why does it feel so incredible?

It's amazing, isn't it?

A soft sigh falls from my chest when I hear him again. I resist the urge to close my eyes at the way it drifts over my body like a feather caressing my every last nerve.

"Why do I feel so good hearing you?" I ask out of pure curiosity.

"It's the bond. I told you it doesn't always have to be strengthened by touching. It can come from connecting through talking or being around each other."

A strange sensation suddenly dawns on me. Am I really accepting all of this like it's normal? My life has changed too many times over the past few years. A part of me doesn't even know what I'm doing anymore.

It would help if I could remember a damn thing. But it's like that part of me has been cut off, and I will never access it again.

"What's the matter?" he asks.

I shake my head. "I don't know. I guess this is a lot to process."

"I know." He nods in agreement. "But nothing has to go

faster than you want it to. Everything will be on your terms. I realise how intimidating this all seems."

"Yeah," I rasp. "A lot."

"Guys!" Lucy's voice booms across the lake. "Come use the swing!"

I glance at her across the lake on a large rock. I tell myself not to dwell on these feelings and to just enjoy today. I'm out. I'm breathing fresh air. I'm swimming in calming water. I'm free.

That's what I need to remind myself. *I am free.*

15

JAXON

Since our trip to the lake a few days ago, the pack house has been fairly quiet, which is a relief as I've wanted to stay home and spend time with Ava. She's been making herself known at breakfast and dinner in my private kitchen, even helping Lucy out with a few things to keep herself busy.

I don't want to put all my faith in the bond because I want to give Ava all the credit for how hard she's been trying to settle—despite this not being her true home—but I know the bond between us is helping her realise she can learn to trust me. I want nothing more than for it to be authentic, but I can't physically slow the bond. It's inevitable.

That's why I'm making sure she knows exactly what the bond is doing between us because I want to be honest. The ball is always in her court; I've made that clear from the start.

Ava is currently in the living room reading a book with a hot chocolate and a blanket. I decide to leave her to it, to give her some time alone if that's what she needs.

Lucy meets me in the kitchen and offers me a smile. "So," she drawls. "Has Ava remembered any of her past yet?"

"No." I shake my head. "Gemma is trying to help, but she's struggling."

Lucy frowns. "Has she thought about Googling herself?"

"I don't know." I shrug. "I haven't asked. I don't want to meddle in her business. If she wants to come to me, she can come to me."

"Maybe we should."

I stare at my sister in disbelief. "Are you serious?"

"It's public knowledge. It might help. We might be able to figure out where she lived before. It could jolt her memory," Lucy suggests. "I'm not saying to do a full background check, but if she went missing, then there might be an article online or something."

I run my teeth over my bottom lip. "I don't know, Luce."

"If we find anything of worth, we could show her to see if it helps."

My eyes close for a brief second. I might have done some questionable things in my life, but this settles awkwardly in my stomach. This isn't how I want her to figure out her past, but at the same time, it might bring her closer to being with her family.

"Fine," I grumble. "But if we don't find anything, we leave it, alright?"

Lucy holds up her hands before reaching into her pocket to pull out her phone. I watch the screen as she types in the search bar, *"Ava missing girl England"*.

A bunch of results show on her phone, but she scrolls and scrolls, and none of them contain anything about Ava. "Not a single thing?" I raise a brow.

"What's her surname?"

"White."

Lucy tries again and scrolls with her thumb. I turn away because this is ridiculous. There isn't a single article, and we shouldn't be doing this anyway. This isn't how I want to earn Ava's trust.

"I found something."

I dip my head beside my sister's and glance at the screen. "What?"

She draws up a social media page, where I immediately recognise Ava's face in the profile picture. There's a bright white smile beaming at the camera, eyes full of life and light. *Happiness.* My heart twinges when my wolf realises how broken she seems now, but I know deep down, she's not broken—she's lost her way and in desperate need of love and affection.

"Oh my Goddess," Lucy murmurs. "Jaxon, look."

I spot the post and frown. "People still use this site?"

"Humans. I don't know."

Posted 2 years ago

I just wanted everyone to know I have decided to leave Russell Vale and travel around the world. I wanted to keep this quiet because I didn't want to say goodbye to my friends and family. This is something I have always wanted to do, and I am so happy I am finally free. Don't try to contact me. I want to start fresh with my life and make new memories.
Ava x

"What the fuck?" I curse.

If that doesn't sound suspicious, I don't know what does.

I glance down to find hundreds of comments. "Click on them."

Lucy scrolls until I tell her to stop. I press my finger to the phone and pause on a comment that stands out.

Kayleigh: *How could you leave without even saying goodbye? I thought we were best friends! How could you leave me, reply to my text now!!!!*

"Well, we know she's from Russell Vale," Lucy comments.

"Which is miles from here."

She hums softly. "Lucien must have done this."

"But why? I doubt he cared about having to erase his footsteps. It doesn't make any sense."

"Yeah." She nods in agreement. "Maybe because she's human. People might have been looking for her, and this gives the police a reason not to search."

I stare at the screen for a moment more.

"Are you going to say something to her?"

"She has the right to see this and to connect with her friends and family. But I want her to be ready to see this. I'm worried it might trigger her if she still can't remember."

"Maybe." Lucy lowers her phone. "But it might help."

I chew on the inside of my lip. "I want to see how her sessions with Gemma are going and see if she's making any progress first."

Lucy sighs. "Your call."

The hairs on my arm stand before I hear my mate's voice. "What are you guys up to?"

I whip my head to Ava, standing in the doorway of the kitchen. "Not much," Lucy says. "Just chatting."

My eyes roam over Ava, wearing a mint-green jumper and a pair of grey leggings. Her dark hair is placed in a high ponytail with wispy bits falling around her face. "You okay?" I ask.

"Yeah." She gives me a small smile. "Are you ready to go, Lucy?"

Lucy hums and jumps up. "Of course."

I frown. "Where are you guys going?"

"We're going into town to get a dress for Ava for the wedding," she says as she picks up her keys from the counter. "I asked Ava if she wanted to have a girly day out, and she said yes."

Ava looks at me timidly. "I hope that's okay."

"You can do what you want. Enjoy yourselves," I say before tucking my hand into my trouser pocket and removing my credit card. "Take this."

Lucy swipes it from my hand. "Wow, you never give me this thing."

"It's for Ava." I shoot her a glare. "Buy whatever you want."

"Really?" Ava's cheeks redden.

"Really."

"Let me grab my jacket," Lucy excuses herself from the kitchen.

Ava takes a step towards me. "Thank you."

We stare at each other for a second, and I'd kill for a moment to give her a hug or a small embrace. But I don't—even though I can see slight hesitation in her eyes. "Bye, Jax."

A shiver runs down my spine at the nickname. "Bye, Ava. Have fun."

I walk them both to the front door before offering a wave.

∼

During the three hours Ava is gone, I have security reports sent to my desk, work around my plan to attack Lucien's pack, and have Kayden lead a hunting session. *Three hours.* Yet, the house feels cold.

I run a hand down my face in defeat. My wolf howls inside me the second they step through the front door. I stand from my desk and head downstairs to find them walking into the kitchen with a thousand shopping bags.

Oh, boy.

Lucy's head twists, and she exhales an exasperated sigh. "Good, you're here." She grins. "You can take these."

I walk towards Ava to take the bags from her hands to find red marks across her palms. "I'll take those."

Ava's big eyes sag with relief. "Thank you."

"Uh. What about me?"

"Am I your housekeeper?"

Lucy rolls her eyes and leaves them at the door to the kitchen.

But my gaze stays firmly on my mate. Her scent is stronger now. The soft smell of vanilla and chestnut hits me right in the sternum. It's like instant medicine for any ache or pain.

"How was dress shopping?" I ask Ava.

She hums gently, the sound vibrating my ears. "Yeah, it went well. We found a dress."

"Yeah?"

Lucy's eyes explode. "She looks absolutely gorgeous in it!"

Ava looks a little overwhelmed with her rosy cheeks and sharpened breath. "Come," I beckon my head to her as we walk into the kitchen. "Sit."

She perches on the stool by the counter as I grab her a glass of water. "Thank you," she says gratefully before taking a couple of large sips.

I watch her intently, and her eyes flick to mine. They move from my face to the counter and back again. "What?"

"Nothing." I shake my head with a smile. "I'm just glad you're back."

"Awww," Lucy chimes behind me. "Miss her already?"

"Yeah, I did."

Ava's cheeks bleed even darker as she covers her lips with the glass once more.

"So." I clear my throat to take the attention away from my statement. "Are you going to show me what you got for the wedding?"

"Nope," Lucy says when Ava opens her mouth. "It's going to be a surprise."

Even the thought of seeing Ava in a dress makes my bones chill in excitement. You would think I had never seen a woman in a dress before. She's beautiful in a jumper and lounge pants —I am not denying that—but I'm dying to see Ava dressed up.

"Well..." I shrug. "I look forward to it."

"You should." Lucy wags her eyebrows at me.

"What are you doing tonight, Luce?"

"Bash is taking me out for dinner."

I nod. "Nice."

"What about you guys?"

My eyes wander over to Ava, who is already staring at me. "I was hoping to cook this one a nice dinner. What do you say?"

The corners of her lips curl subtly, and she nods with bright eyes. "Yeah. I'd like that."

"Cute." Lucy gives me a wink. "Well, you guys enjoy. I need to start getting ready."

When my sister is gone, I focus on Ava again. "Is there anything in particular you'd like for dinner?"

She nibbles on her bottom lip for a long moment. "Surprise me."

My brows raise at her suggestion. "Okay. Surprise it is."

∽

"How was town today?" I ask as we dig into our dinner.

Ava nods and covers her mouth as she chews. "Busy. A little overwhelming, but it felt good to get out. I can't remember the last time I went shopping."

"I'm glad you had a good time."

Her brown eyes lay on mine for a moment. "Is there always a man at the market singing really badly and playing that instrument that has a keyboard and harmonica in one?"

I bark out a laugh, almost choking on a piece of pasta. "Yeah, he's kind of a legend around here."

"Legend?" She chuckles with tinted cheeks. "It was a lot to take in."

"You get used to him and the sound of his voice."

Ava hides her smile. "Maybe it was just me. He did have a lot of coins in his case."

"He works hard and definitely brightens people's day."

"This is amazing." Ava releases a satisfied sigh as she places her knife and fork together. She's practically licked the spinach and ricotta ravioli off the plate. "Thank you, Jax."

"You're more than welcome."

I stand from the table to take the plates, but she rushes to do the same. "I can do that," she says.

"Sit down," I say gently. "I can clear up."

I wander over to the sink to rinse off the plates. "Well, at least let me dry up?" she offers as she appears by my side in a flash.

My eyes flick down to her pleading expression. "Okay."

I clean the plates and utensils before handing them to her. Our arms brush every now and then, and I bite down on my jaw to suppress the instant warmth that rushes over my body. I know she feels it, too, because she gasped the first time.

"Thank you," I say as I hand her the last plate to dry.

Her dainty fingers use the tea towel to remove the droplets before placing it on the counter. "No." She shakes her head. "Thank you for tonight. It was wonderful. It was *normal*." She beams at me with all her undivided attention. "No one has ever cooked me dinner like that."

"Well, get used to it." I flash her a confident smile.

Ava's throat tenses when her eyes roam my face. Her scent intensifies and wraps around my lungs like a crushing blow. It's intoxicating and beautiful.

My hand raises slowly by default, and her lips part when I rest my fingers against her jaw, tilting it ever so carefully. A sound falls from her chest—somewhere between a sigh of relief and a groan.

My nostrils flare at the sound as I step into her, the lower part of her back hitting the counter. My finger trails across her skin softly, over her jawbone and up the pad of her cheek.

All the heat from my body transfers into hers—a live wire between us. Bright colours spiral in my mind at the gentle connection. I can't stop. Her skin is like silk beneath my fingers.

Her heart pounds. I can hear it roar in my ears. I step closer again, testing the waters, and her eyes flutter shut when I flick my thumb over her chin. It's a soft caress, nothing more, but it's euphoric. My blood hums in my veins.

Our chests graze by a millimetre, but I don't move any

closer. Her breathing becomes louder and less controlled. I flick my gaze across her face to find her brows pinching together as if she's in pain.

Before I can drop my hand, she shoves at my chest, but I don't move an inch. Instead, she slips from beneath me and moves as far away from me as possible before burying her head in her hands.

An influx of emotions hit me square in the chest, then followed by thoughts that are muddled and inaudible. "Ava–"

"Do *not* touch me."

I blink at the rawness of her voice. "I'm sorry," I heave loudly. "I shouldn't have touched you without your permission. I'm so sorry."

The back of her head lowers at the same time her shoulders begin to vibrate. Bile rises in my throat. This is the last thing I wanted. I pushed her too far. I didn't think rationally about how she would have felt.

Stupid fucking idiot.

Her entire body trembles. I stay back.

"Ava, please talk to me."

But instead, she shakes her head. "Do not touch me."

"I'm not going to touch you, okay?"

"Don't ever do that to me again."

My heart constricts as if someone has wrapped a hand around it and squeezed.

"Okay," I whisper. "I promise, I won't do that again."

Ava sniffles, and it shatters every part of me. She takes one step forward on shaky legs before she leaves the kitchen without looking back. I know better than to chase her. She needs the space.

But now, I fear I've triggered something, and I don't

know how I can comfort her without scaring her. I drop my head into my hands and release a sigh.

Goddess, why do I fuck everything up?

16

AVA

I can't stop the thoughts that flood my mind. My brain reacts to Jaxon's actions by seizing up like muscle memory. Right now, there isn't a single thought without a filter. I gasp for a breath as I reach my room, sheltering inside for some privacy, but I'm not alone with the loudness inside my head.

One hand presses firmly against my chest, and the other grips my hair. I groan in agony, desperate for these voices and impulses to leave me alone and spare me some peace.

My head whips towards the door, and I lurch forward to lock it. I shove my back against the wood and slowly sink to the floor, sobbing into my hands. As soon as my legs hit the ground, I crumble into a hyper-sensitive state.

I tighten my hands into fists so intensely that my fingernails dig into my palms. My eyes shut as I try to control my breathing, but I can't seem to distract myself. Everything is so loud, and I cannot push it out.

There is an ache between my brows, growing over my eyes and into the back of my skull. I continue to cry, tears leaking with every sniffle. The harder I cry, the clearer the voices in my head become.

It makes me remember what they made me believe.

Whore.

All your body is good for is to be used by us.

It's an object. You are our object.

Dirty whore.

My head shakes desperately, trying to rid myself of these horrid memories, but they don't go anywhere. They linger like parasites by clinging onto my insecurities and making me live through every dreaded moment over again.

I place my hand over my chest and grip my T-shirt; my lungs are seconds away from exploding. My eyes close in an attempt to calm down, but nothing will calm me. *Not a single thing.*

No one would even want you. Useless piece of shit.

Dirty whore.

Give us a show. It's the only thing you bitches are good at.

My fingers claw through my hair as I grip the roots and tug. I grit my teeth and groan in agony as they take away my last breath. It never goes away. I want it to go away.

Please make it stop. Please make it stop. I cry to myself over the volume of my living nightmares.

I can't keep my back against the door as my chest movements become rapid. Nothing is working—not my lungs, not my brain. I am not in control. Have I ever been in control?

Ava. Jaxon's voice enters my head, and I whimper. *Let me help you. I won't touch you. I won't do anything to make you uncomfortable. Let me help you like I did last time. Do you remember?*

I shake my head at the added voice. It's so damn loud. I

want to scream at the top of my lungs to get them all out. I need this to stop *now*.

Ava. Listen to my voice, okay? You need to breathe deeper. Take longer breaths.

Tears drip off my jaw as I turn up my nose at his voice. It makes me feel all sorts of things—things I can't trust.

Leave me alone, I yell through gritted teeth.

Whore. Whore. Whore. Whore. Whore.

The things you are thinking are not *true. You are not those words.*

I choke out a breath and frown at the wall. How can he hear my thoughts?

Please let me in. Let me help you.

Stupid dirty fucking whore.

"Get out!" I scream, pulling at my hair to the point it almost tears my scalp. "Get out of my fucking head!"

Ava– he's quieter this time, but he's still there and still burning a hole through my brain.

"Stop it," I cry into my hands pathetically. My vision is so blurry I can't even see what's in front of me. "Stop it."

Jaxon's voice doesn't come again. I'm left alone with these demoralising words and the sound of my own sobbing. The sound of my own heart beginning to crack erupts in my ears.

I am broken. I am nothing. I am useless.

My body slumps to the side of the door, and I hit my head with a thud. I curl up into a ball and attempt to cry away the pain, but after a few long moments, I realise I don't consume pain; pain consumes me.

∼

SECOND CHANCE MATES

When my eyes flutter open, I feel like I've been reversed over by a truck. My head pounds, and every inch of my body aches, yet I am empty and hollow.

Panic attacks truly use up every last drop of energy.

I push myself up from the floor where I fell asleep or passed out from hyperventilating. It wouldn't be the first time I fainted during an episode—I doubt I'll be the last.

Ava. Jaxon's voice reaches me again. *Are you okay? I'm trying to give you space.*

My lips tremble at his words. At least the voices from earlier are gone, and I can finally think clearly. I could sleep forever, and I'd be at peace.

I'm okay, I say bluntly.

I've had to leave the house for a couple of hours for some duties. I've asked Lucy to check in on you.

I push myself up from the floor on wobbly legs. I make the short distance to my bed before flopping down on the soft mattress. It's definitely different to camping out on the floor; my back is tight in all the wrong places.

My eyes focus on the ceiling as I release a shuddering breath. Why can't I be normal? I'm so fucked up that I wonder if I'll ever stand a chance of going back to how I once was.

Stop saying that, Ava. You are not fucked up. It's Jax again.

He's reading my thoughts. How? I'm too exhausted to argue right now.

I thought you were giving me space, I respond blankly.

Jaxon's voice flitters for a moment. *I'm sorry. I don't mean to hear your thoughts,* he states slowly, and each word sounds so sincere that it's hard to digest. *When you think something with intense passion, it floats into my mind the next second. It's a part of our bond that connects us. I'll teach you how to put your shields up. I don't want to intrude on your privacy.*

I have questions, but I don't have any energy, I mindlink weakly.

Then save it. Please can we talk when I get back?

My eyelids shut, and I twist onto my side, tucking myself into a tiny ball with my head firmly on the pillow.

Ava?

Okay.

I'll see you later.

Once the mindlink between us disappears and the place he was occupying in my brain vanishes, a wave of emptiness settles inside me. One minute, his presence calms me, and I know our bond is a big reason. Then the next minute, the thought of being too close to him makes my skin crawl, and all these memories come flooding back.

I open my mouth and drag my tongue along my bottom lip. Every part is bone dry, and I peel myself from the bed desperate for a drop of water. I unlock the door and slowly descend the stairs, where I approach Jaxon's private kitchen.

But I stop in my tracks when I hear voices.

"Did you hear her scream last night?" asks a voice I don't recognise.

"No, I didn't. Was she alright?" That's Kayden. My body shudders.

I don't dare take another step. I stand right where I am and listen. I shouldn't listen. I should walk away, but something is forcing me to stay.

"I dunno. She's weird, man—like so weird. She's been here for a few months and is acting like some freak."

My heart sinks. I know they're talking about me. "Don't say shit like that," Kayden snaps, his voice bouncing off the kitchen walls. "You don't know her. None of us know her. She's our future Luna. Jaxon would slaughter you for this."

The other guy tuts loudly. "Still, she isn't going to be like

Julia, is she? How could someone like her be our Luna? There is no way Jaxon is going to stand for this. He's nose blind because of how he felt with Julia before. He's just giving anyone a go."

"Stop being a fucking ass," Kayden grumbles. "You don't know if she's going to be like Julia. None of us know that. She's still learning to be around the pack. She's human, remember? This isn't easy for her. Speaking awfully about the Alpha's mate is a low blow, even for you, Sam."

"All I'm saying is Jaxon could do so much better. It sounds like she's got baggage–and a lot of it, too. It doesn't sound fun."

Bile rises in my throat at the harshness of his words. Baggage? Tears well in my eyes, but I tell myself not to start crying here. Not in case either of them catches me with their heightened senses.

"He isn't going to leave her. No matter what you or I or anyone think. Good for him; he should do what makes him happy. She's going to be our future Luna, whether you like it or not," Kayden says, but with more determination this time.

"Well, he should. She's just going to bring the pack down." Sam laughs. "And you haven't even found your mate, and you sound like a love-sick superhero, trying to save the day as always. Grow up."

"Keep running your mouth, Sam," Kayden threatens. "And we'll see what Jaxon thinks of your disgusting opinions."

I cannot control my state of mind as it wanders.
Weak.
Pathetic.
Dirty whore.
The thoughts start invading once more, and I can't remove them.

Weak.
Pathetic.
Dirty whore.
"Stop," I whisper to myself. "Stop it."
Weak.
Pathetic.
Dirty whore.

My feet patter against the cold floor as I make my way back upstairs. I run into the bathroom, and at the same time my knees hit the floor, I throw up my entire stomach's intake. I haven't eaten anything in a while, but it's mostly bile, which stings my throat.

I groan in distress and slump to the side, wiping my mouth with the back of my hand. "Crap," I curse as my stomach growls. I close my eyes at the discomfort.

Are you okay? Jaxon must be able to feel my pain. *What's wrong, Ava?*

I'm fine, I respond before imagining a large brick wall between us.

I don't know if this counts as shielding, but it's the first thing I think of.

My knees quiver as I rise onto them and flush the toilet. I tug myself up to stand on my feet, and then stare at the wall behind hazy eyes. My actions take control of me. I don't even think about what I'm doing next. My fingers lock the bathroom door, and I step into the shower.

I turn on the showerhead to the hottest setting and bend over. At first, it's freezing. But after a few minutes, it begins to heat up until my T-shirt practically melts into my back at the intensified heat. I don't realise I'm crying.

This is the only way to make it go away.

I choke back my sobs, biting onto my bottom lip so sharply I break the skin, and the blood seeps into my mouth. My teeth grit at the heat of the water as it pours over every inch of my back.

Screaming out in misery as I slip to my knees, I grip my soaking hair and bawl as the water scalds my skin. All I can think in my head is—*you deserve this.*

17

JAXON

The second I knew Ava was hurting herself, I abandoned my meeting with the district Alphas and raced home as fast as possible. Despite her unskilled attempt to try and block me out, I could still feel every inch of her physical pain.

I roar at Lucy through our mindlink to check on Ava before it's too late. I won't get home in time, but at least she will be there with the pack doctors on standby. The journey back to the house is silent and agonising. By the time I cross our territory borders and run to the front door, I'm up the stairs quicker than I can blink.

My hand presses to Ava's door, and I find my sister sitting beside her on the bed with Gemma to her left. She's lying on her front, and my eyes roam her bare back. It's clear of broken skin, but it remains red and blotchy.

"Is she okay?" I whisper as my eyes flick to her face.

She looks peaceful, but I can't help but feel she's content being asleep. It makes my chest compress to the point my lungs can't even take a breath. Lucy looks at me, and I don't miss the tears in her eyes.

"She's okay." She nods weakly. "I got to her in time. It was bad."

"Are you okay?" I ask as I sit beside her.

My sister has always had thick skin, but I know when she's sad, she feels it to the extreme. It's connected to her witch powers, heightening everything, including her wolf's senses. I don't know how she handles it some days.

"I-I just can't keep seeing her hurt herself like this, Jaxon." Her lips tremble. "She deserves so much better than this. I don't know what else we can do. Goddess, she was screaming. She was screaming so loud."

I wrap my arm over my sister's shoulder, and I tug her into my side. My eyes close at the description. Her screams destroy me every time.

"You're right; she deserves better."

Gemma walks around the bed after checking on Ava. "Alpha." She bows. "She's stable for now, but I suggest when she wakes up, she comes to see me in my office."

"Thank you," I tell her gratefully as she leaves. "And, Luce, thank you. I mean it. I don't know what I would do without you these last few months. I've been a mess."

She peeks her head up from my shoulder. "You weren't a mess; you were grieving. Now, you're on a completely new journey with your old one still intact. I can't imagine what you're going through."

"What I'm going through?" I repeat. "I couldn't give a shit what I'm going through. That would be incredibly selfish when I know she's struggling."

Lucy gives me a sympathetic smile. "Just because she's struggling doesn't mean your struggles aren't valid."

"I know, but she's the priority."

She grabs my hand to give it a quick squeeze. "Gemma put her in some pyjama pants, but let me wrap her in a cardigan. She said she should wake soon. We should give her some space."

"No." I shake my head. "Not after she's done this for the second time. She could have killed herself, Lucy. I am not taking any more chances. Not when I know her mental state is this fragile."

My sister flashes me a conflicting look. "Jaxon–"

"I am not leaving her alone. I am not letting this happen again. I'll never forgive myself."

"Okay," she sighs. "Be gentle with her."

"I'm always gentle, Luce."

"I know."

Lucy gives me a quick hug before sliding a cardigan onto Ava's arms and over her back as she sleeps softly. "I'll see you later."

"Yeah," I whisper as she leaves the room.

My eyes cut back to Ava. This is all my fault. I set her off in the kitchen. I should *never* have touched her without permission.

I glance at my hands and snarl at my own audacity. That is not how you treat your mate. I wasn't respectful of her wishes.

My legs carry me from the bed to the chair. I'm vibrating, and my wolf refuses to calm down. She was in so much mental pain that she chose to hurt herself again. The static in the room is crying out for me to comfort her, but I've learned my lesson the hard way. I need her consent. I refuse to have another situation like this.

A few minutes pass until she finally wakes up, and I shuffle to the edge of my seat, resting my elbows over my knees with my hands entwined.

"Hi," I exhale.

Her droopy eyes flick around the room before they land

on mine. I expect her gaze to light up with fear, but today, I don't see that; instead, I see a tsunami of sadness, and that cuts even deeper.

Ava releases an uncomfortable whine as she attempts to push herself up from the bed and grabs onto the cardigan to wrap it around her body. "How are you feeling?"

All she can do is shake her head. I frown instantly.

"Take a drink." I gesture to the water on the nightstand. "I know you're thirsty."

Those lifeless eyes move to the bottle, and she leans over with shaky hands to take it. I watch her crack the lid slowly and draw it to her lips, letting droplets roll down her jaw as she consumes it. "Easy," I tell her.

She gasps for a breath before placing it back down. "How is your back feeling?"

Her nose scrunches at the question. "Fine."

Far from it. The instincts from her mind channel towards my own.

"Gemma asked for you to go down and see her when you wake up," I explain. "That's if you want to."

"No," she snaps. "I don't want to."

My lips twist downwards. "Okay, that's fine."

Ava's shoulders droop, and her arms stay firmly over her chest. "I don't need you here."

I sigh. "Alright. You want me to go?"

"Yes."

No.

"You want to be alone?"

"Yes."

No. No. No.

The words make my brain twitch. Goddess. How am I meant to leave when she won't even tell me the truth? She doesn't want to be alone but is too terrified to admit it.

"Can I ask you one question before I go, Ava?"

She doesn't nod or answer; instead, she stares back at me.

I lower my head along with my heavy heart.

"Is there anything I can do to help you through this? Because I feel utterly useless standing by and doing nothing."

She blinks at my question. A gleam reflects in her eyes as she shakes her head once before pausing and then shaking it again. Every inch of me deflates in defeat.

"Okay." I stand from the chair and walk towards the door. Her eyes stalk my every step. "If you need me, you can mindlink me, or I'll be downstairs, okay? If you're not feeling right and can't talk to me, please at least talk to Gemma or Lucy. They are more than willing to be there when you need them."

My eyes are tight when they roam across her face. I offer her a small smile before I open the door and step outside.

"Wait–"

Her voice has me freezing in my tracks. I turn slowly, knowing better than to crowd her. I give her space. I wait and listen. Our gazes meet, and her hands pick at the skin around her nails. I despise the action because I know she does it when she's anxious.

"Yeah?"

A single tear rolls down her cheek. "D-don't go," she whispers tragically, and I sag in relief and torment all rolled into one. "I'm tired of feeling alone."

My fingers itch to lean over and cuddle her. What I wouldn't give to make her feel comfortable enough to hug me—to prove to her all I want to give is affection and care. Nothing less.

"I'm not going anywhere," I whisper back.

Ava's lips quiver until she breaks down, sobbing into her hands uncontrollably. My heart moves to my throat, and my wolf screams at me to do something.

I step towards the bed and bend to the edge to not intimidate her.

"Ava—"

"I couldn't make them go away."

"Make what go away?"

"The thoughts. They were everywhere. They were so loud."

More tears sprout from her eyes as her breathing increases.

"Why didn't you tell me, Ava? I would have been there for you."

"Because I'm scared," she chokes.

I study her pink cheeks and glossy eyes. "Scared of what?"

"Of everything. Of everyone finding out I'm crazy."

"You are not crazy, Ava. That is the last thing you are."

Her trembling mouth parts as she attempts to catch her irregular breath. "All the voices are so loud. They felt so real. I felt them. I *heard* them."

"You didn't," I reassure her. "They were a fragment of your imagination—nothing more. They weren't real. They're not here, and they will not hurt you again."

Ava's head rises as she sniffles softly. "You heard them," she whispers. "The thoughts in my head. Do you think they are true?"

"No." I furrow my brows. "No. Not a single thought is true."

"I feel like they are."

"They're not. I promise you."

Ava wraps her arms around her legs in a well-needed

hug. I wish I could be the one to give that to her, but I keep my distance—as I should have done last night. "Did you hurt yourself because of the thoughts?"

"I know your pack think I'm weak."

"They don't know you well enough to even think that incorrect statement."

She presses a pale hand to her face to wipe a rogue tear. "Not incorrect when I heard them talking."

My back stiffens at her confession. "Who said something to you?"

"H-he said I have baggage, and you would do better without me," she murmurs in a harsh whisper. "I know that's true. I'm only bringing all of you down. Making you weaker."

"Ava." I try to calm the beast swirling inside me. "Who said this to you?"

But she doesn't look at me; she stares at the duvet as she carries on. "He said I will never be as good as Julia. I will never be able to stand by your side. I'm an embarrassment."

Frustration grinds in my bones. "Tell. Me. Who."

"Sam and Kayden. I overheard them talking."

"Kayden?" My brows fly towards my hairline.

Ava shakes her head. "He was standing up for me. It was Sam who did the damage."

I grit my teeth and tell my wolf to halt its paws for a moment before we tear through the house to find the soon-to-be-dead fucker. The audacity to talk about his future Luna like that. I'm going to have him squirming with apologies.

"I appreciate you telling me," I exhale as calmly as possible. "And I promise he's not going to get away with this. It's unacceptable. I'm sorry you heard his bullshit lies. Please do not listen to them."

Ava hops off the bed, shaking out her hands before lacing them through her hair. I rise from the floor. "I feel so out of control all the time," she whimpers. "I just want it all to stop."

"I'm here for you. I know it's not been easy, but I am. Whenever you need me."

Her hands grip her arms as she releases a strangled sound. "I feel their words, I feel their–" she cuts herself off on a sob. "Their hands and their gazes. I feel all of it, and I wish I could turn it off. I want to turn it off."

I walk around the bed with my chest gaping open. "Ava–"

"When they touched me," she murmurs through a cry. "When they used my body. When they took away my own rights, I was nothing but an object to them."

My eyes pinch at the pain behind them, and her shoulders shake in agony. *Fuck.*

"I will never be the same again," Her voice echoes around the room. "I'll never be the Ava I want to be. That's why I don't want to be here in this life...because it's not mine. This isn't what I set out for myself."

She rotates her body towards me. I find her cheeks stained with tears and her eyes puffy and red. "No one will ever want me for the mess they've left behind. Because I am. I'm a mess, and I don't think I'm ever going to get better."

Then she completely breaks down...into pieces. A thousand tiny pieces.

"Ava," I strain. "Please. *Please.* Just let me hold you. I nee–"

I cut myself off and remind my wolf this isn't about me. This is about her choices. Her consent. It'll *always* be about her consent.

"Please will you let me hold you?"

Ava takes a wobbly step forward before crashing her body into my chest. I immediately wrap my arms around her and clutch the back of her head with my large hand. A wave of solace runs through my body at the connection.

She continues to cry and whimper, her hands latching onto the back of my T-shirt in an iron grip. I close my eyes at the soreness of them and the desperation for my body to take away her pain.

"It's okay," I whisper into the top of her head. "I got you, baby. I got you."

An electric force field shields us from everything outside this embrace. Instead, I channel positive thoughts and happy affirmations towards her. I don't want to overwhelm her, but I do it gradually over time.

After a few moments, Ava's breathing slows, and her cries become quieter. I don't let go, not for a single second. I adore the way her body fits against mine like we're two pieces of a puzzle.

My lips press to the crown of her head in a delicate kiss as I hear her release a soft pant into my chest. She doesn't pull away, so I don't make a move to either. My skin tingles from all the comfort that flows between us, and her heartbeat begins to regulate with mine. It's a strange yet euphoric feeling.

A hug with a mate can definitely attempt to heal some scars, but Ava's trauma runs deep, and it's going to take a while for her to find peace within herself—in which I'm ready to be patient. I've got all the time in the world, especially for her. I'll be there through every step she takes.

"You are never alone," I murmur into her hair. "You will never be alone again. I promise."

18

AVA

A stroke of warm sunlight hits my face as I slowly stir from my sleep. My hands lift to rub my eyes, and I slump back into the pillows. I feel somewhat better than yesterday. My body still feels psychologically and physically exhausted, but after my conversation with Jaxon, things felt more doable.

Most hugs say nothing at all, but hugs from Jaxon say a million different things. They might be silent, but I can hear them. Even if the last thing I wanted to do was give into the bond, I can't refuse myself calmness, especially when it feels authentic.

I swipe the sheets from my body and stand on achy legs. My arms lift above my head, and I stretch out to my maximum capacity. I glance down at my bedside table to find a note with a few words scribbled down.

Never forget how strong you are
Jax

I blink at the paper and take it in my hands. A small zap rushes down my spine when I pick it up, like an electrical current that tightens our bond.

My hands press the small note to my chest, and I take a deep breath, closing my eyes. I already know that flashbacks and panic attacks are always going to be a part of my life. They're embedded into my veins. Yesterday was the first time in forever I felt like I wasn't alone in this dark era.

It was nearly impossible to tell Jax I didn't want him to leave. But when I saw him walking out that door, I couldn't bear the thought of actually being alone—especially if those thoughts came back.

I don't want to hurt myself, but sometimes, it's like my body has been taken over, and I have zero control. The pain is so torturous that I'd rather make myself suffer than deal with my loud thoughts. I don't necessarily want to end everything, but I get carried away. It's so easy to give in to the pain.

Deep inside my heart, I want to give myself as much self-love as possible. I've been deprived of it for such a long time. I've forgotten what looking after yourself actually looks like. I want to get better; I just don't know if I'm physically capable of doing so.

I look at Jax's message again. Strong. *Strong.* I am far from it.

My fingers smooth out the note as I pin it back down to my bedside table. I might be in need of reading that later. I know it's only a few words, but it means more to me than I could've known.

After getting dressed and shoving my hair up into a ponytail, I head downstairs for something to eat. My stomach growls at me. I don't remember the last time I ate.

I peek my head inside Jaxon's private kitchen to find it

empty. My shoulders droop in relief as I step inside and work my way around the fridge and the cupboards to throw something together.

Once I've toasted a slice of bread and buttered it, I raise it to my lips to take the first bite. The hairs on the back of my neck stand, and my eyes focus on the counter ahead of me. This feeling isn't like when Jaxon is around; it feels like danger...like *trouble*.

A tall figure appears in the kitchen doorway, and in a flash, I glance over. "Hey, Ava." Kayden's voice traps me in a frozen stance. "How are you?"

I follow him with my eyes like a hawk as he walks towards the coffee machine. My heart pounds against my ribcage so loudly I can hear it in my ears. My fingers seize up around the piece of toast, and I struggle to swallow what's in my mouth.

Just because he's a Beta, doesn't mean he's bad, I remind myself.

Kayden turns around when I say nothing. "Sorry if I startled you," he adds gently. "Even if I am heavy on my feet. Do you want a coffee?"

I can't respond. I can't even move.

Fear paralyses every inch of my body, and I drop my toast to the floor. It hits the ground with a pathetic splat.

"Ava?" Kayden sounds concerned now.

Breathe, Ava. Breathe, I chant in my head. *He's harmless. He's harmless. At least, I think he's harmless.*

My knees wobble, and I know it won't be long until they give out. I'm barely standing as it is. "Take a seat." He rushes forward to pull out a stool. "For the love of the Goddess, please do not pass out on me."

I can't guarantee it.

My backside hits the chair before my ankles snap. I try

to push through the cloud my head is currently in. Everything is so hazy. Oh, God. Why? I want it to stop. Please. *Stop.*

"Here." Kayden is in front of me again and is passing me a glass of water. "It might help."

I raise a shaky hand to take it. My body knows better than I do. My fingers latch around the glass, and I tilt it towards my lips. Kayden doesn't release the cup, and I'm relieved. It would have smashed within seconds.

The water is cold and delicious but does nothing to make my creeping panic attack go away. I pull back the glass, and Kayden places it on the counter before levelling his brown eyes with mine. "Are you feeling okay? You're really pale, and I'm slightly terrified."

I gasp silently. He's so damn close. My throat seizes up.

"Ava–" Jaxon's voice floats into the room. "Did you touch her?"

"What? No," Kayden defends himself. "I don't know what's wrong. I came in, and she started looking real pale, like she was about to faint. I didn't do anything."

Jaxon steps to my side, and I focus on his handsome face. The deep concern on his expression makes my heart beat out of time. As he moves closer, the bond wraps around my lungs and widens them, giving me a chance to breathe properly since Kayden walked into the kitchen.

"Are you feeling okay?" Jaxon asks, flicking his eyes between mine slowly.

I merely nod. My tongue extends to drag along my bottom lip.

"Gemma," I blurt out.

"What?"

"Gemma. I want to see Gemma."

Jaxon nods his head once. "Let me take you there."

I hop off the stool, trusting my legs a little too early. My knees literally cave, and Jaxon grabs my arm gently to stabilise my balance before I hit the floor and make a fool out of myself.

"It's alright," he murmurs when I stare up at him with embarrassment. "I got you."

His hand remains on mine for a moment. All that warmth spreads down my limbs with attention and care. His reflex was so quick I didn't even see his arm shoot out to catch me.

I shake it off and walk out of the kitchen without sparing another look at Kayden. My feet automatically carry me towards the infirmary. I've been here a fair few times now, it's like muscle memory.

My knuckles rise to knock on Gemma's door. A few seconds later, it opens, and she stares at me with a small smile. "Hi, Ava. How are you?"

"C-can I have a session?" I exhale before my chest holds my intentions a secret. "I really need one."

Gemma bows her head and steps out of the way. "Of course. Come in, Ava."

I take one step forward and then glance back at Jaxon, who is smiling at me with support. "I'll wait for you out here."

My eyes don't leave his as I stall for a moment. "Ava?" Gemma says.

"Do you want to come in with me?" I ask Jaxon.

He blinks at my request. "Sure." He nods. "You definitely want me to?"

"If it's too much for you, then you don't have to."

"No." He steps forward immediately. "I want to. I want to be there for you."

I nod and clear my throat. "Okay."

When I turn back to Gemma, she's beaming at Jaxon as I walk inside her office. Jaxon waits for me to take a seat, but he doesn't know I don't like to sit down. I don't like being confined. I express myself better when I'm walking around because it helps my blood flow. It also reminds me I can leave whenever I want. If I sit down, I know my entire body will cramp up from the nightmares of my past.

"Jaxon, please sit." Gemma points at any of the available chairs.

I stand near the window and pace slowly. All the air I suck down fills my lungs. When Gemma casually leans against her desk, legs in front of her with her hands on her thighs, I realise I am in the limelight.

Jaxon sits on the chair directly opposite me and rests his forearms over his knees.

"Ava, why did you want to see me today?" Gemma asks.

I twiddle with my fingers as I stare at the walls covered in quotes and art. Usually, I focus on one and take it in, but today, I'm conscious of Jaxon being here, even though I invited him.

"When I see Kayden, I feel everything inside me freeze," I exhale and close my eyes. "I don't want to associate him with the Beta from—"

My throat feels like razor blades.

"It's okay, Ava. Take your time," Gemma says softly.

I open my eyes to find Jaxon staring back at me with a sensitive expression.

"I don't want to associate him with Damon, Lucien's Beta. He did things to me the others didn't. He hurt me. He took from me. He violated me in more ways than any of the others. And I can feel that Kayden and—" I take a second. "Damon are different people, but my brain seems to think I have to be cautious—just in case."

Gemma hums softly. "And is seeing Kayden a trigger for you?"

I nod. "But I don't want it to be."

"It's something we can definitely work through," she says. "Did something happen before this?"

"I was alone with him in the kitchen. Nothing happened. He saw I didn't look well and helped me onto a chair before I passed out. I wish I could take the reins on these thoughts, but I can't. It feels impossible." I begin pacing again.

"Well, how about you try being around Kayden but with other people present? People you are comfortable with. Lucy, perhaps."

My gaze immediately settles on Jaxon's. "I'm feeling a lot more comfortable with Jaxon now," I admit.

"That's great." Gemma's expression widens. "Taking one day at a time. That's wonderful, Ava."

"If anything is ever wrong, you know you can mindlink me," Jaxon adds, and the smoothness of his voice sends chills down my spine. "I felt your distress. That's why I came down to see what was going on."

I look at Gemma. "Our bond does that now. It's growing stronger than before."

"And how does that make you feel?"

"Good and scared."

"Scared, why?"

"I'm scared I won't know how I'm truly feeling because the bond is masking it," I explain with my fingers entangled. "I know it doesn't tell me what to feel, but I worry it's all an illusion, and I'll be left with nothing at the end of it."

Gemma folds her arms over her chest casually. "And I totally understand that, Ava. I do. But like you said, bonds don't tell you what to feel. If anything, they tell the truth. All the things you feel with Jaxon might seem like they're forced, but they're not. Your body wouldn't allow you to feel him unless you bring your walls down on your own and accept him in."

My brows crease. Is that true?

"Do you remember when you first met?"

"Yeah."

"How did you feel the bond, then?"

I clear my throat. "It was non-existent."

"Exactly, because you weren't accepting it. But now that you've experienced the bond, your body and emotions are letting it in slowly. None of it is fake by any means. Being with Jaxon might calm your panic and help you when you're having a bad day, but you're only accepting his help because your body trusts that it's safe. I think in your subconscious, you think it, too."

"Oh," I exhale and stop pacing.

Jaxon's lip curls. "Everything you've done in the last few months has been down to you, Ava," he states. "I might have helped along the way, but for you to get where you are today, that's all you. It has nothing to do with our bond. You came to Gemma on your own accord, and you've been making an effort with Lucy. Do you have bonds with them like you do with me?"

I let my lashes brush my cheek as an unknown feeling washes over my chest. It feels a lot like pride, but I don't let myself hold onto it for too long. "No," I whisper.

"No," he clarifies with soft eyes, making my knees melt. "You did all of that on your own because you are strong—a lot stronger than you believe you are. And I'll remind you every day until you believe it, too."

My cheeks heat, remembering the note he left me this morning. *Thank you*, I say through our mindlink without hesitation.

Don't thank me for stating the truth. I'm your mate, and I will support you through every wobble, through your tears, through your doubts. All of it.

I can't take my eyes off him when he looks at me like that. He's proud and has a lot of confidence in me. My walls have been falling day by day, but right now, they're on the floor, and every ounce of the bond surrounds me.

My heart glows from the inside out. I admire his kind face while I take a slow breath. I might not be able to trust him with everything yet, but we both know I'm not the same person I was when he first found me.

He's right. I've done most of this by myself, and I recognise the shell I've started to shed. Every day will be different from the last, and I doubt I'll ever get off this rollercoaster, but I need to learn to cope with my irrational thoughts and feelings.

I'm proud of you. Jaxon's voice is smooth like silk.

Tears swim in my eyes, and for the first time in a long time, they're not because I'm sad. It's relieving to let myself go and submit to all the kindness I want to feel for my own sanity.

He stands up, and I crank my neck to meet his gaze. *And I know you're proud of yourself, too, even if you won't give yourself the full credit.*

One day at a time.

One day at a time, he confirms.

19

JAXON

A knock at my office door stirs me from the messy paperwork on my desk. I glance up and stare at the wooden panel. "Come in," I shout.

The door cracks open, and I find Sam stepping inside. "You wanted to see me, Alpha?"

My eyes narrow on him and the way he walks in so casually, as if he hasn't been trash-talking his future Luna like she's nothing. I try to keep my face calm, but studying his ignorant stance has my wolf stirring inside me.

"Close the door," I command and stand.

Sam turns and shuts the door. I step around my desk to take slow strides towards him, tucking my hands behind my back as he follows my every move. "Do you have any idea why I've called you here, Sam?"

"Uhhh...I wasn't doing well in training?"

My lip quirks at him. "Well, I'm relieved one of us finally said it, but no. I haven't called you here because of your lame attempts during training."

Sam doesn't seem pleased by my brash response, but I

wasn't happy with his either when he made Ava feel less than she is. I bet he wouldn't be able to last a day experiencing the abuse and neglect she suffered.

I pause directly in front of him, the tips of our shoes almost touching. Sam's eyes flick upwards to look at me, and right now, he seems small enough to squash under my foot.

"Do you know what I don't like?" I ask smoothly despite the bitterness on my tongue.

Sam seems taken aback by my question. He shakes his head, eyes moving to the left and then to the right as he ponders. "Uhhh...people who are bad at training?"

I laugh, but I'm not entertained. Not whilst he's still none the wiser of the damage he's caused. "Wrong." I flash him a fake smile. "I don't like people talking shit about my mate, let alone your future Luna, who you will one day bow down to."

His eyes widen like he's been caught in a trap. "Alpha, I did–"

My hand raises to silence him, and his voice stops abruptly. "I swear, you say another word, Sam, and I'll have your head on a fucking stick and your body burning on the stake."

Sam presses his lips together and manages to nod in understanding.

"I would ask if you have some kind of excuse for talking down to Ava, but I know there isn't a single one in this world that could explain why you said what you said," I snarl in his direction.

He flinches from the proximity between us, his eyes closing in fear. I grit my teeth at his reaction. As if closing his eyes is going to make this situation any easier; he's just dug himself a deeper hole.

"Look at me when I'm fucking talking to you!" I roar across my office to find him snapping his eyes open. He shudders. He fucking *shudders*. Pathetic.

I turn my nose up at him. "Goddess," I grumble as I take the collar of his shirt and shove him back into the wall. "You're a coward. A fucking coward."

He squirms against me, but his strength is nothing on mine. He knows better than to fight when I lift him off the ground like he weighs a grain of rice.

"Now, if I ever hear you say another fucking word about your future Luna again, I will skin you alive, and I will enjoy every second of it," I hiss through my teeth. "Do you understand me?"

"Yes, Alpha."

I lower him for a second before I release my fist straight into his gut. He releases a gurgling sound before hunching over as he gasps for a breath. I'm certain I felt one of his ribs crack beneath my knuckles. "You can enjoy spending a week in the dungeon. Limited food, limited water, and zero sunlight. I hope it was worth it."

My fists release his collar, and he slumps forward. An arm wraps around his waist as he attempts to straighten, but he can't. I roll my eyes at his weakness.

Guards, collect my newest prisoner.

On our way, Alpha.

Soon, the door to my office opens, and two of my largest dungeon guards step towards Sam, grabbing him roughly by the arms. "Wait–" he heaves. "I'm sorry. I didn't mean to upset her."

My jaw aches from clenching so tightly. "It's a bit late for that. Don't you think, Sam?"

His eyes flash me a look of regret, but he made his

choices. I shake my head once and nudge my head towards the door. "Get him out of my sight before I actually kill him."

As he's being dragged away, he attempts to struggle against their grip, but he's out of his depth. If he keeps this up, I'll make it two weeks, then he'll realise he can't fight his way out of his mistakes. He must learn from them.

After his dramatic exit, I shut the door and sit back at my desk. A long exhale escapes my lips as I lean into my chair, stretching out the muscles in my back. My finger runs along the edge of my hairline in an attempt to help me focus on the work in front of me.

I've sent some of my pack's wolves off to Lucien's territory to suss out his schedule, exit points, weaknesses—*everything*. Since I found out his location, I've had eyes on him. Now we've got a plan, I need to know every last detail of how his pack is run. I will not fuck up this mission. I want Ava to have closure from these monsters who have left physical and invisible marks on her forever.

A thousand thoughts cross my mind, but with Lucy and Sebastian's wedding coming up and Ava slowly but surely opening up to me, I don't want to jump the gun. It's already an overwhelming time for her. All she has to know is they're being watched, and she's safe. If they ever started moving closer, I'd execute the mission in an instant.

My fists clench, and I can't hold back the smile as I imagine them covered in *their* blood. Every single one of them who has touched her. All of them will pay, and I won't be gentle about it.

A knock at my office door stirs me from my work. I shake my head and glance up. "Come in," I yell.

The door handle twists, and my gaze collides with my

mate as she steps inside. Her brown eyes immediately light up the room, and I shiver subtly at her unexpected entrance. "Everything okay?" I ask as I lean forward.

Ava's teeth clamp down on her bottom lip as she steps inside, not shutting the door behind her. "Are you busy?"

"For you?" I quirk a brow. "Never."

Her cheeks spread with a tint of pink, something I always find incredibly adorable. "What are you up to?"

"Alpha duties," I admit. "Nothing you need to worry about."

"Oh?"

"Oh."

A ghost of a smile rests on her pretty little lips. "Where is everyone? The house is so quiet."

"Half the pack are out on an important duty." I stand from my desk and straighten out my shirt. "The other half are training with Kayden."

"You didn't want to go with them?"

I shake my head. "I've been busy with a workload."

Ava flicks her gaze to mine for a second before she runs her finger along the edge of my dark wooden desk. "You seem to work a lot," she comments.

"Trying to stay on top of things. It's literally the least I can do for my pack. They deserve an Alpha who is on the ball, and I'm not falling behind again. I have to be a good role model for them."

"Did you work a lot before?"

I nod. "Yes, but this feels different now. I'm not letting anyone down again."

Ava stares at me for a long moment before a wave of anxiety crawls through my sternum, and I frown at the intrusion of her emotions.

"What's wrong?"

"It's just–" she sighs and finds the words. "Being the only human is a little isolating."

My brows bunch together as I study her for a moment. "Just because you're human doesn't mean you're any different than us."

"I feel like I am."

The room falls to silence for a few seconds. Ava's hand points to the desk where there is an empty spot. "You didn't get a new frame for the picture I smashed?"

"I never got around to it," I say, but she eyes me suspiciously.

"Why? Julia was your mate, too. You don't need to hide her from me if that's what you're doing. I know you loved her, and you still do. That's never going to go away."

Her name is like an unexpected spear to the chest.

"Yeah," I rasp. "I guess I haven't had time to do it."

"I see."

My lips press together as Ava's eyes begin to roam my office, paying attention to a large map on the wall.

"I might still have love for Julia, but she's not here anymore, and I can't keep chasing ghosts. I know she'd want me to be happy; she'd want me to find my peace."

Ava offers me a small smile. "Everyone deserves to find their own peace."

"Including you."

"Yes."

I stare back at her for a long moment. The girl she was when she came here is barely a fraction of who she is now. Pride and warmth burn through my chest like a flickering candle.

"Can I ask you something?" My arms fold over my chest as I lean back against the edge of my desk.

Ava nods.

"Does the name Russell Vale ring a bell for you?"

Her eyelids flutter gently, and she pulls back her head. "Russell Vale?"

"Yeah." I nod. "Does that mean anything?"

She twists to the wall and presses a hand into her hair, spreading it through the strands softly. "I–" she cuts herself off. "Uhh–"

"If it doesn't, it's okay," I reassure her.

I want nothing more than for her to remember herself rather than ambush her with all this information. I don't want to take this achievement away from her—not when she's been trying so hard with Gemma in her sessions.

"Maybe," she exhales with a disorientated expression. "Should it? I can't find a place for it in my head."

My heartbeat pounds in my throat. "It's a popular human town in the north. I was wondering if it meant anything to you. Only a question."

"Oh, okay."

"Do you want to go outside and watch their training session?"

Ava nods in agreement. "I'd like that. I need to get out of this house for a bit."

I walk across my office and beckon my head to the hall. "Let's go, then."

We make our way downstairs through my private entrance and into the clearing at the back of the house. "I've not seen you train with them in your wolf form before."

My lips tip to the side. "You've been watching me, Ava?"

"Well, when you all leave, there isn't much else to do." She covers her embarrassed face with a hand on her cheek. "I'm intrigued."

I release a soft laugh. "I'm flattered." I flash her a small wink. "I don't train with them in my wolf form because since Julia's death, I haven't been able to shift."

She places a hand over her heart and frowns. "He's not there anymore?"

"He wasn't there at all for a while. I couldn't feel him. I couldn't hear him. It was like he was dead when Julia passed," I say slowly before the words become muddled in my mouth. "But when I found you, it woke him up again. I heard and felt him for the first time in nine months."

Ava's mouth falls open in shock. "Because of me?"

"Yeah, because of you."

"But you can't shift into that form?"

"No."

We inch closer into our territory, where Kayden has my wolves running at lightning speed. They're playing one of our favourite training games that involves a lot of defence and ample amounts of competition.

I help Ava up onto one of the boulders so she has a better advantage point. She immediately drops her hands into her lap and glances around at the wolves as they pass. "So, how do you get your wolf back?" she asks curiously.

"I don't know," I admit. "I feel the closest to him when I'm around you."

She blinks in surprise. "When specifically?"

"When I held you. I felt incredibly close to him, then."

Ava's eyes roam my face, and I take in her pure beauty. I adore the way her natural complexion has been restored with a healthy glow and how her eyes seem brighter than when I first met her—like life is blossoming. Even when she smiles, I find myself doing the same, like a goofy idiot who has just learnt to smile for the first time. I can't help it. It's an instinctive reflex I don't want to stop. Her smile is contagious.

"Shall we try it again?" she suggests.

Goddess, she's breathtaking.

She's not looking at me. She's beaming at me with hopefulness in her eyes. She wants to help me get my wolf back, and I can sense him running circles inside me at the thought alone.

"Only if you're okay with it," I say gently. "Don't do it for me."

"Well, you've done a lot for me," she shrugs. "I want to do something for you, too. If it helps. I know you want your wolf back; it's obviously something that makes you, *you*."

My jaw tightens at her selfless statement. I merely nod. She opens her arms, slides them around my back, and buries her face into my chest. I hear her inhale deeply, and I can only presume my scent somewhat reassures her. My hand rests on the back of her head as I keep her close to me. The wideness of my body drowns her. My other arm wraps around her back in an embrace that could tilt the axis of this planet.

I drop my forehead to her crown and listen to the way our hearts thump over and over. She grabs my shirt, and I listen to her soft breathing, making my skin tingle.

My wolf is scratching at the edges to get out. He's there, but it's not enough to break this emotional and mental block I've caused. I let my fingers run through the back of Ava's hair and she releases a shuddering whimper.

I sigh in satisfaction and think about my precious mate between my arms. She's safe here. For a moment, I can't control the thought of her pain, tears, or sadness as it etches its way into my mind.

My wolf growls deep inside me at the agonising thoughts. *No one hurts her. No one will ever hurt her again.* I promise myself and my wolf that. *If anyone lays a single finger on her, I'll kill them without hesitation.*

Then, when I least expect it, Ava's smooth, tranquilising voice echoes through my head. *Is it working? Do we need to try something else? This feels good to me.*

My hand wraps around her back, and I tug her to me. I lower my head so my nose runs along the edge of her neck.

It does. I groan softly. *So much.*

A giggle erupts in my brain that comes out of nowhere, but it makes me short-circuit for a moment. My wolf doesn't just claw at my insides; his whole paw practically rips through my skin—or that's what it feels like.

Our bond, it's...beautiful, she whispers in my mind. *I want to see your wolf. Show him to me. Let me see all of you.*

I pull away from Ava and pant heavily. Her eyes search mine as she grips my shoulders. "Is it working?"

"Yes," I heave, but deep-red pain soars through me.

It's been a long damn time since I last shifted, and I can only imagine how my bones have become used to my human form. I jump down from the boulder and grip my hair as heat tears me from the inside out.

"Jax–" Ava's voice calls from behind me.

Stay back, I warn her.

My back arches with a loud crack at the same time my clothes begin to tear. I heave out shaky breaths as every single bone grows and snaps into a thousand uncomfortable positions. A growl forms at the top of my lungs as fur bursts from my skin and my paws hit the ground.

I take a moment to control my breathing. I turn around to face Ava through my yellow eyes. She's still sitting on top of the boulder, a hand covering her lips.

"Holy–" she cuts herself off.

My paws grind into the dirt, and I exhale through my

snout. I can smell every single thing, including Ava's earth-shattering scent. I thought it was powerful before, but now, it's like she's been laced through my veins and is here to stay.

You're back, I say to my wolf as he stretches out every limb.

He vibrates in response, and I already know what he thinks.

This is all thanks to our mate.

20

AVA

Jaxon's wolf is larger than any other wolf I've ever seen. His fur is black and thick, and his yellow luminous eyes glow back at me. The size of one of his paws is bigger than my head. He's not just big; he's huge.

I jump down from the boulder on shaky legs, and then press my back into the rock. I'm not scared of him, but I've never seen a wolf like his. If I saw him alone in the woods, I'd be running for the hills. But he breathes through his nose softly and takes a step forward.

It's okay, he reassures me through our mindlink. His soft voice wraps around my brain and sends soothing motions through my spine, for which I'm grateful. *I can see the concern in your eyes.*

My head shakes. "Just startled," I admit. "Are Alphas bigger than normal wolves?"

Yes. I'm a lot bigger than I remember. It's been a while.

"Is he a completely different subconscious to you?"

Yes. I believe so. We have separate minds, separate wants. He lives in my human body whilst I live in his shifted body.

"But you have full control of your wolf?" I ask slowly.

Always. His instincts might be sharper and more determined, but I still own the brain to our bodies. It's a complicated idea to wrap your head around, but you can trust me. You can trust him.

I swallow gently. "I know. Your eyes are gleaming yellow."

My parents like to call it a strange mutation, considering I have blue eyes. Lucy's wolf's eyes are blue, and my parents', too. But mine turned out yellow.

"I think it's to make you look fiercer," I blurt. "Like you were born to be an Alpha."

Jaxon's laughter fills my mind. I close my eyes with satisfaction from the sound. *Do you want to come closer?*

I blink once and then twice. "Yeah," I whisper.

His wolf watches me with those pretty eyes and tilts his snout as I stop directly in front of him. *Stroke me.*

A mini pause runs through my veins as I raise my hand and extend my arm. The tips of my fingers lightly graze the edge of his fur, and as expected, it's thick but also incredibly soft. He closes his eyes as I glide my hand across his back, lacing my fingers through the strands until I meet skin.

His wolf takes a step closer, nuzzling his snout into my stomach. He inhales my scent deeply as I continue to stroke him. "He's beautiful, Jax. You are beautiful."

After a few moments, I sink to the ground, bending my knees to admire his face. I could only imagine how vicious he could turn if he felt threatened.

He rubs his snout against my chin, and I laugh softly when his fur tickles me. *I like your laugh—a lot,* he whispers.

I gently cup my hands around his face, grazing over his ears and down to the edge of his jaw. "I'm an extremely ticklish being," I admit with a glint of amusement. "So please don't test me. I won't survive."

His wolf's tongue darts out and gives my chin a lick this time. I pull back, but there is a smile on my face. "Now, you're pushing it," I say with a playful warning. "Does it feel good to be back in this form?"

Yes. I couldn't have done it without you. Thank you.

I snort unattractively. "I doubt it."

Alphas might be strong, but they still need their Lunas at their sides to help with what they cannot achieve themselves. Power comes from emotion, and without them, we might as well be useless.

Luna. *Luna.* The word is a little alien to me as Lucien's pack was strictly males. "Not sure if I'm ready to be a Luna yet. The thought is terrifying. I barely know who I am myself—how could I be someone I know nothing about?"

His wolf nods in understanding. *I know. I would never rush you. Your memories of the past will come back soon. I promise.*

"I want to know who I was, what my life was like before." My shoulders slump as I pull my hand away from his fur. "But I'm also surprisingly content here, even if I feel like I don't belong."

Jaxon nuzzles his snout against my face again. *You do belong. But I'm glad you feel content. That's all I've ever wanted you to feel.*

My lips curl into a gentle smile. "Me, too," I say before clearing my throat. "So when you shift back...are you naked because your clothes have shed?"

Yes. So I suggest you turn around and walk back to the house before I shift.

My cheeks bleed with heat as if I'm already seeing him naked, but instead, I'm just thinking about it. Why on earth am I blushing? This is humiliating.

"Right, I'll do exactly that then."

I stand and give his wolf a once-over before turning away and walking back to the pack house. I'm certain this won't be the last time I see his transformation, and I'm still deeply intrigued.

21

AVA

The stars are bright tonight. Each and every one of them. I'm not usually a stargazer, but right now, it's a beautiful sight. There are constellations in the sky I've never noticed before —glowing like fireworks.

I can't take my eyes off them. I'm in a trance. They make the dark night sky feel warm.

A presence has the hairs on my arm standing, and I turn towards where my intuition directs. That's when I spot a woman with floor-length white hair and eyes that practically glow in the dark. She's not dangerous; I can sense it.

She takes long, languid steps to meet me, her purple and cream dress dragging along the forest floor behind her. Her glittery skin shines in the moonlight. Iridescent and breathtaking.

"Who are you?" I exhale when she stops in front of me.

A line of gleaming makeup runs across her cheeks and over her nose to the other side of her face. The mark is unique. I wonder if it's a tradition from wherever she's from. I know she's not human, but I don't know where she belongs.

"I'm sorry, Ava." Her voice is a velvety whisper of sorrow.

"For what?"

"For not helping you sooner. My powers were misdirected."

My brows pinch together. What is she talking about?

"Who are you?" *I repeat.*

Whoever she is, she's beautiful. Mysteriously beautiful.

She raises her hand and caresses my cheek. I half-expect it to fall through my face with how she looks like a spirit from above, but it doesn't. Her fingers are soft like expensive silk, and I close my eyes to the sensation.

"I never wanted you to suffer. I'm glad you're on the right path now."

"What do you mean?"

When I open my eyes, she smiles, her cheeks creasing around her mouth. "You're home, Ava. You are exactly where you are meant to be. I never wanted it to be through these circumstances, but this is where you belong, where you've always belonged."

I flick my gaze between hers slowly. "Home? I don't remember my home."

"No." *She shakes her head and drops her hand. My cheek turns cold without her magical touch.* "You don't. But that was never your true home. This is your forever home. I know it's hard for you to trust, but trust me when I say you're exactly where you're meant to be. I will keep saying it until you believe me—until you see for yourself."

My gaze turns hazy for a second. "With Jaxon?"

Her smile is calming. "With the family that was meant to be."

"Who are you? Tell me who you are."

"I am always here, Ava. You might not be able to see me, but my energy will always be present."

I blink at her words. "But I can see you?"

The next second, she's gone, and I turn around to find myself alone. I swipe a hand over my forehead. "Hello?" *I call out, but all I can hear is my voice echoing against the trees.*

My hand touches my cheek from where I can still feel her

presence. The moon above me glows so bright I shield my eyes from the sharpness of it. I wince and turn away.

"You're home, Ava."

I GASP a silent breath and sit up in my bed. My head whips around my room, but I'm alone. It was a dream. I press a hand to my chest and listen to my heart rattle against my ribcage.

Although I'm coming to terms with the fact it wasn't real, an eerie feeling buzzes around my head. I close my eyes and attempt to control my breathing with large gulps of air.

She felt so...real. A mythical creature of some kind but, at the same time, a soul with heartfelt emotions. My fingers graze my cheek. I can still feel the warmth of her touch despite her pale skin. She radiated heat—comforting heat.

I've never seen anything like her in my life. She's a mystery to solve. I crawl out of bed and get dressed into comfortable clothes before heading downstairs to the library. My eyes swipe past the clock on the wall. It's barely eight o'clock in the morning, and I doubt anyone will be in the library this early.

My feet creep into the room as I turn on the light and glance around. It's empty, thank goodness. I step forward and analyse the walls of books as high as the ceiling. A lot of them look ancient, covered in years worth of dust.

I chew on my lip. I don't have a clue where to start. My hand rests on my hip as I walk to the furthest ladder. I test out the sturdiness of it before climbing the steps to reach the top. My eyes scan the spines for words that might stick out to me, but I'm not entirely sure what I'm looking for.

It's more of an instinct than actual knowledge.

My fingernail hooks onto a book, and I pluck it from the

shelf. I lean onto the ladder and flick open the pages, eyes scanning the contents. *Pictures.*

I focus on the pages, eagerly sweeping over the drawings in the book, but none of them are what I'm looking for. Instead, it's a bunch of historic werewolf artefacts and heirlooms.

"What are you doing up there?"

The unexpected voice has me jumping out of my skin. I drop the book. My foot slips off the ladder, and I fall. I squeeze my eyes shut and release a squeal, ready to hit the floor, but instead, I land directly into strong arms.

I snap my gaze open to find Jaxon staring down at me with a wide smile, flashing off all his white teeth. A shiver runs through me as he holds me in his arms like I weigh next to nothing. "Hi."

"Hi," I murmur as I take in his handsome face. His stubble is neatly trimmed today, and his dark hair is swept back as if he's styled it for the first time. Those blue eyes simmer against mine with peaceful stillness.

"Sorry," he whispers. "Did I startle you?"

My throat tenses. "I thought I was going to hit the ground."

"Never." He drops his eye into a wink. "I've got you. *Always.*"

For a moment, I forget his arm is wrapped around my back and the other under my legs. My hands grip his T-shirt tightly, and I eventually start to peel them away when I realise I'm safe and not about to break my back.

"I'm going to put you down now," he clarifies, and I manage a nod.

He lowers me to the floor with ease, and my knees wobble slightly. I pray he's none the wiser. "Thanks," I rasp and brush myself off.

"What were you looking for so early in the morning?"

I clear my throat, trying to ignore the tingles that flicker over my body like little fireflies. I've come to the conclusion that I enjoy touching Jax, but I also don't want to get used to the feeling and rely on it when I'm down. I don't want my own emotions to be masked.

"Do you have any pictures of the Moon Goddess?" I ask.

Jaxon's brow quirks, a thousand questions passing his eyes. "Well, there are many different interpretations of the Moon Goddess. Us wolves don't meet her personally; she's more of a spiritual energy. The Goddess is our version of the human's God."

I nod. "Can you show me?"

"Yeah," Jaxon hums and beckons to the other side of the room. "I believe there are drawings in here. Can I ask why?"

My lip finds its way between my teeth. "Just curious."

Jaxon's head moves upwards as he grabs a book I wouldn't be able to reach without the ladder. "Let me have a look," he says before removing a couple and laying them out on one of the wooden tables.

I follow him as he opens the pages to find what I'm after. At first, he shows me a picture of a woman with dark hair. She wears silver beads and charms in her hair with blue eyes. I hum softly, and he flicks to the next book.

"Wait," I say, grabbing his wrist before he can turn the page.

He pauses. I take the edges of the book in my hands and bring it up to my face, shaking at the picture before my eyes. It's not a spitting image of the woman I saw in my dream, but it's very, *very* close.

"That's what we picture her as," Jaxon comments as he stands back and folds his arms over his chest. "White long hair and misty eyes, but no one knows. I don't know anyone who has met her. It's more of an idea, a feeling."

My heart thumps in my throat. I know it was just a dream, but it felt incredibly real. It wasn't like anything else I've ever experienced.

You're exactly where you're meant to be.

Her voice echoes around my head, and I take a shallow breath. No. *No.* I'm going crazy. My dream couldn't have been real. I'm imagining things. It was just a dream—an overstimulating visual dream.

The thought of being visited by her makes my body vibrate. Those words she spoke into existence, I find myself wanting to believe them, as if I've been waiting for confirmation this entire time.

"Ava." Jaxon's voice snaps me back to reality. I look at him. "You okay?"

I flash him a weak smile. "Yeah."

He quirks a brow, clearly not convinced. "Sure?"

"I just had a weird dream," I admit. "It was nothing. Now, I'm just curious."

I shut the book between my hands and lay it back down on the desk.

"Are you hungry?"

"Yes," I answer far too quickly. Jaxon releases a laugh.

"Do you want to make breakfast together?"

I nod. "I'd like that."

It'll certainly take my mind off my crazy dream.

22

JAXON

"I don't think you understand; my wedding has to be *perfect*," Lucy says as she stares at her laptop screen with wide eyes and flailing fingers over the keys.

My eyes roll automatically. All I've heard over the last few months is wedding plans, and I can see her turning into bridezilla within the next few days. The date is getting closer, and she's about to burst.

"*Our* wedding, babe." Sebastian's voice floats through the kitchen. Lucy glances up at him with a sudden nod—it's like she didn't even remember he was here.

Oh, boy.

"Sorry." A hand raises beside her head. "*Our* wedding."

"Well, if you wanted it to be perfect, you wouldn't be looking for the wedding cake nine days before now...would you?" I quirk a brow in her direction.

Unsurprisingly, she scowls at me with heavy annoyance. "Shut up, Jaxon. It's not my fault the original cake company didn't get back to me."

"Yeah," I rasp heavily. "It's called having a backup. I can't believe you decided to do this yourself and not get a wedding planner."

Lucy stares at me like I've stomped on a puppy. "Until you get married, *brother,* you have no opinion. Back. Off."

I glance at Sebastian who rests his head in his hands, muttering words under his breath. The corner of my lips tug. I shouldn't be getting involved, but it's far too easy to get under my sister's skin, and seeing Sebastian fight for his life —and her attention—is something else to add to the morning entertainment.

My head immediately turns to the door. My wolf's senses are ridiculously alert since Ava helped me shift for the first time in a while. She walks into the kitchen with damp hair over her shoulders and an oversized hoodie clung to her body. The sleeves hang over her wrists. *She looks adorable.* I clench internally at how she glances at me and offers me the sweetest smile.

"Morning," I exhale gently.

I flick my eyes down to find her barefoot, the black leggings cutting off at her ankles. The sounds of her footsteps echo in my ears as I watch her near the counter. To human ears, you wouldn't be able to hear a thing, but I hear those delicate steps.

"Morning," she greets.

Lucy suddenly turns to my mate. "Oh, thank the Goddess. Ava! I need your opinion. These idiots don't have the first clue about wedding cakes."

She blinks at her outburst. "Okay." A hesitant laugh falls from her lips. "But I don't know how helpful I'll be."

I watch her as she loops around the counter and settles behind my sister, flicking between different slides on the laptop screen. "Trust me, better than this lot."

"What flavour are you going for?" Ava asks.

"I want it to be three-tiered. The bottom will be raspberry and white chocolate, the middle will be caramel, and the top will be a classic Victoria sponge." Lucy claps her hands together as she lists each one.

Ava smiles in agreement. "Sounds tasty."

"But which style do you think? The decoration of the cake is important to me. It has to be a little out there but also not too much." Lucy bites her lip as if she's about to chew the entire thing off while Ava moves closer to the screen for better assessment. "This with the bright flowers or this one but with a bit of sparkle?"

I study Ava's face as she analyses both cakes with her ultimate thinking expression. My shoulders fall relaxed at the way she wants to help my sister but is obviously out of her depth. I adore seeing her like this. "The second one."

A huge grin stretches across Lucy's face. "I'm so glad you said that because I think so, too!" Her hands clap together like one of those annoying monkey toys. "I'm going to order it now."

Ava huffs out air like that was the toughest decision of her life. She meets my eyes as she walks around the counter and then stops. "What?"

I must look like a Cheshire cat. "Nothing." I shake my head. "Hungry?"

"Yeah."

My hand reaches over to the vacant stool beside me. I pat at the softness and stand from my own. "Come sit. I'll make you something."

She steps to my side and watches me with gentle eyes. "Thank you."

"Why do you never make us breakfast, Jaxon?"

My patience is wearing thin. "Because I like making sure that Ava is fed. I know you can do that yourself. And you guys never fucking tidy up after yourselves. If we worked together, maybe I'd offer you breakfast, too."

She tuts at me before bombarding Ava with a million and one different questions. I absolutely love my sister to pieces, but I can't wait until this wedding is over. Not that I'm jealous of her happy ending, but I've got one too many things on my mind, and once this wedding is out of the way, I can go back to focusing on what's important.

Like taking Lucien and his foul men out for good.

After ten minutes, I plate up scrambled eggs and avocado on toast for Ava. Her whole expression brightens when I place down the food. She's always delighted to have a decent meal, which makes me realise how starved she must have been when she was Lucien's captive.

Malnourished. Neglected. The thought does awful things to my sternum.

"Mmm. Smells delicious."

"Eat," I order as I perch beside her. "Don't let it get cold."

She doesn't need to be told twice.

Ava takes her knife and fork to cut into the toast. Her elbow grazes my arm, and despite it being through the material of her hoodie, it still makes my skin vibrate.

"Oh, for fuck's sake," Lucy curses and hits her laptop.

Sebastian sighs. "What is it?"

He leans over to rub her shoulder, but it doesn't help. She exhales a frustrated groan, and I hide my knowing smile. "I literally just got an email saying those embroidered tablecloths I ordered might be late!"

My head tilts to Ava, who is already looking at me. I'm glad I'm not the only one finding this entire situation comical. It's not new for Ava to smile, but when she does, it's like time stands still, and I can't get enough. I want to take a picture of it and keep it in my pocket. My wolf purrs with possessiveness at the idea.

"It's okay, babe. They're just tablecloths," Sebastian tries to calm her, and I wince.

Lucy recoils like she's been slapped with an iron pole. "Excuse me?"

I brace myself for what's about to unleash. Sebastian might officially be uninvited to his own wedding. Goddess, how does he put up with this crazy woman?

"They're *just* tablecloths?" she spits, slamming the laptop closed. "How dare you, Sebastian? I thought you'd be better than that."

I can't tell if that's fear or frustration behind his eyes. "Luce–"

"Who even are you?"

My hand cups my jaw, but it's too late. The laugh slips out. The look on Sebastian's face and the sheer madness my sister has become is like a reality show, and somehow, I've got a front-row seat to it.

Lucy's death glare flicks my way. "Do you think this is funny?"

My sister is a drama queen most of the time, but this is ridiculous. I flash her a slight grin, which she gapes at. Ava gently swats my arm, but she's also trying her hardest to keep a poker face.

"I'm sure they'll be here in time," Ava says, attempting to console her. "It said might, not definitely. Just remain optimistic. I'm praying for you, Lucy."

Lucy takes a couple of deep breaths and listens to Ava's wise words. I resist the urge to lean over and squeeze her hand. Instead, I focus on Lucy as she closes her eyes and holds her hands up in front of her face, wiggling her fingers.

"Calm down, Lucy. It's all going to be okay." Lucy mutters to herself.

I shake my head. I need to get out of this kitchen now.

"Ooh! I need to go over table plans." Lucy opens the laptop again and starts tapping away.

Ava finishes her breakfast and places her knife and fork in the middle of the plate neatly.

"Good?" I ask.

"Amazing." Her eyes light up. "Thanks again."

She stands to put the plate away, but I grab it before she can and silently usher her to sit back down.

"Are your parents coming to the wedding?" Ava asks curiously.

Lucy looks at me for a moment and sighs, her shoulders tensing. "We haven't had contact with them in a while," I admit. "Remember what I told you before?"

She nods once. "Sorry. It slipped my mind."

"It's complicated. I know they'd want to be here, but they wouldn't jeopardise our safety. Who knows if they're being tracked? It's tough for us without them, especially for Luce with her wedding day, but I know they'll be there in spirit."

"Oh." She frowns. "I'm sorry for bringing it up. I hope wherever they are, they're okay."

Lucy's head shakes, her blonde hair flying everywhere. "It's okay. Bash's family will be there. Some of our cousins and childhood friends are coming, too. It'll be lovely, even if our parents won't see me get married. I know they're happy for us. Everything they did was to keep us safe, and I'll forever be grateful for that."

Ava's lips part to respond, but another voice cuts her off. "Good morning, everyone." I turn to find Kayden strolling into the kitchen with a sweat-soaked T-shirt from his morning workout.

"Morning," Lucy chimes with a smile before sinking her head back into her laptop.

The hairs on my arms tighten, and I turn to find Ava completely rigid. I frown at her body's reaction as she follows his every move around the kitchen, especially when he pauses by the coffee machine to make a drink.

Before I can register what is happening, Ava leans over to take my hand which is resting on the counter. I know being in the same room as Kayden is a huge step, especially when she told Gemma she wants to battle this head-on. I gently run my thumb over her knuckles in soothing motions.

I got you. Our mindlink opens, and I fill the bond with a safety net.

Within seconds, she exhales a sigh that I realise was constricting her chest. She squeezes my hand, letting me know she's okay. I let my gaze fall on her, and she nods to herself. I raise her knuckles and kiss the skin gently.

This distracts her for a moment, and her eyes gleam but not with tears.

"H-hey, Kayden." Her voice is quiet and shaky, but we all hear it.

Kayden looks at us and smiles. "Hi, Ava. Coffee, anyone?"

Lucy points a finger to the sky. "Me, please."

"Always, Luce."

The kitchen then is filled with Lucy telling Sebastian the plan for their wedding day. Ava is still holding my hand, breathing a little steadier than before, and I know this is taking everything out of her right now.

I'm so proud of you, I whisper through her mind with every emotion inside my heart. *I'd never let anything harm you. You know that, right?*

Yes, she shoots back immediately, and it fills me with relief.

"And before you moan, Jaxon." Kayden glances over his shoulder at me with a cheeky smirk. "Training starts at midday. I've got an hour before I take the wolves to the border."

Quite frankly, the thought of training the pack is the last thing I'm thinking of. Ava, in this moment, has my undivided focus until my eyes dart to the counter beside the coffee machine, and I spot the residue of pressed coffee sprinkled over the marble. I twitch. "That's not what I'll be moaning about today," I murmur.

Kayden rolls his eyes and places a mug down next to Lucy. "Sometimes I think it would be better if you had a cleaner."

"Sometimes, I think it would be better if people cleaned up after themselves."

"I'll do it after breakfast."

"Which basically means never."

Kayden releases a laugh. "You're too easy to wind up."

"And you are the biggest pain in my ass."

I turn my attention back to Ava, who is silently watching our encounter.

Are you okay?

Just trying to get used to being around him, she admits.

I appreciate that, and you're doing amazing.

My throat clears, and Kayden flicks his eyes to me, along with Sebastian. "Well, I think now is a good time to tell you about my wolf."

"What about your wolf?" Kayden's brows crease.

"I shifted for the first time in a year."

Sebastian's face lights up with amazement, and my sister's mouth falls open. "No way! How?"

I raise my hand, which is still entwined with Ava's. "Thanks to this one and our bond. She practically drew it out of me. She has superpowers. She's very special."

Ava seems stunned and blinks in shock. "Oh, no." Her head shakes. "I didn't do anything."

"You did *everything*," I tell her before kissing her knuckles again. Those cheeks bloom like roses.

"Pack runs together soon?" Kayden suggests.

I nod, my heart slowly mending together again. "Yes. I need it."

"Good." Kayden steps towards me and slaps my back. "As much as I hate to admit it, it sucks without you, brother."

23

JAXON

It's a few days before my sister's wedding, and tonight is her "last night" of freedom before she becomes a wife. All of Lucy's closest girlfriends from the pack—Ava included—are planning on going out and celebrating in town. And right now, I'm being forced to take pictures of them together.

I mean, I'm not complaining too much because I physically cannot take my eyes off my beautiful mate. Lucy put some makeup on her, making those brown eyes even darker and her pale skin glow.

She's not just beautiful; she's taken my entire breath away.

My eyes roam her face and down her body. In an instant, my gaze hardens, looking at her in that pretty burgundy dress and heels with laces wrapped around her ankles. She's a sight for sore eyes. She smiles gently towards the camera, completely stealing my heart and running away with it.

When I finish my noble brotherly duties, I hand the phone back to Lucy. "Please don't do anything stupid tonight," I say under a hushed breath. "The last thing I need is more trouble."

She rolls her eyes and snatches her phone back. "Like what?"

"Like getting stupidly wasted, getting arrested, someone getting hurt. The list goes on and on and on," I murmur before folding my arms over my chest. "I don't need rumours going around the district, alright? Stay out of trouble."

Lucy groans. "Honestly, you sound so boring. I know you're worried about Ava, but I promise she's safe."

"I know." I nod. "That's why I'm ordering some guards to accompany you. And before you say anything, you won't even know they're there. They won't ruin your fun. They'll only help if anything happens."

The corner of her lip tugs. "You're so concerned about her. It's cute."

She's not wrong, I think in my head.

"Please look after her," I whisper before looking over at Ava as she talks away with Phia and Grace. "Don't leave her out. It's her first time going out with all of you girls, and I want her to feel comfortable and safe."

Lucy places a hand on my arm and gives it a squeeze. "You have my word, Jaxon. I promise. Like you said, the guards will be there, too."

I hesitate for a moment before nodding. "Alright."

"Right, girls, let's go!" Lucy claps her hands together, and the entire room roars with cheers of excitement for the night. I turn to Ava before she can escape out of the front door.

Instinctively, I reach for her hand, and she meets me in the middle. I run my thumb across her knuckles gently, and a zap of electricity rushes through my palm.

Jesus. My chest quivers at the sensations.

"Enjoy tonight," I say softly. "But be careful. I want you home in one piece."

"Who exactly am I being careful of?" Her brows rise curiously.

I offer her a smile before beckoning to the group of girls. "Them. They're all crazy and full of bad decisions."

A bright grin stretches onto her face, and it stops my heart beating altogether. It's completely unreserved, beaming at me for all to see. "I'll let you know how it goes." She nods and squeezes my hand. "We can mindlink, remember?"

How could I forget when it's the most blissful thing to experience?

"Sounds good," I say calmly. "Have a good time. I'll see you later."

She drops my hand, and my skin turns cold. "Bye."

I watch her walk away to join the girls. "Ava?"

"Yeah?"

Those glossy lips are pulled into what I wish was a permanent smile. I pause for another second to take her all in because I'm a selfish man, and I want to admire her for more than this moment. "You look beautiful."

A deep blush appears on her cheeks as she curls a finger around her hair. "Thank you," she replies timidly before exiting out of the door.

∼

KAYDEN SMIRKS from across my desk as he lounges back in the opposite chair. I twirl my pen between my fingers and attempt to focus on the plan in front of me, but we both know it's barely going in. "Something on your mind?"

I press a hand to my forehead and groan. "Please, leave it out."

"I mean, it's eleven-thirty, and you've not heard a word from them."

Don't fucking remind me.

"They're out having fun. I don't need to act like a possessive mate. That's the last thing Ava needs."

Kayden's lip twitches. "I'm surprised you didn't demand you went with them and crash Lucy's night. I see how you look at Ava—even when she was terrified to be around me. You're a lot calmer than I thought you'd be."

Little does he know I'm experiencing a mini-heart attack inside.

"Calm is not what I'm feeling." I run my tongue over my teeth. "When you have a mate, you'll realise how protective you can be of them, even when you know they're safe. It's a fucking nightmare, Kayden. But she needs to live her life. That is one thing I will never take from her."

"The guards would have contacted you already if something was wrong." He shrugs simply, and I know he's right. I trust my guards with my life. Ever since Julia's death, I upped their training and skill set. Now I know they're the strongest they can be. "We both know they're in safe hands. But truthfully, I know you just miss her. You're a big softie at heart. Absolutely smitten."

My eyes focus on my Beta. "You annoy the hell out of me sometimes."

He barks out a laugh. "Got to be here to humble you."

I scowl at him, and he flashes me a boyish grin.

"You are head over heels for the girl." His brows quirk.

"I don't want to talk about this with you."

Kayden scoffs. "Why not?"

"Because it's distracting us from what's really important. Remember?"

"Ahh." He tilts back his head and shoves his sleeves up to his elbows. "Yes. I remember."

"Anyway," I rasp. "We've had eyes on them for weeks now. Once the wedding is over and done with, we take our strongest wolves, and we get that fucker Lucien and everyone else and make them pay."

"What are the guards around his territory saying?"

"Mostly under the radar. But he's been making some suspicious moves."

Kayden's brows raise. "Suspicious how?"

"I've noticed he's been taking his wolves out in groups, like some kind of search party. I don't want to think they're looking for Ava, but they could be."

"Shit, really?"

I nod slowly. "But he hasn't come close to our territory. The second he takes a step closer, I'm launching the attack without hesitation. I'm getting hourly updates of his moves. And I'm not mentioning any of this to Ava. I don't want her to worry."

Kayden nods in understanding. "What are you going to do to him?"

My eyes flare at his question. What *won't* I do to him?

"I guess that's up to my imagination at the time," I say with a focused stare. "Ava will never fret over them again. She deserves her justice. She deserves a lot more, but this is a step in the right direction."

"Agreed. Let's make him wish he was never fucking born."

I'd rather torture him so badly he'll beg me for death.

"Let's go over the duties I've assigned everyone and what

specific tasks I need them to carry out," I clear my throat and shuffle through the notes I made earlier. "I want all of my wolves to know the plan like the back of their hand before it's executed."

Kayden flashes me a knowing smile. "You got it, Alpha."

24

AVA

"Ava! Ava! Ava!"

The girls chant my name as I throw back a rather sweet cocktail. It's been years since I've drunk alcohol, but tonight is the first night I've wanted to let my hair down and have some fun. It's Lucy's night, and I'm not going to let anything ruin it.

I wipe at my mouth when I finish the fruity drink, and the girls cheer. Lucy wraps an arm around me with the world's biggest grin. "Ah, Ava. That was the slowest chug I've ever seen."

"I haven't had alcohol in a *really* long time," I shout over the loud music.

She releases a laugh. "I know. I'm only teasing. Are you having fun? How are you feeling?"

My eyes pulse from the wave of that cocktail. "Yeah." I nod. "So much. It's good to get out of the house and spend time with you girls."

"I'm so glad you can be here." She gives my shoulder a squeeze. "How are you with karaoke?"

"Awful!"

We both laugh. "Me, too," she agrees. "But we leave no woman behind. Come on!"

She latches onto my hand and drags me away from the booth we've been perching in for the last hour. I step onto my heel and sway a little. I don't remember being this much of a lightweight.

"I'm not sure if I remember any of the songs," I admit with a slur.

Lucy shakes her head. "Doesn't matter. They have a screen with lyrics!"

Phia bounces towards us with bloodshot eyes and smudged lipstick. "Who the hell have you been kissing?" Lucy quirks an impressed brow.

"The bartender." She throws her thumb over her shoulder. "He's pretty sexy."

I grin. "Good kisser?"

"Oh, he was divine. He did this crazy thing with his tongue. I'll be going back for seconds later."

Lucy presses a hand to her forehead but cannot fight a smile. "Wow, I already know this night is going to end up in pure chaos."

Phia shrugs. "If you're getting married, then I'm allowed to have a cheeky fling with the hot guy at the bar. It's only fair."

"I guess so." Lucy chuckles. "Right, we've got to decide what song we want to sing. All of us on stage together!"

"Shot, shots, shots!" Grace's voice booms over ours as she walks towards us with a tray in hand.

The alcohol sitting in my stomach does a sudden flip. I know this shot will tip me over the edge, but another part of me wants to have a "screw it" moment. I know I'm in safe hands. All I want is to have fun, and I'm having tonnes of it.

"Ava," Grace beckons to the tray. "Take one."

I take a tiny plastic shot glass and analyse the neon-green liquid. Oh, boy.

"Speech!" Phia screams.

Then all the girls erupt into a loud chant which makes Lucy beam with a smile until she waves a hand to quiet them all down. "Okay, okay," she shouts. "I just want to say thank you for coming tonight to celebrate. I love you all. But here's to falling in love, having the best friends ever, and getting shitfaced!"

Our arms extend to clink our glasses, and I push back the funny-coloured liquid. The taste of sour apple rolls down my throat, and I pull a face, swallowing and sticking out my tongue. Lucy's expression morphs the same before we both laugh.

"Lucy's Bride Tribe," the guy on stage calls into a microphone. "It's your turn to hit the stage."

My stomach warms from the shot I took. I follow the girls with a huge smile. I don't want this night to end. If this is life...I want to continue living it.

25

JAXON

It's late. I know that much. But when my ears prick at the sound of the front door opening, I immediately stand. I purposely kept my office door open for this exact reason. I'm trying my damn hardest to not be overbearing, but I was counting down the seconds until they got home.

I tidy away the notes on my desk before heading downstairs into my private kitchen to find Lucy and a few of the other girls. All of them are chatting away like it isn't the middle of the night. The smell of alcohol wafts from them like they've been out for the past five days. Holy hell. How much did they drink?

My eyes scan the room, but Ava is nowhere to be seen. The hairs on the back of my neck stand in her absence, but I know she's here. My wolf is happily rested but eager to see her.

"Alpha Jaxon!" Phia shouts—or slurs—to get my attention. All of them are grinning ear to ear, swaying slightly.

"Where's Ava?" I ask.

"She's getting changed in her room," Lucy responds.

"Fun night, girls?" I quirk a brow.

"Look what we learnt tonight!" Grace shouts across the space, even though I'm merely a few feet from her. I study her movements as few of the other girls hoist Phia up and hold her by her legs. She's in the air, I'll give them that. Did they accidentally fall into an acrobatics class?

Their laughter erupts, and the next thing I know, they're all tumbling to the floor in a messy heap, all cackling like witches you see in movies. I jump back with a concerned expression.

Oh, Goddess. These girls are a nightmare.

"Ava taught us some tricks!" Grace shouts from the floor.

I arch a brow in utter surprise. "Did she?"

Lucy nods as she stuffs her face with leftover dinner from last night. "Yeah, it was fun. I wish I had filmed it. You would have died with laughter, Jaxon."

Lucy helps the girls off the floor. I turn away from them, head back upstairs, and I walk straight towards Ava's bedroom.

The door is slightly ajar, but I knock anyway. "Come in!" a muffled voice echoes. I step inside to find Ava struggling to put on a jumper. She can't quite find the head hole. I smile to myself as I approach.

"Here," I say, pulling down the material.

Her head bursts through the hole, her hair poking in every direction, eyes bloodshot. "Thank you!"

I blink at the loudness of her voice and the bright grin that doesn't leave her face for a second. My gaze studies her makeup to find her eyes slightly smudged and her cheeks rosy.

All that alcohol hits me in one wave. Goddess.

"Are you drunk?" I ask, cocking my head.

Ava waves a hand in front of her face. "Pfft. Noooooo."

She takes a step back which results in a stumble, so I

lean forward to catch her before she hits the floor. I narrow my eyes at her playfully. "You're not drunk?"

Ava nibbles on her lip and shoots me a finger. "Okay, you got me."

I glance down at the heels that are still on her feet.

"Sit down."

She doesn't protest.

I kneel in front of her and take her ankle in my hand. I tug at the strings before pulling the shoe off her heel. My gaze hardens on the scars around her ankles, red and jagged. I breathe through my nose sharply and press a delicate kiss to the skin. Goddess, I'll never understand how anyone could lay a finger on her.

"These hurt so bad," she murmurs. "Why do people wear heels? They're torture devices."

I smile at her words. "Because they look good—especially on you."

What I wouldn't do to have them over my shoulders, I think to myself.

I shake my head and scold my wandering mind.

Her eyes roll playfully. "You would say that."

My fingers start to undo the next heel, and I match her ankle with another kiss. I swipe my thumb along the tender flesh before placing them down on the floor. I glance up at her to see pure adoration in her eyes.

"Thank you," she whispers.

"Let me get you some water."

I push onto my feet, and Ava follows. I reach down to take her hand, but she moves it away and wraps her arms around my middle instead, snuggling her face into my chest. My head tilts down at the surprising action before I lace my arms around her.

"I missed you," she whispers, leaving my heart a puddle on the floor.

My head rests down on hers, and I leave a kiss on the crown of her head. I press my other hand to the nape of her neck. Her heart beats into my chest. I could live by that beat; it might just be the only thing keeping me alive. "I missed you, too, baby."

When she lets my body go, I do the same. "Stay here for a second, okay?"

Her face falls immediately. "Where are you going?"

"To get you some water to help with your head in the morning."

"Oh." She relaxes. "Okay."

I walk down the hall to my office and open the small fridge I keep here. I reach for a fresh bottle of water and retreat back to Ava's bedroom.

When I return, I find her staring up at the ceiling. "Here," I say. My voice alerts her, and she takes the bottle from my hand and inhales half of it.

She gasps for a breath like she's never touched water in her entire life. "How was your night?" I ask.

"It was amazing! I had so much fun." Her eyes light up with pure joy. She takes a step towards me so we're closer. I enjoy this proximity; it reminds my wolf she's home and safe.

She's with us.

My mouth curls into a satisfied smile. "I'm glad you had a good time."

"I lost count of how many drinks I had...b-but then–" Her words are nothing but a jumbled mess, and it makes me chuckle. She holds up her hands towards my face. "I fell up the stairs. I had no idea stairs could be so dangerous... upwards!"

This is highly entertaining.

"You fell up the stairs?" I ask as she nods. "Are you alright?"

I check her for any visual wounds, but all I can see is intoxication. She sways again, and I take her hand, leading her to the sofa before she falls and actually hurts herself.

"Yeah. It didn't hurt."

"Have you ever been drunk before?"

Ava throws her head back and laughs. No, she doesn't laugh—she *cackles*. "H-have I ever been drunk before?" she slurs before standing up. Oh, Goddess, here we go. "You must think I'm so fucking boring!"

I'm startled for a moment. I think this is one of the first times I've heard her swear.

"I don't think you're boring," I admit.

She ignores me and starts pacing the room. "You know I used to be a cheerleader?"

I instantly lean forward, pressing my elbows to my knees. *Is she remembering?*

Then, she stops to stand in a spot and presses a finger to her delicate lips. "Actually, I was the co-captain!"

I watch in awe as she throws her hand up to the ceiling with force. Her memories are starting to come back, and I'm glad I'm here to witness it. The smile on my face is permanent—practically tattooed on at this rate.

"That explains the circus act downstairs, then." I chuckle gently. "Did you teach them some of your old tricks tonight?"

"Yes, that was all me." Her eyes beam at me with pride. "And, and, and..." she trails off and begins walking again. I lean forward with my arms, ready to catch her if she topples over. "I used to go to parties with my friends. I used to dance until the early hours and drink and regret it all the next day but happily do it all again the weekend after."

A moment of realisation suddenly hits me. Before I met her, she was a normal teenage girl. She's a human and did things that made sense—now she's been thrown into a new world that is completely alien to her.

"I used to be fun!" she yells, but then scowls and points to the middle of her chest. "No, I still am fun!"

She plants her hands on her hips for a second to catch her breath from all the yelling. I think she's stopped, but then she starts again. "I'm sure you think I'm weak and fragile, and you tread on eggshells around me."

"You know I don't think that," I express calmly. "I want to give you the time and space to grow yourself, not through me or anyone else. But you are far from weak, Ava."

We stay silent for a few moments. I fear I've upset her, but when she starts spinning in a circle and laughing to herself, I know that comment has blown over her head.

"Do you remember your friends?" I ask.

"I remember my best friend, Kayleigh. We were like sisters," she says, clutching her hands over her heart. "I miss her. She was like my family."

I clear my throat and have a small flashback to the social media post I saw with a comment from a user called Kayleigh. Now she remembers, I know it's something I'll need to show her. It's her choice if she wants to see any friends or family members. I know I cannot keep that from her.

"Do you remember your parents?" I ask gently.

Her head turns to look in my direction. "My parents?"

I nod and wait patiently.

"I didn't really have any parents. I've been fostered since I was a baby. Never was chosen to be adopted, so I jumped from foster home to foster home." Her lips turn downwards at the thought, and I hate how her emotions make my heart plummet. "Foster care sucks."

She's never had a loving home? My bloodstream freezes.

I open my mouth to respond, but she speaks first. "I wish I could feel like this forever," she whispers, holding onto her neck as she looks up at the ceiling.

"Like what?"

"Like I have no problems. Like I'm normal." She smiles to herself, but it's not a happy smile.

I frown. "You are normal, Ava."

She ignores me again, her eyes wandering over the room like she's deep in thought. "Oh, yeah!" she blurts. "I also had a boyfriend."

My entire throat closes as I choke. "You had a boyfriend?"

A weird sensation of ice-cold water and burning-hot fire rush through my body at once. I shake my head at the reaction and watch her as she swings her arms around her body.

"Mmhm," she murmurs.

"Do you miss him?" I ask out of nowhere.

Goddess, help me get my shit together.

Ava's eyes snap to mine within a second. "Do you miss Julia?"

Yeah, maybe we won't go down that path tonight.

When I don't respond, she wanders back over to the sofa and sits down next to me. Well...half on me, half on the sofa. I never expected her to sit this close, but I'm not complaining. I like knowing she trusts me.

Her hand reaches up, and she traces her index finger over my stubble and across my lips. Her touch is so gentle I barely feel it. I study her face as she analyses mine with big eyes and a pretty smile. The bond is zapping between us like lightning; it's in the pit of my stomach.

"You're a fine specimen," she whispers as her finger pulls down my bottom lip.

My heart thumps in my throat. I grab her little fingers and press my lips to her warm skin in return. "You have a way with words, Ava." I chuckle softly.

She fidgets on her knees and falls back. Luckily, I have a grip on her waist, catching her before she hits the floor.

"Woah!" she shrieks. I pull her back until our chests are flush against one another, then she starts to laugh, and I adore the sound. I'd keep it in a jar if I could and present it on my office desk to be reminded every day.

"Come on." I beckon with my head. "Let's put you to bed."

When she doesn't move, I stand from the small sofa and carry her in my arms to her bed, tucking her beneath the sheets.

"Wait," she mumbles, latching onto my wrist. "Stay. Please. I don't want to be alone."

I flick my eyes over her pleading face. My chest crumbles. There is no way I could say no to her, but at the same time, I want her to be sober while making these decisions. I would never want to push her boundaries and take advantage of them just because she's drunk.

"Until you fall asleep," I eventually land on.

Instead of getting in the bed, I lay on top of the sheets. I face the way she's sleeping and watch her eyes flutter open and shut. She's trying her hardest to stay awake, but I know the alcohol will claim her soon.

When she opens her eyes again, she scowls in my direction. She doesn't look mad; she looks drunk-mad. "Why are you so far away from me?"

I chuckle to myself and shuffle closer. "Where do you want me, Ava?"

"I want to lay my head on your chest," she slurs through tired words.

"Okay," I whisper and move until she curls into my side and rests her head on my chest. I wrap my arm around her back and stare up at the ceiling.

She giggles softly. "I can hear your heartbeat."

"Yeah? Is it racing?"

"No, it's calm," she admits.

I hum softly. "Because you make me feel at peace, Ava."

She stays silent for a few moments, and when I think she's finally asleep, she says, "D-do you wish I was her?"

"Huh?"

Those eyes are half-closed as she speaks.

"Julia," she whispers. "Do you wish I was her?"

Her expression is nearly emotionless. It's a genuine question. I can't help but pull my brows into a deep frown. "Why would you ask that?"

"Because she was your first mate. Because you love her." She pauses. "Now, I've come into your life, and I wonder if you wish she was still alive and you never met me. That we could somehow swap."

Her confession has my heartstrings tugging in the wrong way. Grief is a complicated emotion. Although since Ava has walked into my life, I've found her bond has helped me grow out of my depressive state. I wanted to be present throughout her recovery. I wanted nothing more than to be a good mate.

"I am her replacement," she whispers sadly.

"No." I shake my head. "You're not. I don't wish you were Julia. You came into my life for a reason. I don't expect you to understand, but I'm trying, I'm really trying. None of this has been easy for me, but I've loved spending time with you, getting to know you, and letting our bond grow authentically."

Her eyes quickly look down to my lips and then back into my eyes. "How long were you together again?"

"Two years."

"You must really miss her."

Of course, I miss her. I will always love her, but that doesn't mean my limit for love stops there. The word has complex conventions, and I've been trying to figure out my brain for the last few months while Ava adjusts to this new world.

"I do miss her," I admit. "But my heart didn't halve when I lost her. It doubled when I met you."

A slight smile plasters across her exhausted face. Her eyes close once more, and she rests it back on my chest. I release a soft sigh. I wish when she wakes up, she doesn't regret this conversation or choosing to be this close to me. If she even remembers it at all.

~

WHEN I WAKE UP, I'm in my own bed. I had the willpower and all my morals to leave when she fell asleep. Despite it being difficult, I knew it was the right thing to do.

An unsettling feeling in my stomach has me shooting up in my bed. I groan when a sharp pain races to my throat. I clutch the skin and realise nothing is happening to my body. It's Ava's body.

I leap out of bed and rush down the hall to find Ava's door ajar. The sound of retching has me barging into the bathroom to find her on her knees next to the toilet, groaning before throwing up last night's cocktails, I presume. The fluorescent orange colour makes me slightly nauseous.

My knees hit the floor beside her, and I gather her hair into my hand and rub her back in soothing motions. "Hey," I say softly. "It's okay. Get it up. You'll feel so much better afterwards."

She throws up a few more times before groaning again, and then falls back onto her ass and wipes her mouth with the corner of her hand. Her hair is a mess and the makeup she didn't take off last night is smeared across every inch of her face.

I lean up to flush the toilet and grab the half-drunk water from last night. "Here, drink some. Hydrate yourself."

She sighs uncomfortably before taking a sip and spitting it out into the toilet to wash out her mouth, then she finally takes a few gulps. "Thanks," she whimpers.

"How are you feeling?"

Ava's brown eyes stare at me for a long second. "Are you seriously asking me that question?"

I laugh softly when I know I shouldn't, but this moment is far too adorable. "Sorry if we woke you up last night. I'm sure we were pretty loud coming in."

My brows raise at her statement. "You don't remember?"

Her face pales even more. "Remember what?"

"Us talking for ages." I tilt my head with amusement. "Me putting you to bed, you asking me to stay? I didn't by the way. I waited until you were asleep before leaving you."

"Oh, God," she murmurs and presses a hand to her forehead. "*Oh*, God!"

She glances around the bathroom frantically as if trying to remember what happened. "D-did I say anything embarrassing?"

"No," I reassure her, and she breathes out a sigh of relief. "But–"

Her eyes widen in suspense as I carry on.

"You did call me a fine specimen," I tease with a grin.

"Screw my life." She throws her head into her hands, attempting to hide herself.

I tug at one of her wrists lightly. "Don't worry," I say, finding her mortified eyes again. "I think you're a fine specimen, too."

26

AVA

Today is Lucy and Sebastian's big day. The house has never been this chaotic. Everyone is walking left, right, and centre. In and out of the kitchen. Up and down the stairs.

Lucy demanded everyone but her bridesmaids and I leave the house so she can have some peace and quiet. Of course she doesn't want Sebastian to see her before the ceremony, so he left with Jaxon and Kayden a little while ago.

I stand in front of the mirror in the hallway as I look at the pretty dress clung to my body. I press down against my stomach, flattening the soft material. I don't remember the last time I felt comfortable in my own skin. But right now, I have a spark of confidence in my heart, and I'm enjoying every second of it.

My dress is navy with a square neckline that shows off my collarbones—Phia added a dash of highlighter to make them pop. A small band runs around my waist and pinches just below my bust before the rest of the dress falls down to the floor.

I've been anticipating this day for a while, and I've

voiced my concerns to Gemma in our recent sessions. My brain forces me to overthink every little detail, when in fact I need to take the day as it comes. There's no point dwelling on the future; it hasn't even happened yet. Gemma said not to put pressure on myself, and I'm not. I should take a breath and step away if I become overwhelmed.

But I'm going to enjoy today. I feel pretty for the first time in years, and I don't want anything to dampen this mood, especially since we're celebrating true love.

"Ava!" Phia shouts from the hall. "We're ready to go!"

I quickly grab my belongings and make my way towards them. My eyes fixate on Lucy as she adjusts her dress. It's strapless and tight at the waist, making her hourglass figure look incredible. The dress fans out at her feet with a small trail behind her, and it's embellished with white beads for extra detail. I've never seen anything so gorgeous in my life.

"You look beautiful, Lucy," I say, unable to take my eyes off her.

She squeals with a bright smile. "Thank you." Her hands take mine. "I'm so nervous!"

I squeeze her fingers. "I know, but enjoy it. Think of the excitement instead. This is *your* day."

Lucy's face crumbles, and then she draws me into a hug. "I'm so glad you're here, Ava."

I relax into her embrace. "I'm glad I'm here, too," I admit.

"Let's go, let's go, let's go!" Phia yells as she ushers us out the front door and towards the white cars.

When we pull up outside the manor a few moments later, I stare out the window in awe. I saw the pictures online, but they do not do this place justice whatsoever.

It's a huge white manor with four wide pillars and pink flowers around the walls. A small fountain with a sculpture of a lady sits in the middle, and there's a large set of grand stairs that go up to the building with golden features.

I pop the car door open as we halt to a stop. My head turns to find Jaxon waiting at the bottom of the stairs. I attempt to walk properly in these black heels on the pebbled floor, but my feet haven't forgiven me yet from Lucy's night out.

My eyes take in Jaxon's tall stature. A man in a suit. My goodness.

Handsome doesn't even cut it. He's in a league of his own. *And out of mine.*

His attire is grey with black dress shoes and a dark tie. His stubble is trimmed neatly and his dark hair is swept back and placed with perfection. My mouth turns alarmingly dry.

Lucy approaches him, and he meets her halfway. He smiles at her before leaning down to kiss her on the cheek. Her bridesmaids follow close behind. Once he steps around his sister, his eyes flick to mine.

Those blue eyes dilate in ways I can't understand. It makes my legs clench as he admires me boldly. I slowly make my way over to them, and Jaxon leans forward to slip an arm around my waist. He roams my face, and the corners of his lips flick upwards.

"There are not enough words in the dictionary to describe how beautiful you look right now," he says huskily. "Goddess, I can't believe I'm all yours."

A whimper escapes my throat as blood rushes to my face. "Thank you," I whisper, savouring the placement of his hand on the small of my back. "You don't look so bad yourself."

"I know." He smirks. "I can hear your thoughts."

My gaze widens. Heat spreads across my cheeks,

burning darker than ever. Oh, crap. I'm drowning in mortification—I need the ground to swallow me whole.

He chuckles softly, his nose running along the edge of my cheek. "Goddess, you are so adorable. I think we need to try harder in our lessons on shielding. Two might not have been enough."

"Please," I say desperately. "Save me from this humiliation."

His mouth stretches into a gorgeous grin. "Nothing to be embarrassed about. But once the wedding is over, we can work a little harder on the techniques. I know it will make you more comfortable. Although I have to admit, I'll miss hearing your sweet little thoughts."

I gulp when he winks. "I'm convinced you love to tease me."

"Yeah," he drawls. "Just a little. I like seeing you blush."

"Right." Lucy steps towards us. "They're ready for me."

I step back and press my cheek to Lucy's. "I'll see you guys in there," I say before giving her shoulders a supportive squeeze.

My gaze catches Jaxon's quickly as I give him a soft smile.

I'll see you soon, baby, Jaxon's voice floats through my head as I take the stairs up to the manor, beaming from ear to ear.

~

THE CEREMONY WAS a beautiful celebration of love and tenderness. I couldn't stop my eyes from watering when they exchanged their vows. Never have I witnessed anything so pure, and I'll treasure this day forever. It just might have restored my faith in happy endings.

Jaxon walked Lucy down the aisle and to see their sibling bond was like no other. It must have been hard for them to know their parents couldn't be here to share this special day with them.

After the ceremony, we arrived at the reception, and I mingled with some of Jaxon's pack. We listened to the speeches and raised our glasses. Then, it was time for the cake to be cut and to get drunk—Lucy's words, not mine.

I've seen Jaxon in passing a few times, but this is his sister's wedding. I don't want to get in the way. When everything starts to get a little overwhelming, I step outside to grab some air and refresh my lungs.

My eyes fall on a white gazebo with pink and cream flowers woven into the arch with fairy lights dangling from the roof. I pause for a moment and admire the perfect scenery. A smile covers my lips as I step inside, allowing my fingers to brush the delicate roses and carnations.

Where are you? Jaxon's voice floats into my mind.

A shiver of comfort rushes to my heart. *Outside.*

It doesn't take long for Jaxon to find me. My skin tingles when he's right behind me. I close my eyes at the sensation —the bond growing and glowing and everything in between.

When I turn around to face him, I stop breathing at how beautiful he is. It's a sight that will be engraved into my mind forever.

Jaxon walks towards me. His blazer and tie are gone, and now his shirt sleeves are rolled up to his elbows, showing off his impressive forearms. His gaze roams my face and body agonisingly slow. His eyes turn a notch darker when he meets my gaze. "I'm sorry I've not spent much time with you today, Ava. It's been hectic. Lucy was getting angry because the chef didn't include some special salad dressing, and I had to sort it ou–"

A little laugh rumbles from my chest at his distress. "Jax, it's fine. You are being her fatherly figure today, and everyone is expecting you to sort out all the disasters. It's okay. I've been enjoying boosting my own confidence."

"You never fail to amaze me," he exhales with adoration in his eyes. "Starting now, I am not going to leave your side."

I try to hide my smile but fail miserably. "Good."

Joy swarms my sternum like a big hug.

"I haven't stopped thinking about you all day." His voice is raspy.

My heart pounds against my ribcage, heat creeping up my neck and across my exposed chest. I can't hide from him; it's already too late. He steps closer, his tall frame towering over my body.

"T-thinking about what?" I ask curiously.

Jaxon's eyes flare at my question. "I've been thinking about how amazing you look in that dress." He slides his hand against mine in a gentle caress. "I've been thinking how beautiful you look."

I'm unsure if I'm capable of breathing right now, especially when he looks at me with those soft eyes that I believe were made for me—and *only* me.

My lips part, and his gaze flicks downwards. He pauses for a moment before he says, "I've been thinking about how much I want to kiss you."

Holy hell. My heart clenches like someone has squeezed it.

Jaxon closes his eyes and pulls back, dropping my hand. "I'm sorry," he apologises with a heavy chest. "That was incredibly inappropriate. You're not ready for that."

When he opens his lids, they've returned to dark blue. I shudder and attempt to ignore how clammy my hands have become. I glance at his lips. They look soft and downright kissable.

I remember my sessions with Gemma. I want to claim back my desire and affections with my consent, my body, and my consciousness. It's *my* choice.

"Maybe I want you to kiss me," I whisper.

Jaxon looks at me so intensely, so hard that I lose my breath. "Don't say things you don't mean for the sake of me, Ava," he states. "I don't want any maybes. I want you to know for definite."

"I do," I say fearlessly. "I know what I want. I want you to kiss me. I want to feel close to you. I want to feel empowered."

Jaxon blinks a couple of times at my declaration and then takes a step closer. His hand slides against my cheek, and I shiver. There is a twitch in my brain that is yelling at me to step away, but I ignore it. It's not real. It's my insecurities speaking. Jaxon would never hurt me.

He leans down slightly and brushes his lips over mine in the sweetest kiss. The sparks that ignite inside my body are indescribable. My head swims in the clouds at the feeling of his lips. *Euphoric.*

A few seconds later, he pulls away and looks at me. I know he felt that, too.

All I can think is—it was way too short to be our first kiss. I want more. I need more. I need...*him.*

For once, I pray he can read my mind because I'm sure words will fail me right now. All my limbs are numb from satisfaction and relief. I need him to understand I want more. His mouth fits mine devastatingly well.

The corner of his lip twitches into a gentle smirk before he dips his head back down, tugging my face closer with his palms. His mouth closes over mine, but instead of being sweet and soft, it's deep and passionate. My toes tingle. It's like he's waited years to be able to do this, and right now, he's savouring every single second.

Slowly, his lips start to caress mine, and I kiss him back with urgency. I latch onto his wrists as he walks forward, forcing my legs to move backwards. He gently grazes my bottom lip with his teeth before sliding his tongue into my mouth. I moan at the contact, and every single thought in my head empties.

All I know is *him*.

My back hits the fencing of the gazebo, and I place one hand on the edge to steady myself. Jaxon wastes no time reaching down underneath my dress and hoisting me up onto the ledge, holding me tightly so I don't fall. He positions himself between my legs, angling my head so he can kiss me harder.

My hands snake over his shoulders, and I clasp them behind his neck, sliding them into his hair. He smiles against my lips, which has me shaking. Blood roars in my ears, and I ignore the rest of the world. His tongue slips into my mouth again, gently caressing mine with yearning strokes.

Jaxon bites down on my bottom lip, and I can't suppress the groan that escapes the back of my throat. He grips me tighter and wraps a hand around my back to push us impossibly closer. A light growl erupts from his chest, which catches me by surprise.

My head becomes dizzy. The bond. The connection. The emotion. Everything is getting too much. I slowly pull away, but I keep my eyes closed, resting my forehead against his chin.

I inhale a wave of air and fill my lungs to the maximum. I desperately want my head to stop spinning and to come back down to planet Earth. He presses his lips to my forehead with a feather-light kiss, and eventually, I suck up the courage to look at him. My cheeks redden when I realise what we've just done. I don't regret it—at least, that's a positive. His eyes make me feel seen.

Then his warm, loving lips press to the pulse on my neck. I sigh into his touch and angle my head for better access. All of his kisses are tender and purposeful yet make me hot and bothered at the same time.

The strap of my dress falls down my arm, and Jax uses this as an opportunity to work his way to my collarbone and over my shoulder. I let out a small whimper of pleasure because his lips are like pure fire against my skin.

A spark taps in my head, and everything becomes tighter, louder, and heavier. I'm out of my depth here. This needs to slow down before I trigger myself.

"Jax," I say softly.

He instantly removes himself from my shoulder and glances at me with deep-rooted concern. "What's wrong?"

I shake my head to reassure him. "Nothing," I admit. "Just a bit overwhelmed."

He slides the strap of my dress over my shoulder and offers me a peaceful smile. "Then we'll stop," he says quietly. "Never be afraid to tell me anything. Okay?"

"Okay." I bite my lip. The skin is sensitive from where the memories of his mouth have been. "We should get back to the wedding."

"You're right." He nods.

I jump down from the ledge with the help of his hands on my waist. "Like I said, I'm not leaving your side," he whispers in my ear and squeezes my fingers at the same time.

I'm flushed with a thousand different emotions, but contentment is at the forefront. My entire expression screams—*I've had the life kissed out of me*—but I'm convinced he kissed life *into* me instead.

27

AVA

"Okay, ladies and gentlemen. It's time for the first dance. Lucy and Sebastian, please find your way to the dance floor."

A loud cheer erupts throughout the room. My eyes latch onto Lucy as she bounds towards the dance floor excitedly. Sebastian soon follows, both grinning at each other like they've won the lottery.

In their eyes, they definitely have.

Lucy wraps her arms around Sebastian's neck as the music starts, and they gently sway to the beautiful song playing over the speakers. I watch in awe at their admiration for each other. After a while, people begin to join them with their partners, family members, and friends.

Jaxon's hand slides into mine gently as he tugs at my fingers. "Dance with me?"

"Yeah," I whisper. "I'd love to."

He leads us over to the dance floor with the others, and our bodies mould together to move to the music. I place my hands over his shoulders as his arms wrap around my waist.

My head softly falls onto his chest, and I smile to myself at this peaceful moment.

Jaxon hugs me closer, dipping his head down to leave a kiss to my crown. My eyes focus on Lucy and Sebastian across the dance floor. The way they look at each other, laugh with each other, *be* with each other—it's magical.

Every moment they share is so raw and emotional. *Real.*

It's like the world has slowed down just for them, to allow them to devour this moment for a little while longer. It's more than heartwarming; it feels life-changing to see their love in the most honest form.

Whatever they have, I want.

They must love each other more than anything in this world.

"They do." Jax's voice interrupts my thoughts, which causes me to jump.

I look up at him and his pretty blue eyes that are analysing me. "In my head again," I say breathlessly. "Those lessons aren't working."

If I'm being honest, I haven't thought about my shields because of how secure I am in his arms. Protecting your mind is a lot harder than I thought, but Jaxon reminds me it'll get easier—soon, it'll be something my body does by default. But right now, I don't mind if he hears them.

"You were projecting hard." His hand cups my cheek. "You might want what they have, but trust me, ours will be in a league of its own."

I forget to breathe for a second as I take in his words. I expect to be overwhelmed, but I'm not. Instead, I'm flooded with reassurance, reminding me I'm in safe hands and not just the physical kind.

My head snuggles into his chest once more, and he

holds me tight. Both of us understand we don't want to let each other go. I can't quite grasp how we got to this point in our...relationship? But I can't fight what feels right, even if I'm still finding my feet.

I know nothing between us is rushed like Jaxon said before—the ball is always in my court. There is no pressure, and that definitely helps me sleep at night.

When the song is over, everyone cheers for the bride and groom, and they share a kiss for the whole room to see. Then, Lucy starts running towards the DJ and grabs a microphone. "Hello, everyone!" she yells with the biggest grin I've ever seen. "Thank you so much for coming to celebrate with us. I want to say how grateful we are for each and everyone of you allowing us to share this perfect day with you."

A few people raise their glasses, and others cheer. "The night is still young, and we will make the most of the last few hours we have left! But if you're already wondering when the next wedding is going to be, don't worry because my brother, Jaxon, and his beautiful mate, Ava, will most definitely be the next to tie the knot."

I gawk at her words. Marriage? That is the last thing on my mind.

Jaxon must sense how tense I've become as he dips his head down to the shell of my ear, squeezing my hand in support. "Chill, baby. We are taking it one day at a time. Alright? Our pace. No one else's. Lucy is getting ahead of herself."

I look up at him sheepishly as my body trembles. He reaches to tuck a piece of hair behind my ear. "Okay," I whisper.

Music starts booming over the speakers again, and

people rush to the dance floor with their drinks. Lucy worms her way through the sea of people to get to us, that pristine smile still in place and a champagne flute in hand. "Ava, come dance with me!"

"Uhh–" I turn to Jaxon.

He gives me an encouraging smile. "Go. Have fun. I'll find you later."

I merely nod before Lucy drags me away to the front, where her bridesmaids are dancing. "Congratulations! I feel like I haven't seen you all day."

"That's because you haven't! I wanted to spend some time with you." She grabs my hand and starts moving her hips to the music.

I stare at her for a long moment because I've forgotten how to dance—especially without a drop of alcohol. But then I remind myself I am free. Free to do whatever I want, feel whatever I want, and be whatever I want.

So my body starts moving automatically like muscle memory. I close my eyes and move my hips to the song. Even the smallest things, like dancing to cheesy music, make me feel alive—something I have missed deeply.

When I open my eyes, Jax's gaze bores into mine from the other side of the dance floor. I glance away before I become embarrassed. Why should I? Movement of the body feels incredible, liberating, and *empowering*. I might not have many skills in the dancing department, but it's what it makes you feel inside that matters.

Jaxon's stare is like laser beams, and my body lights up at his attention. I glance down and turn my back to him.

Quit looking at me; you're putting me off, I say through our mindlink.

His laugh vibrates through my head like a deep harmony. *Oh, baby. You've got moves.*

How can he make me blush from across the room? I try my absolute hardest not to let a smile creep up on my face. My curiosity gets the better of me, and I finally turn around to face where he's standing. Those eyes are on me in an instant.

Stop.

Another smooth laugh, something I always find so incredibly comforting.

You're still looking at me, I add.

I'm sorry. My eyes just naturally gravitate to you. He wears a proud smirk.

My entire face burns up. I turn my attention back to the girls, and a song I remember from years ago starts playing—though I don't exactly know the words. Lucy holds my hand as she sings to me and then throws me into a hug by surprise. "Oh, Ava. I'm so glad you're here. I'm so glad you're in our lives," she murmurs before pulling back and gently gripping onto my forearms. "I'm so glad that one day you're going to be my sister-in-law!"

A hesitant laugh escapes my chest. "Yeah," I rasp. "That caught me off-guard a little."

Lucy's face falls with sudden realisation. "Oh, my Goddess. I am so sorry. I didn't mean to make you uncomfortable! I love seeing you guys together. Honestly, you're so perfect. I don't think you realise."

"It's okay," I say with a smile. "I just wasn't expecting it."

"Weddings get me so excited. I love love!" she yells.

My lips spread with enthusiasm. "I'm so glad I met you, too, Lucy." I'm engulfed in another hug before I pull myself away, in desperate need of five minutes to myself. "I'm gonna go grab some water."

She nods before turning towards Phia and Grace. I push my way out of the crowd and approach the bar, and then lean my elbows on the counter and wait patiently to be served.

"Hey, Ava." A soft voice appears beside me.

My head tilts towards Kayden as he approaches the bar. My heart skips a beat as I rest my eyes on his face. I thought my mouth tasted like stinging nettles before; they taste like paper cuts now.

"Kayden," I murmur. "Hi."

I ball my hands into fists to stop them from shaking and force a smile. I don't want to seem rude, but it's obvious that my body language is off.

"I was wondering if we could have a chat?" His voice seems hopeful and harmless.

I swallow back the lump in my throat. "Sure."

"Great." He nods. "What do you want to drink?"

"Um, just water. Please." I say as I play with my fingers. Kayden notices, and I freeze.

Once I have my water and Kayden takes a drink of his own, we make our way to an empty table at the back of the room. I sit down silently and watch Kayden as he perches on the chair beside me.

"I wanted to speak with you properly," he begins. "I feel like we've had some bad encounters, and I would never ask why you act this way around me. I couldn't even try to imagine what you have been through. But I want you to feel comfortable around me, and I don't want to see you almost pass out again. That scared the shit out of me."

My lips press together. "I wanted to let you know that I'm glad you are in a safer place now." His gentle brown eyes are giving me nothing but empathy. "Nothing will happen whilst you're with Jaxon and the pack. We look after our own, and you're one of us. If there is anything I can do to help, please let me know. If you want me to leave you alone for the foreseeable, I will."

I take a moment to gather my thoughts. "I know, Kayden. I trust you're a good person. It's...it's just hard to convince my defence mechanisms that. When I see you, I see him, the only other Beta I've known. Everything comes back to me, and I can't help it. It's hard to block it out, but I've been trying. I've been speaking to Gemma about dissociating things. It's worked with Jaxon so far. I mean, I've managed to have this conversation with you without completely freaking out, so it's going well."

A look of appreciation covers his face. "You are one strong girl, Ava. I think that's something you haven't heard a lot of."

My lips part to reply, but Jaxon's appearance makes the hairs on my arm stand. "What's going on?" His deep voice is full of worry.

I turn in my chair to see his tall frame. His forehead pinches, and his concerned gaze flicks between us before eventually settling on my face.

"We're just talking," Kayden admits.

Jaxon's brow arches. "About what?"

"About being more comfortable in Kayden's presence," I admit. "Trying not to associate him with my past."

Are you okay? Do you need to go outside? We can leave now. Jax's voice is in my head in an instant.

I'm okay, honestly. I know I'm safe with him. He wouldn't be your Beta if you didn't trust him.

We hold each other's gaze for another moment. "O-kay," Kayden says as he slaps his knee and stands. "Whilst you two mindlink about me, I'm going to find my mate."

"You have a mate?" I ask in surprise.

"No," he deadpans. "But maybe by some form of magic, she might be here. I'm sick of seeing everyone all lovey-dovey together. It's sickening."

This earns a laugh from Jaxon. "All in good time, my friend."

Kayden rolls his eyes. "Or no time. I'm going to die alone. Fact." His gaze moves between us rapidly. "You heard it here first."

Jaxon ruffles his head teasingly, and it's the first time I've seen their friendship up close. Before, I believed their relationship to be strictly professional, given they run the pack. "Get off me," Kayden swats him away with a muscly arm.

"If it doesn't work out, I suppose you could always go for a human," he suggests.

Kayden sharply breathes through his nose. "Ava doesn't count. She's actually your mate."

"Just an option, bud." Jaxon shrugs.

A groan floats from Kayden's mouth before he fixes his eyes on mine. "Have any cute friends from home, Ava? I'm getting desperate. Actually don't answer that. I might be desperate, but I'm not *that* desperate."

"Goddess, am I getting the impression that you could be a romantic at heart?"

Kayden scoffs. "I am not discussing this with you."

"Holy shit, you are."

My lips curl into a smile at their exchange.

"Whatever," Kayden deadpans.

"Don't lose faith," Jaxon says again. "Like I said, I'm sure she'll come when you least expect it."

Then he winks in my direction, and my cheeks flush.

If I could remember my friends, that would be a good start, but I can't.

Jaxon takes my hand as he sits opposite me. "Everything okay?"

"Yeah." I flash him a small smile. "Just needed five minutes."

"Want to get some fresh air again?"

I nod. "Sure."

28

AVA

As I lay in my bed, looking up at the white ceiling, I can't stop thinking about what happened tonight. I raise my fingers to my lips and brush the delicate skin. Jax kissed me. *I* kissed him back.

I thought I'd be reeling in shame and discomfort, but if anything, I'm proud of my self-confidence. For claiming my right to my body and what I want.

And boy...did it make me feel things.

A childish squeal rushes through my throat, and a giant smile creeps up on my face. I'm giddy. My head is spinning with a thousand different positive emotions. God, I can't stop thinking about him.

I close my eyes again for the hundredth time and pray I fall asleep. But deep down in my bones, I know I'm far too ecstatic to even think about it. I'm on cloud nine. Tonight was perfect in so many different ways, and I'm growing in my own skin.

I might not ever be the woman I was before, but I like who I'm turning into. It's refreshing and relieving, all wrapped into one.

My stomach growls from hunger and pure excitement. *Ugh.* I toss and turn, and nothing seems to help me drift off. I release an annoyed sigh and slap my arms down on the bed.

What's wrong? Jax's sleepy voice echoes through my mind.

Nothing, sorry. I frown. *Did I wake you?*

My fingers rub against my eyes gently. They're heavy, but my mind is working a thousand miles a second.

You feel distressed. What's the matter?

Another sigh escapes my lips. *I can't sleep, that's all. It's okay. Go back to sleep. I don't want to disturb you.*

Why can't you sleep?

Do I tell him I've been internally screaming over our kiss? Hell no. I've been trying my absolute hardest to block out my thoughts so he can't hear them. From the two lessons he's given me, I'm trying my hardest, but I'm yet to perfect it.

I'm a little hungry.

Meet me downstairs in the kitchen. I'll make you something.

I don't fight it. My heart pounds with the desire to see him. *Okay.*

My fingers grab the sheets to throw them off my body before I creep out of bed and analyse my appearance in the mirror. My hair is a complete mess. I quickly try to flatten it, but it's a frizzball from dancing all night.

I focus on my eyes and swallow a breath. Why am I getting so worked up about seeing him? It was only a couple of hours ago that we arrived home.

I silently creep out of my room and make my way downstairs to Jaxon's private kitchen. I step inside, and he's already here—except he's shirtless. I pause in the doorway to admire his sculpted shoulders and toned torso.

An unexpected shudder runs through me at the sight of

his tan skin and muscles packed over muscles. Werewolves are always in the best shape of their life, but Jaxon is in another realm.

He doesn't look at me, but the corner of his lip quirks. I've been caught red-handed. Of course, his crazy senses would pick up that I was here. I slowly walk over to him as he finally turns to me. "What do you want to eat?" he asks, his voice a little groggy.

I ponder and watch as his eyes wander down my bare legs. My face heats within seconds. "Something with cheese," I say as confidently as possible.

His brow arches. "What about some grilled cheese?"

"Sounds good."

After a moment, he turns around to prepare our midnight snack. I jump up onto the counter so I can observe silently. He slices the cheese against the cutting board, those impressive back muscles contracting with every movement. I gulp at the action. He looks so damn good doing something so simple.

The Greek Gods would be jealous.

My fingers twitch at the thought of running my hand across the skin on his back, how smooth it would feel beneath my palms—

I shake my head. I need to *stop*.

Jax slides our food underneath the grill and turns around to face me. "You know I can still hear your thoughts?" he says playfully.

"Goddamnnit." All colour drains from my face, which is then replaced with a deep blush. "Those lessons were useless."

"Not useless." He flashes me a smug grin. "Although I really don't want your thoughts to disappear. I find them rather entertaining."

I glance down to hide my embarrassment, but Jaxon steps in front of me. He places two fingers beneath my chin and tilts my gaze to his. He gently nudges his way between my bare thighs. Oh, gosh. I'm the temperature of the sun.

"You can stare as much as you want," he says huskily, lowering his head so our lips almost brush. "I'm all yours, Ava."

My lungs decide this is the perfect moment to forget how to take down air. I hesitantly look into his eyes, which are watching me with admiration. Jeez. There is no oxygen left in this room—I'm sure of it.

He glances down to my lips and smiles. "Can I kiss you again? I've been thinking about you non-stop."

I manage a slight nod, words failing me. His hand clasps the side of my cheek gently and presses his lips to mine. This time, it's different. Slower and patient as if we have all the time in the world. And we do. We're alone with no one to interrupt us.

The kiss doesn't turn heated. It's a caress of a touch that makes my heart sing. I clutch onto his wrist, drawing him closer. Our chests press together, his bare skin making my body sizzle beneath the surface.

When he widens his mouth just a little, the alarm on the grill starts to beep. We both pull away at the same time. His forehead drops to mine for a couple of seconds, and I shield my eyes from him.

The moment I open them again, he leaves a simple peck on my lips before making his way over to the grill. I press a hand to my head, knowing my mind is swirling from all the new chemicals.

He plates up our food and slides it onto the counter. "Thank you," I say politely, as I stare down at the sizzling cheese coating the golden bread. We sit and eat in silence despite feeling his eyes on me the entire time.

I eat slowly, my appetite now subsided. If anything, I'm trying to calm my breathing so Jaxon can't hear it, but with his wolf senses, there is no doubt he can hear *everything*.

When I'm finished, he takes my plate from me, and I jump down from the counter. "Come on." He takes my hand and presses a kiss on my forehead. "Let's get you back to bed."

Once he leads me out of the kitchen and up the stairs, we pause outside my bedroom, and I hesitate for a moment. A new wave of self-assurance washes over me.

"Goodnight, baby," he whispers. "Sleep well."

My fingers raise to his mouth, and he leaves a peck on my knuckles. I stare at the action, and my heart flutters like a butterfly. He drops my hand and turns to walk down the hall towards his own bedroom.

I stand there fumbling with my fingers, the words on my tongue. After everything I experienced today, the last thing I want to be is alone. It's a part of the reason why I think I couldn't sleep.

"Jax," I call.

He stops and turns around. "What's the matter?"

"Can I–" I swallow the lump in my throat.

I hear footsteps until he's directly in front of me again. "Tell me, Ava."

"The bed you sleep in," I roll back my shoulders, "is it one you shared with Julia?"

Jaxon blinks at my question, and suddenly, I want the ground to swallow me whole. "No." He shakes his head. "I had it replaced around six months ago. I had to do it for my own sanity."

"Oh."

Why does that flood me with relief?

"What did you want to ask, Ava?"

I flick my eyes between his and decide to grab this moment with both hands. "Can I sleep in your bed tonight?" I ask quickly. "As a one-off only."

Jaxon's smile is instant. "You can sleep in my bed whenever you want."

"W-with you?"

His soft laughter wraps around my sternum. "Yes, with me."

He takes my hand and leads me down the hall to his bedroom. For a moment, I become apprehensive of my decision. He squeezes my hand, and I know he feels my nerves. "If you want to go back to your room," he says before pushing his door open. "You can. I'm not going to hold you hostage in my bed. Although, it's very comfortable."

I merely nod as we enter his bedroom. It's huge with black and grey interior. and very well organised. The best part is that it smells like him, the scent so strong it almost knocks me off my feet. It's deep and musky and earthy.

When I inhale, I close my eyes, the feeling of safety clinging to my chest. Jaxon tugs on my fingers, and I walk towards his large bed. He pulls back the covers for me, and I slip beneath the silky sheets.

A sigh escapes my lips when he joins me from the other side. I rest my head on his pillow and stare back at him—he does the exact same. I chew on my lip gently before I reach out my hand and brush my fingertips across his bare chest. Oh, he's so warm and velvety.

Jax's eyes close in satisfaction when I touch him, his arm slipping around my waist to pull me closer. I lean my face into his neck and smile against his skin. My lips graze his collarbone, and I allow myself to be in this moment.

There's not an ounce of fear in my head or in my body. I am truly at peace.

I'm safe in his arms, yet he's practically a killing machine.

"Can I ask you a question?" I whisper into the darkness.

Jaxon hums softly. "Anything."

"Have you killed people?"

"Wolves," he states. "I've killed wolves before."

I shift my head as he drags his hand across my shoulder blades. "Who deserved it?"

"I've killed wolves that have become a threat to my family and pack. I will never hesitate to kill someone if they're going to try and take anyone special away from me. I'd never kill innocent people. I'm not a monster. I care about everyone here, and I'd do anything for them—like an Alpha should," he says firmly.

"Are packs under threat a lot?"

He clears his throat gently. "It depends. But yes. You never know what's going to happen in our world. Some wolves are power hungry, others are seeking revenge, and others are determined to make people's lives miserable."

"Would I be in danger?"

Jaxon holds me tighter. "No. I'll protect you with my life. But please, never leave the house alone. Even on our territory, you never know who might be out there, and I'm not running the risk of you getting hurt. If you want to leave the house, tell someone first, then a guard or I will escort you safely."

"I want to train," I blurt. "I know I'm not like you, but I'd like to get stronger. I'd like to learn some self defence, some fighting skills. I want to trust my body and my mind."

He nuzzles his head against mine. "Then we'll train together." He pecks my clothed shoulder. "If that's what you want, we can do it. I've told you before, just because you're not a wolf doesn't mean you're not one of us."

"Maybe training will make me feel like one of you."

"Then I'll get you to whatever level you want. I have a lot of faith in you and what you can achieve. Will that make you happy?"

I nod before he even finishes the question. "Yes. Very. I want to surprise myself. I want to prove to myself that I'm strong. That I'm able. I'm tired of being the damsel in distress. I want to save myself, and this feels like a step forward."

Jaxon exhales a sound from the back of his throat. "I want that for you, too, baby. We'll do whatever you want."

"Did you have a good time today?" I ask.

"I had the best day *ever*." A full grin stretches across his face. "And that's all because of you."

I melt into his words, our bodies moulding into one. My head rests against his chest, and I close my eyes. I'm at home in his arms, and I never thought I'd be able to experience this level of security—not with my past. I thought I would be broken to accept care. But I'm not broken; I'm healing.

That is true power.

"Goodnight, Jax."

"Goodnight, my love."

Love. My entire body tingles like fireworks exploding in my skin. I release a silent breath, knowing I am going to have the best night's sleep ever.

"Oh." Jax leans down to my ear. "And for the record, I am one hundred percent going to make you my wife."

The bond between us heats up so intensely that I'm burning from the inside out. Tears well in my eyes, and I can't remove my smile, no matter how hard I try. The idea of marriage is terrifying because I am so young, but his words don't feel like a prison sentence; they feel like a lifetime of happiness.

29

AVA

It's been a few days since Lucy and Sebastian's wedding. Whilst they are off enjoying their honeymoon, Jaxon is whipping the pack back into shape. A few days off doesn't mean they slack for a second—only now have I realised how determined he is as an Alpha. Always striving for the best.

I've been building up the courage to join in with group training, and I told Jaxon I wanted a few sessions with him alone first. I asked him to take it easy because my stamina and strength will be at the other end of the spectrum.

On Monday, we start with core training with balancing and slow movements. On Tuesday, I attempt a stamina session in which I end up on the floor in a heap of dirt from how weak my legs are. On Wednesday, we start with self-defence and practising getting out of certain grips and positions—always finding a way, even if it seems impossible.

Having the Alpha to myself whilst Kayden takes on the rest of the pack has my cheeks heating. I have to admit I love it, selfishly. He's their leader, and I'll have to share him eventually, as I'm not the only one who needs him.

By Friday, Jaxon persuades me to join in with group training. I know most of their sessions involve being in their shifted form, but today, he's going to cater it towards me—even though I told him I want to be as invisible as possible.

He rounds us up in the clearing outside the house. "Alright." His loud voice booms across the trees, making the leaves quake. "Everyone, listen up. We're going to train in our human forms today. It's wise to keep up our natural strength as well as our wolves. It's going to be a little different, but it's going to benefit us all."

I suck down a breath and clench my fists together. Jaxon's eyes meet mine, and he gives me a supportive nod. "I'm going to split you up. Half of you will follow me, the other half will follow Kayden. We're going to do a light trail run to get warmed up, and then we'll move on to the good stuff."

My eyes glance around the group and I'm relieved to find none of their attention is on me. Why would it be? They're here to train.

Jaxon splits us up, and thankfully, I'm in his group. They lead off down two different paths. He remains at the front to keep everyone running in the right direction. I stay at the back and try my hardest not to die.

You've got this, beautiful, Jaxon's voice echoes through my head.

My lungs hurt.

Warmth spreads through me as if he's attempting to take away some of my pain. I rub my chest as I run. The ache isn't as intense as it was a few seconds ago.

Take it easy. You don't have anything to prove. You're doing so well.

How did you do that?

Less talking, more running.

I roll my eyes. *Bossy.*

Once I make it to the end of the trail and we're back in the clearing, I press my hands to my knees and breathe as deeply as possible. Jaxon tried to mask some of the stabbing motions in my lungs, which I am eternally grateful for—I doubt I would have finished otherwise. I definitely need more training sessions to improve my stamina before I'm puking up my guts.

You okay? he asks.

I raise my thumb in a "good" gesture whilst I fight for my life.

"Okay, good warm up," Jaxon shouts, and everyone turns deathly silent. "We're going to do some light sparring to start, and later, we can get into some physical contact."

My eyes widen. *Physical contact?*

Don't worry. I won't let you do anything you're not ready for. Light sparring will be enough for today.

I gulp back my sudden wave of anxiety. *Okay. Sure.*

Have more faith in yourself. This is practice, remember? The pack aren't enemies; we all want each other to do better.

I let his words ease me. He's right. They train for a reason, not to hurt each other.

I listen as they're split into pairs whilst the rest of the pack facilitates the sparring. My eyes immediately float to Jaxon as he teams up with Kayden, both of them smirking at each other with their dominant personalities. I'm not entirely sure what sparring should look like, but once they start going for each other, I realise it's less serious than I imagined.

Their laughter filters through the air, along with playful insults as they throw punches and dance around each other.

It doesn't take long until both of them are dripping in sweat. There are a few close calls, but no blood to be seen.

Jaxon strips off his T-shirt, leaving his abs on full display. Kayden does the same, but I barely notice him. My eyes travel down Jaxon's long torso and rippling muscles. His sweat gleams off the sun, biceps bulging and his broad shoulders rolled back but ready for action.

His chest heaves as he catches his breath, droplets rolling down his tanned skin. His hair is tousled and messy. They're both covered in dirt as they continue to joke around light-heartedly. Goddamn. My body begins to tighten.

There is a sharpness in my crotch, and I shift to relieve the pressure building unexpectedly. The feeling is so alien that my forehead aches from how hard I'm forcing my brows together. I close my eyes to gather these erratic thoughts.

My mouth parts as I attempt to calm down. I can't believe this is happening to me right now of all places. I whimper when my thighs roll together, and I finally look back to Jaxon, who is wrestling with Kayden against the dirt.

A part of me wants to be disgusted for having such thoughts, but then I remember back to a session with Gemma when I asked about female pleasure. She reassured me that having any sexual thoughts shouldn't be seen as shameful—despite what I might have been told in the past.

Every woman has a right to pleasure, whether that be sexual or not.

I tell myself to ignore this sudden rush of fire. I can speak to Gemma once this training session is over—she will help me dive deeper into the cause.

A girl beside me begins to fan herself as she watches Jaxon and Kayden fight. I narrow my eyes as she bites down on her lip and releases a whimper. My face twitches at the sight of her gaze on Jaxon—she's no better than me, but it triggers a wildfire in my heart.

An unsettling feeling ripples through my stomach, and I hate that it tastes like jealousy. Her eyes flare with excitement every time Jaxon throws Kayden down onto his back. I tighten my fists at my sides and find my entire body vibrating.

Time is called for the first groups of sparrers, and Kayden calls out the next pairs. I stand back as they weave in and out of the clearing. "Ava," he shouts. "You're up."

My eyes widen, not expecting to be next. Jaxon appears at my side. "It'll be okay," he says, and I glance at his sweaty stomach. "It's sparring, not actual fighting."

"Right," I whisper with a nod.

"Hey, Alpha Jaxon," the girl calls over to him. "Nice fight."

Jaxon releases a long breath. "Thanks, Rachel."

Rachel. *Rachel?*

He turns his attention back to me and gives me a quick wink. "You got this."

Suddenly, a wave of anxiety rolls through me. I'm no Luna. I can't even believe I'm meant to be their future Luna. My mind instantly switches to the thought of Julia. I wonder what she was like beside Jaxon.

Did she train regularly with the pack?

Was she a strong Luna?

Are the pack going to compare us?

I'll never be able to live up to someone like her.

"Rachel," Kayden calls and beckons her over.

I glance across the clearing as she steps forward. My fists clench when I study her face. I'm boiling over the edge, and I can't seem to control it. It's like there's a ticking time bomb inside my head.

Rachel's black hair is scraped back into a high ponytail. She has the most haunting green eyes. They are so pale they almost look white. My lips curl into a forced smile, and she greets me with one, too—she seems kind, but I'm not feeling kind.

Jaxon's hand presses to the small of my back encouragingly. "Come on. You've got this," he whispers in my ear and then his attention is turned towards another pair. "*Hey!* None of that. If you want to fight, do it outside of my damn territory."

I watch him leave before I focus back on Rachel. "Light sparring," Kayden clarifies again before moving on to the next group.

We step towards each other, and I take up my fighting stance. I inhale some air and shake out my limbs.

She flashes me a genuine smile. "Come on. Show me what you've got."

The thought of Rachel dragging her hand down Jaxon's sweaty abs crosses my mind, and it makes me flinch. I grit my teeth and shake my head. No. No. I'm making up fake scenarios. Heat explodes in my sternum.

Breathe, Ava. *Breathe.*

I hear Rachel's whimper in my mind, but this time, she's on top of him, running her fingers through his hair with desire in her eyes. She dips her head lower and lower until I'm ready to explode.

A spark lights up inside me, and without grasping my complete self-control, I lunge forward and push her to the floor. Never in my life have I felt this level of rage and envy—it makes my skin itch. All the adrenaline in my body is about to burst from the top of my head. I didn't know I could possess this sort of strength.

Rachel squirms against me as she knees me in the ribs. I

gasp in a breath from being winded, but I twist and pull back my fist and punch her. Immediately, my hand begins to burn from the sensation of hitting someone. It's an alien feeling. I don't think I've ever been in a fight in my life. This doesn't feel natural.

It doesn't take her long to flip us over. She uses her impressive muscles to hit me twice as hard. Blood dribbles down my nose and over my lips, the coppery taste invading my tongue.

Then, everything starts to move in slow motion. I somehow reach up to grip her ponytail and throw her onto her back with all the blood and anger pumping through my veins. I grit my teeth. All I can hear is ringing.

Our hands fly in all sorts of directions, especially when she lands a punch to my already bruising ribs which causes me to groan.

"I said that is enough!" Jaxon's voice bellows across the clearing, and two people pull us apart before we end up killing each other.

Everything is on fire. Never have I felt this...territorial.

Over Jaxon.

My eyes find Rachel's as she scowls at me. I ball my fists together at my side.

"She fucking attacked me!" Rachel snarls, and I stupidly lunge forward, but I'm pulled back. "I didn't do anything."

"Hey," Jaxon's voice snaps. "I said enough."

I attempt to catch my breath and finally rip my gaze from Rachel. My body shakes away the person's grip, who turns out to be Kayden. I raise my hand to wipe my bloody nose. I wince at the way it twinges when I touch it.

"Inside. Now," Jaxon says as he steps to my side. "And Rachel. Go to my office, and don't move until I get there."

Rachel huffs and storms back to the pack house. I keep

my head low despite everyone's eyes on me. I move towards the back door once she's out of sight.

I know Jaxon is right behind me because the hairs on my neck are standing up. "What the hell was that all about?"

I brace my hands on the counter for a second before turning to look at him. His nostrils are flared, and his brows are dipped, but once his eyes roam my face, concern washes over his features. "Fuck, Ava." He steps towards me. "You're bleeding."

"It's just blood," I say dryly before rinsing my hands in the sink. "I've had much worse."

Jax's fingers are underneath my chin, forcing my eyes to his. "I don't care if it's just blood, Ava. You're hurt."

I roll my eyes. "It's fine."

"Don't ever roll your eyes at me." He pinches my chin, making me gasp quietly. "Not when it's about your wellbeing. Now, let me clean you up."

My mouth parts as I stare up at him. "Jax, honestly. It–"

"*Sit.*"

I don't object. I perch on the edge of the stool and watch him pull out antiseptic wipes and tissues. He peels the box open and starts cleaning the wound. "I think you're okay. No broken bones. The skin has just split. One of the pack doctors can heal you."

He throws the bloody supplies away, and I remain silent.

"So, are you going to tell me what happened?" he asks, leaning onto the kitchen island.

I peek my eyes up at him. "I-I don't know what came over me."

"So, you hit her first?"

My hands cover my face, and I wince. I'm still shaking from excess adrenaline, but I'm finally managing to take a few calm breaths. "I felt this way towards her."

"What did you feel?"

"She was looking at you, and I-I didn't like it."

Jaxon pulls back in confusion. "You attacked her because she was looking at me?"

"Oh my God." I laugh sadly to myself. "I sound insane."

"Ava, I know you're adjusting to new emotions, new surroundings, and our bond. But we don't do things like that here. Not to pack members." His voice isn't as gentle as I expected it to be. "We treat each other with respect."

I bite on my lip and nod. "I know. I'm not proud of it. In that moment, I was fuelled with these emotions I couldn't control. They literally took over. I know I attacked first, but trust me, she got in more punches than I did."

Jaxon analyses my expression for a long moment, and I feel all that jealousy flood out of me. Why am I even jealous? I know deep down that Jaxon wants me and no one else. He's made that very clear. His reassurance is one thing I don't need to ask for.

"I feel so bad," I confess. "I don't want everyone thinking I'm a bitch."

Jaxon runs his tongue across his bottom lip. "Look, none of us are perfect, and sometimes we let our emotions cloud our judgement of what's right and wrong. I trust you won't do anything like that again, and if you feel like that, then you take five minutes for yourself."

"All my emotions have been incredibly heightened lately."

"That's being around werewolves for you."

I want to laugh at my pathetic actions, but my ribs ache. I can't believe I did that. My fists throb, and I know I need to work on my technique. I definitely could have broken my wrists. I'm surprised they didn't snap in two.

As if on command, he reaches for my hand and raises

my bruised knuckles to his lips, leaving delicate kisses along my fragile skin. "You put up a good fight," he confesses.

My heart beats out of time at the intensity in his gaze. "I bet she hasn't got one scratch on her."

"Hey." He angles my face towards him. "She is a wolf who has been training for years; you've only just started your training journey. You can't compare the two of you. For how little we've trained together, that was incredibly impressive."

"I'm sorry," I murmur.

His thumb grazes my chin. "Why are you sorry?"

"I don't want to embarrass you."

"You could never embarrass me, baby. *Never.*"

Those sapphire eyes hold mine hostage for a few moments. My entire body seizes up, and I will never grasp how nervous he makes me. His smile grows, and he leans in to leave a delicate kiss on my lips.

"I should apologise to her, too," I confess. "Now that I can actually think with a clear mind, I feel so guilty."

Jaxon nods. "I think that's a good idea, baby. But first, please go and see the infirmary and ask the healers to help. I can't bear to look at the bruises forming on your face."

I chuckle gently. "Does it not make me look cool?"

Jaxon's jaw tightens. "No, it turns my stomach."

"I'm fine," I reassure him again for what feels like the hundredth time.

"You're not fine. Let me take you there," he says. "I won't rest until you're healed. And I'm not letting you fight me on this."

This time, I don't protest.

As I lay in bed thinking about today's events, my brain is more than scrambled. It's like I've latched onto a livewire, and I'm still feeling the aftereffects. I'm over what went down with Rachel. I've been thinking non-stop about my reaction to seeing Jaxon sweaty, shirtless, and fighting instead.

But that pressure inside my core continued through his care and attention towards me. The way he speaks to me, touches me, and reassures me. It's incredibly intense but in the best way.

Another image of his perfect body flashes in my mind. His muscles flexing, those big strong arms wrapping around me...wait, what?

My entire body erupts into endless flames. It's not just him. It's thinking about *us*. What is happening to my body right now? I've been turned on before, but I'm on literal fire.

I clamp down on my bottom lip and twist in the sheets. My hand slips over my stomach, under the fabric covering my skin, I slowly dip my fingers into my pyjama shorts and inside my underwear. I lightly brush the tips over my core, and I gasp at the connection.

I don't even remember the last time I touched myself and allowed myself to have this private and intimate moment alone. Wow. It was a long time ago.

I close my eyes as I gently rub my fingers across my sensitive clit. More images of Jaxon's half naked body show clearly in my head. The last thing I want to do is objectify him, but he's beautiful—in every sense of the word.

The way he makes me feel safe. The way he positions his hands with respect. The way he cares about my wellbeing more than his own.

It's not just his appearance. It's *everything* else.

My lips begin to tremble as I rub harder, arching my

back into the bed. I slap a hand over my mouth to stop the whimpers that fall from my deepest pleasures. But I don't stop because it feels blissful and freeing all at once.

This is my body, and I get to do whatever I want to it.

It doesn't belong to anyone else. It belongs to *me*.

30

AVA

Lucy and Sebastian have been home from their honeymoon for an entire day before Jaxon drags Sebastian away to train. I take a walk with Lucy through the town for a change of scenery. Every last detail of their honeymoon? I hear about it.

I swear this woman doesn't have a filter, but I appreciate her willingness to share. It makes me feel like I've been here all along. I smile listening to her; it's nice to hear happy stories and exciting memories being made.

"Anyway." She waves a hand in her face. "Enough about me. How was it whilst we were away?"

A soft hum vibrates off my lips. "Yeah. It's been good. Jaxon's back to training everyone until they bleed internally."

Lucy snorts. "Sounds like my brother."

We fall into a comfortable silence for the first time since we stepped out of the house, and I let my boots kick the leaves that have fallen on the path.

My head tilts towards Lucy, who is smiling up at the blue sky. I part my lips, the question on the tip of my tongue.

She's the only person I feel comfortable enough to have this discussion with—apart from Gemma, but I'd like to get a friend's opinion.

"Lucy," I say. "I wanted to ask you about something."

Her eyes light up. "Yeah, go ahead. What's up?"

A knot twists in my gut, but it's been playing on my mind for the last few days, and if I don't talk about it, I'll start overthinking. "I know this is a bit awkward because I'm mates with Jaxon. But recently, my body has been getting all hot and flustered, especially when I'm around him. I've never felt anything like it before, and I don't know if it's normal or if I need to get checked out at the infirmary. It's like I'm being sizzled from the inside out."

We pause at the entrance of a spacious field. Lucy shakes her head. "It is normal, Ava. It's called heat."

"What?"

"Heat," she states again, and I stare at her dumbfounded. "It's what we go through when we find our mate. It's the bond's way of getting us to mate quicker."

I frown at her words. "But I'm not a wolf."

"Maybe it's because Jaxon is an Alpha. It makes the bond stronger and the urge more prominent," she offers simply.

I'm quiet for a few moments, taking in her words. "And the mating process..."

"You know about it?"

"Briefly," I confess. "Jaxon has explained what it means and so has Gemma. I asked her to give me a breakdown of what's expected of the Luna, but she didn't mention the heat side of things."

Lucy nods, and we start walking again. "She might not have expected you to experience heat. I mean, I'm not entirely sure what would happen if Jaxon marked you anyway. I don't know what a mark could do to a human. He would never want to hurt you."

My mouth turns bone-dry at this conversation. I already know I'm incredibly out of my depth. I take a sharp breath, and Lucy links her arms with mine as if registering my sudden distress.

"Don't overthink it now, Ava," she says softly. "You don't have to think of mating, marking, or any of the intimate stuff if you're not ready. Jaxon would certainly not pressure you, and everything else will make more sense as time goes on. What's most important is that you feel safe and comfortable. There is no rush, so don't pressure yourself."

I nod and swallow back the lump in my throat. "And the heat?"

"If it becomes unbearable, a pack doctor might be able to give you medicine to help calm you down. But it's nothing to be ashamed of. It intensifies emotions you already feel. It's similar to a period. Some women's sexual desire peaks when it's their time of the month. Heat is similar, and it doesn't last forever. It comes and goes, but medicines can help."

I knew I found Jaxon attractive before, that's a given. Now, when I see him—especially with his T-shirt off—my entire mind goes on a journey, one I thought I would be afraid of, but I'm slowly accepting that being turned on is okay. I'm still safe in my bubble, and that's what matters.

"Thanks, Luce," I tell her gratefully. "For being the kindest person."

She releases a laugh. "Sebastian wouldn't think so, not after the dramas I caused at the wedding. But I appreciate it, Ava. And I'm always here if you want to ask me anything. *Always.*"

TODAY IS JAXON'S BIRTHDAY. I slightly despise him for not telling me, making me find out through Lucy only a couple of days before. His reasoning being he didn't want me to feel stressed.

So we decided to throw him a party at the pack house. Considering I don't have a single penny in my pocket, this was the least I could do to let him know that I'm thinking of him. I'll have to make it up to him another time.

"Do you think this dress is too much?" I ask Lucy as I push down the red hem.

She stares at me in the reflection of the mirror with clenched brows. "No, you look incredible. It's a party, Ava. Everyone is going to be dressed up. Let's go. We're already late."

Crap. I gather my things, which include a lip gloss and a pair of heels.

"Jaxon is probably wondering where the hell you are," she says as she holds the door open for me. I follow her out into the hall, tucking my feet into the heels and stabilising my balance before heading downstairs.

The noise from the kitchen is loud, with a choir of chatting and booming music blaring throughout the room. Now I think about it, I can't imagine Jaxon enjoying a party. I suppose it's the thought that counts, right? Everyone agreed to help clean up early tomorrow morning before Jax sees the damage.

I reach the doors to the kitchen. People are flowing in and out of the room. I take a moment to pause and steady my breath.

Lucy stops beside me. "You good?"

My eyes float over the sea of people. A strain of anxiety

crawls up my throat at the sight. "Yeah." I nod. "Just a bit overwhelmed."

She takes my hand and gives me a supportive smile. "You've got this. Come on. Let's go."

"Okay." I nod as she tugs me towards the kitchen.

I immediately start panning around the room, my eyes settling on people I haven't met before. Lucy was in charge of the guest list. I merely helped with decorations and food orders.

My head stops turning when it lands on Jaxon. His back is towards me, but he's facing a woman who I've never seen before. Her hair is cut into a short bob, and she has gleaming eyes. She rests her hand on his forearm, but he pulls away as soon as she makes contact.

My stomach churns, and I don't know why. Lucy seems to sense the tension in my body. "Hey, it's nothing. They're just talking," she says softly.

Exactly, they're just talking. So why the hell do I feel like this?

I learnt my lesson before. I have to control my emotions.

The last thing we need is a catfight at a birthday party.

I turn and force a smile in her direction. "I know."

"Just go over. He's dying to see you, Ava. Knock him dead." She winks.

She gives my hand a squeeze before dropping it, and I straighten my spine for fake confidence. I make a beeline towards them.

Just put on a brave face, I tell myself.

"Hey," I call when I appear beside him.

Jaxon's eyes flick to mine, and he takes a moment to analyse my face before they move down my body. "Holy fuck," he whispers to himself.

My cheeks burn so painfully at those two words. His

eyes literally turn black as he looks over me again, in which he takes his sweet time, devouring me with his intense gaze.

"Ava, you look incredible."

He places a hand delicately on my warm cheek and brings our lips together in a featherlight kiss. Oh, goodness. This is *everything* I need right now. I'm flooded with reassurance.

We pull away, but he keeps us close as he beams at me. I smile back when a set of unwanted eyes lands on us. The girl he was talking to is watching us like a hawk.

I'm convinced she's trying to hide the daggers she's aiming at me, but her expression is all over the place. I move away from Jax and hold out my hand. "Hi, I'm Jax's mate, Ava. And you are?"

I didn't know something so sickly sweet could come out of my mouth. She glances down at my hand and shakes it sloppily. "Maddy."

"Nice to meet you," I say, twisting my head.

She drops my hand and flashes us both a tight smile. "Have a good night."

We watch her walk away, and I shoot imaginary lasers into the back of her head. Jaxon stares back at me with a knowing smirk. "Who are you, and what the hell have you done with my Ava?" he says teasingly.

"I just wanted to say hi." I let my lashes brush my cheekbone in an innocent gesture. "I thought it would go down better than what I made Rachel endure. I'd like to keep my eyeballs. Did you see the length of her fingernails?"

Jaxon barks out a laugh and cups my cheek again. "If I knew better, I'd think you were jealous."

"Not jealous, just staking my claim," I admit.

His eyes blow up in flames. "Goddess," he hisses and

dips his head to mine. "Is it bad that seeing you like this turns me on?"

My whole body betrays me by jolting at his words. The heat between my legs spreads, and I whimper silently. Goddamn this heat. I can barely survive this torture.

Instead of responding, I clear my throat and attempt a covering smile. "Happy birthday again. We promise to tidy up in the morning. It's going to be a mess."

He grunts and runs his lips over mine. "Couldn't give a shit about the mess when I've got the best birthday present ever."

∼

All night, I try my best to mingle at the party, but realistically, I just want to be by Jaxon's side. I remind myself it's his birthday and *everyone* here wants to speak to him. I have to learn to share.

"How's it going?" Lucy pops up beside me with Sebastian on her arm.

My lips curl at their presence. "Good. How about you guys?"

"Oh, you'll never guess who turned up," Lucy begins to ramble, but I zone out when my eyes rest on Jaxon across the kitchen. He's standing with Kayden and a few other wolves from the pack.

My eyes study him intently, occasionally humming towards Lucy so it sounds like I'm listening. His dress shirt is rolled up to his elbows, thick forearms on full display. My parted lips close in case I start drooling. He looks ridiculously good. More than good—*divine.*

I focus on his face and watch as he laughs towards the group, showing off his perfectly straight teeth. He reaches up to swipe his thumb across his bottom lip. Ugh. Why is he so attractive? I wonder if he knows what sort of power he possesses in a room like this. I shake my head. Of course, he does. He's an Alpha.

Stop eye-fucking me, baby. Jaxon's voice is loud and clear through the mindlink. He's laughing away with his pack—I didn't think he noticed me.

How does he know I'm checking him out?

Unless you want me to do something about it, then I suggest you stop.

I blush furiously and look down to my feet. *Sorry,* I say timidly.

My chest can barely keep up. I wait for my anxiety to hit me, but it doesn't. Instead, it does something weird to my insides. Lucy is somehow still talking. "S-sorry, Lucy," I murmur to her. "If you'll excuse me."

I quickly push my way out of the kitchen. Lucy calls after me, but I don't turn back. My skin is about to melt off the bone. I climb the stairs faster than I've ever moved before stepping into my bedroom and running to the ensuite.

I bend over the sink and splash my face with cold water, but it doesn't help. I'm burning up. *Sizzling.* I look at myself in the mirror. God, I am beyond flustered. I barely recognise myself with pink-tinted cheeks and dilated pupils.

I curl my fingers around the basin and grip, taking steady inhales until I calm down.

Or don't.

31

JAXON

Oh, shit.

I've really done it this time.

I watch as Ava darts out of the kitchen, and I mentally scold myself for being so crude. The way her shameless gaze lay on me, like I had no idea, but I did—I felt *everything*. It sent my wolf wild, and I let a stupid thought slip through the mindlink. I'd be an awful liar if I said I didn't mean a single word because I did. Goddess, the things I would do to her with her full consent. My wolf claws at me desperately.

I excuse myself from the group and follow Ava. Oh, Goddess. I've got a lot of making up to do. I told her I'd go at her pace, and now, I'm jumping the gun because of everything she makes me feel when she looks at me.

I follow her scent and find myself walking straight into her room. I notice the bathroom door is ajar. My knuckles raise to brush the wooden frame as I look at her through the tiny crack. Her hands wrapped around the edge of the sink. "I'm sorry, Ava," I blurt. "I should not have said that to you. It was wrong and completely out of line."

Ava jumps at my voice. She must be drowning in her

own head. She presses a hand flat to her chest. "Crap, you scared me."

After a few moments, she emerges from the bathroom and stands in front of me. I glimpse her face and acknowledge how small she is compared to me now her heels are off. I expect to see concern or sadness on her face, but I don't see any.

"It was extremely inappropriate, and I–"

"Jax, I don't care about what you said," she cuts me off.

My brows clench. "You don't care? Because you literally ran away."

She breathes out a string of air. "Okay, I did care," she agrees. "But not in the way you think. I wasn't offended by what you said."

"Then why did you run off?"

Her hands fumble as she looks up at me. "I-I just got a bit...hot."

"Hot?"

"Yeah." She rubs the back of her neck. "Apparently, I'm in heat."

I take a step towards her, and I'm immediately hit with the scent of her arousal. It almost blinds me and knocks me sidewards. Holy shit. She's turned on. I pause for a moment and think through my next words carefully.

"You know what heat is?" I ask.

"Lucy explained it to me."

"What I said made you feel hot?"

Ava nods with wide eyes and rosy cheeks. I shove my hands into my pockets before I reach out to touch her. "Yeah," she whispers. "My entire body."

"When did you start feeling like this?"

"Mainly the first day I joined pack training."

The night I heard her quiet whimpers of pleasure.

Fuck. Fuck. Fuck.

I lower my gaze and tighten my jaw.

"Ava, I heard you. I felt you."

"What?"

"That night. You were thinking of me, and–"

She gasps to herself, eyes widening in shock. "I-I blocked you out."

"Not well enough."

A hand claps over her mouth. "I completely objectified you. I'm sorry."

My lips release a soft laugh. "Baby, I am honoured."

I step forward to clasp her cheeks. I expect her eyes to dart around the room with hesitation, but she doesn't. In fact, she stares right back at me with every ounce of confidence. Instead of any negative emotions, I'm flooded with her heightened arousal instead.

Fuck.

My eyes flick between her frantically. I glance down at her lips and groan quietly at the soft gloss on them. I lower my head to kiss her because it's all I can think about.

Her small hand bunches into my shirt as I cradle the back of her head, caressing her lips with mine. I push her backwards until she hits the wall. I sigh into her mouth when she twists her head and attempts to widen the kiss.

Easy. I coax my voice through her mind, earning a whimper of pure bliss. *We don't have to rush. I'm right here.*

Ava slows down for all of three seconds before she devours my lips again. Her tongue slips into my mouth with eagerness. I smile into the kiss and hold her delicately between my hands.

After a moment, I pull away, and she leans forward, chasing the kiss. Her brown eyes are as dark as midnight, lips swollen and chest heaving—a sight that will put me into an early grave.

"What do you want, Ava?"

My fingers stretch through the back of her hair, tilting her head to continue meeting my gaze. "You. I want you."

I fight the urge to claim her now. But this isn't a race.

"You want me to do what?"

Ava's throat contracts as she swallows, releasing a shuddering breath. "I want you to touch me."

My eyes flare at her declaration, but I quickly mask it. "Where?"

"Jax," she whimpers in protest.

"Tell. Me. Where." I run the tip of my nose along her jaw in a gentle caress.

Her hand begins to trail down her body. "Here," she says as she rests her fingers between the satin material of her dress, over her crotch.

I hum in understanding, my eyes soaking up the beautiful sight of her.

"I'm not going to touch you," I rasp, and she frowns. "I want you to show me what you did the other day. I want to see what you like, what makes you comfortable, what turns you on. Will you show me, baby?"

"I–" she pauses.

My lips meet hers once more. "Only if you want to."

She blinks up at me with those big eyes and fanned lashes. "I want to. I want to show you."

"Then, get on the bed and show me."

Ava bites her lip before slipping by me and climbing onto her perfectly made bed. I tell myself to keep composed. This moment isn't about my desires; it's about Ava claiming hers.

I watch as she pushes her back into the headboard and spreads her legs. I grab the corner chair and perch it at the foot of the bed. When I take a seat, I lean back and enjoy whatever she's willing to share with me.

She hikes up the material of her dress and dips her hand between her thighs. I eagerly admire her fingers as they brush her nude underwear. At first, she rolls her index and middle finger over the hood of her clit through the fabric.

A soft noise escapes her parted lips. I flick my gaze to her face to find her eyes focused on mine. My wolf howls so deeply it almost tears me off this chair and into a frenzy of heated lust. But I keep my ass firmly planted and watch.

"How does that feel?" I ask, barely recognising my voice.

She hums with a nod. "Good."

Then she slips those fingers under her panties, rolling the tips in a circular motion over her clit. Her hips buckle at the new sensation, and she moans towards the ceiling, fighting to keep her eyes open, but the pleasure is taking over.

I lean forward, unable to sit back calmly. My eyes move from her reddening face to her rapidly moving chest and her nimble fingers making quick work on her wet pussy.

My hand runs over my jaw and mouth in pure agony at the devastating sight, especially when she cries out in the most beautiful harmony of comfort and pleasure. I grit my teeth at the way she moves faster until she releases a strangled cry.

"Jaxon, please," she begs. "I want you to touch me. I can't–" she cuts herself off with a long exhale. "This isn't enough. I need more. I need *you*."

My hardened eyes watch her as she slumps back, her hand now still. "I don't want this to be your heat talking. I want to know *you* want this and not because the heat is encouraging you to. I will never take advantage of you, Ava."

Those pretty lips tremble, and she shakes her head aggressively. "It's not the heat," she pleads. "Okay, maybe a part of it is. But I know this is what I want with you. I know how I felt about you before. You make me feel safe, wanted, and desired. Lucy said heat only intensifies what's already there. Oh, my God. Please, just touch me. Finish me off."

My fists ball together. "I don't want you to regret this."

"I won't. I'm ready. Let me be in charge of my pleasure. *Please.*"

"Ava–"

"I trust you. I want to try. Please."

"Fuck." I stand from the chair and crowd over the bed. I have self-control around Ava, but when she says things like that, I only want to please her. "Put your arms above your head."

She does as I ask within a split second. I grab the hem of her dress and whip it from her body in one swift movement. A flash of apprehension covers her eyes when I focus on her naked torso and strapless bra. I leave a kiss on her lips to remind her she's the most beautiful thing I've ever seen.

"If you want me to stop, you tell me right away," I murmur against her lips. "Do you understand me?"

Ava's heated eyes find mine, and she nods in agreement. "Yes."

I glance down at her half-naked body and internally groan. The scars on her body are beginning to fade. My wolf cries out at the reminder of others putting her through pain, but I know no one will ever hurt her again.

"Are you sure you want this?" I ask quietly.

She releases a jagged breath. "Just touch me, Jax."

I smile at her order and lower my face to her neck,

leaving a trail of kisses across her collarbones and down her chest. I can hear her heart pound outside her body, but the glow of the bond tells me she's excited.

Good. Let's keep it that way.

My mouth drags down to her stomach when I realise she's stopped breathing. I glance up at her. "Breathe, Ava," I whisper, and she instantly inhales.

I slide my hands down the curve of her ribs and over her hips until I'm pinning them down gently. I let my mouth tease her for a few more moments, basking in the soft whimpers that erupt into the room.

I nudge apart her thighs with my hand and drape my fingers around the outside of her underwear. She jolts at the sudden sensation. I pause and wait before carrying on. When she pushes her core into my hand, I know what to do.

My fingers gently press against her slit, feeling her wetness against her panties. Another moan. "Is this what you want?" I ask before pressing my lips to her stomach.

"Mhmm."

"Words, Ava. I need words."

"Yes."

I begin to rub her clit through her underwear. I take my time and do exactly what she showed me—not crossing any other boundaries. Her legs spread wider. "Shit," she murmurs.

My cock stirs in my pants. Turning her on is turning me on and absolutely killing me from the inside out. I build her up until she's quivering against the sheets and clawing at them for leverage.

I push her panties to the side and massage her clit without the added layer in the way. "Oh, my God!" she cries out at the top of her lungs. I smile at her reaction.

My lips press to the inside of her thigh. "Take it, Ava. It's all yours."

She chews on her lip so hard I think she's about to rip it off. "More," she begs. "More. *More.*"

I quirk a brow at her request. "More?"

"Please. *Please.*"

"You want me to put my fingers inside you, Ava?"

Her head peeks up from the bed. "Yes," she whispers. "Please."

I nod at her request and slip a finger inside her slowly. Her entire body arches as I ease it in, pulling out and going deeper each time. I kiss up her sternum. She throws her head back to the bed, and those lips part to release endless moans that will haunt my dreams—both awake and asleep.

My pace begins to pick up gradually, using my thumb to rub over her throbbing clit. She cries out, "Oh, Jax!"

Her entire body quivers beneath mine. I add another finger and curl them at the right angle. "Oh, my God," she heaves when I find her G-spot with the tips of my fingers. I keep moving at the same pace, making sure I don't overwhelm her. "Jax. I'm gonna come."

I place a delicate kiss on her collarbone, leaving my lips by her ear. "Then come for me, baby. Come for yourself. Give me all of your pleasure."

She shakes violently, riding out her orgasm on my hand. I focus on her face and the way she splutters all sorts of words mixed with whimpers and groans. My head spins from the sensuality of this experience.

When her chest starts to calm and she raises her limp arms to push her hair from her face, I gently remove my fingers from her. She shuts her legs with a tremble and peeks up at me with huge eyes.

I place my fingers inside my mouth and suck around the skin to taste her. My eyes never leave hers as I swirl my tongue around her wetness—Goddess, she tastes beautiful. A woman. A pure woman with a heart of gold. *My* woman.

Ava's cheeks bleed at my actions.

"You okay?" I ask.

"Yes," she says weakly. "I had no idea pleasure could feel like *that*."

"Best birthday ever," I exhale with a wink.

Sometime in the early hours, I'm called from my bed with Ava snuggled between my arms. I struggled to leave until my guards told me they had urgent news on Lucien.

I burst through my office to be met with Kayden and my head guard, Jon.

"What's going on?"

Kayden folds his arms over his chest and shakes his head. "Lucien and his wolves are getting closer to our territory. They were spotted going into town earlier, asking around."

"Asking about what?" My pulse thrashes in my throat.

Jon releases a harsh breath. "They've been asking about a girl. We don't know if it's Ava they're specifically referring to, but they're looking for someone."

"Fuck," I curse and shake my head. "Where are they now?"

"I suppose they didn't get the information they were after. They headed back to their pack house. Our guards are still keeping an eye on them there," he clarifies.

My blood begins to hum in my veins. I grit my teeth.

"Goddess," I mumble. "We're not waiting any longer. I'm not chancing them moving any closer. If they step foot on our territory, I will fucking lose it. I'm not risking it now. We move at sunrise."

Kayden nods in agreement. "With the original plan?"

"Got it set in stone."

32

AVA

Jaxon's birthday was a night to remember. I could see the reservation in his eyes when he woke me; he didn't want me to regret sharing that intimate moment with him. But there wasn't a single regret in my body.

Early this morning, Jaxon left with half of his wolves. He kissed me goodbye in his bed, and I could tell in his focused, bloodthirsty eyes where he was going. I didn't have to ask. Instead, he devoured my lips and promised he will never let anyone harm me again.

I shuddered at the intensity in his voice and the way he held my head like a precious gemstone. I asked when he would be back. We've never been apart for longer than a day. He responded with, "When the job is done."

Later that morning, I went down to the infirmary to ask for a medicine to help calm my heat, and eventually, my heightened emotions and desires began to align—but one thing was very clear...I still want him more than ever.

I had a session with Gemma, which allowed me to dive deeper into my emotions and generalised fears around sexual encounters. Although with Jaxon, it felt like I was experiencing it for the first time again.

What I'm doing doesn't make me feel like a whore or a slut. It makes me a woman who is powerful enough to admit she wants pleasure for herself. The thought of doing it again isn't something I dwell on. This is one tiny step. Right now, I'm holding onto what we shared together and using it at the forefront of my mind to push the bad memories away.

A part of me is relieved I have Gemma to help me through these new emotions because she reminds me that everything I feel is valid. And I realise all I've ever wanted to feel is true validation—especially from myself. I'm welcome to be my own person here, and I am forever grateful for every ounce of support.

After my session, I head downstairs to the kitchen, kneading my fingers into the muscles behind my neck. I wince at the tenderness of my flesh. I know I overdid training a few days ago, and I'm still paying for it.

When I step into the kitchen, the smell of bacon and eggs instantly swarms me. Lucy is facing the stove, humming to a song I don't recognise on the speaker. "Hey, Luce," I call out to her.

She whips her head over her shoulder. "Hey! Want some breakfast?"

"Sure, thank you. Do you want me to help?"

"It's almost done."

Once she starts plating up, I meet her at the counter and inhale the delicious smell. "Mm. Thanks, Luce. You're honestly the best."

"Bon appetit." She winks.

"The house is quiet," I comment.

Lucy glances at me. "Did Jaxon tell you where he was going?"

"Not entirely, but I got the jist."

She reaches over to grab my arm soothingly. "He's been planning this for a long time, Ava. Are you worried?"

I meet her gaze and nod. I didn't want to admit it to him because I know how powerful he is. But I also know what Lucien can be like. My stomach rolls at the thought.

"Don't be," she reassures me. "Jaxon knows what he's doing. He's had his eye on the pack for a while. He was just waiting for the perfect time to attack. He definitely wanted you to be more comfortable here first, too."

I hum softly and cover my mouth with a glass of orange juice. "I don't want anyone to get hurt because of me, especially Jaxon."

Lucy frowns. "You're going to be our future Luna. The pack will go above and beyond for you."

That word makes me flinch. I don't know if I'll ever react normally to that title.

"I'm sorry," she says, registering my sudden change. "I mean, we are a family, and you are a part of our family, too. I know this is probably a scary time, but they're doing this so those vile creatures can never hurt anyone again."

I nod at her words. That's one of the only reasons I'm not breaking down at the thought of Jaxon encountering Lucien or...Damon. My eyes close at all the different scenarios running through my head.

"Let's change the subject," Lucy declares. "How are things between you and Jaxon?"

"Yeah," I rasp, staring down at my half-eaten plate. I want to eat, but there is a ball lodged in my throat now. "Things are good. I'm feeling a lot more settled."

She smiles brightly at me. "I love that. I'm so happy for you."

I shove my fork around my plate. Luna. *Luna.* The word

keeps buzzing around my head like an annoying wasp. I want to slap my head to empty these thoughts.

How can I be their future Luna? I barely know anything about myself.

Julia must have been an incredible role model, and I'm... just me. My stomach tightens at the thought of being compared to her, but I try to push it away, even if I'm not fully convinced.

"Lucy..." I blurt. "Can I ask you a question about Julia?"

Lucy seems startled by my outburst but nods. "Sure. What do you want to know?"

"What was she like?" *Will I ever be as good as her?*

A small chuckle passes her lips. "Let's just say Julia and I didn't always see eye to eye."

I frown at her statement. "What do you mean?"

"I didn't really get along with her. I didn't agree with some of the choices she made. But, of course, I couldn't say anything." Her lips slowly swish to the side.

"What happened?"

Lucy sighs. "I don't wish to talk badly about the dead, but it doesn't change how I felt about her. She was always up her own ass, and sometimes, she treated Jaxon super unfairly. He didn't see it. He let her treat him like crap because the vision of being mates must have clouded her vile actions."

I glower at the thought of anyone treating Jaxon badly. He's an angel.

"What sorts of things would she do?"

"She would make him do everything for her. She'd make rude comments about him being Alpha. I've honestly seen manipulation at its finest with her. She loved to belittle him, but he passed it off as constructive criticism." Her eyes roll.

"It didn't make sense to me at all, but it wasn't my relationship. I let them get on with it."

I chew on the inside of my lip. "But why would she treat him like that? I don't understand."

"Me neither." She shrugs simply. "When I saw them, I thought to myself, that's not how you treat your soulmate. All her spiteful intentions were there, and he defended her every time. I will never understand."

My eyes blink in surprise. "I can't believe he would endure that."

"She helped him through the aftermath of becoming Alpha," she explains. "I think he held onto that."

I nod once. "What was he like when she—" I pause. "You know...died?"

Lucy flashes me a sad smile. "A mess. I was worried about him."

"I see."

My chest turns to cement. Why did I ask that question? Of course, he would be a mess. They were together for a long time, and he loved her. Losing someone special to you is something you'll never get over.

We both remain silent for a moment as Lucy takes our plates and places them in the sink. I bite my tongue because I'm full of a thousand questions, but I know I should be talking to Jaxon about this.

Yet, the thought of bringing Julia up makes my heart ache.

"Lucy." I twist in my seat. "Why do you think we were given second chances?"

She meets my gaze across the kitchen. "Because I think the Moon Goddess got it all severely messed up in the first place, and she had to put it right. When I see you together, the way he looks at you, the way you look at him. The development your relationship has taken. I just know you two are meant to be together."

A quick flash of the dream I had a month ago sparks in my mind. It might have been nothing, but it felt personal. *I'm on the right path.* I definitely feel like it, even if I can't explain it.

"You are everything Jaxon has ever wanted. You're down to earth and real. You make an effort with the pack. You are so different compared to Julia, and honestly, you are a breath of fresh air." Lucy gives me a supportive smile.

My heart thrashes against my ribcage.

"You two have been building genuine trust. You didn't submit to the mate bond right away. Instead, you let it guide you," she carries on.

"Yeah," I whisper. "It's been an emotional and taxing journey."

Lucy purses her lips to hum softly. "Yes, it might have been taxing, but everything you've done, you've done because you are a strong woman who deserves to be happy."

"I'm getting there," I admit.

Not everything is perfect inside my mind, but it's a work in progress, and I'm preparing myself for the hurdles along the way.

∼

LATER THAT NIGHT, I toss and turn in my bed. I shove my head into the pillow and close my eyes as tightly as possible, but nothing is allowing me to sleep. I release a frustrated groan and roll onto my back.

I stare at the ceiling for what seems like hours before I build up the courage to throw the covers off my body and walk down the hall towards Jaxon's bedroom. He's not here, so I shouldn't be apprehensive.

He said I'm welcome to sleep in his bed any time, and I know for a fact his smell will calm me enough to send me to sleep. I press my fingers down onto the handle and step inside. His deep scent immediately crashes over me like a wave, all earthy and natural.

I shut the door behind me and walk to his wardrobe. My fingers brush over the edges of his T-shirts. I don't hesitate before pulling one from the hanger and raising it to my nose to inhale. My eyes close with satisfaction. I take off my pyjamas and slip it over my body, and then I tuck myself between the sheets. They're cold, and I wish for nothing more than his body heat. It's been almost twenty-four hours, and the bond is beginning to tighten. At first, the sensation was dull, but now, I'm aching to be with him.

Hey, I say through our mindlink. *Are you there?*

For a few moments, my mind is silent. I rub my hand down my face and exhale a long breath.

Goddess, I've been dying to hear your voice, Ava. Is everything okay?

My skin rises in goosebumps at the way his words wrap around my heart.

Everything is fine. I wanted to hear your voice, too. Make sure you're in one piece.

He chuckles softly. *I'm safe. I'll be home soon, I promise.*

I shudder in the sheets. *Your bed is cold without you.*

You're sleeping in my bed?

Not sleeping. Lying wide awake. I needed the comfort.

Goddess, he groans. *You are killing me.*

Should I tell you I'm wearing your clothes, too?

A groan makes my core twitch. *I can't wait to hold you.*

Then, all of a sudden, warmth spreads around me, and

the sheets turn from cold to a luscious hug. I snuggle my head into the pillow with a heavy smile. *Are you doing that?*

Yes.

How?

Our bond. I'm using my energy to charge the sparks that connect us. It'll stay warm enough for you to fall asleep.

So you're actually heating me from the inside out?

Essentially, yes.

Thank you.

Does it feel better now?

So much, I admit.

Dream of me, baby. I'm always dreaming of you.

33

JAXON

I had already planned out what would happen when I came into contact with Lucien. I told myself I'd remain calm and do everything necessary to stick to the mission ahead. But now I'm staring at him from across the grand hall—chaos breaking out around us—and all I want to do is rip his throat out with my teeth.

Getting into their pack territory was too easy. They think they're bulletproof, but they're lazy idiots who didn't see this attack coming. Panic erupted, and I've never been so joyous to hear the sound of true fear.

Blood splatters across the granite floor, limbs and organs following in its wake. I trained my pack well. I trained my pack to kill. None of them will let me down. My only wish is to keep the Alpha and Beta alive for my personal entertainment.

Lucien's dark eyes are misty and full of hatred. I growl at his presence and remind myself if I kill him, it'll ruin our entire plan. But when I look at him, I think about all the tears Ava has shed, the times she's purposely hurt herself, all of the pain she's been through.

I launch into action, darting towards him in my shifted form. My legs move so quickly that he barely has time to jump out of the way. I clamp my sharp canines around his leg and drag him to the floor.

My jaw bites down, and blood seeps out of his wound and into my mouth. He screams in pain.

Good. I want to make him beg for his pathetic life.

A quick death is too kind for someone like him. He deserves hours and hours of torture until there is barely anything left of him. I bite harder, almost ripping his leg off.

Stop. Kayden's voice echoes through my mind. *Don't kill him. I know how badly you want to, but we've got bigger plans ahead. Remember them, Jaxon. Don't let your anger win right now.*

A snarl rips from my throat as I pull away, blood dribbling down the fur on my chin. I'm on the verge of letting my wolf go, but I keep control of his actions by masking them with my own emotions. He's bloodthirsty. He wants the fucker dead *now*. But I want revenge. I want true justice for Ava.

Lucien squirms against the floor, clutching his wounded leg. A puff of air rushes through my snout in his direction. *Wrap him up in silver,* I tell Kayden. *Get him out of my sight before I kill him.*

You got it, Alpha.

I turn around to find the majority of Lucien's wolves dead. Sebastian is downstairs in the basement, helping girls who have been chained up and used for Lucien's sick desires.

We've got the Beta out here, Kayden informs me.

Good. Don't let go of them for a single second.

Never. I'm looking forward to making them pay.

The room quietens down, and I hear the last breaths

some of these low lives will ever take. I prowl down the hall, checking to make sure they're all dead.

A noise behind me pricks my ears, and I whip my head to the sound. I focus my eyes on the royal blue curtain that is fluttering slightly. A soft whimper erupts into the room. I move forward until I rip the fabric away to find a young boy cowering in the corner, knees drawn up to his chest as he sobs.

His terrified blue eyes move towards mine. He flinches from my presence and pushes himself into the wall desperately. My gaze holds on his face—he's nothing but a kid. "Please," he trembles. "Please, just make it quick."

My wolf growls inside me, but I keep myself still. He doesn't look like the other men we slaughtered. He's a teenager.

"Jaxon," I hear Sebastian's voice behind me. "I've got a couple of girls outside. They're humans. We're going to take them to the nearest hospital."

I nod. *Good.*

Sebastian's eyes flick to the boy hiding away. "Another?"

I'm not sure. Ask him who he is.

"Who are you?" Sebastian demands, and he jumps at the echo of his voice.

"E-Evan. I'm Evan."

"They hurt you like the girls?"

Tears cloud his eyes. "Lucien is my brother," he whispers. "B-but I am not like him. I could never be like him."

I glance at Sebastian, who merely nods. *Let's take him with us.*

"Got it. Come on, Evan. Let's go."

His eyes flash with white fear. "Where are you taking me?"

"I'll answer your questions later."

I study them as Sebastian guides Evan out of the blood-splattered hall. I take a moment to glance around at the lifeless bodies. I wish I could have taken my time with each and every one of them, but at least I have the Alpha and Beta to myself. I can't wait for their torturous nightmare to begin.

~

It's into the early hours when we get home, and all I've been thinking about is how desperate I am to see Ava. To hold her in my arms and never leave her for another night. I had a mission to uphold, and as much as our bond was tugging due to our distance, I had to keep focused.

My hand gently presses against my bedroom door to find Ava asleep in my bed. A strange sensation washes over my chest, sharp but bright. I study her sleeping face and steady breath. I wish for nothing more than to crawl in beside her and wrap her up in my arms, but I'm a mess.

I stare down at the dirt and blood on my body, silently draw the door shut, and walk towards the guest shower. I scrub every inch of my body three times. I don't want any of their scents lingering on my skin. Ava shouldn't have to endure that possibility.

When I return to my bedroom after getting dressed, I peel back the duvet and wrap my arms around Ava from behind. She jolts when I touch her.

"It's okay," I whisper in her ear. "It's only me. I'm home, baby. I'm home."

She instantly rolls in my arms to look at me. Those pretty eyes are tired and begging for sleep, but it's replaced with relief when she sees my face.

"You're back," she murmurs.

I kiss her forehead with a nod. "Yeah, I'm home. Are you okay?"

"What happened?" she asks, avoiding my question.

"We can talk about it when the sun rises. Get some sleep."

Ava shakes her head. "I won't be able to—not now. Please, tell me what happened. Are they dead?"

I raise my hand to brush a lock of dark hair behind her ear. "All of the pack are dead," I state. "But I kept three of them alive, and I'm keeping them in a dungeon out in the warehouse on our territory."

Her face pales. "They're still alive?"

"They're being watched by multiple guards. They're not going anywhere. They won't be able to escape. They won't be able to harm you," I try to reassure her, but those brown eyes start glazing over.

"W-why would you bring them here?"

I cup her face gently. "Because I wanted to give you the opportunity to have closure, if you want to. And killing them quickly didn't seem fair to me. If you don't want to see them, I won't make you, but I will make them pay for all the pain they've caused you. I want to see them suffer."

"Oh, my God," she trembles.

I push myself up on an arm as she swipes her legs over the edge and paces. "They're here. They are *here*."

"Not in the house," I say. "I would never let them anywhere near you without your permission. If you don't want to see them, then that's okay. But I wanted to be transparent with you. I had to be honest and give you this chance before I took it away forever."

She cups her hands together and starts pulling at her fingernails. "I-I don't know if I can face them," she murmurs. "I don't think I can stomach it."

I scoot to the edge of the bed. "Then you don't have to."

Her breathing increases, and I stand. "No." She holds out a hand when I approach her. "Just give me some space for a second. Please."

"Okay," I say carefully. "I'm not going to touch you. I just don't want you to start panicking. I'm sorry if I overstepped a line."

Ava presses her face into her hands and releases a soft cry. "I've spent so long trying to keep my progress going," she whimpers. "I'm worried this is going to push me right back."

"No, it won't. It will remind you of how far you've come. That you are capable of doing anything you desire," I remind her. I wish she could see how strong she is. Not every day is going to be perfect, but she needs to see the strength she possesses. "You have the upper hand. You have all the power. It's in your hands."

She turns to me slowly, two tears rolling down her cheeks. "Then why do I feel so weak?"

"You're not weak. What I told you is a shock, and you don't know how to digest the information. We don't have to do anything right now, but whatever you want, it's yours to take," I whisper, my fingers itching to reach out and hold her.

"I need longer to think," she sniffles.

I nod. "Of course. There's no rush. I promise."

Ava wraps her arms around herself, and I frown. "Okay."

"Will you let me hold you now?"

Her glistening eyes meet mine. It takes a moment for her to speak, but when she says, "Yes," I gather her in my arms and wrap her up in the safety of our bond. I kiss the top of her head over and over until she settles into my embrace.

"I'll never let anything happen to you. *Never*."

SECOND CHANCE MATES

Two days later, Ava bursts into my office. "Sorry I didn't knock."

I shake my head. "You don't need to knock. What's the matter?" I ask, my eyes quickly assessing her to make sure she's not hurt.

"I want to go see them. I want to talk to them." She throws back her shoulders and straightens her spine.

I stand from my desk and walk across my office towards her. "Are you sure?"

"Yes," she whispers. "I had a session with Gemma today, and we made a pros and cons list. I realised what you said was right, if I get closure then it might allow me to fully move on. My trauma will never be forgotten, but I can try and close that chapter of my life and look to the future."

My lips curl at her bravery. "I'm so proud of you," I say sincerely. "But as soon as you want to leave, say the word, and we'll be out of there in a second."

She sucks down a breath and nods. "I haven't thought about what I should say. I don't really know how I'm going to feel when I see them."

"You don't have to plan anything." I take her hand, running my thumb across her knuckles soothingly. "If you want to say something, you'll know what to say at the time. Try not to dwell on it."

"Okay," she rasps.

I place my hands on her cheeks and bring her forehead to my lips. I leave a simple kiss that lasts for a couple of seconds. "Let me know when you're ready, and we'll do it. Together."

Her head tilts slowly, and I see a wave of concern past

her eyes. "Sooner rather than later. Otherwise, I'll end up overthinking it."

"Then, let's head out now." I entwine our fingers. "You've got this, baby. I'm going to be right by your side every step of the way."

34

AVA

Jaxon holds my hand the entire walk to the warehouse I didn't even know existed. Nausea creeps up my sternum, and I attempt to push it away without any luck. Oh, God. What am I doing?

His eyes focus on the side of my face, giving my fingers a light squeeze. "You don't have to do this," he says carefully. "We can turn back. It's okay to change your mind."

Once the guards come into view, I realise how protected the building is. It gives me a small sense of security. I pause before the door and inhale so deeply that I almost fall over. Jaxon stabilises me and kisses the back of my hand.

"If you want to leave at any point, we can," he reminds me, and I flash him a forced smile.

Inside, I'm a wreck. Blood roars in my ears, and my mouth is bone dry.

Every time I consider walking away, I remember what Gemma told me earlier about how closing this door with a firm slam could help my recovery. I know she will be there if it triggers me—Jaxon, too. I'm in safe hands. I have been since he brought me here; I just didn't want to believe it at the time.

"They're going to be behind bars and chained to the walls. They won't be able to get anywhere near you," he says, but I can barely focus on what he's saying.

Everything makes my head spin, and I'm pushing down the bile that crawls up my throat. "I want to get this over and done with."

"Okay, baby," he says.

I let him guide me into the warehouse and down to the basement. In each corner, there is a guard. Jaxon nods at them, and they greet him with his title. We stop behind a door, and he gives me one last glance. "You ready?"

"Yes."

He pushes the door open with a quick shove. I step inside after him and find myself facing large metal bars and the grimiest dungeon I've ever seen. The smell of sewage makes nausea curl inside me like a rotten egg. But the thought quickly passes when my eyes fall on Lucien.

I'm frozen in place for a few seconds until Jaxon squeezes my hand. *Breathe,* he reminds me. *Breathe, Ava.*

I do as he says because I am incapable of a single thought right now.

My eyes flick over Lucien as his legs are chained to the wall at his ankles, but there is a large flow of blood trickling down his thigh, a wound so big I can see his insides.

I finally focus on his face to find his dark eyes in tight slits, aimed straight at me. My knees wobble at the intensity of his stare, but he can't hurt me from here. He can't hurt me ever again.

My free hand balls into a fist to stop it from shaking. I don't want them to see my struggle. I am strong. I can do this.

After a few moments of composing myself, I finally look over at Damon and heave at the sight of his face. What makes it worse is that he has the audacity to smirk in my direction. My chest tightens, and I pray I don't start to panic —not here. Not in front of them.

Jaxon gives my hand another squeeze, and I love that he keeps reassuring me that he's here. I'm not alone. My lips part, and I release a shuddering breath as I focus on the third person in the cell.

I frown when I see a small boy bundled up in a ball in the corner with his head tucked into his knees. My heart cracks. Evan?

"You vile creatures are lucky to even still be alive right now," Jaxon says suddenly, which makes me jump out of my skin. He smooths over the skin on my hand with his thumb once more.

Damon smirks with his scarred lips. "Came for another visit, sweetheart?"

I hold my breath. Jaxon steps forward. "Keep talking, and we'll see how long I can keep you alive while I carve you apart."

My eyes hold onto Damon's stare, and I shake my head. *No.* No. He isn't going to taunt me. He isn't going to make jokes on his deathbed.

"Let me in there," I shout.

Jaxon's head whips to me quickly. "What?"

"Let me in there."

"What are you thinking, Ava?"

I chew on the inside of my lip hard enough to draw blood. "Ask the guards to hold them back. The pair of them. I know I'm safe. Aren't I?"

His eyes waver for a second. "Are you sure?"

"I'm positive," I say, even though my gut is flooded with tremors.

Jaxon curses softly before gesturing to the guards to open the bars and hold Damon and Lucien. I take two steps to the entrance before looking at the floor. It's now or never. This is the only chance I'll ever get.

I walk towards Damon first. The sight of his face makes me want to run. I refuse the horrific memories to haunt me. I only allow this new thought of knowing they're about to be killed in the most gruesome of ways. His lip continues to curl as he eyes me up and down.

I have the upper hand. I have the upper hand.

"You coming back for more, pretty girl?" he grunts with a wink. "You used to scream for me to stop–"

My knee raises and connects with his groin so hard I think it might split him in two. The loud groan of pain gives me a burst of satisfaction. Before his legs can buckle, I raise my knee and do it again, twice as hard. I use every ounce of frustration and hatred I have for this man who ruined my life.

He cries out, struggling against the two guards who refuse to let him go. "Fuck you, asshole," I snap. "You will never touch me again. Especially after I make Jaxon chop *everything* off."

My heart pounds in my chest like an alarm, but I hold onto the adrenaline that is coursing through my veins. I turn towards Lucien who is staring at me from under hooded eyes. I glance down at his wound and grit my teeth. He deserves worse than I'm planning.

I lean down and stick my fingers into his open wound, scissoring them as quickly as possible. His blood leaks down my hands as I push the wound wider. I've never heard a man scream the way he does. "You fucking bitch!"

"This is not even a fraction of the pain you made me feel," I spit through my teeth. "But I know your fate will be worse than mine. Jaxon will not take it easy on you. I hope he makes you suffer until you're pleading for him to finally kill you. It's what you deserve."

Lucien growls, "I should have killed you when I had the chance."

I dig my fingers deeper, and he cries out to the ceiling, gritting his teeth together to relieve some of the agony. "You should be very," I push harder until I hit bone, and he hisses, "*very* scared."

"Fuck you."

"It's not nice being helpless, is it?"

My eyes burn, but I will not shed a single tear for them. I stand, ripping my fingers from his wound. My entire body trembles as I balance back on my feet and walk out of the cell.

I don't meet Jaxon's eyes. I exit the dungeon and rush up the stairs until I can see sunlight. My eyes glance down to find my entire fist covered in his blood. Once I hit the fresh air, I take down a large gulp, shaking uncontrollably.

My throat tenses, and I buckle. I drop to the floor on my hands and knees. Bile shoots up from my stomach and lands on the forest floor. I groan at the acid that burns my insides and makes my body slump forward. Jaxon is behind me in an instant, tugging my hair into his hand and rubbing circles on my back.

It was only a matter of time before my stomach decided to empty itself, but I did it. I faced them, and now, I'll never have to see them ever again. I'll never have to worry about going back to that hellhole.

"I got you, baby," Jaxon whispers.

My abdominals clench, but nothing else comes up. I

groan and wipe my mouth with my clean hand. Then, I start sobbing. Fresh, hot tears fall down my face. Jaxon rolls me into his side and wraps me up in his large arms, cradling me close to his chest.

"It's over." He kisses my head. "You did it. They will be gone by tonight, okay? I am so proud of you. I know this is hard, but you did it because you are the bravest person I know. I am so grateful to call you my mate."

I sob harder at his words and latch onto him.

"I hate them. I hate them. I hate them," I chant breathlessly.

Lucien's blood is *everywhere*. The thought makes me gag, and I need to get it off now. I can't bear another second, knowing it's on me.

Jaxon takes off his jacket. "Here," he murmurs, noticing my distress. He begins wiping at the blood with the material, but my skin is stained. I watch him ruin his jacket for me, but I've never felt more relieved. "Is that better?"

"Yeah," I whisper.

We sit amongst the leaves for a while until I pull myself together. Jaxon studies me carefully. "Come with me."

He slides his hands under my arms and tugs me onto my wobbly legs. I wipe my face. "Where are we going?"

"Somewhere to release all this anger." He threads his fingers through mine, and we begin walking deeper into the woods. "It might help."

Once we reach a large boulder, he bends down. I stare at him with a raised brow. "What are we doing?"

"I'll boost you up."

I don't protest. He hooks his hands together, and I wedge my shoe into his palms before he hoists me up without a struggle. I claw my way to the top, and he joins me the next second.

"Now what?"

"Scream."

"What?"

"Scream," he states again. "Let it out. All of your negative emotions. To the top of your lungs."

I blink once. My eyes scan the trees and the deserted forest. No one is out here.

With one last determined nod, my lips part, and I scream so loud that my ears almost burst. I clench my fists at my sides and let everything out until I need to take a breath. My body is vibrating when I turn to Jaxon with a wide gaze.

"Feel good?"

"Yes," I admit with a pant. *Holy. That felt...incredible.*

"Again."

I scream and scream until the birds flap from the trees.

The next time I do it, Jaxon joins in with me, and our choir of chaotic voices fill the air. I imagine every breath is a wave of my anxiety I'm removing from my life.

I won't let them take control anymore. *I'm in control.*

My throat burns but in a satisfied way. I slump back, letting my shoulders droop. I never knew something so loud could help me in this moment.

"It makes me feel alive," I admit.

"I read up on scream therapy."

"I've never heard of it, but I approve."

Jaxon offers me a simple smile that calms the blood in my veins. But everything is far from normal. They're still here...and Evan. My heart twitches, and I close my eyes. He shouldn't be here. He's the only reason I'm alive. I owe him everything.

"You captured Evan," I murmur. "Please don't hurt him. He didn't do anything to me."

His expression hardens. "He's Lucien's brother, Ava."

"He's not like them. I promise you. He got me out. He probably got hurt because of me. He deserves better. He's only a kid. Please, Jaxon."

"I'll focus on him later," he dismisses my pleas. "He's not a priority. You are."

I swallow back the lump in my throat. "I'm okay."

His brows raise as if he knows better. "We both know this is going to take some time for you to adjust to, Ava. Please, let me focus on you for the next few days."

A sigh escapes my lips. There is no point arguing with him when he's like this. I've seen the protective side to him, and I know he will go to the ends of this earth to make sure I'm okay.

"Can you get him some food and water?" I ask. "He deserves that at least. He deserves more."

Jaxon stares at me for a long moment before nodding. "Okay. I'll make sure he's seen to once the others are gone and I have a chance to think about it."

"Thank you."

He jumps down from the boulder and holds out his arms. "Jump."

I do because I trust him. He catches me effortlessly in his muscly arms and carries me back to the pack house. I lay my head on his shoulder and inhale his scent. My eyes close when it hits my nervous system. The beat of my heart begins to slow, and despite being told I'm strong, I'm glad I have Jaxon to help me through it.

Soon, I'll believe it for myself.

I did what I thought was impossible today.

That is something I will be forever proud of.

35

JAXON

"They're ready for you, Alpha." Jon bows his head.

Kayden approaches my side as I breathe raggedly through my nose. "Thanks, Jon," he says. "You ready for this, Jaxon?"

I grit my teeth so hard I hear them grate. "Ready as I'll ever be."

"Then, let's make them suffer."

We head down to the dungeon in silence. I don't speak in an attempt to keep my head clear. I don't want this to be quick; I want this to last all night. It won't make up for the years of pain Ava had to endure, but I'm going to make it feel like an eternity.

Lucien and Damon are strung up by their wrists to the ceiling. The silver digs into their skin, leaving red marks across their hands. Both are naked. Both are unconscious. Both have no fucking idea what I'm going to do to them.

"What's the plan?" Kayden asks darkly.

I stroll forward through the cell door and push my sleeves up to my elbows. "This," I murmur before tightening my fist and punching Lucien in the face with racing adrenaline.

Blood splats the air, and within seconds, Lucien takes a choked breath. I hear his lungs start to work and his throat hiss when he tugs on the silver restraints. He glances up with his bloodshot eyes.

"Fucking bastard," he heaves, blood dribbling down his chin.

I don't waste my energy talking. I'll only wind myself up further. I stand back as he attempts to steady himself in his uncomfortable position. My head twists towards Damon, who is still asleep in his magic-induced state. I don't hesitate to meet him with the same fate.

The sound of bones crunching meets my ears, and I already know I've broken his jaw beneath my knuckles. Blood coats his face, and he releases a groan of pure agony. My nose twitches in disgust as his lifeless eyes find mine.

"Do your worst," he grits, blood smearing his deteriorating teeth.

I push my sleeves up further and compose myself. Kayden moves to my side, and I spare him a quick glance. "Hand me the knife."

The corner of Kayden's lip tips an inch. He steps back to the tray of objects, weapons, and tools. The sound of the sharp edge brushing the metal table rings in the cellar until he places it in my hand.

I take one step towards Damon, whose eyes flare at me with anger. I raise my knife in my right hand and bring it towards his face. He flinches, and I tut at his attempt to delay his doom. "Hold him still," I command Kayden.

My Beta uses his strength to stop his body from wriggling against the silver chains. The edge of the knife presses to his forehead as I begin to carve out a four-letter word.

Damon curses as blood drips over his eyebrows and into his eyes. I tell myself not to dig in too deep. If I kill him now, I'll never forgive myself.

I step back and smile wickedly at my handiwork. Kayden releases him and takes a look for himself. "Branded like the cunt he is," he laughs.

My attention turns towards Lucien, who is watching us intently. Kayden holds him back as I bring the knife to his forehead and begin spelling out my next word–*BITCH*. Each letter releases endorphins in my brain, but it doesn't make what they did any better. I can only make them suffer and bring Ava justice.

Lucien growls but grits his teeth when I finish. Kayden stands beside me once more and smirks at the word. "Yeah, our bitch," he snickers. "You belong to us, and you're going to beg for mercy."

"All this over a girl?" Damon bellows and tugs on his chains.

I shake my head and stroll towards him, letting the edge of the knife trail carelessly across his jaw. He freezes when he notices I barely have a grip on the handle, and a trickle of sweat rolls down his temple.

"A girl?" I repeat ominously. "Do you mean my Luna?"

Lucien glances at me, but I don't take my eyes off Damon. The knife nips at his skin, bringing beads of blood to the surface. "Women are nothing," he bites shakily. "Women make men weaker."

"No." I release a chuckle that's void of any humour. "In fact, they make us stronger. It's you that is pathetic and weak. To abuse women for your own sick, twisted fantasies —I think that proves a lot about your bruised masculinity."

Damon's eyes glow with rage, but when he jolts forward, the knife slices into his face. He howls in agony as he tugs back, a flap of skin now dangling over his stubbled jaw. "You motherfucker."

I fake a yawn. "I'm tired of hearing your bullshit."

Kayden moves past me, and I meet him at the metal table. I grab onto the mouth clamp and position it between Damon's lips. He attempts to struggle, but his strength has nothing on mine. Once his lips are spread, all his muffled words are inaudible.

I release a breath. "That's better. Be prepared for when I cut it out later."

Damon attempts to spit at me, and I shake my head in disgust.

Kayden grabs a set of pliers and craftily twirls them in his hands. "I think it's my turn."

I stand back and let him have his fun. Damon shakes his head in protest as Kayden latches the pliers onto his bottom teeth. His tongue attempts to push him off, but Kayden tuts and stares up at him. "You're only making this worse, *cunt*."

Kayden's forearm tenses, and he grabs Damon's face for leverage before pulling out one of his teeth. A deafening scream erupts into the cellar around us. "Oh, quit whining," Kayden grumbles with an eye-roll. "Fucking baby."

My eyes take in the sight of Damon's tooth falling to the floor beside his feet and more blood trailing off his chin onto his bare chest. "Ahh," Kayden grimaces as he inspects his mouth. "You really need to floss better. Your teeth are nasty."

He wastes no time in latching onto another tooth and ripping it from his gums. He screams louder than the first time.

As Kayden takes care of Damon, I walk towards Lucien with a screwdriver. He stalks my every move with his dark eyes as screams of desperation echo around us. I suck in a breath and study the word on his forehead, thinking how happy I am that his body will not be able to heal, thanks to the silver wrapping around his body.

My fist pulls back, and I slam it into his ribs. He attempts to fold himself in half, but he can't. A groan erupts instead, and he curses quietly. "The more I look at you," I say through clenched teeth. "The deadlier my imagination becomes."

Lucien takes a moment to recover before coughing. "I-I didn't feel anything for her."

"I know you didn't, you son of a bitch."

I stab the screwdriver through his shoulder without a second thought. "Ahhhh," he bellows as I rip it from his flesh. "Fuck you."

"Did you think you would get away with every vile action you committed?"

"Yes," he hisses. "That's why we did it."

My head shakes once. "Not anymore," I mumble before replicating the same puncture but through the opposite shoulder. "You'll never hurt her again. She was meant to be your mate. How could you treat someone like that?"

Something waivers in his expression, and I pull the screwdriver from his arm. His head throws back as blood trickles down his skin. "W-when I saw her," he groans. "I didn't feel anything."

"What the hell is that supposed to mean?"

Damon's screams heighten as I hear Kayden's morbid laugh.

Lucien's wrists tug against the chains. "The bond, it–"

"It what?"

"It was pathetic," he spits.

I suppress a growl and the desperation of my wolf to shred him to pieces. Instead, I lean up to grab his wrists and stab the head of the screwdriver against his index fingernail. It cracks and chips off within seconds. His finger is practically split in two, and he yells out curse words. The sight of his tendons pouring out of his ripped skin is something I'll never get out of my head.

Like Kayden, I don't wait. I hit the next nail and the next.

Lucien's head hunches over, and I step back when yellow, mushy liquid escapes his throat. My nose retracts quickly, and my stomach clenches at the foul stench.

"Goddess," I grumble. "You're fucking pathetic."

He continues to whine from his mutilated fingers.

"We haven't even got to the best bit yet," I say, using the screwdriver to tilt his chin. "Wait till I chop off your nonexistent cock and make you fucking eat it."

I throw the screwdriver to the floor and glance over at Damon, who is missing half his teeth and crying thick tears. Kayden hooks his pliers into the belt hole of his jeans. "You got a new idea?"

"A part of me wants to slit their Achilles heel and watch them attempt to crawl their way out of here. Now, that would be entertaining."

Kayden flashes me a crazed smile. "I think I've seen that in a movie before, sick bastard. Let's do it."

"You're enjoying this."

"A little too much," he agrees.

I walk across the cell and pull on a lever, which tightens the chains a couple of inches. Lucien groans at the new strain on his arms. Damon's moans aren't even human. Their feet barely graze the floor, and they begin to twist from side to side, all their weight hanging off their wrists.

Kayden steps forward, and I grab his shoulder to tug him back. "Leave them for now," I state. "We keep on like this, and they won't last the next hour. We leave them for a couple more minutes and resume."

"Alright," he sighs. "I think it's time to get more creative."

I nod once. "I'm open to all ideas."

My blood thrums in my veins like a shot of adrenaline. I flick my eyes between the two monsters and smirk at our devious work. It's only the beginning. I don't want a single regret from this situation, so I'm going to take it in my stride.

This is for Ava. This is for my future Luna.

36

AVA

"I'll go easy on you, I promise." Lucy flashes me a playful smile.

I groan. "Don't make me regret this."

"Where are you guys going?" Jaxon's voice interrupts us.

We both glance at him as he steps out of the kitchen door and onto the patio. "Lucy is taking me for a run," I say, lifting my hands to tighten my ponytail. "I needed time to stretch my legs and get out of the house for a bit. I still need to build up my stamina."

Jaxon's eyes sparkle at my new determination. "That's my girl."

My cheeks flush at those three simple words. "Be ready to pick me up from the floor when I get back because I might be unconscious."

"Have more faith in yourself." He walks towards me and slips an arm around my waist. "I do. I always have."

I flick my gaze between his dark blue eyes. There is a huge smile on his lips that encourages me to believe in myself—if he can, why can't I? Today is a chance to prove it's mind over matter, even if my lungs want to give out.

"Come on. Let's go." Lucy beckons her head towards the trees.

I step away from Jaxon's grip and give him a firm nod. He shoots me one right back. "See you later."

Lucy sets the pace, and I attempt to keep up despite being torn from the inside out. I breathe as deeply as possible, but I'm definitely not cut out to be a marathon runner.

"It's all about practice!" she shouts as we run—more like jog slowly—through the trees. "You won't improve if you don't practice."

And she's right. Practice is what makes us better, and I want that for myself. My mind. My health. My self-belief.

"I'm dying," I exhale through a jagged breath.

I keep up with Lucy's pace—*barely*. She could run round the perimeter of their territory twice before I even get to the next tree. When I feel like my lungs are about to burst, I halt in the dirt and press my palms to my knees.

We've been running for at least thirty minutes. That's a record in itself.

"Ava!"

"Go." I wave her off. "I'll catch up. Promise."

She hesitates before turning back. "I'll do a lap and meet you."

I don't think my legs are going to last another lap. My chest constricts and puffs out at a rate I've never seen it move before. I place my hands on my hips and glance around the forest.

In the distance, I spot the warehouse. Jaxon told me Lucien and Damon are dead. Jaxon and Kayden took turns tearing them apart little by little. I didn't want to know the gory details, but I knew it wasn't quick and it certainly wasn't pretty.

Curiosity peeks inside my brain, and I start walking in

the direction of the building. Jaxon hasn't mentioned Evan since I was last here, and I pray he's in better conditions—he should never have been dragged into this.

A guard stands in front of me as I approach. "Can I help you with something, Ava?"

"Is there someone still inside the cells?"

He stares at me for a long, hard moment. "The Alpha grants access to the cells."

I narrow my eyes. "I am the Alpha's mate, if you didn't already know. I want to go inside. Let me inside."

"Ava–"

"*Now*, please."

He hesitates for a moment before nodding. I follow him down to the dungeon, and I'm hit by that hideous smell. The first cell is empty, but when I step closer, I find Evan in the same position as before.

"Evan," I murmur and step towards the closed bars.

His legs are chained to the wall, and his body is covered in dirt, shivering from the coldness of this disgusting basement. I didn't think he heard me until his head slowly peeks up.

My lips part at the glumness of his face. His eyes are burning red and sore.

How could they leave him like this? I grit my teeth.

"Ava," he chokes out.

"Are you okay?"

He shakes his head, tears streaming down his pale face. I see the fear in his eyes. It's a similar representation of how I used to feel. Helpless—absolutely helpless.

I twist my head down the hall of the dungeon to find a bottle of water and a paper bag on the floor outside of his cell. I furrow my brows and lean over to look inside. *Food*. I glance at the guards. "You had food and you didn't give it to him?"

None of them speak. Fury burns inside me so bright it hurts.

"Don't," one of the guards barks. "He's dangerous."

A hand lays on my arms in a firm grip. I turn to him, my throat clenching. "I suggest you take your hand off me," I hiss through my teeth. "He's not dangerous. He's a child. Touch me again and the Alpha will be the first to know."

I've never seen someone retreat so quickly, but he scowls under his dark lashes. I couldn't give a crap what he thinks. This isn't any way to treat someone who hasn't done anything wrong.

"Here," I say, poking my hands into the cell doors and cracking the lid of the water. "You must be so thirsty."

He pushes himself up from the floor on wobbly legs. I break at the sight of him. Once he takes the bottle, he downs it so quickly that most of it splashes over his face. "T-thank you," he rasps.

"I'm sorry they kept you like this, Evan," I say as gently as possible. I reach for the bag of food and pass it to him. He sinks his teeth into a sandwich like he's never seen food before. "I told Jaxon to get you out."

He chews for a moment before swallowing. The darkness under his lashes make his bloodshot eyes stand out. "It's okay. I've been waiting for my execution."

"I'm not going to let them hurt you." I shake my head. "You should *not* be in here."

Evan shrugs and continues to eat the sandwich slowly. "I won't have anywhere else to go. It's probably best if they put me out of my misery."

"Don't say that," I whisper. "We'll work something out."

He scoffs. "The Alpha hates me."

"Well, we'll–"

"Ava!"

My name is shouted at the top of Jaxon's lungs as he rushes down the stairs to the dungeon. I glance over my shoulder when he bellows my name again. His footsteps echo through the emptiness of the space, and then he steps into view, his face struck with worry until he locates me.

"What are you doing down here by yourself?"

"What the hell is this, Jaxon?" I point towards Evan. "They didn't even give him water or food; they left it outside of his cell so he couldn't reach it."

His forehead creases. "You should not be here, Ava."

I pull back from him slightly. "You've left him down here for what reason? I told you not to hurt him. He doesn't deserve this. He let me go. If it weren't for him, I would be dead."

Jaxon flinches from my declaration. The word clearly triggers something in his brain. "You put yourself in danger."

"The guards are here." I gesture to them down the hall. "We can trust Evan. He's safe. If you don't believe me, ask Lucy to look into his past. She'll show you exactly what happened when he let me go."

"We can't trust him regardless," he grunts.

My eyes begin to sting. "We haven't even given him a chance. Jaxon, please. I am literally begging you."

He breathes through his nose heavily, and for a moment, I think he's about to shake his head without any negotiation. But when his dark gaze flicks to mine, something in them simmers. "Fine."

Soon, Lucy joins us and holds out her arms. "What the hell, Ava? You disappeared. I couldn't find you."

"I was down here," I murmur.

"I see that now. Why am I here? It stinks," she says before pinching her nostrils together and wafting a hand.

Jaxon turns to her. "We need you to look into Evan's past. I want you to tell me what happened when he let Ava go. If he's hiding anything."

She sucks in a breath and narrows her eyes at him. "Ugh, you owe me for this."

"I know," he grunts.

Lucy approaches Evan, who's silently watching this entire encounter. "Hi," she greets him politely. His body trembles as she steps closer. "Hold out your hands."

He moves his fingers towards her, and despite how dirty and pale they look, she latches onto them and closes her eyes.

Evan whimpers, his eyelashes twitching. Lucy holds her focus and doesn't move an inch. Jax's warm presence alerts me, but I won't rest until he grants Evan freedom. I stand like stone, watching the silent encounter—it might sound stupid, but I trust him with my whole heart.

After a few minutes, Lucy opens her eyes and takes a step back from Evan. His entire body slumps forward, barely giving himself a chance to grab onto the bars. Lucy grabs his wrist. "Easy," she warns. "Reading your memories will have worn you out. Rest, okay? You'll need to sleep it off."

He sinks to the floor, legs muscles failing him. My fingers itch to help him, but I know I'll be pulled back before Lucy has the chance to explain what she saw.

"Well?" Jaxon asks.

"Good as gold if you ask me." She shrugs simply. "And he did let Ava go and almost got killed because of it. He hasn't done wrong, Jaxon. He's a kid who was brought up in an environment that was toxic."

I sigh a breath of relief. I never doubted him. Now, Jaxon has no choice but to let him go and treat him with the respect he deserves. "Fine," he snaps. "He can stay, but he's still going to be under watch until I trust him. He's related to that monster, and I won't ever forgive myself if something happens to Ava or the pack."

"Do not keep him in the dungeon." I shake my head. "Move him to the annexe at least where he can be watched."

"He is not to be alone with Ava or any of the other girls, not until I can completely trust him. I'm not taking any chances." He flicks his eyes between us and the guards before they land back on me again. "Especially not where you're involved."

I huff. "Jax–"

"Do I make myself clear?"

My core tightens at the tone of his authoritative voice. "Yes," I whisper because there is no point arguing with him right now.

"Great." He nods.

"He needs a shower," Lucy says with her lips twisted downwards. "And a hearty meal."

Jaxon turns to the guards. "Take him to the annexe and don't let him out of your sight. He is to wash and have food brought up to his room. If he wants to leave the annexe, then he must be accompanied by at least two guards. Do you understand?"

"Yes, Alpha."

"If I see him walking around without guards or in places he shouldn't be, I will gut each and every one of you," he threatens in a lethally calm tone.

I shudder watching him. "Yes, Alpha."

"Good," he rasps before turning back to me. "Let's head to the house."

Jaxon takes my hand and leads me out of the dungeon in silence. I peek up at him, but his eyes are set forward and narrowed. I frown at the moody expression.

"I take it you're pissed at me."

"For going down there without telling anyone first? Yes."

My eyes flicker at his sharp tone. "I knew I was safe. The guards were there."

He pauses and turns to me suddenly, his tall stature backing me into the nearest tree. My spine hits the bark with a light thud. "What if something happened to you?"

"But it didn't." I tilt my chin towards him.

He breathes through his nose heavily. "That is beside the point, Ava. Do not do that again. Do not scare me like that again."

Within the flash of a second, fear and relief cross his eyes like a blur of light. My lips twitch downwards at his reaction. "I'm sorry," I whisper. "Evan crossed my mind and my curiosity got the better of me."

Jaxon's hand slides across my cheek, and his fingers lightly grip the back of my hair. "I would never forgive myself if something happened to you, Ava. *Never.*"

"I'm okay." I press my face into his hand. "I'm right here."

"Please, ask me to come with you when you want to explore."

"I knew you'd say no."

"I wouldn't have said no." He shakes his head firmly. "I wouldn't have agreed with it, but I would never stop you from doing it. I've told you before, we are equals."

My throat contracts. "I didn't mean to scare you."

Jaxon rests his forehead against mine and closes his eyes. "I know, baby."

"I'm sorry." I lean up onto my toes and kiss the corner of his mouth.

He presses me back into the tree and claims my lips with every ounce of energy he possesses. I sigh, feeling all of his emotions flood out of him when he kisses me deeper, and I don't want to make him feel like this again.

37

AVA

I pace Gemma's office as she watches me closely. Blood pumps around my body, and I'm convinced it helps calm me. She never questions why I don't like to sit down and accepts me for who I am. This isn't a safe space; this is a safe haven.

"And how do you feel knowing Lucien and Damon are gone?" she asks.

My tongue extends to lick my bottom lip. "Relieved," I admit. "I did think it would give me closure, but I'm not really feeling anything yet."

Gemma's mouth curls into a soft smile. "It's barely been a week, Ava. Closure doesn't have to happen the next second. You are probably still digesting what happened, and that's okay. It might take time, but don't be frustrated with yourself."

I nod once. "I know." I raise my thumb to my lips to chew on the nail. "It felt surreal seeing them again."

"Did it upset you?"

"At first, yes. It felt like someone had punched me in the throat and I couldn't breathe. But I knew they were going to die, and I wouldn't get the chance again. That's why I decided to do what I did," I sigh and drop my hands to my sides, flexing my fingers. "It didn't fulfil me with the satisfaction I thought it would."

"Why do you think that is?"

I meet her gaze. "Because the pain I made them feel in those short seconds is nothing compared to the years of abuse they gave me. It put things into perspective for me, and I've never been so angry."

"And you have every right to be angry," she states, leaning forward in her chair. "What other emotions did you feel?"

My body turns towards the window, and I stare out at the cloudy sky. I fold my arms over my chest and release a heavy sigh. "Fear. I feared them, just like I did when they kidnapped me from my school–"

I cut myself off and blink. *School?*

"I haven't heard you mention your school before, Ava. Would you like to elaborate?"

My eyes dart from tree to tree as I search my mind for the memory. I swallow back the lump in my throat. I close my eyes, letting the memories flood towards me.

"I-I was at school. I was in my final year, a few months away from graduating, and they took me...in the car park. There was a white van. A white van," I murmur as the memory replays in my head like a movie. "And..."

Gemma waits patiently for me to carry on. I turn around to face her as she watches curiously. I keep my mouth parted, but for a few moments, nothing comes out. The words are all jumbled in my mind.

"And..." I rasp through trembling lips. "I was there with my friends."

"Do you remember the names of your friends?"

I nod slowly. "Kayleigh. She was my best friend."

Tears well in my eyes as the memories become clearer by the second. I take down a shuddering breath and slip a hand through my hair.

"I spent a lot of time with her because I hated my foster parents," I whisper. "Her family was like my true family. I loved them to pieces. They treated me like their own—like everyone does here."

A hand covers my mouth. "Oh, my God," I gasp. "I remember. *I remember.*"

"How does that make you feel, Ava?"

"Weightless."

"In a good way?"

"In a good way."

We're silent for a few moments, and I wipe my eyes. "I need to tell Jaxon," I blurt. "I'm sorry. I need to go."

"Go." She stands and urges me out of the door with a proud smile. "You did this, remember? You did this all by yourself."

Warmth swirls in my chest. "Without you, I wouldn't have been able to do it all."

Then I dart out of her office and run through the infirmary into the house. "Jaxon!" I shout, my voice echoing around me. "Jaxon!"

I stumble out into the hall and call his name one last time. He emerges from the stairs in a hurry. "Ava?" His voice is laced with alarm. "What's wrong?"

When he reaches the bottom step, I crash into his chest. His arms engulf me in a tight embrace. A hand cradles the back of my head as he inspects my face, but I'm beaming. "What's wrong? You scared the shit out of me."

"I remember," I whisper, clinging onto the back of his T-shirt. "My past. I remember."

Jaxon exhales out through his nose and drops his forehead against mine. "That is incredible." He relaxes into me. "I am so proud of you, baby."

My lips remain in what feels like a permanent grin despite my glassy eyes. "I had to come tell you. I needed to find you."

"Please, never shout my name like you're in danger again. Ava, I–"

I frown and lean up to peck his lips softly. "I'm sorry," I murmur against him. "I was excited. I wanted to tell you. Gemma helped, but I wanted you to be the first to know."

He releases a soft grunt and kisses me again. "Thank you for wanting to share it with me. Do you want to talk about it?"

My head moves into a nod. He takes us to his private living room, and I explain everything I remember—right down to the last detail.

Jaxon's eyes hold mine as I speak, and he moves his thumb across my knuckles. "I am so proud of you, you have no idea. I had every faith in you."

I press my head against his shoulder. "It feels good to remember. It feels like that part of my mind has opened up."

"Ava." He slips an arm around me and tugs me up so I'm looking at him. "I have something to confess."

My lashes brush my cheek as I blink a couple of times. "Okay?"

He inhales a large gulp of air. "The night you went out for Lucy's girls' night before the wedding," he starts. "When you were drunk, you mentioned a few things, including Kayleigh and your foster parents, but with nowhere near as much detail as you just explained to me."

A gash strikes my heart like a spear. No. No.

"What? Why didn't you tell me?"

"Because you didn't remember in the morning, and I wasn't sure if it would trigger or upset you. I wanted you to do this by yourself. I didn't feel like it was right to start meddling in something that meant a lot to you." He places his hand on my face delicately. "I didn't do it to keep it from you maliciously. I wanted you to have this moment like you did with Gemma just now. I'm sorry."

I stare at him. "It's been ages since that night."

"I know." He nods and caresses my face with his thumb. "I'm sorry. I didn't do it to upset you. I did it so you could remember in your own time. The alcohol must have opened up a part of your memories, and in the morning, it sealed back up again."

My body shifts backwards, and I move out of Jaxon's reach. I run a hand down my face. "I understand why you did it," I admit with lowered eyes. "But it hurts to know you knew and kept quiet about it. All this time, I could have known. Did you think I would run away and leave or something?"

"Not at all." He shakes his head.

I turn my gaze away because my eyes ache.

"I'm sorry, baby," he says sincerely. "I didn't want to take this moment away from you. Please forgive me. I should have been honest, but when I once asked you about Russell Vale and you said it didn't ring any bells, I didn't want that to be a repeat with mentioning Kayleigh or your foster parents. I didn't want to confuse you further."

I clear my throat and straighten my spine. "I see."

We sit in silence for a long moment. I can't believe this.

"I didn't know what to do," he rasps. "I should have told you."

"It's fine." I force a smile. "It doesn't matter now, right? I remember, so it's fine."

"Don't say it's fine because it's not." Jaxon frowns. "I want to show you something."

"What?"

He grabs the laptop sitting on the coffee table. He opens it up and taps away at the keys before turning the screen towards me. I move my eyes over the laptop to find it open on a site. Another memory I had completely forgotten.

Posted 2 years ago

I just wanted everyone to know I have decided to leave Russell Vale and travel around the world. I wanted to keep this quiet because I didn't want to say goodbye to my friends and family. This is something I have always wanted to do, and I am so happy I am finally free. Don't try to contact me. I want to start fresh with my life and make new memories. Ava x

"Oh my God," I mumble under my breath. I move forward to scroll through the endless comments I had no idea people would make. I read them as quickly as my eyes can move until one comment stands out.

Kayleigh: *How could you leave without even saying goodbye? I thought we were best friends! How could you leave me? Reply to my text now!!!!*

A million questions fly around my head. Nausea creeps up my throat and claims me in a chokehold. Jax's hand grips my fingers gingerly. "Ava?"

"She thought I left." I stare at the screen blankly. "No one knows I was taken. No one looked for me."

Tears swim in the crevice of my eyes once more. Jaxon moves the laptop away and twists his body towards mine. He doesn't smother me in affection, which I'm grateful for.

Instead, he takes my hands again. My brain has barely processed any of this information. It aches between my brows.

"Do you want to contact her?" he asks.

I glance at him in a dazed surprise. "Really?"

"Of course." He brushes a strand of hair from my eyes and tucks it behind my shoulder. "I'd do anything to make you happy, Ava. If you want to contact her, visit her, or *anything,* you can do whatever you want. I kept this from you, and I want you to be able to see her as soon as you can. If that's what you want."

I release a quiet whimper and lean forward to wrap my arms around him, burying my head into his neck. "Thank you," I mumble inaudibly as his arms secure around my back. "Thank you for not giving up. I know I've not been easy to deal with."

"Ava." He kisses my cheek. "I would have been there for you no matter what it takes. Don't thank me for allowing you to see your friend. You don't need permission for these things."

I hold onto him for dear life.

Now that I can remember my past, I think about Kayleigh. I miss her. I miss being with her—more than I could ever comprehend. I pray she wants to see me after all these years and that she'll give me a chance to explain.

38

AVA

Today is the day I'm going to see Kayleigh after two and a half years.

After my conversation with Jaxon, we got in contact with her. We video called each other because I don't think she believed I was real. When her face popped up on the screen, tears started to flow.

I found out she's attending a university sixty miles from here. Jaxon said she could come to the pack house to see me while being trailed by our guards for safety into the district.

The intense butterflies make my stomach churn. I know I need some normality from my old life.

Kayleigh wasn't just a best friend to me; she was like a sister.

Jaxon kneads his thumbs into the muscles on my shoulders. "Relax, baby," he whispers, giving my cheek a peck. "This is good. This is exciting."

"I know." I chew on my lip. "I'm apprehensive."

He hums against my jaw gently before wrapping his arms around me from behind. I latch onto his arm and smile at the warmth of his body. A moment to embrace his calmness—God knows I need it.

"She's here." He kisses the back of my head. "Guards have informed me."

I jump from Jaxon's arms and start shaking out my limbs. My throat tenses, but I force a gulp of air down anyway. He gives me one firm nod before I make my way to the front door. I take hold of the handle and swing it open. My eyes immediately fall on my best friend. Her expression is weary, but as soon as she sees me, her mouth bursts into a grin. Then, I glance to the right of her, not having noticed a second person.

"Danny?"

Holy hell. What is he doing here?

Danny doesn't say anything for a few moments. Instead, he watches me with sadness and relief in his eyes. My heart aches at the expression. "Hi, gorgeous." His lips tremble as he speaks. "I've missed you so much."

He steps forward to wrap me up in a hug, but it doesn't even compare to an embrace from Jaxon. I tilt my head and return it gently. "Hi," I exhale.

When he lets me go, I turn back to Kayleigh, who has tears in her eyes, but her smile hasn't faltered. "Hey, Av," she murmurs before bundling me into an embrace that almost knocks me over.

I chuckle and hold her tight. "Hi, Kayleigh. It's so good to see you."

We stay like this for a few seconds, and I close my eyes and savour our reunion. The bones in my body begin to relax, and I can't stop the pressure behind my lids. Nothing beats this moment—especially now I'm coming to terms with who I am.

I pull back and hold her at arm's length. Goodness, she's

still as beautiful as ever. Blonde wavy hair hangs around her shoulders and pale blue eyes are sparkling at me with joy. I glance down at her signature nose ring she's had since we were sixteen.

"Come in," I say before guiding them down to the kitchen.

Kayleigh and Danny's eyes glance around the grand hall in awe. "So, this is what you left us for then, huh?" Danny laughs hesitantly.

I flick my gaze to Kayleigh, who is beaming along. I didn't tell her where I had been on our phone call. They think I left Russell Vale by choice.

"Not quite," I admit and step into the kitchen. "I want you to meet someone first."

Jaxon is leaning against the counter with his arms folded over his chest and biceps bulging out of his black T-shirt. His head turns towards us as soon as he notices we're in company.

"Kayleigh, Danny, this is my..." I glance between them. "My boyfriend, Jax."

Danny's brows pinch together at my words, and it makes me wince inside.

"It's Jaxon, actually," he clarifies.

Kayleigh takes a few confident strides towards him and holds out her hand. "Nice to meet you." She grins, and Jax shakes her hand.

"Likewise, Kayleigh."

Then Jaxon's eyes instantly move to Danny. His expression hardens like stone.

Please don't tell me that's who I think it is? he says through our mindlink.

Guilt churns my stomach, but I had no clue. I didn't specify to Kayleigh not to tell anyone, so that's my fault.

I hold his stare. *I'm sorry. I didn't know he was coming.*

Danny scratches the back of his head before reluctantly holding his hand out to Jaxon. "Nice to meet you, man," he says with a struggle.

"Yeah. You, too, Dale."

"Danny," he corrects him with an edge to his tone.

Jaxon looks unphased. "Right...that's it."

I squirm at their exchange and how long they awkwardly shake hands for. Kayleigh clears her throat, sensing the tension. "So, how did you guys meet? What's the story?"

I urge them both to sit down at the kitchen counter. Danny sits down beside me and Jax narrows his eyes at the action. "Uh, well," I say with a shallow breath. "I didn't choose to leave Russell Vale. Things happened to me over two years that I cannot quite vocalise yet, it's too painful. I'm getting help for it. I've got a therapist, and I found Jaxon. I'm happy here, and that's what matters."

Kayleigh's face drops, and her lips part, but I can tell she doesn't know what to say. "I'm sorry, Ava," she whispers carefully. "How are you now?"

"I'm getting there." I swallow the rough lump in my throat. "I have my good days and bad days. I'm taking every day as it comes."

Danny leans over to take my hand, which catches me by surprise, and I blink at the action. "What happened, Ava?"

"She just said she doesn't want to talk about it," Jaxon's voice booms across the kitchen, which makes Danny flinch. "So *don't* push her."

Then he glances down at the grip he has on my fingers, and my chest tightens. His eyes darken and not in a good way—he looks murderous.

If he doesn't take his hands off you in the next second, I will happily break both of his wrists. Jaxon's words are calm but full of deadly determination.

I slowly pull my hands away from Danny's touch because I don't want any broken bones here. "Yeah," I rasp with a forced smile. "I don't want to talk about it. Please respect that."

Danny nods. "Of course. I'm sorry."

"But I'm here now. I'm safe. I had nothing left for me in Russell Vale. This place feels like my home," I admit to them and myself.

Because it is your home, baby. Jax's words wrap around my heart.

"I'm glad you're safe," Kayleigh says. "I missed you so much. You have no idea."

My head tilts to my shoulder and I blink back my tears. "I missed you too."

"So you didn't write that post?" Danny asks, and Jaxon shoots him a glare.

"No, I didn't. They probably wanted to cover their tracks. Must have made sure that no one started looking for me." I shrug simply.

Kayleigh brushes a finger over her lips in deep thought. "When you left, I went to your house and saw your foster parents. They kept deflecting everything and seemed so angry. They said you were eighteen now and could do what you wanted."

"They didn't care about me."

"They moved away shortly after you."

I'm desperate to change the subject. "Sorry. I'm an awful host. Do you guys want something to drink?"

Kayleigh nods. "Sure, thank you."

"Yeah, that'd be great," Danny says.

"It's okay, I'll do it." Jaxon moves towards the counter. "Is coffee okay?"

They both agree, and Danny glances over his shoulder before turning to me, his face inches from mine. "I don't understand this, Ava. So...you guys meet, and now you're all happily ever after?"

Kayleigh gasps and scolds him.

"All of this seems strange and very out of character for you."

I narrow my eyes at him. "I'm not the same person I was when I was eighteen, Danny. Things have changed. I have changed."

"Have you seen this house? It belongs to a billionaire," he whispers under his breath. "You cannot tell me you just fell into his arms."

"Danny–"

He leans impossibly closer. "Is this a cult? Because if it is, we can get you out."

My brows widen at his accusation. I watch him carefully as he pulls away and focuses on a spot on the floor. "Although I've seen some seriously messed-up documentaries, and they did not end well."

"This isn't a cult. None of this is strange—not to me anyway. I get it from an outsider's point of view. But I didn't have anywhere else to go, and I've found peace here. Without Jaxon, I probably would have been dead."

Jaxon's shoulders tense. Despite us speaking quietly, his sensitive hearing means I'm probably shouting. I grimace at my choice of words.

"Well, I'm glad you're happy, Av. I'm just so pleased to have you back in my life." She leans over to take my hand, and I give it a soft squeeze. "Please tell me we can see each other more."

I nod without hesitation. "Of course. I would love that."

"Our university isn't too far away." She nods. "Maybe you could come up and see it."

"Sure," I agree as Jaxon sets down their drinks on the counter.

Kayleigh thanks him before her eyes settle on the kitchen window. "Oh my," she murmurs. "Who the hell is that?"

We all turn our attention to the window. It's Kayden. He's on his way back from a run, and his whole body is glistening with sweat, dripping off his large forearms. He tugs his T-shirt off his back, exposing his toned body.

"Oh," I say, turning back to her, but I can see the love hearts blooming in her eyes. She's in a Kayden-induced trance. "That's Kayden. Jaxon's B–"

"Brother," he cuts over me, and I freeze. That was a close call. *Crap.*

Danny's brows crease as he glances from Jaxon to Kayden. "Funny, you guys don't look alike."

"Ever thought about the fact adoption exists, Dale?"

"Danny," he says through gritted teeth.

Jaxon rolls his eyes. "Yeah, yeah," he mutters. "He's like a brother to me. We're friends, but we're not related."

Kayden then strolls into the kitchen, and I glance at Kayleigh, who is composing herself. He notices we have company and raises his brows.

"Kayden, these are my friends from home," I say. He glances at Danny first and shakes his hand. "And this is Kayleigh."

"Hey," she greets him politely.

His eyes roam over her face as she sits on the stool. "Hey, nice to meet you."

Kayden's hand extends for her to shake, and she takes it

delicately. The encounter goes on for a few seconds too long, like no one else in the room exists. Danny clears his throat, which snaps them out of their daze, and Kayleigh looks away, cheeks reddening by the second.

"I'm gonna go clean up," he says, dismissing himself, but not before he looks over his shoulder to take one last glance at Kayleigh.

"So, what do you do for a job, Jaxon?" Danny quizzes.

Jaxon leans his hand on the island. "I invest in property."

"Like this one?"

"Yes." He nods.

"And you own it?"

"Yes."

"And who exactly lives here? This place is a goddamn mansion."

"Danny," Kayleigh snaps. "This isn't one hundred and one questions. Cut it out."

His head whips in her direction. "I'd like to know more about Ava's boyfriend, if that's okay with you."

I press a hand to my head and close my eyes for a second. "Please," Kayleigh hisses. "Stop. Just stop."

"Fine," he grumbles. "Can I use your bathroom?"

"Sure. I'll show you." Jaxon's voice is low.

I jump off of my stool faster than lightning. "No. I'll show you."

There is no guarantee what would happen if I leave Jax and Danny alone, but I can imagine it won't be pretty. I catch Jaxon's eyes on the way out and raise my brows at him.

I show Danny down the hall to the bathroom, and then as I'm about to turn, he takes my wrist. "Ava, wait," he pleads.

My eyes meet his, and I pull back at the devastated expression on his face. Those eyes don't lie. He's hurting right now. "Are you sure this is what you want?" he asks. "Do you remember what we had? That we loved each oth–"

I pull away from his grip, shaking my head vigorously. "Danny, stop. Stop." I hold up my hands. "I'm sorry this is how you had to find out about us, but it's been two and a half years. I'm not the girl I was in school. I don't mean to hurt you. Things have changed. I have changed."

"What you and this guy have had for God knows how long was better than what we had in two years?"

I release a tight breath. "We were kids, Danny. I'm sorry. I never want to hurt you."

"I still have feelings for you, Ava."

My eyes close in defeat, and I chew on the inside of my lip. "Please, don't do this. Please respect that I've moved on and I'm trying to let go of my past. I need it for my recovery. I'm sorry for being selfish, but it's what I need."

He lowers his head, covering the look in his eyes. "Right," he rasps. "Sure. I can respect that. I can respect whatever you need. I'm just hurt."

"I know. I'm sorry."

When I make it back to the kitchen, Kayleigh and Jaxon are laughing away as they crowd around Kayleigh's phone. "What are you guys doing?" I ask suspiciously.

Kayleigh turns to me with a wide grin. "I'm showing Jaxon videos and pictures of you from school from our cheerleading days when you face-planted the floor at Lydia's party."

I laugh hesitantly, my face on fire. Jaxon's eyes glitter with amusement. "O-Kay, I think that's enough," I say, reaching forward to take her phone.

"Fine, fine." She swats me away gently. "I thought Jaxon would like to see."

"I did." He nods in agreement.

Danny makes it back to the kitchen, where he sits in silence. Jaxon quirks a brow in my direction.

I'll tell you later, I shoot down our mindlink.

They stay for another hour before they head off, and I give Kayleigh a much-needed hug goodbye—one I couldn't give her before. But this won't be our last.

She pauses by the door as Danny starts the car. "Oh, I'm sorry I brought him unexpectedly. We're both at the same university, and I got excited. I had to tell someone. If I knew you were with Jaxon, I never would have done that. I'm sorry if I pushed any boundaries. I assumed you might have liked to see him, too."

I shake my head. "It's okay. I still saw you. It doesn't matter."

"Bye." She waves with a beaming smile. "It was super nice to meet you, Jaxon."

"You, too. Drive safe."

I return to the kitchen when they leave, and within seconds, I sense Jaxon's eyes on me. "What did he say?"

I sigh and fill the dishwasher. "He still has feelings for me and doesn't understand how this happened so quickly between us."

Jaxon leans against the counter with a firm nod. "How did you feel when you saw him?"

"Surprised," I admit. "But I didn't feel anything—not a single thing."

He holds out his hand for me, and I take it, and then I'm tugged to his side. "Not even a sliver of something?"

"No. I felt nothing. But when I'm with you, I feel everything. This is right. I'm still getting my head around it all, but I couldn't imagine being anywhere but here. Does that make sense?"

Jaxon leans down to peck the corner of my mouth.

"Makes more than sense," he whispers. "You're meant to be by my side. This is your home. It will always be your home."

"I've never really had a home," I confess heavily. "Jumping around in foster care didn't give me much security. Nothing was stable. Nothing was forever. It was continuous false hope, and I hated it."

"Well, you have indefinite security here because this can be your first true home. I'm glad I can be a part of it," he says so softly it makes my eyes water.

A smile possesses my lips. "Me, too. I don't want to be anywhere else."

39

AVA

I never really took myself for an affectionate person. That's until I met Jaxon. There is nothing I enjoy more than waking up to him in the morning with his strong arms secured around me. Every day, I acknowledge how far I've come with my recovery and how I grow to trust Jaxon more and more each day.

A hand reaches up to push away a strand of hair that covers my shoulder. My eyes are still firmly shut, but a smile covers my lips as Jaxon's warmth swarms me. "Morning, baby," he whispers.

I release a slow grunt and open my eyes to meet his handsome face. "Hi."

He cups my jaw and brushes his thumb over my cheek. "You okay?"

"Yeah." I nod. "You?"

He hums softly. "More than okay when I wake up to your beautiful face."

My skin flushes at his compliment. "Likewise."

Jaxon grins softly and leans forward to press a kiss to my chin, then my jaw and my neck. I slip my hand over his bare shoulder and close my eyes when he kisses my pulse and over my collarbones.

A flutter of warmth shoots across my abdomen and through my core. I clench my thighs together. I've grasped the concept of my heat with the help of medicine, but when Jaxon touches me like this, it awakens my desire in the most intimate of ways.

"Is this okay?" he whispers.

For a moment, my brain hesitates, but I know what I want. Jaxon will never push my boundaries. I am safe. I am in control. I have the right to pleasure.

I purse my lips and nod. "Yes."

My fingers slip into the back of his hair as he peppers kisses across my hot skin. I part my lips and release a tremble of satisfaction that crashes over me. I squeeze my thighs together at the placement of his lips and the tenderness of each peck.

"This is my favourite part of the day," he murmurs into my neck. "Knowing you're in *our* bed. The sheets are covered in *your* scent. You're in *my* arms."

I shudder at the sound of his deep voice. My fingers knead into his biceps, and I clutch onto him as he kisses lower...over the tips of my breasts. "This still okay?"

"Yes," I say desperately with a nod.

It's more than okay. It's divine. It's magical.

It doesn't feel anything like my bad memories because he is worshipping my body, mind, and soul. I've never been worshipped in my life.

The trail of soft pecks he leaves behind makes my head spin. "More," I plead.

His eyes peek up at me. "Yeah...you want more?"

"Please," I exhale. "I want to feel everything."

The corner of his lip twitches. "Can I taste you?"

I can't even remember what it's like to receive oral sex. It's been so long since I experienced it that the idea sends a shiver down my spine. His eyes are determined but soft—there's no pressure.

"Yes." I manage a nod. "Please. I'd like that."

Jaxon grins and kisses the centre of my sternum. "Good," he rasps. "Lay back and let me pleasure you. If you want me to stop, say the word, and I will. All of this is in your hands, Ava. Okay?"

"Okay," I whimper at the adoration in his eyes.

I don't have to ask Jaxon to understand me, be patient with me, and not push my boundaries. He already does it because he knows it's the bare minimum—nothing more. He never allows me to thank him for asking me for consent or if I'm okay. It should be a given, not a praise.

He pushes up my T-shirt and slips his hands over the curve of my hips. I study his eyes as they focus on my stomach. He kisses my belly button and then down each of my ribs until I throw my head back.

I bite my lip in anticipation as he sinks lower. The bottom of his lip grazes the tip of my underwear. An unexpected groan falls from the back of my throat as he teases the sensitive area.

"Does this feel okay?"

"Mmm. Yes," I moan.

He slips his fingers inside my panties and tugs them down my legs until I'm bare. I peek at him, and he gives me a second to compose myself before he slides his hand between my thighs and parts them.

The sound of his body shuffling down the bed until his face is parallel to my core makes me throb. I let my fingers run through his hair as he opens his mouth and closes it around my clit. I gasp and slam my head back down into the cushion. All my nerve endings burst from the warmth of his tongue.

He rolls it around the hood slowly, and my legs spread wider subconsciously. I tremble when he sucks on my clit again. He groans as he licks my wetness that is pouring out of me.

My lungs gasp for a breath at the same time I release a pant of pleasure. He eats me harder, holding my thighs back so he can feast on me like his own private meal. "Jax," I whimper. "Oh, gosh."

You taste beautiful, baby. His voice etches its way into my mind.

I arch my back off the bed and reach for his hand on my thigh. He entwines our fingers, and I grip onto him for support. "Yes," I cry out as he sucks harder and then releases. "Please, don't stop."

Everything he's doing makes my world tilt.

I'm shaking. I can't stop shaking.

My eyelashes flicker when I tense my core at the way his tongue works over me. It's like he's known my body for years. He answers my body language, and I'm full of pure ecstasy.

Let go for me, he whispers again and heightens our intimate moment. *Come for me, baby. Let me hear how good I make you feel.*

His tongue flicks over my clit until my eyes are swimming with tears and my legs quiver. Pleasure builds in my core so quickly my vision turns blurry. I can't even stop myself. I fall headfirst over the finishing line.

"Fuck," I scream. "Jax. I'm coming."

I clamp a hand over my mouth to stop the cries of paradise erupting around the room. My hips grind over Jaxon's mouth as I ride out my orgasm on his face. Every part of my body is weightless. I'm numb all over yet sensitive.

Holy crap.

My high begins to subside, and Jaxon pulls away from my core. My hazy eyes find his. Those lips are glistening with my orgasm proudly. I press my shaky legs together, and he grabs a blanket to wrap me up in.

"How was that?" he asks huskily.

I'm lost for words.

I don't think I'm on planet Earth. I'm on planet Jaxon.

My lips part, but I laugh instead, pressing a hand to my forehead. "I can't even comprehend."

"I have one suggestion," he whispers, and I glance at him. "Next time, don't put your hand over your mouth to muffle your moans. They are beautiful and so damn sexy. I want to hear it. I want to hear how you feel."

A blush creeps up my neck until it reaches my face. "I was conscious of how loud I was being."

"Be as loud as you want." His eyes glitter. "Trust me. I don't mind."

I bury my head into his neck and chuckle softly. "Okay. Noted."

His hand smooths over my shoulder as I stare up at the ceiling. "Would you like to shower with me?"

"With you?"

"Yeah. I'd like to give you the proper aftercare."

I press a hand to the bed and sit up. "What's that?"

"Where I look after you when we've been intimate together." He cups my cheek with his large hand. "We don't have to shower together. I can do it here."

The stickiness between my legs is evident. "We could save water?"

Jaxon beams at me with bright eyes. "If you want to, then we can."

He stands from the bed and holds out his hand. I take it and let him guide us to the en-suite. As soon as we're inside, he turns on the waterfall shower and starts to strip himself of his boxers.

I try my hardest not to look, but my wandering eyes are curious. He turns towards the shower and holds out his hand, letting the water hit his palm. Once it's warm enough, he ducks beneath the showerhead. Those impressive back muscles flex as he runs his hand through his hair.

After shamelessly checking him out, I pull my T-shirt over my head. I hesitate for a second, but I remind myself it's okay. If I want to leave, I can. No one is stopping me.

I slide in next to the wall, and he turns towards me. He keeps his gaze above my collarbones, which flushes me with guilt after I checked him out brazenly. The hot water hits my skin, and I close my eyes.

"Are you working today?" I ask breathlessly.

"I work every day."

I frown at his statement. "I know you need to keep the pack in line, but you work so hard all the time. Do you ever take time for yourself?"

"I do, especially when I'm with you."

"That's not the same."

"It is."

Jaxon's cheek grazes mine softly as he presses a kiss to my lips. I smile and tilt my neck to meet his height. "You okay?" he asks.

"You don't need to ask if everything is okay, Jax."

"I do." He nods. "Because how will I learn boundaries?"

"I trust you."

My head glances down between us, and I almost gasp at

Jaxon's half-hard cock. It's thick and veiny. *Big.* So fucking big.

One of his arms rests on the wall behind me, and I flick my gaze to his. His eyes are now pitch-black with desire. The bond sizzles between us. I run my teeth over my bottom lip.

"Ava," he says hoarsely. "I'm not asking you to do anything to me. I'm hard because tasting you was the hottest thing of my life."

I stare down at it. It's growing by the second. How much bigger can it get?

My hand reaches to grip his length. Jax releases a shallow grunt but then shakes his head. His fingers find my wrist. "You don't have to do this, Ava," he warns me. "I promise you. I'm not expecting anything. I would never pressure you into doing it."

I look up at him under damp lashes. I swat his hand away with my fingers. "I want to," I whisper. "Can I? I should have asked. You always ask me first. I'm sorry. I would like to touch you. Will you let me?"

"Fuck, Ava," he groans and lowers his forehead to mine. "I..." he pauses. "This..."

"Yes or no, Jax? Can I touch you?"

His eyes move between mine in a conflicting battle. "Yes."

I'm filled with a wave of assurance. I waste no time in gripping his girth. His head is thrown back in immediate pleasure. My hand begins to work up and down him as he presses his other arm against the wall, caging me between him.

Jaxon's breathless moans are pure heaven. They're like sweet harmonies—deep yet completely unleashed. His forehead rests back on mine. He doesn't hold back his pleasure. It makes me realise I don't need to be embarrassed about how loud I am because I get it. He wants to hear me like I want to hear him.

My wrist moves quicker, and I grip his cock tighter. One of his hands slides into the back of my hair, tangling my hair between his fingers. He pulls me to his lips and kisses me desperately, fiercely, devotedly.

I roll my thumb over the head of his length, and he moans into my mouth. "Oh, Ava," he says before clamping down on my bottom lip. "Oh, fuck. That feels so good, baby. Holy shit."

His mouth pulls away from mine, panting like he's lost all sense of himself. I study his shattering face as I keep up the pace. I can't take my eyes off him. The way his entire body hardens and shivers is alluring.

A few pumps later, his cum squirts across my stomach as his loud groans fill the air. I don't stop. I don't want to. He is a masterpiece.

He releases the grip on my head. "Oh my Goddess," he mumbles. I smile and drop his cock. The water washes away his climax from my fingers. "Ava. Ava. *Ava.*"

I bite back a grin.

"Fuck..." He lowers his lips down to mine and captures them in a passionate kiss. "That felt incredible. Perfect. You are perfect."

My eyes flutter closed as he devours my mouth. He presses his forehead into mine as we catch our breath. Water droplets roll off his nose and onto my face.

"You know, I never expect you to do anything to me because I do it to you."

I frown and shake my head. His black gaze returns to dark blue. "I did it because I wanted to, not because you did it to me. Every moment I have with you is like I'm overwriting all the bad memories. Instead, I'm associating moments in my life with happier ones."

Jaxon nods. "I understand," he whispers before kissing me again.

"Sex isn't a bad thing," I admit. "These moments I have with you are nothing like what I've experienced in the past. Now, I'm choosing for myself. If I can replace the old memories with ones that make me feel in control, then I will take it."

"Okay," he murmurs against my lips. "I want nothing more than to be a part of your new memories, Ava."

"I associate these moments we have with feelings of contentment and joy. I want these emotions to remain. Nothing else. Not the bad stuff," I confess. "I want to do this more than anything because I really, *really* want to pleasure you and because I know I'm strong enough to accept what I truly want."

His hands wrap around my jaw and he kisses me one last time. "Yeah. You are. My mate. My Luna. My life."

I lean into his kiss with a smile. Those words used to trigger me, but now, I welcome them. I'm slowly accepting who this world wants me to be. A part of me believes this has always been my destiny.

40

JAXON

A muffled cry wakes me up from my sleep. I twist beneath the sheets and open my eyes to the dark room. Ava shuffles around the bed, releasing a distressed moan from her trembling lips.

"No," she whimpers. "No. No. No. Please. Don't. Please. No!"

"Ava." I take one of her hands but she bats me away.

Her eyes are firmly shut as she squirms and shakes her head aggressively. "No. Please. Leave me alone. Please. Don't hurt me. *Please.*"

"Ava."

I cup her cheek to find her skin burning beneath my palm. "No!" she yells as tears escape from her closed lids. "Get away. Get away."

"Ava. Baby." I attempt to pull her close to my chest, but I only make it worse.

Her eyes fly open, and she screams at the top of her lungs, fear etched onto her face. She extends her arm aggressively, which ends up knocking into my jaw, sending my lip into my teeth. Blood invades my mouth as I listen to her erratic breaths.

Ava scurries back into the headboard, eyes shot wide with terror. "He's here," she trembles. "He's here. *They're* here."

"No." I shake my head and wipe my mouth. "No one is here, Ava. No one is here. I promise."

"They are," she sobs. "I saw them. They're here. They're back. They're taking me away again."

I lean out to take her hand, trying anything to calm her down, but she leaps off the bed. Her body collapses onto the floor as endless tears fall down her cheeks. "No," she gasps. "Don't touch me. I don't want you to touch me."

My hands retreat carefully as I study her face. I clench my jaw at her petrified state, but if I do anything more, I risk breaking her trust. My wolf howls at me to do something, but I have to put her first. She's safe here with me, that's a start.

"It was a nightmare, Ava," I whisper. "They're not here. Okay? Whatever you saw, it was a dream. I promise they're not here."

She clamps her eyes shut and pushes her back into the wall, wrapping her arms around her legs. I drop to the floor and face her from across the room, listening to the sound of her blood pounding through her veins.

"Ava, listen to me." I try to get her eyes to focus on me, but she's not thinking right now. "Listen to my breaths, okay? You're going to make yourself panic. Please, listen."

Her throat tenses before gasping. "Come on, baby," I drop my tone and push through the bond to calm her mind, wrapping a wave of security around her nerves like a soothing blanket.

For a few moments, her eyes glaze over and she takes

her first calm breath. But then she shakes her head. "Stop doing that," she shouts. "Stop messing with my head!"

She entwines her fingers into her hair and starts tugging at the strands. "Don't hurt yourself." I move forward, but she watches me with terror in her eyes. "Ava. Please. I'm sorry. I only want to comfort you."

My heart strains. I've never acknowledged this agony before. Seeing it right in front of me, but not being able to do a single thing about it. I want to wrap her up in my arms and hold her until she knows she's safe again. It's my only wish.

"I felt them," she whimpers. "On my skin. They're always around me. I'll never be able to escape them. They made me like this."

A light of fury ignites in the pit of my stomach. I know they're dead, but I'd do anything to bring them back and torture them all over again.

"Baby," I whisper. "Listen to my breaths. I want you to copy me."

She's already beginning to hyperventilate, and I don't want it to escalate.

Those glossy brown eyes locate mine before she looks down to my lips. I breathe in for four long counts before exhaling as long as possible. I keep going until Ava copies my actions, but her chest quivers with her breathing pattern. "That's it," I encourage her. "Deep breaths. Fill your lungs, then breathe out like you're trying to blow out candles. Yes. That's it."

Once her breathing slows down and the bond is begging me to give her some kind of affection, all I can offer is a smile. "Good. You've got it."

Ava nods and presses a hand flat to her chest as she takes control. Her cheeks are still stained with tears, but as soon as she gives me her consent to comfort her, I'm wiping them away.

Her gaze flicks down to my lip and she frowns, shaking her head. "I'm sorry," she sniffles. "I'm so sorry."

"What for, Ava?"

I scoot closer so we're only a metre apart, but I keep my hands to myself. "For hurting you." She points to my bust lip that I had forgotten all about. "I-I didn't mean to. The dream felt so real. I saw them. Then I saw you. I flinched. I'm so sorry."

My brows crease. "You don't need to apologise. It'll heal in the next few minutes. It's fine. I'm fine. You didn't hurt me."

She wraps her arms around herself once more and releases a few more tears. Her eyes are so sore that I can't watch her cry anymore. I will break. This is *destroying* me. "I can't go back to sleep." She shakes her head. "I can't. I don't want to."

"Then, we'll stay up and talk," I suggest. "Would you like that?"

Ava's exhausted eyes sweep the room as she remains silent for a few moments. Then, she nods. "Don't leave me. I don't want to be alone right now."

"I'm not going anywhere," I promise.

Neither of us say anything more. I listen to her undisturbed breaths and sigh in relief because I know she's calmer. Her fingers twitch around her legs.

"Can I hold you now, Ava?"

There is zero hesitation when she nods. My wolf cries in desperation to touch her, to soothe her, to take away her pain in any way we possibly can.

She pushes up onto her knees and bundles herself into my arms. I cradle the back of her head and secure the other around her lower back. I press my lips to the side of her face.

"I've got you," I whisper. "I've always got you. You're always safe with me."

Ava clings onto me as I rock us from side to side, still positioned on the floor. I press her chest against mine and let the beat of our hearts synchronise. She releases a soft sound and then an exhale of ease. "I'm sorry for using our bond to calm you. I realise now that your head must have been a very overwhelming place."

She pulls back, but I continue to hold onto her. "No." Her voice is strangled. "I'm sorry. You were trying to help, and I was pushing you away."

I raise my hand to brush away her hair in front of her eyes. "You've got nothing to be sorry for." I kiss her temple.

"I wish I could go back to being normal. Every time I believe I'm doing well and getting better, something like this happens." Her eyes fall to my chest. "I know I'm not back at square one, but sometimes, it feels like it."

"Your recovery doesn't have a timeline, Ava." I stroke my thumb across her cheek. "You don't need to put pressure on yourself to feel good all the time. It's normal to have hiccups. But keep being vocal about them, if not with me, then at least Gemma. I know you've grown a strong relationship with her. I never want you to struggle in silence. It's one of my biggest fears."

She nods slowly. "Yeah, I have grown a strong relationship with her. She's taught me to open up and that my feelings are always valid."

"Because they are," I state.

Ava purses her lips, and we stay in silence for a moment. I stand from the floor and hold her close to my chest. I walk us to the bed and tuck ourselves beneath the sheets.

"How do you know how to deal with panic attacks?" she asks with her head on my chest and our fingers entwined over my stomach.

I drag my tongue across my lip. "Because when Julia passed, I used to get them. I didn't know what was happening to me, and it felt like I was dying. But then I realised it was pure fear, anxiety. I taught myself breathing techniques because I didn't want to feel like that again."

She nods once. "Do you still get them?"

"No. I only got them a few months after her death. It's been a while since I felt like that."

"Thank you for being honest with me about her," she whispers.

I tilt my head towards her with a frown. "What do you mean?"

Ava looks away with a shrug. "She was a big part of your life, but when I ask you things, you talk about her. You don't keep that part of your life from me. It's nice to know you're transparent about it. Your life isn't a secret."

"I don't keep any secrets from you, Ava."

"I know."

I lean over to kiss the crown of her head. "Tell me something."

"Like what?" She looks at me.

"Something. Anything. Now that you remember your past, I'd love to hear whatever you're willing to share."

Ava sucks in a deep breath. "Okay," she hums. "When I was seven, I entered a talent contest at school. It was the Christmas show, so I did a dance to 'Rockin' Around the Christmas Tree'. I honestly thought it was great, the best thing I had ever choreographed. The prizes were given out, and I won nothing but a good-effort medal. I cried for a week."

A small chuckle passes my lips. "That's sweet. I would have loved to see the footage."

"Oh, there was no footage." She shakes her head. "My foster parents at the time were too busy with all the other kids they took in. I'm sure they turned up late and missed my performance anyway."

The thought makes my heart strain. She never had a loving family growing up.

"Were all your foster parents like that?"

Her head shakes. "Not all. Some. I never understood why we couldn't stay in one place for longer than six months."

"Tell me something else."

"I'm quite fond of spiders," she blurts.

My eyes widen in surprise. "Really?"

"Yeah. A kid brought his pet tarantula to school one time, and I asked to hold it. It was pretty cute. Its name was Kinsey. I remember because I looked at it and thought, 'How can anyone be afraid of this adorable spider called Kinsey?'"

"And now you love them?"

Ava snorts quietly. "I wouldn't say I *love* them, but I'm not terrified of them like other people are. I will happily place them outside if they're in the house. Some people kill them, but they're good for our ecosystem."

I grin at her. "That was totally unexpected."

"Please don't gift me a tarantula any time soon, that is not what I'm suggesting."

A deep laugh rumbles from my chest. "Noted. No spiders for birthdays or Christmas." I stroke my hand over her shoulder in soothing motions. "Are you feeling better now?"

"Yes." She nods. "I like feeling calmer with you like this.

Sometimes when you're in my head, it's very intense with everything else going on."

I press my lips to her forehead. "I'm sorry. I should ask before I make things worse. I trust our bond, but I realise it isn't always what you need."

"I'd prefer that," she whispers gratefully, then sighs. "I don't want to close my eyes and slip back into that dream again."

"Will you let me project images into your mind instead?"

"So you were doing that, too?"

My lips quirk to the side. "I did it at the start when you had your nightmares and you wouldn't let me near you. It was the only way I knew how to calm you because hearing your screams killed me."

"It helped a lot," she admits. "I didn't fear sleeping as much."

"Good. Will you let me tonight?"

"Please." She looks at me with grateful eyes. "But what about you?"

"The bond will keep them going while I fall asleep." *Although I know I won't.*

Ava flicks her eyes between mine slowly. "Are you sure?"

"Positive, baby." I wrap her up in my arms and pull her body on top of my chest. "I'm not going anywhere. Remember that. Now, close your eyes and let me help you sleep."

Her eyelids flutter shut on command and there is a soft smile on her face. I watch her for a few moments before flashing images of golden beaches and shimmering lakes through our bond.

I wait until she's fast asleep and then stroke back her hair with my fingers.

"Goodnight, my love."

41

JAXON

Ava's strength over the last few weeks has improved vastly, and I can see the drive in her eyes when she joins in with pack training. At first, she was apprehensive, but now, she's in her element.

I stand back and watch as she runs through the trees. She digs her fingers into a large boulder before climbing to the top and jumping down onto a smaller rock. Her feet move quickly and every choice she makes is with precision.

Sweat trickles down her back and off the edge of her jaw. I adore seeing her like this—with focused eyes and eager to outdo herself from the last training session. She's pushing herself out of her comfort zone and challenging her body with new skills.

Kayden guides Ava through her obstacle course while encouraging her as she succeeds in every direction. She starts to climb a tree before swinging from a branch and landing directly in the middle of a stream. The water splashes up her legs, and she takes a large breath as her lips spread into a bright grin.

"Yes, Ava!" Kayden claps loudly. "I told you you could do it. That was fast as hell."

She releases a long laugh and places a hand on her hip. "Thanks," she rasps. "I tried."

Lucy cheers alongside her, raising her arms in the air to clap with Kayden. "My Goddess, you are literally incredible. Your stamina is out of this world, Ava."

That smile remains on Ava's face as she nods. Her skin is flushed, but I see the pride burning in her eyes. Kayden gently pats her on the back. "Don't push it anymore," he warns her. "Take tomorrow off. Rest. Your muscles need time to repair."

She frowns. "But I like training."

"Alright, teacher's pet." He releases a laugh with a subtle wink. "You might be one of my best students, but you're coming off a little needy, and it's not a good look."

Kayden's playfulness makes Ava shove his shoulder. "Needy, my ass."

He laughs. "But seriously, you need to rest, and I personally don't want Jaxon beheading me for burning you into the ground. You did good, but I'm looking for a personal best next time."

"A personal best? You said that was fast!"

He shrugs teasingly. "Could be a smidge faster."

She rolls her eyes. "Alright, fine. Next time. You're on."

"You're on." He holds a hand out to her, and she shakes it. "Thank you for training with me."

"Thank you for not killing me," she says with a smile.

"We've always got next time." He points a finger at her.

I narrow my eyes at my Beta as he chuckles deeply. "No jokes about death, please. Thanks," I murmur.

Kayden tuts with a smug smile. "Spoilsport."

Lucy flashes Ava a thumbs up before she turns with

Kayden to start walking in the direction of the house. I step closer to her as she looks up at me, her chest returning to a gentle rise.

"I'm proud of you," I state simply.

"Me, too. I want to do well for the pack."

I fold my arms over my chest. "Ava, you have nothing to prove. To them. To me. To anyone. You should be doing this for yourself, not for anyone else."

"I am." She nods. "But I'd like your pack to look at me with at least a bit of hope."

My hand stretches to take her chin between my thumb and index finger. "Trust me, they're impressed. We're all impressed. I love your drive and determination and the fact you always show up for yourself. It is so damn attractive, and I'm lucky to have you as my Luna."

A deep pink blush bursts across her cheeks. "I'm lucky to have you, too."

"Since you came here, I can sense there is a new atmosphere within the pack."

"Good or bad?"

"Good, of course."

Ava smiles to herself. "How so?"

"I guess I might have been a little harsh on my pack, even before Julia. When I became Alpha, I was thrown into it. I wasn't a very good leader, but with you by my side, things seem clearer. For the first time, I feel like we're really forming together as a pack, and I believe that's down to you."

"You can't give me all the credit." She shakes her head.

I shrug once. "Things have shifted since I met you, and it's obvious in the satisfaction of the pack. Not only did you help me get my wolf back, but you also integrate yourself into the pack where you can, you want to help others, and you want to learn about our culture. We all see it and appreciate your efforts."

"Well, it's clear they enjoy seeing their Alpha more," Ava says. "Respect goes both ways. You knew you weren't giving them your all while you were grieving, and you decided to turn that around. You've worked hard to prove to your pack you're going to be the best you can from now on."

I nod. "Agreed. I never want to let them down again. I never want to let you down either."

"You could never let me down."

My lips meet the top of her head.

"Can I ask you a question?" she asks.

We both start walking back to the house, the sun glittering through the trees. "You don't need to ask." I laugh softly.

"Oh, well." Her throat tenses. "I know you've told me briefly before, but to officially be Luna, we need to mate with each other?"

"Technically, yes. But together, we can decide what it truly means."

She licks her lips. "And the mating process, we have to–"

The words die in her throat as she speaks, and I slip my hand into hers, gripping onto her fingers tightly. "Whenever you're ready. There is no rush. And if you don't want to, then we won't."

"And you mark me?"

"Yes."

"Like actually biting into my neck with your teeth?" Her eyes widen.

I release a low chuckle. "Yes."

Ava runs a hand along her neck, touching the delicate skin. "Really?"

"It's normally incredibly pleasurable. You would mark me, too."

She turns towards me as we continue walking. "How can I mark you if I'm not a wolf?"

"I don't know," I admit. "But we can work something out, I promise. I'll do my research and make sure whatever we do, it's safe for you. I would never want to put you in danger. I don't know how your human body would take a mark from a wolf, and I don't want to put you at any kind of risk."

"I know. I trust you."

Those three words set my world alight in the best way. I give her fingers a squeeze before bringing them up to my lips for a kiss. "Good," I whisper against her skin with a smile.

Once we get closer to the pack house, I spot Evan sitting outside with his two guards. He's staring down at the patio floor with his shoulders slumped. "There's Evan," Ava comments, spotting him at the same time. "How's he settling in?"

I shrug. "I don't know."

Ava shoots me a look. "What do you mean you don't know?"

"I told the guards to look after him. I've got more important things to deal with."

She walks ahead of me. "Let's invite him for lunch."

"Ava," I call out to her as she looks over her shoulder at me.

"I'm capable of making my own choices, Jax," she murmurs. "I owe him my life. I want to get to know him better."

Before I can protest, she approaches him and invites him inside for some food. At first, he's concerned by the offer, but soon accepts and they walk into the kitchen.

I follow and glance at the situation. "Come take a seat, Evan." Ava pats one of the stools. His emotionless blue eyes flick to her hand before he sits down hesitantly. "How are you today?"

"I'm okay, thanks." He looks lost as his hands fumble in his lap.

Ava's eyes cut to mine and widen subtly. I sigh and turn to the guards before dismissing them while he's having lunch with us. If it makes Ava happy, then I guess I'll have to deal with it.

"I know what happened with your pack...but do you have any other family?" she asks him.

Evan shakes his head slowly. "I don't."

Ava's lips curve downwards. "I'm sorry for what happened to them."

"He deserved it. They deserved it. You don't need to apologise. What they did was unforgivable, and they belong in hell." His words are sharp.

"I know," Ava whispers. "But he was still your family."

His mouth presses together, but he doesn't say anything more. "I'm glad I'm not there with him anymore, but at the same time, I have nothing."

"You have us now, Evan." Ava offers.

I turn to her with a puzzled look. *What are you doing?*

Her face falls into a frown, but she still doesn't look at me. *He saved my life, Jaxon. The least we can do is help him. Did you not hear him? He has nothing, no one. He's innocent. I know you're playing the protective mate, but he is not dangerous.*

I'm not playing anything. I am the protective mate. I'm sorry if it comes across as overbearing, but I can't dissociate him from his brother as easily as you expect me, I shoot back, and she finally meets my gaze.

"That's a nice thing to say, Ava, but I don't want to be a burden." He forces a sorrowful smile.

Her head shakes. "You would never be a burden. Where would you even go?"

Evan shrugs after thinking for a moment. His home is destroyed. He has nothing. A pang of guilt hits my chest, but I still have my walls up just in case. I'm not taking any chances.

"How old are you, Evan?"

"Seventeen."

I merely nod before joining Ava at the counter. We start preparing lunch as I listen to Ava make small talk with Evan, but he's quiet and doesn't say much back. I imagine myself in his shoes—the isolation, loneliness, and fear of not knowing where you belong.

Ava places down a sandwich in front of him as we sit around the kitchen counter. *Talk to him,* she urges me.

I sigh and chew on my food. *And what would I say?*

I dunno. Guy stuff?

My brow quirks in her direction. *Guy stuff, huh? And what would that entail?*

I don't know. Make something up. Please.

She stares me down, but I smile back at her with amusement.

"So, Evan," I say, my voice catching both of them by surprise. "Do you have a mate?"

"No. I don't."

I study his face and glum expression. "Oh. That's a shame. I'm sure she'll come along soon."

Evan clears his throat and looks to Ava. "Actually, I–" He pauses and pinches the bridge of his nose with his fingers. "I don't want to be mated to a girl."

"What?"

"I'm–" he sighs as if he can't get the words out. "I'm gay."

Oh, Goddess. I'm hit with a wave of regret for assuming.

"Oh," I murmur quickly.

"Yeah..." he trails off and itches the back of his head. "I hope that's okay with you guys. I never told Lucien because I knew what they would have done to me, but things are different here, and I don't want to hide anymore. I'm tired of pretending to be someone I'm not."

Tears glisten in his eyes, and Ava leans over to take his hand. "We support everyone and anyone here. Whoever they like, love, want to be with, that's none of anyone else's business," Ava states with sincere eyes. "Thank you for feeling comfortable enough to share it with us."

"This is completely different to the hellhole you saved me from," he sniffles. "I know I have restrictions here, but I've never felt freer."

Ava's chest quivers, and I look at her. Okay, maybe I've been too harsh on the poor kid. Maybe he deserves a new start. He's only seventeen—he's got his whole life ahead of him.

"I'll take away the guards," I blurt. "You can have more freedom within the house, but I'll assign someone to watch over you."

"Who?" Ava asks.

I chew on my lip for a moment. "Sam. Sam can look after you. He owes me."

Evan blinks and a tear rolls down his cheek before he wipes it away. "Thank you," he mumbles. "I will do whatever I can to help out. Anything you need. I will be here. Thank you again, Alpha."

I nod at him and point to his half-eaten sandwich. "Finish your lunch. You need nourishment."

He immediately digs in, and Ava beams at me from

across the counter. *Thank you,* she mindlinks me. *He needs us.*

One slip up and he's gone.

I know. He deserves a chance to change his life.

My eyes cut back to Evan as he munches on his sandwich with a relieved smile on his face. I exhale a quiet sigh. I never thought I'd be taking in a homeless rogue, but it's Ava who is making me softer by the day. This is one of the reasons I need her by my side. She balances me out. But at the same time, I hope nothing happens that will make me regret this.

42

AVA

I've been in desperate need of a girly day out with Lucy for weeks—anything to get out of the pack house for a breather. A little retail therapy and some overpriced smoothies. I adore Lucy's company. Even when she's bossy with our itinerary.

Everything is going perfect, until Jaxon's panicked voice floods my mind urging us to come home. Apparently his guards are on the way to meet us. He doesn't explain what's going on, he says he'll tell me when we get back. An unsettling feeling swirls in my stomach.

Now I'm filled with dread.

"Lucy!" I yell across the packed market.

Her blonde hair flips over her shoulder with a beaming smile. "We're going to miss it," she murmurs. "Come on."

This place is heaving. I never knew there would be hundreds of stalls and even more people coming down to buy all sorts of arts, crafts, and different animals strung up by their feet.

"Lucy, wait." I push through the crowd. "Jaxon."

"What about Jaxon?"

"He said we need to go home. I don't know why. Something isn't right."

Lucy flashes me a puzzled look. "He probably just misses you, Ava. Insufferable asshole. How dare he ruin our girl time. I knew he'd pull something like this."

"No." I shake my head. "I could hear the worry in his voice. Please. He said he's sending the guards to get us home. I don't think we should be here."

Her lips press into a flat line. "Fine, but–"

The crowd in front of us erupts into deafening screams. We flinch and turn to the sound before people start running, pushing, and shoving. An elbow collides into my back, and I hiss as I fall into a table full of fresh produce.

"Ava!" Lucy yells as we're split up between the sea of people running.

The hairs on the back of my neck begin to stand, and panic rushes through my veins. What is happening? I twist around to find Lucy, but she's gone, and I'm being pushed. My feet rise from the floor.

A distressed shriek escapes my lips as I'm directed towards a narrow path and then pressed up against a brick wall. My arm is scratched as I'm squished between a bunch of strangers and someone's house.

The stampede only gets worse, and I slip down an alleyway before I'm crushed to death. I swallow down the bile in my throat and press a hand to my chest.

I glance down the dark and gloomy alley. "Crap," I murmur to myself.

When I turn back to the rush of people, something is wrapped around my neck, and I'm shoved backwards. I exhale a long scream for a hand to slap over my mouth. I kick and struggle against the weight that is pulling me away from the market.

"Shh, sweetheart," they coo, but I don't recognise the voice. "You're not going anywhere."

My teeth clamp around the flesh on their fingers to find the taste of their salty sweat on my tongue. Blood seeps into my mouth, and they hiss, dropping their hand for a second. "Ah. You fucking bitch."

My body twists, and I step back as quickly as possible. I stare at the man I've never seen before. He's huge, bulky. His arms are practically the size of his legs. I have two seconds to decide where to run before he catches me.

I don't think. I run in the opposite direction.

The crowd of the market is still rushing by in heaps, not knowing which way to run. As I reach the end of the alleyway, I gulp when another man steps into view. "Nice try," he snarls. "But you're ours now."

My head shakes vigorously. "Screw you."

"Sure thing." He grins before flashing me his gold-capped teeth.

I step back to find an arm being wrapped around my chest tightly. I gasp for air as I watch the guy in front of me take out a syringe with the largest needle I've ever seen. My elbow wriggles from his grip, and I jab his ribs as hard as I can. The man buckles, and I lurch forward, breaking free. Without hesitation, I turn and punch him, using all the techniques Jax has taught me during training.

Blood bursts over his lips as he staggers into the wall, and I begin running.

Loud footsteps behind me make me cower. I have nowhere to go.

Shit. Shit. Shit.

My fingers tingle as I look between the pair of them, backing myself towards the stampede of the alley. "Get back here," the man with the needle spits.

I push myself into the crowded market, only to be pulled back a second later. I release a loud scream, and my body's instincts take over as I kick and struggle as fiercely as I can.

"Fuck sake," one of them grunts before his fist lands against my cheek.

Pain explodes, and I slump until I see the syringe inch closer to my exposed neck. "Wait," I cry and attempt to fight my way out of his hold. "No."

He swings it directly into my neck, and I scream out in agony. "That's it," he whispers against my ear as he empties the syringe. "Go to sleep. You're going to need the rest for what we've got in store."

The next second, my entire body slumps. I stare at the man who watches my strength deteriorate. Suddenly, I start seeing two of him, my vision deceiving me. "Close your eyes."

I fight. I fight as hard as I can to stay conscious, but my limbs won't cooperate.

My eyelids fall heavy, and I hate my body for betraying me. I inhale a breath, but I'm completely numb. I slip through his grip to the floor, and darkness consumes my mind.

∼

THERE'S an ache inside my skull that jolts me awake with a groan. I attempt to open my heavy eyes, but it's nearly impossible. My entire body is numb, but the pain thumping against my head is very much alive.

I eventually pry my eyes open and glance around but don't recognise my surroundings. My skin is littered with goosebumps as a light draft whips past my chest.

My hands are chained to a pillar with large metal

clamps around my wrists. I lift my arm, but it weighs a tonne, and I have zero energy. I take a couple of deep breaths and try to regain my full consciousness—whatever they injected me with, it was strong.

I drag my tongue along my bottom lip, but it's as dry as a desert. My throat closes, and I release a cough as I try to swallow. Instead, I start gasping. "Oh, fuck," I murmur to myself, blinking through the fog that clouds my head. I need to get my shit together. I need to get the hell out of here.

The room is empty.

After a few moments of gathering at least two thoughts, I start tugging on the chains, but there's no way I'd be able to break through them. I don't possess that kind of strength.

No. No. No. No.

I shake my head over and over. This isn't happening again. This can't be happening. Tears build in my eyes, but I refuse to let them fall.

The door to the grimy room opens, and I twist my head to the sound, backing into the pillar. I stare at the woman as she steps inside. My heart stops in my chest. Her eyes level with mine, blonde ponytail swishing behind her like a runway model and bright red lipstick drawn over her mouth. Tanned skin. I've never seen her face to face, but I remember seeing her photograph.

I pale at the sight of her. Julia. *Julia.*

43

JAXON

While Ava is out with Lucy having a girls' afternoon, I take the time to catch up on work. There is a committee meeting next month, and I'm desperate to have everything done before then.

I run my fingers along my forehead as I read through the latest regulations for our district. I note down any questions I wish to raise when all the Alphas meet together.

A knock at my office door stirs me from my train of thought. I clear my throat. "Come in," I demand as I twirl my pen between my fingers.

"Alpha." Sam's voice is hurried as he steps into the room. "Your shields have been up. I've been trying to mindlink you."

"I've been busy focusing on work."

"I need to tell you something."

I sigh. "What is it, Sam?"

"Alpha Jaxon, when I tell you this, I need you to hear me out." He steps towards my desk, and I lean back in my chair, already losing patience. "I know this is going to sound crazy, but you need to believe me."

My teeth grind together. "For Goddess's sake. What is it, Sam?"

I drop my pen onto my desk and fold my arms over my chest, quirking a brow in frustration. There is a look of distress that crosses his eyes before he closes them. and when he opens them again, he shudders. "After training with Evan, Kayden and I took him into town to show him around, and we–" He pauses to drag a hand down his face. "We saw someone."

"Who?"

"Alpha, I know this is going to sound crazy–"

"Who, Sam?" My voice bellows across my office.

He gulps once. "Julia. We saw Julia. She's still alive."

No.

No.

No.

My blood runs ice cold. There is no chance. I saw the life leave her eyes. I watched as she was murdered by those rogues in the most brutal attack. I saw limbs. I saw blood. I heard her scream for her life.

For long moments, I say nothing. Processing. It's impossible.

I stand from my desk on shaky legs. "That can't be," I state with confidence. "I saw her die. I was there when she died. There is no chance she could still be alive."

Sam holds up his hands. "I know this sounds insane, but it was her. I swear on my life."

"Where is Kayden?" I heave.

"With Evan. They're coming now."

I lick my bottom lip. "It can't be her. You must be seeing things."

"Alpha–"

Kayden steps into my office a second later, his eyes

flicking over my expression—I presume to see how I've taken the bullshit news. It can't be true. How can it be true? I'd know if she was alive. I'd feel the bond.

Wouldn't I?

"You saw Julia?" My voice wobbles despite the heaviness of my chest.

Kayden's dark eyes find mine as he nods. "Yeah. It was her."

I stare at my Beta. Those words coming from his mouth makes my back turn rigid. My lungs constrict. He would never lie to me. He's my second-in-command who I trust more than anyone in this pack.

My throat tightens around a ball of wariness.

"Did you speak to her?"

"No, we didn't get close enough to speak to her."

There is no way this is happening.

"I have to see her," I blurt. "I need to know if this is real. I need to know what the fuck is going on and why I didn't know a thing about it."

My wolf is on edge, and I have to clench my fists to stop myself from shifting.

"Jaxon." Kayden steps forward. "You need to listen to us."

"What?" I snap. "What else do I need to listen to? You come in here and tell me my first mate is alive after being dead for over a year? Tell me how any of this makes any fucking sense!"

All the air in the room seems to have evaporated, and I'm barely holding on by a thread. I run a hand through my hair and grip the roots. No. This must be some misunderstanding.

"Something was off," Kayden's voice levels with mine. "She was with a few men we've never seen in town or the district before. She looks different. I didn't get welcoming vibes from her at all."

"Something was off?" I repeat with a scoff. "What does that even mean?"

"Well, why would she fake her own death?" Sam shouts over me. "If she was still alive, wouldn't you be the first person she came to? This isn't adding up, Jaxon. None of it is. You would have felt something. Don't you think?"

Sam's words trigger something inside me. My wolf hasn't even flinched, and I would have felt something. If she was still alive, she'd come back for me. She knows where to find me. She knows how devastated I would have been.

My hands tremble with the need to smash my fist into something. I can't grasp this situation. I can't grasp my emotions. But something settles in my stomach like an anchor. This can't be right.

Why hasn't she come to see me?

A million questions fly through my mind, and I itch my head, but it doesn't relieve anything. I'm bound by dread and panic. This doesn't make sense.

I can't ignore the way my wolf is clawing at the idea of being with Julia's wolf again. But that's only because he's heard this information, not because of feeling her. Instead, we both feel *nothing*.

I hate the guilt that crashes over my sternum.

My entire life has changed in the last few months. The grief I endured to meet the most courageous and wonderful woman. We helped each other out of our darkest times. We found peace within our sanctuary of one another. Our safe space.

"Something didn't feel right," Sam says, snapping me back into the room.

"Did she see you?"

Kayden shakes his head. "She was gone in a flash. We couldn't get to her."

"Shit," I rasp.

"And you've felt nothing?" Sam asks.

I shake my head. Nothing. Not even a twitch or an inkling she could be alive.

"Where is Ava?" Kayden asks suddenly.

"Out with Lucy."

Sam and Kayden share a glance. "In town?"

My throat tightens. "Fuck."

All of this must be a coincidence. A stupid, unbelievable mix-up. Nothing more.

Ava, are you okay?

Yeah. We're just in town. Lucy's been—

I'm washed with reassurance when I hear her delicate voice.

Leave. Now, I cut over her.

What? Why?

Please don't ask any questions. I need you to get home as soon as possible. I'll explain everything then.

There is immediate panic through our bond. *Jaxon, you're scaring me.*

I clench my fists and order guards to escort them home from town. I refuse to take any chances, especially when I have no idea what's going on. *Baby, please just listen to me. Leave town. Come home. I've sent guards. I need you here with me right this second.*

Okay. Her voice is shaky.

I close my eyes, but I won't rest until she's home. My head spins in different directions, but I know the bond I've grown with Ava over the last few months shines above it all.

A wave of nausea strangles me, an eerie sensation creeping up through my spine. "Once Ava is home and I know she's safe, we're going to get answers."

"Yes, Alpha." They both nod.

44

AVA

No. This can't be real. I must be dead. There is no explanation.

A smirk covers Julia's lips as she stops in front of me, a freshly manicured hand on her hip. "Well, well..." Her voice echoes around the derelict room. "What do we have here?"

I remain silent, flicking my eyes between hers sharply. My pulse pounds against my neck, and I clench my hands together to stop them from trembling around the chains.

She bends down to my level and analyses my face. "A human," she exhales with a sour laugh. "That makes this a thousand times better. I thought Jaxon's mate would be a warrior, an Alpha's daughter, or a legacy. But no, she's nothing but a worthless human with no strength whatsoever."

What's going on? My head spins.

"What do you want from me, Julia?"

Her eyes flare at me. "Ah, I'm relieved you know who I am. Jaxon talks about me, huh?"

My jaw clenches at her patronising tone. The drugs that pump around my system are forcing bile up my throat, but I push it down before I show how weak and terrified I am. I'm tired of being the fragile girl who needs saving.

"Jaxon said you died."

"I did," she sighs and inspects her blood-red fingernails. "Well...that's what he thinks. This has been going on for three years too long."

I narrow my eyes at her. "What is going on? I don't understand what's happening here."

Julia throws her head back and releases a loud cackle. "Oh, Ava," she coos. "How stupid could you be? You think I was Jaxon's first mate? I wasn't his mate at all."

I blink in confusion. "What?"

"I had a spell cast on Jaxon and spent years trying to infiltrate myself into his life, family, and pack. I had myself killed in front of him and the make-belief spell left his poor heart broken." Her evil lips curl into a smug smile.

My arms begin to tremble. No. This can't be real.

Julia's eyes flicker over my face slowly. "Oh! And don't think I forgot about you. I couldn't have you getting in the way of my mission. I had a spell cast on you, too, and then I directed you to the vilest creatures to ever exist. I hoped they would break you, but they didn't. You had to run straight into Jaxon. That's why I had to intervene."

I lower my gaze and tell myself not to throw up. She had something to do with my capture from Lucien? Fuck. Fuck. I release a low grumble, and she continues to laugh at me.

"Ow, look how cute you are when you get angry. No wonder Jaxon fell head over heels for someone as pretty as you." She leans forward to drag one of her talons across my cheek. "But I'll give it to you, I'm surprised you survived that hellhole. I've seen the way they treat women, and I know it's not pleasant."

My wrists tug at the chains. "Fuck you."

Julia gasps. "Now. Now. That's no fun, is it?"

"Why would you do this?"

"Because revenge is best served ice-fucking-cold."

I pull back and shake my head. "How could a spell be powerful enough to mess with a true mate bond? The Moon Goddess cannot be manipulated."

Julia cackles unattractively. "Witches are incredibly powerful. They've been crafting for centuries. There is always some kind of loophole, and I'm lucky I found my way in. It took me a while to find a witch who had the abilities to find you through Jaxon's soul—even if none of us knew who you were. I convinced him it was fortune telling; instead, it was a con to get inside that heart of his to find you."

My throat burns from the dryness. How is that possible?

"The second she sensed you, she bound you to Lucien by false pretences. It took weeks. *Weeks.* But it was worth every damn second." Her eyes grow darker. "I even had to chance my luck by taking a sample of his hair for the ritual."

I clench my jaw so tightly it creaks. "I don't believe whatever Jaxon did made you do all of this and waste years of your life."

"Do you know what I had to sacrifice for those spells? I had to give up my wolf, and I didn't do that lightly." She takes a fistful of my jacket and yanks my face to hers. A whimper falls from my lips. "You are not in any position to judge. You didn't lose what I did. We don't forgive and forget; we get even. Now, we're finishing with you."

Before I can say anything in response, she raises her fingers and backhands me across the face. The blow was so quick that I didn't have a chance to blink. The taste of copper fills my mouth, and I stare at her through my hair that's fallen over my eyes.

"The drugs should be wearing off now. Mindlink Jaxon

and tell him you're at the derelict building up on High River Way. Tell him to come alone, otherwise, I'll gut you the second he goes back on his word." Her nose twitches. "And I know he'll do anything to keep his precious human mate safe. I know exactly how protective he is."

I shake my head. "No."

Those icy-blue eyes harden at my simple statement. "Excuse me?" she roars before smacking me again. I groan, my head falling to the side. Her werewolf strength stings, but I'm not going to let Jaxon end up in this mess. It's a trap. She'll kill us both. I know we're not alone. Those two big guys from the market are most likely hanging around and possibly more. "Do it now, you stupid cunt."

Her hand fists into the back of my hair as she scrunches up her face in pure disgust. I grunt in pain when she tugs at the roots, ripping some of the pieces from my scalp. "I said do it now," she yells as blood trickles down my chin. "Or I will make this worse for you, for everyone. You don't want me killing Lucy, Sebastian, and Kayden. All I want is Jaxon. So mindlink him. *Now!*"

Jesus. I trust she's crazy. I also trust she'll kill anyone in her path to get to Jaxon. My jaw aches from how tight I'm biting down. I'll never live with myself knowing the rest of them got hurt.

I push into the bond that's been masked by the drugs in my system. *Jax...*

Baby, where the hell are you? Are you okay? Are you hurt? Tell me where you are, please.

My eyes hold Julia's stare. *I don't know if you're going to believe this, but it's Julia. She's got me. She's still alive. She's wanting revenge.*

Fuck. Are you okay? Are you hurt?

Yes.

To which question? Fuck, Ava. Don't do this to me. Are you hurt?

No. I'm okay. She wants you to come to the derelict building by High River Way. She says to come alone. If you don't she'll kill me. But it's a set-up. She'll kill us both. She has other people here, too. She's insane. Don't buy into it.

Jaxon scoffs, but it sounds like he's about to lose his mind. *If you think for one damn second I am not coming to get you, then you've got another thing coming.*

She'll kill us both.

No. She's not going to stand a chance. I promise. Hang in there, baby. I told you I wouldn't let anything happen to you, and I am sticking by my word. You hear me?

My lips tremble. I wish he was here now. *Yes.*

I tilt my head towards her. "It's done."

A look of triumph covers her face before she grabs me by the throat and shoves me. My skull hits the pillar behind with a loud whack. I breathe through my nose, but I don't release a sound. She studies my face and then pouts before standing up, her fingers pressing to her mouth as she whistles.

The two men from the market step in, followed by two more. I flick my weary gaze between the five of them. "Let's roughen her up." Julia taps a finger against her lips. "We want Jaxon to be in the worst pain possible."

My throat clenches in fear as they crowd around me. The first punch knocks me onto my side, and I feel the coldness of the ground scraping against my cheek. All of the adrenaline in my body masks the pain, but when the next blow comes, I wheeze in misery.

I despise the sound of Julia's heinous laugh. She stands back and watches the show with her arms folded over her chest, those dark eyes lighting up with amusement. I spit blood from my mouth onto the ground only to be punched in the stomach.

My body folds over, and I groan, tears releasing from my eyes.

I take hit after hit until I'm numb and non-responsive to their violence. Julia whistles again, and they back away. I shudder and glance up at the wicked woman through hazy eyes.

"Think that'll do." She smirks. "For now."

My ribs ache when I attempt to move, and blood invades my tastebuds. Bruises are already forming across my arms and legs. "Aw, come on," the largest man grumbles. "We barely got a chance to see her break."

Julia rolls her eyes. "She's human, Pike. If we do any more damage now, we risk killing the pathetic being. We've still got the main act to come. I know you're hungry for some real blood."

"Bones and limbs more like." Pike flashes her a grin through his tangled beard. "This better be worth it."

"Don't worry." Julia pats his shoulder before focusing her eyes on mine. "It'll be worth all of your precious time. Jaxon losing everything twice? It's like music to my ears."

45

AVA

Blood drips down my lips and over my chin, and my throat tenses like I'm breathing through a straw. Pike glares at me from across the dimly lit room, his fingers itching to get in another punch, but Julia wants to keep me alive.

The past few minutes have felt like hours, but I know Jaxon should be here any second. He won't let me down—not after his declaration. But by the looks of these five evil wolves, I fear he won't make it out either. What if he comes alone and she hurts him? I didn't want him to get into this—not when I can take the fall.

Julia releases a long sigh at the ceiling. "How long does it take?"

I pray he's making a plan, stalling. He wouldn't be careless about this situation; he'd think it through like a headstrong Alpha. I know he cares about my safety, but if he makes one mistake it could cost us both our lives.

There is a warmth in my brain, wrapping around my aching nerves in a soothing motion. I smile down at the ground, trying to conceal it before Julia sees. Jaxon can feel my pain, and he's taking it away. He's silently reminding me he's here, and I'm not alone. Tears swim in my eyes, but it's not from what I've endured; it's from knowing our bond is strong enough to coax me through this nightmare.

"Why don't we see if we can make her cry again?" Pike flashes another devilish grin.

Julia rolls her eyes and swats her hand into his broad chest. "No. Stop getting ahead of yourself. This is my plan. No one else's. Don't ruin it before it's even begun. What did I promise you all?"

My gaze follows Pike's as his shoulders dip and he nods. "I remember."

She walks towards me in long, purposeful strides before I look up at her through my blackened eyes and blood-smeared face. My pain is numbed, but that's because Jaxon is here with me mentally.

"I wonder," she slides her sharp nail over her lips, "how much would it take to break you? If you survived Lucien, then your fight must be better than I imagined."

My eye twitches at the mention of his name. Julia's face brightens, and I despise myself for reacting. "Oh..." She trails off. "Is that a trigger for you? Lucien?"

"No," I spit.

"What did they do to you? Hmm, poor little Ava. I knew exactly what that man was capable of, and I directed you straight to him. It's amazing what a little magic can cause."

My nostrils flare at the tone of her imperious voice. "They taught me to build resilience against people like you."

Julia releases a loud laugh. "Did you build resilience when they raped and abused you?"

"Shut up," I hiss through my teeth.

That word. *That* word.

My stomach gurgles, and I press a hand to my neck to keep the bile back.

She sinks down to my level again and gives me a once-over. "Did they ravish you, Ava? Did they make you scream and cry? Did they make you wish you were dead?"

I ball my hands into fists that are bound to the chains. "Fuck you, Julia."

"Oh, I hit a little nerve." She wipes her hand over her blonde hair. "Do they still haunt your dreams? I bet you can't get away from them, no matter how hard you try, because you'll always be nothing but a useless, pathetic fuck doll."

My jaw clamps down as darkness clouds my mind. I'm fuelled by deep hatred and fire that roars in my soul. "I'm not pathetic," I seethe. "I'm not useless."

"No? You haven't stopped to think that Jaxon needs a Luna that is strong and powerful. You are neither of those things, and you're kidding yourself if you believe he's going to stick around for you. He's in the honeymoon phase, and it'll wear off." She releases a morbid sigh. "Once the bond settles and he realises you have nothing of worth to bring to the pack, the relationship, or his life, he'll drop you faster than you can blink."

A heaviness sits on my chest. "You're lying," I snarl, my voice ten notches deeper than it usually is. "You're trying to fuck with my head. I'm not falling for your manipulation."

"Mmm, am I?" She slides her lips together. "Do you know what Jaxon used to tell me?"

My throat releases a growl that comes out of nowhere. I don't shake my head or speak. She's going to tell me anyway, and I have no choice but to listen.

"He told me I am the love of his life." She claps a hand over her heart and wipes away fake tears. "He told me I am the most beautiful girl he's ever laid his eyes on. He told me that nothing and *no one* could replace me—no matter who came after me, they'd never compare."

I attempt to calm my shaking body, but I can't. I'm trembling all over in red-hot rage. My eyes flick down to her throat, and I want to rip it out and tear off her head. Then, I'll cut open her stomach and empty out her insides until her intestines are splattered everywhere.

"That I have the most perfect body, perfect lips, perfect face," she carries on, and my vision becomes blurry and unfocused. "That the sex we have is out of this world. That he loves the way I taste. That he loves to make *love* to me."

My mouth opens to release a scream in her face, but she only snickers in response. The blood inside me turns to lava, and my fingernails begin to claw at the ground in desperation. It takes over my body with anguish. It's electrifying and foreign all at once.

"Look how upset you're getting." She stares back at me with wild eyes. "Don't like hearing that I am the best he'll ever have? You're nothing but a side piece he has to entertain, otherwise, the bond will actually kill him."

"Fuck you," I yell. "Fuck you. Fuck you. *Fuck you.*"

A wheeze falls from my throat. It's rough and husky. My body doesn't feel like mine—every instinct I have makes me want to act out of character. Julia stands and turns her back on me, peering over her shoulder with a slick smirk.

"The second he gets here," she sways her hips, "is the second I destroy everything in his pathetic little life."

A noise I never knew I could make escapes my throat. My spine straightens at the same time my neck snaps in a fashion that makes my eyes water and a scream erupt into the room. The chains from my wrist burst open as my arms bend and crack in positions I had no idea was possible.

The deep-rooted pain in my veins is almost unbearable. I can't see. I can't breathe. My throat aches from how loud I screech as my body warps and moves, and I'm left trying to catch up because my head is reeling.

My ears prick, and I hear, "Oh my Goddess." It's sharp against my eardrums. The vibrations make me wince at the heightened sensation.

I tilt my gaze down, and I'm met with paper-white paws. My eyes widen in fear and surprise. No. I must be dead. For real this time. I must be.

"Holy shit," Pike's voice is so loud I almost cower.

I raise my head in the air to find my back bending in an arch. My senses intensify; I can smell *everything*. The body odour from Pike's damp armpit stains, the sweet perfume on Julia's neck, and the murderous blood in my veins.

My claws spread against the floor, and I launch myself at Julia. The first instinct that takes over my new form is to attack. I don't know how to use this body, but I let it guide the way.

Pike pushes her out of reach, and I open my jaw to take a bite of whatever falls between my teeth. I clamp down on his shoulder as he attempts to push me off, and his blood swarms my mouth. It's a foul, bitter taste that invades my tongue, but it's the least of my worries when I hear his agonising screams. With all the strength I can gather, I tear his shoulder from his body without hesitation.

The two men shift into their wolves, while the other attempts to protect Julia. She's my target, but I'll take them all out. They will pay. They will see the wrath of my wolf and her years of suffering.

A growl vibrates through my nose as I stare back at the two dark brown wolves. I don't think. I attack. The adrenaline that pumps through my body encourages me to do what will keep me alive. Yet, there isn't a guilty bone in my body. I'm ready for the consequences, though not a single one has crossed my mind.

I'm not thinking logically; I'm thinking on impulse.

They both run towards me, paws grinding against the floor. I swerve out of the way at the last second but extend my front leg, claws flying from the tips of my paws. When I turn around, I swipe at the wolf closest to me, dragging my paw down his hind leg. Blood trickles down his fur towards his feet.

Their growls are vicious, but I act quick on my feet, ignoring their attempt at intimidation. I lunge forward to attack him again. I aim for the neck. One bite and his veins are spread across the floor with blood squirting in every direction. He stumbles back, but I'm already onto the next.

His jaw snaps in my direction, his teeth sinking into my side. I howl at the sharp twinge but kick him off with my legs. His body flies across the room. My bones sting from being in this form for the first time. I twist on my paws and dart towards him, despite my convulsing joints screaming at me for a break.

I let my canines do the damage. Blood drips everywhere, and I'm swarmed with the taste of copper. I rip and pull at his flesh, tearing his organs out one by one until there is nothing left and he takes his final breath.

My head glances around to find the three dead bodies, but I find Julia shortly after. She shoves the guy forward, and his clothes begin to rip as he shifts.

My snout twitches. Once I've taken him out, I'll have her all to myself.

He races towards me, but I meet him halfway. There isn't a single part of my mind that feels sane. My veins are overflowing with a desire for revenge, for blood, for their pain.

I'm so damn close.

We clash together and struggle on the floor. I try to press down on my legs, but his claws slip down my ribs. A pang of tenderness makes me howl. I move my paw and aim it towards his cheek, ripping off the flesh on his face with my sharp claws. My back scrapes against the uneven floor, and I kick my legs as hard as possible. He yelps when I wind him, knocking him onto his side.

My claws swipe and slash his face and neck until his eyes glass over with his expected fate. I keep going, even when his body lays still, trying to maintain the build-up of craze in my body. I step back and turn towards Julia, her perfume stronger than the stench of their rich blood.

I don't have time to blink. She's right behind me. Before I can claw her eyes out, she shoves her hand towards me. My gaze barely notices the reflection of the large knife in her hand. She plunges it deep in my abdomen.

Everything freezes for a long moment. The look on Julia's face is victorious. She releases the knife that's still deep inside me, and I stumble back. I hear my bones snap, but I'm desensitised to everything except my stomach.

My head rocks against the floor, and I groan, blood seeping out of my mouth. I shiver when I glance to find my bare human arm against the cold ground. Julia stands over me with pure hatred in her eyes.

"I wanted to wait for Jaxon," she huffs, sticking her tongue into her lip. "But I guess this will have to do. It'll still destroy him. You might be a wolf, but you're not strong enough to tear me down, too."

I raise my shaky hands to my wound and wince when she grabs onto the handle again. I stare at her as she shoves it deeper and twists. My throat closes around the blood flowing up my windpipe.

There is an urgent tapping against my head. Jaxon is trying to get in. But the torment my body has endured shut off our connection. My lips tremble, tears finally escaping my eyes. Julia bends down and smears her thumb across my cheek. "Poor baby," she pouts. "I can't wait to watch the light leave your eyes...and his, too."

My body wants to let go, but I force my mind to keep fighting. Jaxon will be here soon. I know it. Even if his face is the last I see, it'll be a sendoff worth waiting for.

46

JAXON

"Julia has her."

"What?" Kayden's face recoils.

I grind my teeth together so harshly the sound grates my ears. When Lucy lost Ava at the market, I went out of my damn mind, and the guards searched everywhere for her. Our mindlink connection was down, and when I heard her voice pop into my head, I wept with relief. But this is far from over.

"Julia has Ava. She said I need to go alone. She's wanting revenge," I state loudly. My wolf is on the edge of ripping through my skin. "Revenge for what, I don't know, but we need to make a plan. They're at High River Way."

Sam and Kayden share a glance before we get to work quickly. Within minutes, we have a solidified plan that will get my mate back where she belongs.

I need everyone in the grand hall. Now! I mindlink the entire pack.

The three of us approach the hall in a flash.

When the pack starts to filter into the room with urgency, I take down a few breaths to stabilise myself before

I lose control. My eyes scan the hall as Kayden and Lucy join my side.

"I need everyone to listen to me very carefully," I bellow and watch as everyone's attention focuses on me. The room turns deadly silent. "Ava is in trouble. *Our* future Luna is in trouble. Julia is alive, and she has my mate. She's planning on hurting her, but I won't stand for it. We need to get her to safety."

Whispers and gasps filter across the crowd. Lucy spares me a sympathetic glance and nods in encouragement. "I need back-up. I need all of you to pull your weight. I have no idea what we're up against, but I am bringing Ava home. Lucy, I need you to take the witches and cover our tracks and scents so we cannot be detected."

She nods in my direction. "Of course."

"I need you all to trust me. I need you all to fight for this pack. That's all I ask."

"Let's fucking do this." Lucy's voice is dark although her eyes glass over with tears. The close friendship she has made with Ava is like no other, and I know my sister would do anything for her.

Kayden orders the pack into groups while Lucy works closely with the witches. Evan darts towards me, and I blink at his presence. "I'm helping," he demands.

"No way," I grumble, pushing past him and towards Kayden.

"Why not?"

I turn around to face him with blazing eyes. "Because I don't trust you, Evan!"

"Then make this my test!" he proposes, grabbing my sleeve to stop me walking away. "I want to help Ava. Let me do something. I can't stand here and do nothing."

My eyes flick between his for a split second, and I can

see the determination in his gaze. I clench my jaw. "Fine," I mutter. "You prove your bravery and loyalty to me, and you'll be welcomed into this pack for good. You stick with Kayden and do everything he says. You fight with everything in you."

Evan flashes me a smile, but there is raw sadness in his eyes. "I won't let you down, Alpha. We will bring her home. No matter what it costs."

Once we head on our journey and I lead the pack, pain etches across my abdomen and chest. A grunt leaves my throat, and I scrunch up my snout. Kayden turns to me. *What's wrong?*

We race through the trees to get to Ava's location as quickly as possible. *They're hurting her,* I growl and clench my muscles to dull the pain. My mind focuses on Ava's, and I attempt to mask her suffering with the power of our bond. *We need to hurry.*

I sprint faster. Paws grinding into the dirt and eyes set ahead of me.

Hang in there, baby, I send through our mindlink.

As we inch closer, the scent of unknown wolves floods my nervous system. Seconds later, we spot them. At least a hundred of them stand on their paws, protecting the derelict building, and as soon as they see us coming, they pounce into action.

Take them all out, I shoot through the mindlink.

Claws and canines begin to clash, and blood is shed against the forest floor. I snarl and fight until organs are splattered and limbs are isolated. Ava needs me, and she is my only priority right now.

The taste of blood coats my tongue as I rip out a wolf's throat with my sharp teeth and ravage their body until they are barely recognisable. I twist my head to spot Kayden and Evan's wolves fighting off a pair together.

Go! Kayden shouts in my head. *She needs you.*

I don't waste any time. My pack is behind me, ready to fight for their Luna. As I move closer to the building, I howl out in sudden distress. It sends my body to the floor.

What's happening, Jaxon? Lucy's voice echoes in my head.

The lower part of my abdomen is on fire. Bleeding. I'm bleeding from the inside out, but there is no wound. My bond with Ava begins to shake, and I stand on trembling legs. They've done something to her. They're killing her. I can hardly catch my breath.

I change our plans at the last moment.

I need wolves helping me attack the building. Now!

Moments later, we charge into the building with force. There isn't a second to waste. I scan the room quickly but growl when I spot Julia hunched over my mate's naked body, a knife deep in her gut. Blood is pouring everywhere, through her fingers as she holds them to the wound. I stare back at them in horror. My heart slams into my chest, almost knocking me over.

Ava! I yell so loudly it makes my vision blurry. *Ava!*

Julia whips her head at the sound of our entrance. There isn't a single bone in my body that wants her. Even the sight of her face has me snarling in disgust. There is an evil sparkle in her eyes as she takes a hold of the knife handle and rips it from Ava's flesh. Her body jolts from the force, and she continues to lay there lifelessly. I seethe at the action, but I can make out the jagged breaths on her chest.

"Well, well." Julia's red lips lift into a smirk. "Isn't this a nice surprise? But you're a little late, Jaxon. The damage is already done. Now, you get to lose everything all over again. Watch her bleed out. It's real this time."

I bare my canines at the woman I hardly recognise. *Get her,* I order my pack. *Don't kill her. Save the rest for me later. I want to make her pay.*

Then they pounce, dragging her away as she shrieks in defence, but no one is coming to save her. I rush to Ava's side, her eyes falling shut. I shift back into my human form and scoop her up into my arms, pressing down on her wound to stop the bleeding.

Oh, Goddess. What have they done to her?

Her pale skin wears black and blue bruises, and blood trickles out of her mouth. Scratches cover her entire body. I swipe her hair away from her face. *Don't you dare leave me, Ava. You hear me? Don't you dare.*

I'm sorry. Her voice is weak in my head.

"No," I heave. Tears build behind my eyes. "Don't say you're sorry. Hold on for me, baby. Hold on. Please."

My sister slides to my side and inspects her wound. "Oh, fuck. Oh, fuck," she rasps. "She needs medical attention. Now. She's going to bleed out."

"Heal her."

"I can't," she says frantically. "I can't heal injuries this seve–"

"Just try! Fuck. Lucy, just try. Please. *Please.*"

Lucy doesn't hesitate; she leans over to Ava's wound and cups her hands across the oozing skin. Her eyes close as her arms begin to shake. "Come on, baby," I whisper. "Don't give up. Don't you dare."

Ava's blood covers Lucy, but she doesn't give up. She keeps going. I study the stab wound, but nothing happens. It doesn't start closing up. It doesn't heal. Nothing. Nothing is happening.

My sister slumps back with a groan, sweat covering her brow. "Fuck. I'm sorry. I can't do it. I'm not strong enough."

"Where are the healers?"

"Coming." Lucy nods and keeps her hands pressed to her wound to try and stop the bleeding. "They're almost here."

I cradle her closer to my chest and kiss over her frozen face. The bond stretches uncomfortably, and I can't grasp it. I can't slow down time. This isn't going to be the last time I see her beautiful face. No. It's not. I hold onto every last hope.

I study her angelic face, and my heart cracks inside me. I smooth back her hair when more tears threaten my eyes. She's a fighter. My girl is a fighter. I know it.

"I love you," I whisper along her forehead. "I love you, Ava. Please hold on. We've got so much to experience. So much life to live. This is not the end for us."

My sister releases a sob from beside me, but I don't look at her. I don't glance away from my mate for a second. I press my palm to her cheek and hold her impossibly closer, attempting to warm up her ice-cold body.

The bond is barely hanging on by a thread. All of Ava's pain is making my head throb, and I can't take it away. I want to take away every last piece. Because she's endured too much in this lifetime.

Ava's eyes flitter open for a second weakly, meeting mine before they shut once more. *I can't.* The words make my brain deteriorate. The lack of hope. The lack of strength. *I'm sorry, Jax.*

"No, no, no, no," I chant over and over. "Ava? Ava!"

She falls completely limp in my arms. I press my forehead to hers, a tear rolling off my cheek and onto her broken skin. This isn't even pain anymore; it's suffering. With her, I am living. Without her, I'm merely existing.

"Please," I beg. "Please, hold on. The healers are going to be here any second."

My fingers slide across her slender neck, and I press down, searching for a pulse. That's when I realise she doesn't have one. My heart is ripped out of my chest and thrown across the room. My wolf claws at my skin, howling in despair and devastation. I bellow at the top of my lungs until my throat burns red.

"Ava," I shake her body, but I know the truth.

I don't want to accept it.

Lucy places her hand on mine. "Jaxon."

"Ava," I say through gritted teeth. "No. *No.*"

I groan at the torture that deteriorates my emotions. Tears leak from my eyes endlessly as I shake my head. I break down into pieces. I hold her body tighter and cry into her neck. The agony is ready to rip me apart and throw me into the deep end with an anchor and no way of resurfacing.

"She's gone," I yell through a haunting sob as Lucy slides a shaky arm over my shoulder. "She's gone, Lucy. She's dead."

47

JAXON

The pack doctors spent what felt like hours trying to resuscitate Ava as she lay on the cold floor. Lucy held me back as I handed them over to the healers. I didn't want to let her go. I didn't want her to be alone.

My entire body turned numb.

Never have I ever felt so empty in my entire life.

No matter how hard they tried, she wasn't taking a breath.

I watched beneath glassy eyes and through a shattered heart. Her body twitched with each compression, but she remained lifeless.

Realisation started to dawn on me.

They can't save her. I was too late.

I failed her.

But then finally...finally she took her first breath, and I sagged in relief and agony all at once. I barely remember how we got home. All I cared about was that she was safe and receiving the best care. She deserves better than this. She deserves the brightest future with endless joy. Not this fate. Not at the hands of someone who deceived me for three years.

My fingers grip Ava's hand gently, running my thumb across her knuckles. The machine beside her beeps at a regular pace. The doctors did all they could to stop the bleeding and make her stable, but she fell into a coma shortly after. That was five days ago. She hasn't opened her eyes since.

There is a spark inside me where the bond is tugging, but it's weak. I know Ava needs all her strength, so I don't blame the mate bond for being nearly non-existent, even if it feels like my ribs have been ripped open and my heart is on full display.

I raise her fingers to my lips and kiss the delicate skin. My eyes roam her peaceful face, but it breaks me knowing what she's endured. "I'm right here, Ava," I whisper. "I'm right here, and I'm going to be here when you wake up. Okay?"

I'm met with silence and the machine reminding me her heart is stable. I sigh and bury my head into my hands. All I'm holding onto is the fact she's home.

When I close my eyes, I see the disturbing, heartbreaking image of her lying on the floor, covered in her own blood. I can't get it out of my head. It possesses me, and I despise the gut-wrenching twist inside me.

The look on Julia's face when she pulled the knife from her abdomen.

But she didn't win. She didn't accomplish what she wanted.

The door behind me creaks open, but I don't look to see who it is. A chair drags up beside me, and Kayden moves into the seat. "How you holding up?"

I shake my head. "Until she wakes up, I won't rest."

"I see that." His lips pinch into a thin line. "You should sleep, eat. You're not looking good, man."

"Can't," I murmur and keep a hold of Ava's hand. "She needs me."

Kayden nods. "Of course, but you need to keep your strength up, too. She wouldn't want to see you like this."

I release a long sigh. "She died, Kayden. She died in my arms. I'm not going anywhere."

"Alright," he says after a few moments. "I've got the pack under control. Take your time. You don't need to worry about them."

"Yeah," I rasp. "Thanks."

Kayden gives my back a small slap, and I glance at him for a split second and catch the grim smile he tries to paint on. He leaves, and I'm met with an eerie silence once again. I stand from the chair, slant over my mate, and leave a kiss on her cold forehead. "You're safe," I whisper into her skin. "You're safe. I should have been there sooner. I'm sorry you had to suffer. I wish it had been me. Goddess, I'd do anything to swap positions."

There's a knock at the door, and I huff out a breath. I can't go five minutes without someone checking on me like I'm some liability. All I want is time alone with my mate in peace.

"Jaxon." My sister's voice floats into the room. "You should take an hour, even half an hour. She's going to be here when you come back. You haven't left this room in days."

"Because I have to be here in case anything happens," I say through gritted teeth.

Lucy walks around to the other side of Ava's bed. She offers me a smile that I despise. I don't want her pity. It's like history is repeating itself, but this time, I know what's real.

The pain I endured when Julia died is nothing compared to the suffering I'm experiencing right now. With Julia, I felt out of control and angry, but right now...I am empty.

Without Ava, I am soulless.

"I'll watch over her for a little while," she says. "Take an hour. She'll be here. I'll make sure she's okay. If anything happens, I'll mindlink you, okay? Please. You need to shower and eat."

I stare at my sister, and she stares right back. "Lucy–"

"Jaxon," she huffs. "Please. Trust me. You need some time to yourself."

My eyes shoot back to Ava. The machine reminds me she's stable, but the sound of the beeping is close to sending me over the edge. I hate to admit she's right, but leaving her alone...

No. I can't.

"Jaxon. Go."

I'm stuck to the ground, and I'm certain I don't smell good either. My hand drags down my face in defeat. "Alright," I rasp and stroke my finger down the curve of Ava's cheek. "I'll be back. If anything and I mean *anything* happens, you tell me straight away. Alright?"

"You have my word." She smiles softly and takes a seat beside my beautiful mate. I study their hands as she entwines them and gives her palm a squeeze. "She's safe with me, Jaxon. Do you not trust me?"

My chest aches. "I do, but I want to be here when she wakes up."

"I understand." She nods. "Go. The quicker you leave, the quicker you can come back."

I leave before I change my mind.

The second I'm out of the room, my wolf is begging me to go back. But I keep my head forward, despite how difficult this is. It's a constant mental battle with my own subconscious.

Once I'm upstairs, I shower and get dressed into fresh clothes. Guilt races through me like a river, and when I think about eating, my stomach flips. I head down to the kitchen and make myself a coffee—caffeine being my best friend right now.

I stare out of the window and into the back garden. The trees sway in the wind as the sun ducks behind a sky of dark clouds. I gulp down my coffee, allowing the liquid to burn my throat.

Before I can think about my next decision logically, I walk out the back door and head into the trees. When I reach the rotting building surrounded by endless guards, I shove open the door and head down to the basement.

Adrenaline pumps through my bloodstream as I walk towards the barred cell. Julia sits against the back wall with her legs stretched out and her ankles chained. She hasn't noticed me yet. I haven't seen her since we captured her.

I didn't trust myself not to kill her. But now, I want answers.

My knuckles bash on the metal bars, making her jump. Her shoulders raise, and she cups her arms to her chest. She's definitely seen better days. I haven't laid a finger on her, but keeping basic needs from her has definitely taken its toll.

"Ava dead yet?" Julia smirks in my direction and attempts to stand on her weak legs. "Is that why you've decided to finally grace me with your presence?"

I growl and slam my fist down against the metal once more. "She's a fighter. You tried Julia, but you fucking failed."

She scoffs and wipes at her dry lips. "Time will tell, Jaxon. Time will tell."

"Why the fuck did you do this?"

Her head tilts backwards, and she laughs. "You were always so oblivious to everything. I didn't know magic could work so well, but when you fell head over heels for me and the fake mate bond, I decided I could do anything and you'd still love me. A spell for idiots in love. But I never loved you."

My eye twitches at her words. "You faked our mate bond."

"We were never mates, Jaxie." She flashes me a feral grin with an annoying voice that makes me want to smash her face into the wall. "All I wanted was to fuck with you, and it worked better than I imagined. I had you wrapped around my little finger until the very last moment. Did you cry for me, Jaxon? Did you weep and sob and feel like you couldn't go on?"

I tighten my jaw and remind myself not to bite. Goddess, fuck. I had no idea a spell could cause so much deception for this long. I didn't once question how she treated me or what I felt. She tricked me. She made me believe things that weren't even real.

My fingers itch to brush over my head, but I refuse to let her know she's still fucking with my brain.

"Faking my death and watching you suffer was the icing on top of the cake. We cut off the spell but left you with the excruciating pain of a deceased mate. It was all a lie. Every last bit of it," she hisses through her teeth.

Ava. Ava has and always will be my *only* mate.

Fuck.

Fuck.

"You tried to kill her," I spit.

She snorts and paces with trembling knees. "She was

never part of the plan. I put her in Lucien's path for a reason. I didn't think she would escape their pack, and I never thought she'd run into you. But when I had people keeping a close eye on you, I knew I had to finish you both off."

"Why?"

Julia barks out a laugh through her dry lips. "Why? Are you seriously asking why I did this, Jaxon?"

"Yes," I grumble under hooded eyes. "Tell me why."

"Because of your father and the pain he caused so many people."

My head shakes before she finishes speaking. "No. He didn't do anything wrong. It was a misunderstanding. He never wanted to hurt anyone. He was trying to help the district, but those rumours got out of control."

Julia lunges for me, but she can't go anywhere. "How dare you," she yells. "He killed people he thought threatened his life, his pack. In. Cold. Blood. Why do you think your parents ran away into hiding?"

"They were banished. They had to leave because people were after them. We were exiled. We had to leave our homes."

"That sounds like something someone who is guilty would do."

"They weren't guilty."

Julia growls, "I lost my little brother because of your father. I saw the state he left him in. Sick creature. My parents couldn't live with the grief and went off the rails. I wanted him to go through what it felt like to truly lose someone. And because he decided to fuck off, you were the next best thing."

I stare back at the woman I shared too many years of my life with. "You're not going to believe what I say," I snarl at her. "That's fine. But it doesn't matter anymore because you're not leaving this cell. You are not getting out alive."

Julia breathes heavily. "I still got to see you suffer."

"Ava did nothing to you."

"She existed, which was bad enough. I couldn't let you get on with your life after your father destroyed mine. Eye for an eye."

My gaze narrows at her. "Fuck you."

"Yeah, you did that." She flashes me a cunning smile. "You made *love* to me."

"Love isn't even close to what I felt for you. It was a deception. That's not a true representation of my feelings for you. I never *loved* you because it wasn't real. None of it was."

Julia's expression hardens as my words sink in. "I made you feel things."

"By manipulating my mind," I seethe. "None of it was true. Everything I feel with Ava is authentic because we built a bond on trust. The love I have for my mate is beyond time and measure. It could never compare. It's not even on the same scale."

She growls, "I should have slit her throat right there and then."

I almost reach into the cell and tear her head from her body. "But you didn't. You're never going to touch her again. But unfortunately for you, your fate is going to be a lot worse. You wanted me to suffer? Well, I'm going to fucking torment you until you are begging and screaming for mercy. Even then, I'm not going to give it to you. I'm going to let you burn, Julia. Then, I'm going to spend the rest of my life happy and in love with my Luna."

48

AVA

A wave of heavy discomfort flows through my body. I try to open my eyes, but they remain glued shut. All of my limbs weigh a tonne. I attempt to move my little fingers, but it's no use. I can't move.

Why is this so hard?

A harsh thumping in my head has me flinching, but I don't move. It's a mental reaction. My body doesn't feel like my body. My mind doesn't feel like my mind. *Nothing* is right.

This time, I attempt to curl my fingers as they twitch in desperation to move. I groan internally, which makes my chest burst into heated flames. My nostrils flare.

One eye cracks open, and a few seconds later, the other. It's like I'm seeing for the first time—which is definitely made worse when I'm met by blinding bright white lights. I whimper and shut them again. The soreness makes me wince. I squeeze them tight and try not to focus on the pounding inside my head. The beeping beside me isn't helping either.

Turn that shit off. It hurts.

My throat attempts to swallow, but my mouth is bone dry. I almost choke. Instead, I peel my eyes open again with all the strength I can muster. This time, I take a drowsy sweep across the room.

I'm in a bed. I'm...in a hospital bed.

Wires hang out of my arms, and there is something funny sitting between my nostrils. My skin becomes highly sensitive, making me twitch.

"Ava." I hear my name and glance at the sound. Lucy leans up from her chair. Her face is flushed with empathy, but my sight is blurry, so I'm not sure if I'm seeing right. "How are you feeling?"

I lick my lips. "H-hi," I croak.

"Here." She passes me a cup of water with a straw. My eyes thank her because I can't quite find the strength to talk and move at once. It's like someone has hit me with their car repeatedly.

My mouth latches onto the straw, and I drink down the cool liquid. Pressure builds behind my eyes as it slips down my throat and hydrates my mouth. I drink until it's empty and rest back into the bed.

Pain shoots through my abdomen, and I groan. Lucy shoves the cup down. "I'll go get the pack doctor," she murmurs.

"Wait–" my voice sounds like I haven't spoken in five years.

"What?"

All I can do is shake my head and that's a struggle.

"W–" I dampen my mouth and try again. "W-what ha-happened?"

Lucy frowns and turns back to me. "Do you not remember anything?"

I pause for a moment to think. The last memory I have is

being at the market, and then being cornered by those men. Everything else is a blur that I can't quite piece together.

"T-the market," I whisper.

Her eyes roam my face. "That's all you remember?"

I nod.

She presses her lips into a thin line and sits back down, taking my hand this time. "Ava," she starts. "A lot happened after the market. Jaxon is going to be here any second, alright? We can talk you through what happened together."

I flick my eyes frantically between Lucy's. My arm moves, but it's like it's made out of paper, ready to break any given second. I tilt my head to look down at the gown covering my body. My fingertips graze the edge of my stomach, and I hiss unexpectedly.

"Don't do that," Lucy gasps and moves my hand away. "You're still healing. Let me get the doctor, and Jaxon will be here any second."

I don't fight. I don't have the energy to. My head rests against the pillow, and I glance up at the ceiling. My eyes continue adjusting to the harsh light. One of the pack doctors steps in to check how I'm doing, but my head is racing with blank memories.

Why is my brain not cooperating?

The door to the room flies open, and I meet Jaxon's blue eyes. For a long moment, we stare at each other. The room turns silent, and there is only him. There is pure relief and devastation on his handsome face, yet the dark circles under his eyes tell me he's not had a good few days.

"Ava," he whispers and steps to my side. I can't reach for him. His warm hand cups my face, and I close my eyes at the sensation of our touch. "Oh, Goddess. Are you okay? Are you in pain?"

When I don't say anything, Jaxon takes the other side of

my cheek and an electric force field shoots up around us in the form of our bond. My eyes ache, and I'm too dehydrated to cry, but I can feel *everything*—especially him. Especially our unique bond. It drapes over my tender arms in a soft kiss and wraps me up with a simple breath.

"Baby." He presses his forehead to mine, and I finally open my eyes.

"Give her some time, Alpha," the doctor instructs. "She's just woken up, and it's going to take a while to get used to talking and moving."

Jaxon glances at him and nods, throat tensing. "Thank you. For everything you've done."

"You're stable, Ava. But keep resting and take it easy. I'll check on you later. Okay?"

My head attempts to move, but it's stuck. Jaxon offers him a smile that doesn't reach his eyes. "I'll be with her," he rasps. "Thank you again."

When the doctor leaves, Jaxon perches on my bed and looks at me. He takes my hand and rubs his thumb into my skin. Lucy clears her throat. "Ava wanted to know what happened," she starts. "She doesn't remember anything past the market where I lost her."

Jaxon's jaw tightens. "Okay," he whispers. *Do you want us to tell you now?*

Yes, I plead. I want this fuzziness inside my head to leave.

"Do you remember seeing Julia?" My brows pinch together slightly. I open my mouth, but Jaxon squeezes my hand. "Use our mindlink if it's easier. Don't strain yourself, baby. Take it easy like the doctor said."

Julia? I thought I was confused before, but now I'm dazed. *What do you mean Julia?*

Jaxon looks to Lucy with hesitation in his eyes, which

makes my heart rate spike. The machine beside me starts to beep aggressively.

"Okay, okay," Lucy holds up her hands in defence. "Take a breath."

I do, but my blood feels thick in my veins. I glance down at my arms. They seem different. This doesn't feel right. It's like I'm in someone else's body, and I've done a life swap.

Once my heart rate calms down, Jaxon carries on. "Julia faked her death," he states slowly. "And she kidnapped you at the market. We found you later in a building where she had you captured. She wanted to hurt you, hurt me, hurt *us*. She stabbed you, Ava. You broke a couple of ribs, too."

My vision blurs. His words slam into me like a concrete wall.

"Y-you–" Lucy stops to find her words. "You weren't breathing for like ten minutes, Ava. The doctors had to resuscitate you."

I part my cracked lips and attempt to shake my head. I died?

The urge to itch my head is intense, but I can't even lift my arms to do so.

How long have I been asleep?

"A few days." Jaxon offers me a comforting smile, but I can see the pain behind his eyes. "I'm sorry I wasn't here when you woke up. I promised I'd stay by your side. I'm so sorry, Ava."

He raises my hand to kiss my knuckles, a cannula hanging out the back of it. "But I'm here now. I'm not going anywhere. Okay? Anything you need, I'm right here."

I drag my tongue across my lips and part them. "J-Julia," I croak. "S-she–"

"Mindlink," he whispers. "Save your strength for your recovery."

My throat swallows around the words as I hold his gaze. *Julia, she faked her death?*

Jaxon nods slowly. "She was never my mate, Ava. She cast a spell to make me believe we were mates for revenge. She faked her death to make me suffer."

I close my eyes trying to digest all this information. *Why?*

"It doesn't matter. I'll explain another day. I want to focus on you and your recovery. Nothing else."

Where is she?

"She's been taken care of. She's not coming back to hurt us ever again." His voice is rough around the edges. "I know you have a lot of questions, but I don't want to overwork your brain."

I manage a nod. My entire face is melting from exhaustion, but I've been in the deepest sleep for days. I sit back while Jaxon and Lucy help me with eating and getting into a comfortable position. Yet, there's a tapping in the back of my mind, telling me that something isn't right.

∾

WHEN I WAKE up the second time, I'm not as stiff as before. I reach for a cup of water beside my bed and take a long sip. I glance across the room to find Jaxon asleep in the chair beside me.

I don't know what time it is, but from the position he's sleeping in, I know this is probably the first time he's actively closed his eyes. It doesn't look comfortable, but he's out like a light.

For a moment, I don't wish to wake him. I let my gaze slowly drag over his face. I take in every little detail. My mouth curls, and I release a quiet sigh as I get a better look at him.

My eyes float down to his lips. Beautiful lips.

He loves the way I taste.

I flinch from the sudden voice inside my head. But then I realise it's not a voice. It's something I've heard before. My heart pounds against my ribcage, and I twist off the clip on my finger to stop the machine from going crazy.

My eyes ping to his, and this time, they're open and looking straight at me.

He told me I am the most beautiful girl he's ever laid his eyes on.

"Ava?"

My eyes cloud with tears within seconds. A hand presses to my chest, and I can't catch my breath. All of the air has been sucked out of my lungs.

"Baby." He moves forward instantly. "What's the matter?"

I love you.

Tears stream down my face at the memory of Jaxon's voice.

He told me I am the love of his life.

No one could replace me. They'd never compare.

No matter who came after me.

My hands fly to my head, and I cry out. "Stop. Stop," I chant to myself.

Jaxon hovers over me and reaches for my arm, but it burns. It aches. "Ava, look at me. Please."

I shake my head.

He told me I am the love of his life.

Love of his life.

Love.

Love.

Love.

My throat releases a sob as Jaxon wraps his arms around me, attempting to calm my emotions, but it only heightens them. "Talk to me." He tucks my head under his chin. "Ava. What's going on?"

I grit my teeth and shove at his chest with all my strength. He barely budges, but he glances down at me with pinched brows. "Baby–"

"Please," I whimper. "Please don't touch me right now."

Jaxon stands back with clear distress in his eyes. "Okay. I–"

"Do you love me?"

The room turns silent.

"You said it to me," I whisper. "I heard you say it. Did you even mean it?"

He pulls his head back an inch, eyelashes twitching at my sudden question. "Of course I meant it, Ava. I have been in love with you for a long time."

"More or less than you loved Julia?"

Jaxon's forehead creases. "Ava–"

"Answer the question."

"I didn't love Julia. How could I love someone if the relationship was a lie?"

My lids release more tears. "Did you tell her she was the love of your life?"

He looks like he's about to have a heart attack, dismay etched onto his face. "The things I said to her were because she used magic to manipulate my thoughts, my feelings, and emotions. Ava, what we have is not like what I was forced to experience with Julia. I might have said those things, but I did not mean them."

I choke on a sob. My heart stings. The room spins.

"Baby, please let me hold you."

"I didn't want to be second best," I whisper beneath

trembling lips. "I didn't want to be your second choice. *Your rebound.* I never wanted to be the other woman you settle with because you have to."

Jaxon's chest quivers as his head shakes with determination. "You are none of those things because you are my *only* mate, Ava. It's always been you. No one but you. When I'm with you, everything feels right. You bring out the best in me. You are my anchor. You are everything I have ever wanted."

"No." I shake my head. "I can't be."

He steps forward, but doesn't touch me. "You are. I've been waiting my entire life for you, Ava White. I fell in love with you. *Real* love. Authentically. In our own time. The mate bond might have helped, but everything I feel for you I know is because we've built our own special bond. It's based on trust and safety and communication. It has nothing to do with the Moon Goddess. It has everything to do with *us*. It's special because it's ours, and I know it's real. Every emotion is real."

My heart glows at his words because I thought that, too. The mate bond helped, but it has nothing on my own development with my trauma and trusting again. I lower my head into my hands and release every last emotion.

"I know you probably won't believe me right away, and that's okay. I will spend the rest of my life proving it to you. I know in my heart the limit of my love for you does not even exist," he whispers, and I finally glance at him through blurry eyes. "I will wake up beside you, and I'll love you more than I did the day before. It might seem impossible, but I know it's true. I've felt it over the last few weeks. I love you so much, Ava, and I'm not going to let you forget it."

The bond grows tighter and stronger within seconds. It sends goosebumps down my arms. He wraps an invisible tender hug around my brain, calming my cries, and I accept it. I accept his love.

He slows down my panic attack before it even reaches my nervous system, and I'm eternally grateful for his abilities. Right now, I need it. I don't know if my body can take any more trauma.

We stare at each other for a long moment. Jaxon's eyes glimmer as wetness coats his lash line. My cheeks are stained with tears. It takes merely seconds to believe him. I let my insecurities win for a moment. I won't let *any* of them win.

Julia tricked him. Julia messed with us.

It was always meant to be *us*.

"I'm sorry." My lips tremble.

"No," he heaves. "Don't say you're sorry. You have nothing to be sorry for."

My hand stretches towards him, and he slides into the space within seconds. I sob again when he touches me. This time, our connection doesn't burn; it flourishes.

His warm arms wrap me up as he moves onto the bed. I cling onto him and bury my face into his chest, letting my last few tears dampen his T-shirt. He strokes back my hair in soothing motions and kisses my forehead.

"Julia's gone," he murmurs. "She's never coming back. I made sure of it."

I inhale a shuddering breath and relax into him completely.

I don't belong anywhere else.

He is my home.

49

JAXON

The doctors helped Ava with her mobility after her coma. I stuck by my word and didn't leave her side for a second. I wanted to help in any way I could without being overbearing, but I knew she was grateful for my company.

I make us both some lunch in my private kitchen as she stares out the window, her eyes glazed over and expression blank. Of course I've been keeping a close eye on her. I can't help but suspect that she's hiding something. The pack doctors told me not to probe her for more answers and let her come to me when she's ready. What she went through was extremely traumatic, and I know it's not something she'll be able to let go of easily.

"Do you have a session with Gemma today?" I ask.

Ava remains silent, completely on-responsive to my voice. I frown.

My throat clears. "Ava?"

"Huh?"

She snaps her attention to me, her eyes wide like she's been caught red handed doing something bad.

"Do you have a session with Gemma today?"

"Uhh." She pauses and runs a hand down her face. "Yeah. In thirty minutes. I moved it forward."

"Everything okay?" I ask without trying to sound too weary.

Ava nods once and flashes me a smile that is the epitome of forced. "Yeah. I just spaced out. Sorry."

"Thinking about anything in particular?"

She runs a finger over her lip as I plate up our lunch. "Just about that night with Julia. What I can piece together anyway."

I hum softly. "You think of anything new?"

"No," she exhales.

Her body language is odd, and her face is struck with emptiness. I know she's beating herself up about what happened, and I don't know why. "Do you remember me telling you that when we arrived, there were deceased wolves in the building? They'd been killed and ripped apart."

"Yeah."

"Do you know what happened to them? Did Julia do something to them? Did she demonstrate what she'd do to us?"

Ava stares at the wall. Hard. "No." Her voice is a whisper. "I don't remember anything apart from her words. I can't even remember her face. I don't remember waking up. I don't remember her hurting me. None of it."

I didn't have much time to look at the monstrous scene, but afterwards, Kayden explained the dead wolves didn't make sense. Either something went wrong and Julia slaughtered them or someone else was there when it happened. The hairs on the back of my neck stand. I've had the house and our territory doubled with guards. I had my wolves search the surrounding area for anything they deem suspicious.

We sit and eat our lunch together. Ava's distracted mind pains me to watch. Even her mental walls are sky high, and there isn't a chance of seeing in. But I know to respect her boundaries.

Ava offers me a sweet smile. "Thanks for lunch. I should go see Gemma now. I don't want to be late."

I hop off the chair. "I'll walk you there."

Our fingers lace together as I walk through the pack house and down to Gemma's office. As we turn the corner, my eyes collide with Evan. "Ava," he calls out with a relieved grin. "How are you?"

"Hi, Evan." She drops my hand to give him a hug. "I'm okay. Taking it slow."

"Good. You should be resting. I wanted to make sure you're okay." He gives her a once-over with his soft eyes, and now I believe that he truly cares for her. "Alpha Jaxon and I were talking. He said he'll officially let me into the pack."

Ava's eyes light up with joy. "Really?" She glances at me in surprise. "Oh. That's amazing. I'm so happy to have you here. *We're* so happy to have you here."

He glances between us and nods. "I'm very happy to be here, too."

Once Evan dismisses himself and I slip my arm over Ava's shoulders, she smiles up at me. "You have a soft spot for him," she murmurs.

I snort quietly. "Soft spot is an exaggeration. He wanted to prove himself by getting you back home safely. He listened to Kayden's orders and showed his bravery. He stuck to the rules and acted accordingly, and I trust he will work hard within this pack. He needs a lot of training and one-on-one sessions, but I'm sure he'll get there with time."

Ava snuggles closer into my side. "Thank you for welcoming him into your pack, Jax. It means a lot to me."

"*Our* pack, baby. It's ours."

She peeks her pretty brown eyes up at me, and I'm relieved the bruising on her face has improved with the help of the healers. I couldn't stomach looking at her black eye and busted nose, knowing how much violence she had endured in the past.

My girl is a fighter, a damn warrior.

We pause outside Gemma's office, and Ava sucks in a breath, shoulders raising as she stares at the door. "You want me to come in with you?" I offer.

"No. I can do this alone. Thank you, though. I like it when you come with me, but today, I want to do it by myself," she answers with clarity in her tone.

I press a kiss to the crown of her head. "Proud of you."

When she steps forward to knock and Gemma opens the door, she gives me one last glance over her shoulder with slight reservation in her eyes. "I'll see you later."

"Yeah, baby. I'll see you later."

~

WHILE AVA WAS in her session with Gemma it gave me some time to sit down with Kayden and complete Alpha duties that have been pushed to the side for far too long. He's kept this pack going while my attention has been on Ava, and he always does an amazing job. I trust him with my life, even if he makes me question our friendship on a daily basis.

After a group training session and an early dinner, I find myself upstairs with Ava when it approaches seven o'clock. She still needs a good night's sleep to help her body fully recover with her pain medication.

I lay back on our bed with my hands behind my head. Ava's been in the bathroom for the last twenty minutes, but I haven't heard the shower turn on. I stare at the half-closed door and narrow my eyes.

"Ava?" I call out to her. "Everything okay?"

She doesn't respond, which alarms me immediately. I hop off the bed and walk towards the en-suite. I rap my knuckles on the door and step inside to find her facing the mirror.

"Ava?"

It's like I'm not here. She can't hear me. She can't sense me.

I lean on the doorframe and watch her for a moment. Her eyes are staring straight through her soul, her expression void of any emotion, and for a moment, it terrifies me. I've never seen her like this.

My wolf runs circles inside me and drags his claws through my insides. I slide a hand through my hair at the invasive feelings. He howls as if he's desperate to tell me something, but I know we're both concerned. Ava's mind has been elsewhere.

Eventually, she dips her head and raises her arms, scanning them as if she's looking for something embedded on her skin. I watch silently as she swipes her fingers over her wrists and across her forearms before reaching her elbows. She does it again and again.

She stops, freezes.

I shift on my feet but stay back.

Then, she starts pinching and pulling her skin before releasing them. At first, it's slow and gentle, then it's harder and aggressive, as if she's trying to tear off her skin.

"Hey, hey," I raise my voice and move closer. "Stop. What are you doing? *Stop.*"

Ava doesn't acknowledge me whatsoever. I grip at her hands to stop her from hurting herself as red patches rise on her skin from where she's been pinching too hard. But she attempts to bat my hands away and continue.

"Ava," I rasp her name. "Stop it. You're hurting yourself."

Her head shakes, and she snaps herself out of whatever trance she was trapped in. "Jaxon–"

I stare at her for a long moment, and it's clear as day that she doesn't remember what happened. But her subconscious does. What was that about?

"Baby." I drop her wrist and press my palm to her cheek. "Are you okay? Did something happen today with your session with Gemma?"

Ava furrows her brows. "I-I–" She licks her lips and pauses. "I'm okay."

"Do you feel like you need to hurt yourself?"

"What?" she recoils. "No."

I take a quiet breath. "Okay."

She stares at me through her dark lashes until her face is a scowl, but she's not angry at me; she's confused by the situation. "What just happened?"

"You were tugging at your skin, pinching it. I don't know. You weren't responding to me," I answer honestly. "Ava, if something is wrong, you can tell me."

I study her throat as she attempts to swallow. "This won't make sense to you."

"Try me."

Ava turns away, and I drop my hand from her face but slide my fingers down her wrist instead. "My body doesn't feel like my body. It hasn't felt like my body since I woke up in the infirmary."

"How so?"

"I don't know." She shrugs, her frustration getting the

better of her. "Something doesn't feel right, and I don't understand why. As soon as I woke up I felt this way. Like someone has swapped my body, and I'm in another person's shell."

I notice her trembling legs so I back her up onto the edge of the bathtub and kneel down, collecting her hands in her lap. "You stopped breathing, Ava. You died, and the doctors brought you back. It might be something to do with the resuscitation. They said it might take a while to come to terms with what happened because parts of your memory aren't there. Do you think it could be that or is it something else?"

She chews her lip subtly. "I-I don't know."

"It's okay," I reassure her.

"I don't want to feel like this."

I raise her knuckles to leave a kiss. "I know you're struggling, and I wish I could do more. What can I do, Ava?"

"Nothing," her voice cracks. "I'm so confused."

My expression crumbles. "Come here." I open my arms as she slides into my embrace. I tug her up and cradle the back of her head before walking us towards our bed. "I've got you, baby. I've always got you."

I move us onto the bed and keep her close to my chest. "I know you do," she whispers. "You're the only thing keeping me sane right now."

"I promise whatever this is, we're going to get through it. There is no pressure for your recovery or your therapy. Everything is at your pace."

Ava nods. "Yeah." Her breath tickles my neck.

"I'm going to stay right here and hold you like this all night."

"Thank you." She drops her head onto my shoulder, and I listen until she's firmly asleep in my arms.

50

AVA

My recovery over the last three weeks has been going better than expected. Every now and then, I have a minor blip, but then I remind myself where I am and all of the support I'm surrounded with.

Jaxon's eyes watch me when I'm silent, and he holds me at night when I cry. But these last few days have felt a lot better than when I first woke up. My mind is a little clearer, and I'm slowly accepting what happened to me—Gemma said it's my first step to putting it behind me and looking forward.

And that's exactly what I want to do. *Look forward.*

Today, Jaxon decided to take me out of the pack house in hope of a change of scenery. I adore the place I can finally call my home, but sometimes, comfort spaces can become overbearing when it's all I rely on.

"Will the pack be okay if we leave? I know you have a lot of work to do," I say softly.

Jaxon spares me a glance. "You told me to take it easy, and that's exactly what I'm doing. Kayden said I shouldn't burn myself out, and spending time with you helps me recharge. He's taking order while I'm gone."

"You seem a lot calmer recently," I comment.

"Because I know you're home and safe."

I shake my head. "I mean with the pack. Things are starting to fall into place."

"You think?"

"Yeah." I smile. "I saw you guys training, and I see how the pack looks at you. It's like the bond between you all has intensified. I think you're finally finding your purpose as an Alpha. You're all connecting."

Jaxon's head tilts. "I like that." He nods. "You're right. I used to be uptight and focused on only one thing. But now, I've learnt that listening to their needs goes a long way. Before I ignored that, and it wasn't a good trait to have."

"What made you change?"

"You."

"Huh?"

"You did. Being with you. It put into perspective that I can help them blossom into the best versions of themselves if I give them the attention and care they need. I think about you and how I always paid attention to what you needed the most, and eventually, I earnt your trust. Now, I'm doing it with the pack but with their doubts, fears, and weaknesses. It's a conversation that never ends, and they feel comfortable enough to discuss it with me so we can all improve. They see me as a helping hand, not someone to fear."

My expression lights up. "That sounds incredible. You all help each other."

"Exactly. It's still a work in progress, but I don't plan on changing. I've seen improvements already, and I want it to stay that way. This is the Alpha I've always wanted to be, the pack I've always wanted to have. Now, I'm going to continue working hard and give them the best version of me in return."

"I love that, Jax."

He flashes me a grin. "I deserve a day off now, and we both deserve to go on our first date."

My chest warms at the idea of our first date.

"Are you going to tell me where we're going?" I ask as we drive.

I adjust the hem of my yellow sundress covered in white flowers. We've been driving for at least twenty minutes, and I have no idea where we are. "Stop trying to ruin the surprise." He leans over the centre console to take my hand. "You'll see when we get there."

A wave of excitement and anticipation splashes over my chest. "A surprise?"

"Yep," he says, winking. "Trust me, you'll love it."

"Just us?"

"Yeah, baby. Just us."

Eventually, we slow down as we enter a small dirt track. I glance out the window at the large trees swaying in the wind and the sun gleaming down on us. It's a beautiful day for a surprise that makes me want to burst out of my skin.

We both climb out of the car, and Jax moves around to the boot and pops it open. He pulls out a cooling box and a blanket, which he throws over his shoulder.

"Are we going for a picnic?"

Jaxon's lips curl as we walk, and he threads his fingers through mine. "What gave it away...the blanket or the box?"

I bump his hip playfully, and we both release a laugh. "I haven't been for a picnic in a long time, okay? It's a nice surprise. I love it."

"Good." He presses a kiss to my temple. "You look beautiful, Ava. You do every day, but I love this dress. It suits you."

My cheeks bleed as usual. "Thank you. Lucy took me shopping."

Jaxon guides us through the trees until we reach the top of a hill that overlooks the entire district. "Wow," I exhale at the breathtaking view. "It's pretty up here."

His eyes gleam when he looks at me. "Yeah. It's peaceful. Away from all the chaos. But my view will be prettier."

I smile as he lays out the blanket on a fresh patch of grass in direct line of the sunshine. He holds out his hand, which I take and perch on one end of the blanket. "Are you trying to be romantic?" I ask, crossing my legs.

Jaxon sits opposite me and begins to open the box. "Is it working?"

"Completely."

To some people, a picnic might seem like a small gesture, but to me, it's *everything*. He wanted to take me out of the house to be together, but it wasn't about money or anything materialistic. It's about our quality time.

"I love when you smile," he says as he watches me.

"I love that you've done this. I'm grateful for you. Thank you."

He spreads out the food across the blanket and pours us two cups of something pink and fizzy. "I know the pack house is a lot right now, and I thought this would help clear your mind. It's also an excuse to get you to myself."

"Yeah." I blow out a breath and run a hand through my hair. "I've been getting a lot of attention from your pack members."

Jaxon smiles. "Because they want to know their future Luna. They look up to you and your strength and bravery."

My face heats with a blush at his confession. They look up to...*me?*

"Not sure there is a lot to look up to."

Jaxon pauses and pins me with a stare. "Don't do that. Don't dismiss the amazing qualities we all see in you, including how strong and determined you are."

I swallow once and nod. "It's still taking time to get used to."

"I know." He smooths a hand over my knee. "But soon, you'll realise how remarkable you are, Ava."

A warmth floods my chest, and I allow his comfort. I've realised the more I push him away, the worse everything is. We work together as a team. Our bond thrives off one another, and I accept all of his honesty.

We sit and eat for a moment as I stare into the distance of the district. A part of me can't believe this is my life. That I've ended up in a place I didn't know existed as a child. My entire world has turned upside down and for the better.

"What are you thinking about?" Jax snaps me out of my trance.

I quirk a brow. "Not reading my mind?"

"No. Your mental walls are a lot stronger since you woke up. I can't hear a single thing."

"Did you listen to my thoughts often?"

He chews on the inside of his lip for a moment. "I didn't want to. I tried so hard not to so I could give you the privacy you deserved. But other times, I couldn't control it. That's why I taught you your mental defences as soon as I could. I wanted to earn your trust authentically."

"Yeah, I think I have the hang of it now."

Jaxon eyes me for a moment, and his expression softens.

"This past year has been very bitter-sweet," I exhale and lower my sandwich. "It's been high and low continuously. I still don't feel one hundred percent right from when I woke up from my coma. But things are finally going in the right direction. I'm trusting the universe to guide me to what is meant for me."

His hand slides over the blanket, and he takes my fingers once more, kissing over my wrist and knuckles until it tickles. "You are destined for great things."

"Let's hope." I laugh hesitantly. "Your pack are lucky to have an Alpha so caring for each and every one of them and their wellbeing."

"Well, of course. If I respect them, they'll respect me. It's an easy process. We need to work together as a team." He shrugs. "I am also very lucky to have you alongside me with this pack. You've helped me to see the changes I needed to make."

His words of affirmation make me feel lighter, as if he can blow all of my problems away with his caressing words. They make me feel seen and heard. They make me feel like I matter.

Because you do matter, I tell myself. *You have always mattered.*

A ball of emotion forms in my throat, and I press a hand to my neck. Jaxon studies the action and scoots closer, wrapping an arm around my shoulder.

No one has ever made me feel the way he does. No one has ever cared for me the way he does. No one will ever compare to him. It's simple.

I stare up at him and those dark blue eyes full of adoration. His hand raises and he brushes back a few strands of hair on my cheeks and gives me a stomach-dropping smile. I blink back the tears forming in my eyes, and he immediately notices. "Hey." He tilts my chin and inspects my face. "What's wrong?"

"I love you, Jax."

His mouth parts as I choke back the heaviness on my chest.

"I haven't been able to say it because somewhere inside of me, I'm terrified if I voice it, then I'll lose you. I'll lose everything good in my life. But now, I realise the world isn't against me. I'm allowed to love; I'm allowed to be loved," I say through trembling lips.

Jaxon closes his eyes and presses his forehead to mine. "Baby," he whispers.

"I love you more than I thought I could ever love anyone or anything. You've shown me that life isn't just pain and suffering. It's so much more than that. It's something I have never truly experienced before. I will cherish your love forever because it is one of a kind," I state with truthfulness. "You breathed happiness into me, and you brought me back to life. You've taught me how to truly live."

He clenches his jaw, only to release it seconds later. "Ava."

"Most people think home is a place, but to me, home is a person."

I nuzzle my head further into his. He peppers kisses over my cheek and the curve of my jaw. "The universe led me into your path," I whisper. "And you never gave up, no matter how difficult I've been."

Jaxon's strong arms cage around me and tug me onto his lap. I wrap my hands around his neck and hold him close. "Because we are made for each other, Ava. I couldn't give up on the best thing in my life. Not even when things got rough. We worked together; we grew *together*. You are not just my mate; you are the reason I exist. You brought me back to life, too. You make me want to get up and be a better person than I was the day before."

I glance down at his lips and kiss him. I kiss him with all the passion, desire, and love I have in my body until we both lose our breath. His large hand cups the back of my head while my legs straddle his thighs.

The kiss is slow, perfect, and everything in between. He sensually devours my mouth as his tongue slips inside ever so carefully. I whimper.

I need you, I beg through the mindlink. *I need you so badly.*

There's fire inside my heart. A deep desire for us to be as close as possible.

You've got me, baby. He nips my bottom lip, and I moan.

The centre of my core begins to burn, and I clench my thighs together. Jaxon fists my hair and inhales deeply. My arousal floods us both. My heat is blossoming, and I want him.

My hands slide into the back of his hair, and I angle his head to kiss him harder. His hands trail heat across my skin with a brush of his fingertips.

"I'm ready," I whisper against his mouth.

Jaxon pants and looks up at me through dark eyes. "What?"

"I want you. I need you. I want to be close to you. I trust you with my life, Jax. Please. *Please.*"

He pauses for a moment and swipes his thumb across my bottom lip. "Tell me exactly what you're saying, Ava."

"I want to be with you. Intimately. I want to feel you inside me."

Jaxon searches my expression carefully. "Are you sure about this?"

I nod. "I've never been so sure of anything in my entire life."

"The first time I make love to you isn't going to be out in

the open," he rasps against my lips. "It's going to be in our bed, where I can worship you and we can take our time. I don't want a single distraction because all my focus is going to be on you."

My legs quiver beneath me and I nod, eager for it. "Please."

Jaxon smiles before capturing my lips between his.

51

JAXON

Ava slips into the shower when we get home. The sound of pattering water from the en-suite echoes into the room. When I shut the door, it turns off. I perch on the edge of the bed as Ava steps out with a white fluffy towel wrapped around her body. Steam wafts from behind her, and when our eyes meet, she offers me a smile. I strain at the sight of her like this.

"Come here," I beckon, breathing through my nose heavily.

If I don't have her in my arms in the next five seconds, I might die.

Ava's cheeks heat—and not from the temperature of the shower.

My eyes remain on her face as she takes three steps towards me before she stops. Her fingers clutch onto her towel at her chest. I keep still as she climbs onto my lap, her legs straddling my thighs like earlier.

I press my palms to her back, where the towel has dipped and I can touch bare skin. She slides her hands over my shoulders and gives me a gentle smile with her eyes. "I loved today," she whispers. "I love spending time with you."

My lips press to the tip of her shoulder. "I love spending time with you, too."

"I want you to make love to me." She dips her head to my neck, and I have to stop my eyes from rolling into the back of my head. "I'm ready. I trust you so much."

I release a shuddering breath and hook my arm over her shoulder. "Are you sure?"

"Yes."

My eyes trace her lips, and I nod once. I lean in as my mouth covers hers. My hands remain on her, but not tightly, a soft caress to remind her this is about love and nothing less. I scoop her up under my arm and twist, pinning her to the bed.

Those big curious eyes look up at me as I break the kiss. My heart almost bursts there and then. I allow my fingers to dance along the edge of her towel softly as I listen to her breathing. "Can I take this off?"

She nods, burying her teeth into her bottom lip. "Please."

I pull it off her body, leaving her exposed and completely beautiful. My gaze trails across her chest and over her pink hardened nipples. I groan internally as I cover her body with mine, pressing my lips to her neck.

"Goddess," I whisper beside her ear. "You are divine, baby. *Perfect.* So damn perfect."

Ava whimpers as I pepper kisses across her collarbones. She throws her head back in blissful pleasure. I smile into each kiss I leave. Her body trembles, and I peek up at her, my bottom lip skimming her belly button.

I place my hands between her thighs and gently pull them apart, her fingers sliding over mine. *You okay, baby?*

She presses her lips together in a soft hum. *Don't stop.*

My hand parts her legs, and I press my face into the centre of her thighs, my stubble grazing her legs. She gasps at the sensation as I kiss lower and lower.

"Jaxon," her voice pleads.

I move closer to her core and my cock throbs at the sight of her wetness. I widen her legs and waste no time in placing my mouth over her throbbing clit. The hands that were over my fingers are now buried into the back of my hair.

My tongue glides down and back up through her centre. Her breathing hitches as I taste how heavenly she is. I groan into her core. I'm not able to get enough. I inhale her into my system and keep hold of her thighs.

I gently rub two fingers over her pussy and push them in. Her chest rises off the bed. "Oh, God," she cries. "Jax."

The way she moans my name has me growing even harder.

She pants as I begin to pump my fingers in and out of her, continuing to swirl my tongue around her pulsing clit. Her smooth legs tremble as she whimpers out loud. It's my favourite thing to hear—knowing she feels safe and comfortable enough to share her pleasure with me.

I curl my fingers and press them directly onto her g-spot. I want to bring her to the edge so she can shatter into ecstasy. I glance up and find her already looking at me with dilated eyes and parted lips. Her cheeks are pink, and her throat is tensing in desperation for a release.

Her entire body quivers as I suck on her clit once more. She's close. "Are you gonna come for me?"

"Yes–" she gasps.

I lower my head back down and listen to her body language, the pattern of her breathing. I respond to her reflexes, what her body wants. My mouth clamps around her again when her orgasm starts to heighten.

Her hips grind down onto my lips and fingers. She explodes.

Ava moans my name over and over until it's a weak whimper. Those delicate fingers grip onto my hair for leverage as she rides out her climax on my face. I swallow every last drop of her sweetness and continue licking until she's withering into the bed.

I slowly remove my fingers and slip them inside my mouth to lick them clean. *Fuck.* She tastes like mine.

Ava's hair is splayed across the pillow messily. I crawl up her body and brush a few strands from her eyes, seeing a ghost of a smile on her lips. "You okay?"

"Very." Her eyes glitter.

Then, she leans forward to grip me through my jeans. I take her hand, and she looks at me like she's done something wrong. "This whole thing is going to be about you and only you," I say sincerely. "You are my focus. Is that okay?"

I swipe my thumb across the inside of her wrist. "Yeah. But I want to touch you next time."

"Deal." I peck her lips.

I push back onto my knees and begin to shed my clothes until I'm naked. Ava's eyes trail over every exposed part of me, and she shudders as I lean into my bedside table to take out a condom. "Wait," she whispers. "It's okay. The doctors gave me contraception to take, and I'm back on it now. We don't have to use a condom, not if you don't want to."

My eyes flare at her. "Are you sure?"

"Positive." She nods.

I search her face for any hesitation but find none. My throat works around the ball of desire forming. "Okay," I whisper as I push her legs apart again and shuffle closer to her core. Our eyes meet. "You tell me if you want to stop, okay? If it hurts or you need a second. You. Tell. Me."

Ava's fingers entwine with mine. "I know. I meant it when I said I trust you."

My chest quivers, and I stroke my cock before slowly pushing inside of her. She sucks in a breath, and I pause, caging my arms around her in a gesture of security. It's only us.

When I slide further in, she rests her hand on my chest, and I stop immediately. "Are you okay?"

My fingers take hers delicately. She shifts her hips slightly and nods. "You're big," she exhales as I press my mouth to her palm. "Please, just go slow."

"Of course, baby."

I stay still for a moment and allow her to get used to the feeling before I start to move. I rest down on my elbows and drag my lips across her neck, and when she melts into me, I thrust slowly. She gasps into my ear and clings onto my biceps. I pause and wait until her legs start parting further, and I smile into her neck.

My hips move again and again until she brings our lips together in a fiery kiss. She moans against my tongue and sends vibrations straight down my spine until I'm clutching her face and angling it towards me so I can taste every inch of her.

"Better?" I rasp as I pull out and sink back in.

She nods desperately. "Better."

Then I rest my forehead down on hers. My hips move a tiny bit quicker and deeper, and I watch her face for any slight twitch of discomfort—but instead, her lips are parted, and her beautiful eyes are closed in elation.

She digs her fingernails into the skin on my shoulders. I look at her as she throws her head back with a cry. I speed up. She moans into the room without reservation, and I groan silently, knowing she's allowing me to see this vulnerable side to her. *Because she wants me to.*

The sound of the bed bangs against the wall lightly. Her hands move to grip the bed sheets, knuckles turning white. "Oh my God," she cries out, and my lips find hers.

She groans into the kiss before taking my lip between her teeth and gently biting. My eyes roll in pure pleasure. Goddess, she's about to be the death of me.

Then she presses her palms flat to my chest, and I stop, concern builds in my heart that I've somehow hurt her. But I'm wrong. So incredibly wrong. She pushes me back gently so I slip out of her. Then I'm on my back, and she positions herself on top of me.

This burst of confidence throws me, but I lay back and stare at her through surprised eyes. She hovers herself above my cock and sinks down onto it, her lids fluttering shut as she rocks her hips.

I'm still trying to wrack my brain from what the hell just happened, but I'm not complaining, especially when my hands automatically move to her hips and she rides me with long movements. I watch her in awe. She bounces and grinds and stretches her neck to release a beautiful moan that brings me dangerously close to the edge. But I tell myself to be a team player.

This is about her.

Her head rolls back to face me, strands of dark hair gliding across her eyes, and she leans forward to press her palms to my chest. She takes me deeper at this new angle, and I am in fucking heaven. The way her lips tremble with desire has me forgetting how to use my lungs altogether.

She clenches around my cock as she curls her fingers into my skin, and I know she's close. I slip my hands up her ribcage and hold her there as she grinds down on me, hips speeding up. Then she lets go. She rides out her orgasm. Her pretty mouth exhales unexpected curse words that make my heart pound in my chest.

I can't take my eyes off her. My wolf itches to lean forward and mark her as ours, but that's a conversation for another day. I hear my name slip off her lips as she shudders on my cock.

My arms cage around her back while I tug her chest into mine. I listen to her rapid breaths and racing heart. "You like being in control?" I ask, barely recognising my own voice.

She nods into my neck. "Very much."

"Good."

"But I want you to be in control now. I want to see you."

Her words spark a match inside my soul. I study her face to find a lazy smirk on her lips. I groan and kiss her passionately. Then I flip her down onto the bed, her stomach pressing into the sheets with her leg hitched up half way. Her eyes turn dark at the new position, but she doesn't protest.

I grip under her thigh and place my mouth next to her ear. "I'll put my pride aside and let you be in control anytime you want," I rasp. "But when you ask me to be in control, best believe I am going to make you come so hard that you forget your own name."

Ava gasps at my statement and bites her lip. *"Holy fu–"*

I push myself into her again and slip my hand down her stomach and in between her legs. My fingers run circles around her throbbing clit as I thrust from behind. I hold onto her tightly, pressing my lips to her shoulder blades.

My hips gradually speed up, and she muffles her moans into the duvet. *Don't do that,* I send through our mindlink. *Let me hear you, baby. Let me hear how good you feel.*

She twists her head, and our eyes meet. She moans. She moans so loud that my cock twitches inside her. I wasn't far off when she was riding me. but now...*fuck*. I want to fill her with my cum and listen to her as she explodes with me.

I grip onto one of her ass cheeks and squeeze lightly. "Jax," she pants.

"Tell me how that feels."

"Mmmm." She nods. "So good."

Our skin slaps together as I speed up, and I pinch her clit between my fingers. She cries out. "Jax," she looks up at me, and I see raw vulnerability in her eyes. "Oh, God. I think I'm–"

Ava comes again. Her body jitters, and she grips onto my wrist, pulling me impossibly closer. I press my lips to her ear and drown in the sound of her pleasure. Her eyes roll back, and she glows through her climax. "That's my girl." I nip at her lobe. "Look at you. So fucking beautiful."

The headboard bangs harder this time, the legs of the bed squeaking against the floor. I grit my jaw, and it takes two more strokes, and I'm flying across the finishing line. My throat tenses, and I release a deep groan as I continue to thrust, filling Ava with every last drop.

I slow down and wrap my arms around her. I pull out of her and scoop her up into a blanket. Her eyes fall droopy, but there's a ghost of a smile on her face. I push away a few pieces of hair. "Are you okay?" I ask as her head rests onto my shoulder.

Her eyelashes flutter open and closed. "Mmm."

"Mmm, isn't good enough for me, Ava," I say as she looks at me properly. "Are you okay?"

"Yes, Jax. I'm okay. I'm more than okay. I'm perfect. I'm whole."

I cradle the side of her head and bring it into the centre of my chest. "I love you," I whisper.

"I love you, too. I love everything we've made together."

Our bond tightens as if we're now bound by a lock. Nothing can break what we have. Nothing can break *us*. We are indestructible.

52

AVA

Jaxon had an early meeting this morning. He asked if I wanted to join, and I said I'd leave the business side of his pack to him. He wants me to be more involved and grow into my position as their Luna, but I'm still learning the ropes and need more time.

Instead, I'm in the kitchen with Evan, teaching him how to cook. Sam supervises us, and it's obvious he doesn't want to be here from his glowering. I ignore him, but Evan's shoulders are slightly tense.

"How are you settling in?" I ask.

Evan hums softly. "A lot better now. I'm finding my feet, but I'm ready to learn."

My face stretches into a grin. "Good. I'm pleased, Evan."

His hand takes hold of a large knife and slices through a bell pepper. I nod at his positioning until he slices a little too hard, and the tip of the knife swipes down his fingers.

Blood trickles onto the cutting board, and he drops the knife onto the counter with a clang. He jumps back, eyes slightly horrified. "It's alright, it's alright," I say calmly as I grab his wrist and pull him over to the sink.

"Oh my Goddess," he says as he shakes. "I didn–"

I turn on the tap and let the water mix with his blood to slide down the plug hole. "It's okay." I hold his hand. "You'll heal. It's a small cut. Are you okay?"

His eyes are glued to his fingers, and after a long moment, he nods. "I think so."

Once the blood is gone, he pulls his hand away and wipes it on a clean kitchen towel. We get back to cooking, but when I peer over, I find his fingers are still bleeding. I frown at the sight. When Jaxon or Lucy get a small graze, it usually starts to heal within minutes. But Evan's...it's not healing at all.

I clear my throat, and he turns his attention to me. "Let's put a plaster on it," I say with an optimistic smile. "We don't want it to get infected."

Evan doesn't even nod. He stares at his bleeding fingers. I patch him up in no time, but his eyes are glassed over with clear devastation. My heart strains at the sight of him, and I almost draw him into a hug but stop myself.

"Ready to keep going?" I ask.

He meets my gaze, but he's reserved for a moment. "Yeah."

When Jaxon comes back from his meeting with Kayden and Sebastian, Lucy meets us in the kitchen, along with Grace and Phia. Everyone's eyes light up when they find our food sitting on the counter. Jax slides an arm around my waist and kisses my temple. "Nice job, baby," he murmurs into my hairline. "I can't wait to dig in. I'm starving."

I grin at him. "Then, eat."

We all sit around the counter, and I give Evan a small thumbs up for the help in making everyone a delicious lunch. Kayden walks towards me with a mouthful of pasta. "Holy shit," he murmurs. "You guys made this?"

"No," I deadpan. "We ordered it from the North Pole."

Kayden stops chewing, narrows his eyes, and swallows. "I was going to say it was delicious, but I take it back. It's awful."

I snort. "Yeah, right. Tell that to your empty plate."

"Because I didn't want to hurt your feelings." He pulls a fake frown.

I flip him off.

Kayden's mouth falls open. "Jaxon, did you just see that?"

"Children," Jax mutters. "I'm living with actual children."

"Okay, guys." I hear Lucy shout, and we all turn our attention towards her. She swallows down her large mouthful of pasta and holds her hands up. "Talking of children, Bash and I have some fantastic news we want to share with you."

All of us remain silent as her eyes practically glow, her smile so big it takes over most of her face. Sebastian sinks into the space beside her and places his arm around her shoulder. "Go on," Jaxon urges.

"I feel like after what has happened recently, we are all in need of good news. Something to look forward to." Lucy glances at all of us. "I'm pregnant!"

My hands fly to my mouth at the same time tears swell in my eyes. The room erupts into claps and cheers, and I can't help the sob that falls from the back of my throat. I push myself off the stool and hug them both.

"Congratulations!" I murmur with a smile. "I'm so happy for you guys."

Lucy hugs me so hard I almost snap in half. "So are we. Thank you. You're going to be an amazing auntie to our bundle of joy."

I squeeze her back at those precious words. "And you're going to be the best mother *ever*."

After everyone says their congratulations and we all toast to the new parents-to-be, I'm filled with joy, love, and contentment—so many emotions I never thought I'd be able to feel again. I'm so full and warm, I could burst.

Jaxon takes my hand and guides us into the living room alone. I sink down onto the sofa beside him as he tugs a blanket over us, my legs resting across his. We watch a movie together, but every time I glance at Jax, he's staring at the wall.

I nudge him gently, and his eyes find mine. "What's the matter?" he asks.

My head shakes. "What are you thinking about?"

"Nothing. Just work stuff."

My brows clench. "You sure? You were quiet when Lucy and Sebastian announced their news."

"Yeah." He gives my calf a squeeze. "I wanted them to have their moment."

"You're going to be an uncle. Don't you think that's exciting?"

The corner of his lip twitches. "Yeah...I guess it is."

"You guess?"

He shrugs once, which is not at all convincing.

"Do you not want kids?" I tilt my head.

"Yeah, I do. At some point. Not anytime soon. It feels like I've been with you for five minutes, Ava. The last thing I want right now is to think about someone else, other than you. I want to enjoy as much alone time as I can with you before we decide to start the next steps. If we agree to have any." He smooths his thumb across the fabric on my shin.

I chew on the inside of my lip. "Yeah," I agree. "That's true."

He takes my waist in his hands and tugs me up onto his lap. "Good because I want as much time before we have any little devils running around."

"Did you just call our unborn children 'little devils'?" I release a soft laugh.

"Sure did." He grins.

My forehead presses to his and he leaves a kiss on my lips. "Hey, so I've been thinking."

"About what?"

I clamp my teeth down on my lip as I admire his dark blue eyes. "The next time we have sex," I pull my head back slowly, "I want you to mark me. I want us to be mated."

Jaxon doesn't blink, but he holds me close to him. "Ava—"

"I know what you're going to say. I'm a human, and you don't know what will happen if you do it. But I want you to. I want to experience it. Let's see what happens and pray the mark accepts me."

"Ava, I am not taking any chances if I don't know what the consequences are."

"It's a bite."

A slash of pain etches across his face. "I could hurt you, Ava."

"Or it could be incredibly pleasurable." I lift one shoulder. "Worst comes to worst, I'll be healed by the pack doctors. But it's something I want. I trust you. I trust this world. Why would I be in it if we can't officially mate?"

Jaxon's expression warps into one of internal conflict. "I want that, baby. I want to mark you. I want to complete our mating process, but I will *never* live with myself if I hurt you or do something to you that I can't change."

"So, what?" I murmur. "We'll never be officially mated because you don't want to take that chance."

"Ava, that's not what I mean, and you know it. I want to

be marked and mated to you more than anything, but your wellbeing is the priority. That's the only reason why I'm sceptical." He laces his fingers through mine.

I sigh in defeat. "Okay."

"I'll find out more about it," he counters. "Do some research because I am not putting you at risk before knowing the outcome. I'm sorry. I know this isn't what you wanted to hear, but I don't want to take any chances without knowing the outcome."

My body sinks back into his with a nod. "I know. I'm just desperate to be closer to you and your world."

"You don't need to be a wolf to be close to this world. I promise you. You are already in this world, and you have been welcomed with wide arms," he murmurs against my head. "Being a human doesn't make you any different because we know that you're meant to be here."

"Yeah, I know. Is it greedy to want more?"

Jaxon shakes his head. "No. You deserve everything good in this world, and I won't rest until I see you have it all."

My cheeks bleed with a blush. "I already have everything I need."

"Me, too," he whispers against my jaw, trailing up to my lips. "But it's my goal to make you happy every day for the rest of my life."

"I forgot what happiness was until I met you."

He smiles, and I lean in to kiss him this time. "And you're never going to forget again."

53

AVA

Kayleigh invited me up to her university to spend some time together. As much as I love the pack, I definitely needed some time away.

Jaxon drops me off and reminds me the guards would be following discreetly for my safety. He wants to give me my own space, but I can see the fear in his eyes. He almost lost me once; he doesn't want to lose me again.

The kiss he gives me in his car is like no other. Every ounce of emotion pours from his mouth to mine. I smile against him and remind him I'll be coming home to him.

When I step out of the car and meet Kayleigh, we throw ourselves at each other and embrace for a few minutes. "Ah, I can't believe you're here," she mumbles into my hair. "It's so good to see you again. How are you?"

I nod with a smile so big my eyes water. "It's so good to see you too. I'm good. How are you?"

Kayleigh pulls back and holds my shoulders at arm's length. Her eyes roam my face, and I do the same. "I'm amazing. I can't wait to show you around campus!"

"It's nice to get out," I admit before linking my arm through hers.

"Jaxon didn't want to come?"

I shake my head. "He said he wanted to give us some girl time. He'll pick me up later."

"Well, you definitely scored with him. He's a very beautiful man," she admits, and I laugh at her statement.

"I know." I brush my hair over my shoulder. "But he's beautiful on the inside, too."

Kayleigh turns to look at me with hearts in her eyes. "Oh my gosh, you are so totally in love with him."

"Yeah. He's helped me a lot with my trauma and my recovery." I raise my shoulders. "He's been like a rock to me. Patient. Understanding. Loving. Everything I needed to face things I didn't want to. He's a saint."

Her gaze glitters as she listens to me speak. "I'm glad, Ava. You deserve happiness—always. I'm glad you've found it."

"Me, too."

We lighten up the conversation as Kayleigh takes me on a tour to see some historic educational buildings, along with the library and other facilities that make this university so incredibly breathtaking. A twang in my heart makes me frown. I missed out on this. I missed out on going to university like I always wanted.

We pause by a fountain and perch on the ledge as the sun beats down on us. "So, you go here with Danny, huh?"

She scoffs. "No. I've always wanted to come here. Danny just so happened to rock up. We don't see each other often if that's what you think. I feel like he followed me here so he could find out information about you from me, which he did. I'm sorry. I never intended to do that."

"I know, I know," I reassure her. "It's fine. I don't mind. How are your parents?"

Kayleigh's eyes drop to the pebbled floor. "They're not together anymore."

"Oh." I frown. "I'm sorry. I shouldn't–"

"No, they loved you. They treated you like their own. It's okay to bring them up. They miss you so much." Her eyes crinkle at the sides.

My chest warms. "I'd love to see them soon."

"They'd love that, too."

"Are you dating anyone right now?"

She's quiet for a long moment, and I inspect her face. There is an edge of slight discomfort at the question. "No," she whispers. "Not anymore."

"Oh, what happened?"

"I was with this guy, and he–" she struggles to find her words as she shakes her head. "He treated me like shit. I don't really want to talk about it."

I slip my arm over her shoulder and tug her towards me. "That's okay," I whisper with a squeeze of my hand. "I'm glad you're out of it if he wasn't very nice to you, Kayleigh. You deserve someone who is going to worship the ground you walk on because you are too amazing for this world."

She chokes out a laugh, and I see tears swimming in her eyes. "Sometimes it's so hard to believe when I'm constantly doubting myself and who I am. I am lost a lot of the time, and I hate it."

"Me, too," I agree and rest my head on her shoulder. "But it comes with self-love. I know it's easier said than done, but a little self-love and self-care can go a long way."

Kayleigh raises a shaky finger to her eye and wipes her tears before they fall. "Yeah," she rasps. "I kind of do this thing when I'm sad or lonely. I attach myself to the first person who gives me attention. It's toxic and completely unhealthy, but it's a way for me to cope."

"Well, you have me now. I'll come up and visit as much as I can. You can come down and visit us, too."

"Yeah." She nods with a trembling smile. "I'd like that a lot."

I clear my throat gently. "Have you ever had therapy?"

Kayleigh shakes her head. "Never had the courage to go."

"Well, a lot of people seem to think there is a stigma around therapy and it must mean you're crazy. But what's so crazy about talking through your thoughts with someone who knows how to give you realistic solutions and honest questions?" I admit. "I thought therapy was terrifying when I first started going, but now, I realise it's important to my mental health. Sometimes it's just a chat, nothing about my trauma."

She hums softly. "Maybe. I don't have the time now. University work has swamped me."

"I'm always here for a chat."

"Me, too." She turns with a smile that finally meets her eyes. "It was nice coming over to see your house and meeting Jaxon."

I nudge her shoulder. "Yeah. He loved meeting you."

"And that other guy there...Kayden? He's Jaxon's brother."

"No. They're not related. They're just like brothers. Super close," I state.

Kayleigh nods and licks her lips. I study her expression.

"You seemed to have a moment, huh?"

A flashback of the pair of them shaking hands for a second too long projects into my mind. It was a sweet moment. Kayleigh looked at him like she'd never seen a handsome man in her life.

"What?" she exclaims a little too quickly. "No."

I laugh. "It's okay. We all saw it. Whatever it was."

Kayleigh's cheeks turn red, and she stays silent for a moment. "It wasn't a moment. He probably has a girlfriend or boyfriend. No one *that* good looking is single. Honestly."

"He's single, Kayleigh."

She blinks once and stares at me. "Oh. Well. That's nice. Good for him...Come on, I didn't show you the gym!"

We both stand and start heading towards a large building with people flooding in and out. "You have a gym membership?"

"Nope. Haven't stepped foot in there once. I probably should. I'm so unfit. Two flights of stairs and I'm out of breath."

"Relatable." I chuckle.

At least my training with Jaxon has made my stamina better, and I don't feel like I'll die after running for twenty minutes. It's a work in progress.

"I wanted to enquire, but I like to inspect first," she says as we approach the doors. "I like knowing what I'm getting myself in for."

I nod in agreement. "Sure."

Once we're inside, there's a buzz of people talking in the foyer and loud music playing over a tannoy. I glance around. This is overstimulation central.

"Do you ladies need any help?" A deep voice appears next to us, and we both turn towards them.

My eyes roam his face and then his body as he leans against the wall. All his muscles flex in his tiny vest and gym shorts. The skin around his arms look like they're about to rip from how big he's built. There is a lanyard around his neck, and I presume he works here, otherwise, this conversation would be weird.

"Umm...yeah. I'm thinking about joining," Kayleigh says.

"I see, I see." He winks at her, and I find it incredibly uncomfortable. "You guys know we have personal trainers here, too?"

Kayleigh shrugs, and the guy's eyes flick to mine. The back of my neck starts to hunch, and I instantly get bad vibes. "No, but I have no idea what I'm doing in the gym." She laughs.

He nods at her, but his gaze finds mine again. "Yup. I'm one. I could, uh...teach you guys a thing or two."

When his eyes dip down my body, I grasp we're no longer talking about hiring a personal trainer. He's suggesting that we'd climb all over him like a jungle gym. My stomach churns at the realisation.

He flashes us both a million-dollar smile. "If you know what I mean."

I release a hesitant laugh. "I don't think my boyfriend would appreciate that."

"What he won't know won't hurt him." He gives me another wink.

My arm takes Kayleigh's, and I attempt to drag her away. "Yeah but when he finds out—which he will—it'll be you who is struggling to breathe through a tube in a hospital bed."

The expression on his face warps, and I turn away, taking Kayleigh with me. "That guy was weird," she comments. "Does he really think that sort of approach works?"

"For some girls, I bet it does," I exhale.

"I mean, he was kind of sexy though."

I stare at her like she's lost her mind. "But his personality makes him a zero out of ten."

"True," she sighs. "Sometimes, I like the idea of a big muscly man to throw me around a bedroom, though. That turns me on. Do you know what I mean?"

I nod before I register what I'm doing.

My cheeks heat as I think back to my own intimate moments with Jaxon. Since we started having sex, he's been incredibly gentle and loving, which I adore. But another part of me wants him to be a little rougher. The sex we have is out of this world, but now, I want passion in a different sense. But I understand why he hasn't with my past.

I trust him. That's the crucial aspect. I trust him completely.

He would never hurt me. He would never even dream of it.

But I want more between us.

I want to watch him lose control. I want to watch him fall apart. I want to watch him take order of my body. And I'll fall into an endless pit of bliss because I know I'm safe with him.

Kayleigh is still talking, and I pretend to listen while I slam up the walls of our bond so he can't hear my thoughts —if he hasn't already heard them. I press a hand to the back of my neck and take a shallow breath.

I want him to fuck me. I want him to claim me. I want him to mark me.

God, I want him to act like I'm not going to break—instead, I want to shatter into a thousand pieces of pleasure.

54

AVA

When I travel home later that afternoon, there's a huge smile on my face from how fulfilled I am. My old life might be nothing but a distant memory, but Kayleigh shines above all. She's one person I'll never be able to forget.

As the car drives through our gated community and pulls up outside Jaxon's private entrance to the house, I hop out. I'm desperate to share everything that happened today with him—because he is *my* person.

I wander through the front door and into the kitchen where the smell of food hypnotises me. I'm not even hungry as we ate a few hours ago, but it smells divine.

When I enter Jax is standing there *shirtless.* My feet halt at the sight of his muscly back. He's standing over the stove, using one hand to stir whatever he's cooking in the frying pan. I scan his skin as the muscles contract and relax with each subtle movement. My lips part, and I'm certain I start drooling.

I had no idea I had a thing for backs.

"Are you going to stand there and ogle me?" Jaxon's deep

voice makes me jump. "Or, are you going to come over here and give me a kiss?"

My face starts burning up as I walk towards him. He's not glanced over his shoulder yet, but I already know there is a shit-eating smirk on his lips.

I glide one of my hands across his bare back and press a kiss to his shoulder blade. Electric sparks shoot down my chest and into the depths of my heart when I kiss him again.

He turns, and I'm met with a grin. "Hey, baby."

"Hey." I match his smile.

His body bends, and he leaves a peck on my lips. "How was your day?"

I nod once. "It was good." I wander to the sink and fill up a cup with water. "I loved spending time alone with Kayleigh. It's like no time has passed between us."

"I'm glad." He turns back to the stove, and I get a side glance of his rock-hard abs. My eyes close for a moment to compose myself. "You okay over there?"

I snap open my gaze to his to find a glint of amusement on his expression. "Huh? Yeah. I'm good. I'm good."

"What's campus like?"

"It's super nice, big, and modern but still has historical buildings and culture. Kayleigh always wanted to go to that university, so I'm glad she got in." I take a sip of my water and place it down. "She showed me the English block and where all the parties on campus happen. Then we went to the gym, and–"

I stop speaking immediately.

The most amazing yet daring idea pops into my head. A wave of confidence crashes over me, and I have to stop myself from smirking. It's a childish move, but I'm willing to chance it.

"Oh, yeah?" Jaxon calls out to me.

My teeth clamp onto my bottom lip as I gaze out of the kitchen casually. "And there was this guy at the gym. He said he was a personal trainer."

Jaxon's eyes move to mine within milliseconds. I can see him, but I don't look at him. His jaw clenches. I try to keep composure for my petty trick—I never said I was mature.

"He said he'd be our personal trainer. He was big, you know? Like impressively big and super stron–"

I don't have time to finish my sentence because Jaxon is in front of me. He laces his fingers through the back of my hair and grips, forcing me to look at him. I shudder at the intensity in his blue gaze.

Boy. He didn't like that.

"Say that to me again. I dare you."

My lips part, and he studies the action. "He was big–"

The grip on my hair tightens, and I release the tiniest moan. My legs press together at the shockwaves that invade my nervous system. "He might have been big, but he's nothing compared to you–"

My eyes flick between his as I suck down the last breath of courage and watch his eyes morph into darkness.

"*Alpha.*"

He presses me back into the counter within a fraction of a second. I gasp as his body covers mine with possession and dominance. My neck cranks to meet his eyes, and I find myself turning sheepish yet my arousal floods out of me like a river. It's clear he senses it because his nostrils flare, and I can practically see his heart beating outside of his chest.

"You have no idea what you've got yourself in for," he grunts huskily.

Before I know it, I'm hurled over his shoulder like a sack of potatoes. I yelp out in surprise as he carries me away. My eyes are level with his bare back and then they wander down to his ass. *I'm helpless.*

Jaxon carries me upstairs without saying a single word. We enter our room, and he throws me down onto the bed, my hair sprawling out across the sheets. He stands at the foot of the bed, looking down on me with dilated eyes.

He kneels onto the mattress and leans over me. At first, he trails his lips across the skin on my neck that's hot like lava. Both his hands begin to fumble with the buttons on my summer dress. Not being able to wait any longer, he rips the dress open, and the buttons ricochet against the floor.

I release a shaky tremble as his mouth drags across the tops of my breasts—I'm completely exposed because I hate wearing bras. He nips at the skin and removes the rest of the dress from my body. Each kiss is firm and determined. Perfectly placed. I throw my head back against the bed and sigh in satisfaction.

His fingers find my underwear as he pushes them to the side and caresses my core. I moan out loud and spread my legs. I clutch onto the bed sheets when he slips a finger inside me and then another. He doesn't play around. He quickly thrusts, and my hips buckle. "Holy shit," I cry out.

My eyes close in shuddering pleasure as he eases his way out and then in. A kiss is pressed to my sternum and over my nipples that are as hard as rocks. He sucks one into his mouth at the same time he curls his fingers inside me.

The sound that comes out of my mouth isn't human.

"That feel good, baby?"

Our eyes meet, and I bite on my lip hard enough to draw blood. I nod, incapable of words that will make sense as he works his fingers inside me like magic. He tugs and sucks my nipples gently, which makes me jolt, but he holds me down.

Wetness coats my thighs as he works faster and my head is lost in the clouds. He works his way up my neck and over my jaw, where he watches me with adoration and a sprinkle of lust. His lips claim mine, and he knocks all the air out of my lungs when his tongue sweeps my mouth.

I'm on the brink when he speeds up, and I clamp down on his lip, desperate to fall over the edge. I'm building and building. I groan into the kiss—seconds away from absolute pleasure.

Then he pulls his fingers from me, and I glare at him in desperation. I hate the smirk that sits on his face. "W-wha–" I can hardly get the words out as I watch him suck on his fingers. "Jax, *please.*"

He quirks a brow in my direction as he sits back on his knees, staring down at me with misty eyes. "You think I didn't hear your little thoughts earlier today slip through our bond?"

"I used my barriers," I heave.

Jaxon releases a wicked laugh that sends shivers to my toes. "Not well enough, baby."

"What did you hear?"

"Most of it."

I throw my head back to the bed. I'm pooling with heat. My heart rattles so loud I'm sure he can hear it. He crawls over my body once more and kisses me with rough passion. "You tell me the fucking second I cross any boundaries. Do I make myself clear?"

"Yes."

"Good," he grunts against my mouth.

He flips me around so I'm face-down in the bed and slaps his hand across my ass. I moan into the sheets as the pain spreads into warmth and pleasure. My fingers curl into the duvet for leverage.

When he slips my underwear down my legs and presses his finger against my slit, I groan loudly. He pulls my hips back so I'm now on all fours with a handprint branding my ass. A liberating thrill rushes down my spine, and my core throbs in desperate need to finish.

He spanks me again and then rubs his hand across the skin with reassurance. I scream out in pure ecstasy. "Fuck, baby," he rasps. "You're so wet for me."

The spot on my ass burns but in a way that reminds me I'm alive. I don't like it; I *love* it. He's driving me crazy, and he's barely touched me. This is everything I wanted and more.

I crank my neck backwards to look at him as he discards his trousers and boxers and fists his cock. I quiver as he kneels behind me and positions himself at my entrance. For a few moments, he teases me, I try to push back in anticipation, but he tuts, and I'm met with another spank.

"Jax," I cry.

"You okay?"

My teeth sink into my lip as I nod. "Please. I need *you*."

He pushes into me, and my entire world stops. My lips part, and I exhale a deep moan of pleasure. His hand presses down on my waist, pinning me to the bed as he sinks further. He fills me until I'm full and squirming under his weight.

"Jax," I say breathlessly.

I'm already close. After being teased, I'm ready to detonate.

My eyes begin to water with how perfect he feels inside me. I listen to the groan that escapes his lips, and it's almost enough to shoot me past the finishing line. But he starts to speed up, his skin slapping against mine. His other hand pins my neck down as he rests his lips against my ear. "Is this what you wanted?"

I whimper. "Yes."

His cock fills me with each thrust, and I'm floating. Physically floating.

"I want you to come for me. Right. Now."

Those thrusts are strong and powerful. It takes seconds for me to do as he says. I come. I come so hard I don't even register the words that are falling from the back of my throat. My mind erupts with stars, and I burst.

"Good girl," he rasps. "*Good girl.*"

Pressure builds along my lash line as I gasp for breath. My body is still jolting as he continues to fuck me. "Fuck, Jax."

He slows down so I can finally suck some air into my lungs. He flips me back over and praises my body with eyes that remind me of a hungry lion. *Primal.* He wants me, and it's written all over his face.

I press my palm to the centre of his chest, feeling the warmth and hardness of his muscles. He pushes back inside me and hoists one leg over his shoulder. He presses his nose against mine and watches my facial expressions as he pounds into me with sharp and determined thrusts.

Every inch of me melts into the bed as he presses my other leg down by my knee. It gives him deeper access, and I'm ready to lose my mind entirely. His pace is slower than before but enough to make me lose my train of thought.

His hand slips up my sternum, grazing my nipples on the way. He wraps his hand loosely around the base of my throat, and I almost come there and then. My lips tremble as my walls tighten around him, eager for my next climax.

"Goddess, look at you," he rasps. "So fucking beautiful. You were made for me. All for me."

Jax growls when I moan. "Oh my God."

His hand around my throat tightens an inch, but it sends a thrill down my spine and makes my pussy throb. He looks me dead in the eye.

"Who do you belong to?"

"You."

His eyes turn impossibly darker. "I want you to say it."

"I'm yours, Jax. Only yours."

The hand around my neck is replaced with his lips. He kisses across the base of my throat as he continues to hit my g-spot with every movement of his hips. I wrap my arms around his shoulders and dig my nails into his skin. He hisses into my neck but doesn't complain.

"That's right. You're mine. *Only* mine. And I am all yours, baby. Every inch of me is yours," he grunts intensely. "We belong to each other."

I gasp when his canines lightly graze my sensitive flesh. My hands grip onto him urgently. Tears swim in my eyes as my orgasm explodes, and he plunges his teeth into my skin.

For a split second, I am in agony. My heart clenches and stops until my body bursts into endless rapture. He continues to pound into me. Everything trembles with my climax heightened. I'm certain I levitate at some point or have some out-of-body experience. I'm swarmed with all of his emotions—my head pivots as I tremble.

Jaxon starts to lick and kiss where he marked me, treasuring the bite with everything. His lips vibrate against my tender mark as he comes shortly after me. My arms drop to the bed, unable to move a muscle.

Suddenly, a gust of cold washes over me like a bucket of ice. My vision becomes hazy and Jaxon's touch starts to feel numb. He pulls himself from me before wrapping me up in a blanket and tugging me onto his chest. "Baby." His voice sounds concerned. "Your skin is boiling."

He raises a hand to my forehead and flinches from the heat. I can barely keep my eyes open. I shake my head at his words. It's like I'm neck-deep in a pile of snow. "I'm so c-cold."

"No, Ava. You're on fire," he murmurs. "Do you feel okay? Did I hurt you?"

His fingers move a piece of hair clung to my forehead. "No, I–" I whisper weakly. I can't even finish my sentence.

Jaxon kisses my forehead and holds me impossibly tighter. "Your body is most likely adjusting to my mark. I'll run you a bath."

I smile as best as I can with my eyes still shut.

"I love you," I say quietly.

He rests his forehead against mine. "I love you, too, baby."

55

JAXON

After running Ava a luke-warm bath, I perch on the edge of the tub and study her drained face. Her skin is still on fire, despite the fact she's shuddering as if we're in the Antarctic. Guilt rides my chest like a wave. I'm not sure if her body is rejecting my mark because her human body isn't strong enough to accept it. I don't want to think about that fate.

"Ava," I whisper and caress her face.

Her hand splashes into the water, and she retracts as if it's toxic. I calm her by stroking back her hair and sending as much comfort through our bond as possible. Although, I can sense a barricade.

"How are you feeling?"

Ava's eyes open, and they're lazy, her lids almost shutting again. "C-cold."

I examine her lips and move closer. The corners of her mouth are starting to fade into a light blue. Something is definitely wrong. Her body continues to shake, rippling the water aggressively. She wraps her arms around her legs in an attempt to keep warm.

My hands reach into the bath, and I pull her out. The bath isn't working. Her wet hair rests against my bare chest as I wrap her in a towel and rub up and down her arms.

Gemma, can you come up to my bedroom? Something is wrong with Ava. I need her to be checked over.

Of course, Alpha. I'll be up right away.

I carry my mate back to our room and dry the rest of her body before sliding an oversized T-shirt over her head and loose pants on her bottoms. "Ava." I cup her face, but her head rolls. "Baby, I need you to tell me what's wrong."

Ava's pain doesn't flicker in my body. I'm numb to it, and I don't understand why. She's burning up, but I feel *nothing*. I release a frustrated sigh.

"Nothing's wrong," she says breathlessly. "Just tired. So tired. And cold."

I frown at the same time there's a knock at the door. "Come in," I shout.

Gemma steps inside and glances over at Ava. "Alpha. What's the matter with Ava?"

"I marked her," I admit. "She's not accepting it. Her body is hot, but she keeps telling me she's cold. I did my research. It said humans should heal like wolves do, but it'll take longer. I never expected for this to happen. If I knew, I would never of–"

Gemma offers me a smile. "Let me take a look at her."

I stand back while she does everything she can. Fuck. I shouldn't have done it. I shouldn't have let my possessiveness get the better of me. No matter how pretty her mark looks on her neck, it's not worth her wellbeing.

"She's weak," she states slowly. "She needs rest and water. Don't cuddle her up in blankets, even if she says she's cold. It's like she's got a fever, and we need to make sure she doesn't overheat."

My eyes flick between the doctor's. "What if her body is rejecting it?"

"I'm not sure, Jaxon. I haven't dealt with something like this before. But from what I've heard, a rejection isn't always the end result. With time, you can try again, and her body might accept."

I almost scoff. There is no way I'm chancing this again. What if it kills her next time? My heart strains at the morbid thought. I blink it away in an instant.

"But that might not be the case. Keep a close eye on her. I'm sure it's her human body getting used to the mark. The saliva from your canines is flooding her bloodstream. Her body may be reacting in a way to protect herself, but eventually, her body may end up accepting the mark," she states, and I listen to her words carefully. "If you're concerned, please don't hesitate to mindlink."

I nod despite being on edge. "Alright. Thank you, Gemma. I appreciate it."

When she leaves, I lay down next to Ava and delicately brush my fingers across her arm. I listen to her hoarse breathing and pray when she wakes up, her body has accepted my mark.

∼

THE NEXT MORNING, Ava is covered in sweat from head to toe. Strands of dark hair clung to her beading face and her lips part, trying to draw in air. I didn't sleep. I couldn't. I watched her all night in case anything happened. But she slept like a rock.

I admire the mark on her neck once more, but it doesn't quite fill me with the delight I expected. The red blotches around her skin look sore and unsettled. It churns my stomach.

It was too soon. I shouldn't have done it at all.

Fuck.

Terror settles in my gut like a punch. I hear her grunt beside me as she rests in our bed. Her arms shiver harshly, but her eyes are clamped shut. A tear rolls down her cheek. Then another. And another.

"Baby?" I whisper, but she doesn't react to my voice.

She grits her teeth at the same time her eyes squeeze shut. I hear the sounds of screams in my mind, and I flinch. I scoop her up in my arms and rush down the stairs.

Gemma. Something is happening to Ava.

I take her to the infirmary without a second thought and place her down on an empty bed, but her head rolls. "Ava. *Ava.* Look at me."

Her eyes don't even twitch.

Gemma rushes over behind me and presses a hand to her forehead. Ava's body vibrates aggressively before she opens her mouth and releases a blood-curdling scream.

A slash of pain hits me square in the chest, and I clench my jaw in an attempt to ignore it. My eyes water at the sight of her thrashing against the bedsheets, her cries becoming louder by the second. The distress on her face shatters my soul into pieces.

"We need to get her outside!" Gemma exclaims. I stare at her, deeply confused. "She needs fresh air. She's burning up."

My arms slide around her body as I take us outside. She squirms against me, and I push all of my calming abilities into her body, but nothing works.

I'm right here. Okay? I've got you.

Gemma guides us towards the grass, and I kneel with her still in my arms. She jerks to one side and then another until she bursts through my strong hold and rolls onto the grass.

Holy fuck. She rattles. I've never seen a body react like this.

I rush to her side in a panic. "Leave her," Gemma calls out.

My head turns to her with weary eyes. I'm not going to leave my mate when she's having a seizure.

Lucy appears beside us. "Shit. What's happening?"

"Do something, Gemma," I say through gritted teeth. "Use a sedative. *Something*. She's going to hurt herself."

"Wait." She holds up a hand.

I groan in frustration. "For what? She's hurting!"

My gaze lands on my mate's strained face, and I try to cuddle her into my chest with no support. Her body doesn't stop moving. Those tears don't halt for a second, and I'm breaking all over again. No. I need to do something.

Gemma is right beside me and yanks me back. "I said leave her!"

I open my mouth to shout back, but the mark I left on Ava's neck last night starts burning red and bright until it's glowing like gold. I shield my eyes from the unexpected flash—we all do.

Another deafening scream leaves Ava's mouth. When I glance at her, I watch as her neck snaps at an angle that makes my heart slam into my chest. Her arm bends at an awkward angle and then her legs and her stomach. A groan mixed with a scream fills the air, and birds start flying from the trees.

All of her clothes begin to shred onto the floor, and she shifts into the most beautiful white wolf I have ever seen. Her fur is lined with gold strands that shine against the sunlight. I stare in shock. My wolf howls at me to move closer. He spins and claws at my insides.

But I can't. All I can do is stare in awe and satisfaction.

A tingling sensation shoots through my body when Ava's wolf opens her eyes. They're dark yet ringed with a deep honey colour that glows when she looks right at me. She stands boldly on her four paws and takes a moment to look down at them, admiring in astonishment.

She's a wolf. She's been a wolf this entire time.

Ava, I shoot to her mind. My knees almost snap at the look she gives me.

Perfect. She's beyond perfect. She's mine.

I move towards her and kneel in front of my Luna. My fingers slide through her fur as she nuzzles her face into mine. Her scent of warm chestnut and vanilla infiltrates my veins, and I gladly inhale. It's stronger than ever. My eyes almost roll behind my lids at the way it makes me tremble.

Hey. Her voice is quiet.

I crack a smile. *Hey.*

Guess what?

Ava's fur is so damn soft I can't get enough. My fingers massage through her skin, and she licks my chin. I release a thick breath of gratification. I never knew my heart could feel this full.

What?

I stare into those honey eyes and realise that she's completely stolen my heart and run away with it.

I'm a werewolf.

A large grin spreads across my face. *No shit, baby. Not just any werewolf. A badass white wolf with golden features. Beautiful. So fucking beautiful.*

She presses her soft forehead against mine, and the strands of her fur tickle, but I don't move. I savour this moment. My eyes close at the same time hers do. My wolf howls in approval and acceptance.

I'm so happy, she whispers through my mind.

Our bond connects on a level I never knew it could reach. Heights beyond my belief, but I welcome all of it with wide arms because it's *ours,* and it's perfect.

56

AVA

My ankles are submerged in mild water. The bottom of the lake is clear, and fish swim around my feet. I release a soft chuckle as they tickle my skin. My head tilts towards the sunset as it sits perfectly along the horizon.

I open my lungs and take down the fresh air. A presence behind me makes me tingle, but I'm not afraid. My head looks over my shoulder to be met with luminous eyes and long white hair. I relax.

"Ava." She reaches out to touch my cheek.

My eyes close at the sensation that washes over my skin.

I remember her from my dream before. She came back.

"You're here."

When I open my eyes, she nods, and I study the pretty markings on her face. A triangle with circles glimmer across her forehead, and her eyelashes are a metallic blue. She takes my face between her warm hands, and I exhale a breath of relief.

"Do not forget your power."

I frown. "What power?"

"Do not forget the strength inside your soul."

"What do you mean?"

She offers me a sweet smile. "I would never want you to forget that you are a force to be reckoned with, Ava."

"I'm trying. I've got a lot to learn," I admit.

"That may be true." She smooths her thumb across my cheek. *"But you are surrounded by people who will go to the ends of this universe to support you."*

My lips curl. "I know."

"You might feel at one with your body, but it's not the first time you've met."

My brows crease. "Met who...My wolf?" All she does is nod, and I stare back at her with uncertainty. "I don't remember."

"No. But you will."

"Okay."

"You might look different to the rest, but this is my blessing to you."

My lips purse. "My blessing?"

"An apology for not helping sooner. I know this won't make up for anything, but now your heart of gold will shine from the inside out. You possess your own strength, but this will only intensify it."

I stare at the beautiful woman in wonder.

"This is your home now. This has always been your home. I'm happy to see you thriving in the way you always should have been. I wish to take away your past pain, but I would never meddle with the healing you've given to yourself. You are the strongest wolf I know. Even if you don't believe it, you will soon. I'll make sure of it." Her misty eyes twinkle at me. *"Now, go and live. This life will cherish you."*

The second her hands leave my face, the sky transforms into a show of shooting stars. I take it all in. My mouth falls open in surprise. I smile up at the universe and take in her words.

This life will cherish me in the same way I'll cherish this second chance at living.

SECOND CHANCE MATES

A GASP LEAVES my lips as I sit up. The bedsheets fall around my waist, and I press a hand to my pounding chest. Jaxon stirs beside me. He rubs his eyes as I sink back into the headboard. "What's the matter?" His voice is groggy but alarmed. "Nightmare?"

I shake my head and calm my rapid heartbeat. "Something else."

His eyes roam my face carefully before his arm slings around my shoulder and brings me towards him. "You're safe," he whispers against my head. "With me."

My eyes close, and I picture her face. I play back everything she said to me. *Don't forget. Don't forget.* I snap my gaze open as something tightens around my throat.

"Ava—"

"I remember," I blurt.

"Remember what?"

My eyes flick over the duvet in the darkness as I wrack my brain for all the details of *that* day. The reason the other wolves were slaughtered was because of...me. I turn to Jaxon and he stares back at me with a concerned expression.

"What do you remember?" his fingers stroke my arm.

"The night with Julia. When they took me back to the warehouse. She was taunting me about you, saying things to get under my skin, and I snapped. I shifted. I killed those wolves." I clap a hand over my mouth, and my stomach clenches. "Oh, God. *I* killed those wolves."

Jaxon tugs me onto his lap as soon as he senses my panic brewing. "Breathe," he states. "Breathe, Ava."

I inhale sharply as harsh emotion slashes at my sternum. I accept his comfort through the bond. I'm a murderer. I murdered people.

"Baby." He brushes back my hair. "You did all you could to survive. You did what you did to protect yourself. I know this might be a bittersweet moment, but I am so proud of you for taking out those wolves who hurt you."

My lungs suck in air, and I shake my head. "I know they were bad people, but they were still people. I took away their lives."

He offers me a soft, sympathetic smile. "It's not easy to kill, but when we're brought into these impossible situations, we have to. I remember the first time I killed another wolf, it didn't feel good, but I knew it had to be done. The wolves I kill now deserve to be killed, and I don't let guilt swarm me."

"It's hard to accept," I hiccup. "I literally have their blood on my hands, even if they deserved to die."

Jaxon kisses my cheek softly. "Don't let any guilt sit with you, Ava. You killed them so you could get out of there and get to safety. It was a natural instinct from you and your wolf. It's who we are, Ava. We're natural born killers, and I know that's probably not what you want to hear, but it's the truth, and it'll never change."

I take in his words for a long moment before nodding. "Yeah," I rasp. "I guess you're right. I'm new to this world. For you guys, this is probably child's play."

"It gets easier. I promise."

We lay back down in bed, and I rest my head on his chest. "I can't believe I forgot. I've been a werewolf and shifted, and I still didn't know."

"You lost a lot of blood and were in a coma for a few days, Ava. Don't beat yourself up for not remembering. I think in a way, your memories come back to you when you're ready to face them," he admits, and I think about that for a second.

He might be right. *He's always right.*

I stay silent as he wraps me up in his strong arms. "Sleep, baby. It's still early. We can talk about this in the morning."

My eyes flutter shut, and I inhale the scent wafting from his neck. I smile at the way it invades my bloodstream. My senses have heightened in ways I couldn't even imagine.

∼

LATER THAT DAY, I find myself in the library with Evan and Sam close behind him, looking as bored as ever. I reach up to find books on werewolf ancestry because I feel like I'm missing a piece of my history. My parents abandoned me when I was a baby, and now I don't even know who I am.

"Is it true your wolf has gold lining in its fur?" Evan asks as he stands up on one of the ladders.

I quirk a brow at him. "Gossip travels fast, huh?"

"Oh. Is it a rumour?"

My head shakes. "No. I'm a white wolf with gold in my fur. Yes. But I'm not entirely sure what it means. That's what I'm trying to find out. I know nothing about my parents or where I'm from."

Evan steps down from the ladder and meets me at one of the mahogany tables. "Does it matter where you're from? You've found peace and your family here. I get that you don't truly understand your heritage, but at the same time, you can make your own history."

"I guess I'd like to know," I admit. "It's not super important right now, but it feels like I'm missing out on knowing the truth. But at the same time, they left me in the human world when I needed to be guided, so they suck."

He perches beside me and laughs. "I get that. I couldn't

give a shit about my past. I only want the future and to look ahead."

Sam scoffs behind him, and we both shoot him a glare. "Me, too," I agree. "I'm curious, that's all. What about white wolves? What is their ancestry like?"

"White wolves aren't rare. There are thousands of white wolves across the country. But I don't know any wolves that are infused with gold." He gives me an impressive smirk. "That's what's interesting."

I pull the book away from my eyes and stare at the wall.

Your heart of gold will shine from the inside out.

This is my blessing to you

I blink once, twice. Then a smile tugs at the corner of my mouth.

I'm invaded with reassurance. She thinks I blame her, but I don't. I'm relieved she can make her presence known. That I could come face to face with the Goddess that mated me to Jaxon.

"What?" Evan pulls back suspiciously.

"Nothing."

The door to the library opens, and I glance over at my mate. I smile in his direction as he studies the books spread across the table. "There you guys are. What are you doing?"

"Just some reading," I state simply. "Research."

"Research?" his brow quirks.

Evan gives me a soft smile before leaving with Sam. I stand from the chair and put the books away. "Yeah. Reading on how to be the perfect Luna."

A hand wraps around my waist and tugs me backwards. I release a shriek before laughing. "Don't need to do that. You are already perfect."

My face heats. "Well, it's a little biassed coming from you."

"Nope." He buries his face into my neck and licks my mark. "I state facts."

I shudder and push back into him. It shines gold to this day. The best gift anyone could ever give me. "I'm intrigued about my heritage, I have to admit."

"Of course you are." He pulls back. "Anyone would be. You want to find out more information about it?"

I'm nodding before he finishes his question. "I think it'll help me come to terms with everything a little more."

"Then, we'll find out whatever you want."

My lips curl into a smile as I stare up at Jaxon. It's taken me a while to come to terms with becoming their Luna, but now, I want nothing more. "Remember when we were talking about a coronation? Well, I want to have one. I want it to be official."

Jaxon stops and turns me around to face him. "Baby, I want to put you on my throne and call you my queen."

"I'm being serious." I swat at his shoulder playfully.

"So am I."

"We don't have thrones here."

"Well, we can buy one. Next-day delivery. Sorted."

A small laugh passes my lips as I lean up to wrap my arms around his neck. "I want to officially be the pack's Luna. I want a big party. I want celebrations. I want stupidly long speeches. I want all of us to come together."

Jaxon's hands slip down my waist. "I think we can arrange that."

"I also want to go for a run. Just us. Our wolves."

His eyes darken as his fingers knead into my skin. "Goddess. *Yes.*"

"And–"

"Go on." He leans in.

I lick my bottom lip as fire roars in my soul. "I want to mark you tonight."

"Fuck," he rasps and presses his mouth to mine. "Yes. *Yes.* To all of it. You can have anything you want, baby. It's all yours."

A victorious grin stretches across my face. "I want to make you mine as much as I am yours."

Jaxon grunts and leans down under my legs to hoist me up, my legs clinging to his waist. He pushes me back into the shelves. "I've been yours since the day I was born, Ava White. Never forget that."

When he lays his mouth over mine I melt into his touch. I won't forget it.

We are *made* for each other.

The End

THANK YOU FOR READING

If you enjoyed reading Second Chance Mates, I'd greatly appreciate it if you left a review on Goodreads and Amazon.

You can find future updates on book 2 in the Fated Souls Series over on my Instagram at savannaroseauthor. Don't miss out!

ACKNOWLEDGMENTS

Firstly, I want to thank everyone who has been on this journey with me over the last six years. Jaxon and Ava have been in my head for so long, and I'm so grateful for each and everyone of you who have been here from the start. Without you I wouldn't be able to publish this book. So thank you! I'll never forget your kindness and patience.

To G, my best friend, my motivator. I don't think this book would be here without you. Thank you for always pushing me and helping me get back up when I have my bad days. My number one cheerleader. Thank you for listening to my endless rants, story ideas, and always being so enthusiastic and invested. I love you so much.

My parents, thank you for always supporting me pursuing my dreams—you've never doubted my abilities. Thanks for the endless bacon sandwiches for writing fuel.

To all my lovely best friends from home who always ask me about my writing journey, and when you can read my book as I've kept my identity a secret this long. Well guys, here it is! I hope you enjoyed it. There are too many of you to list, but you know who you are. You all hold such a special place in my heart.

To my beta readers, Josie, Jessi, Tylar, and Kat. Thank you for helping me shape this book into the best version it can be. I'm extremely grateful for you all. I'm blessed that the world has brought us together.

E, thank you for letting me ask you ten thousand questions a day about how to publish a book. You have truly been my anchor. I'm so grateful to have met you. I adore you the most!

Kate, thank goodness I met you at that party and chewed your ear off about writing. I asked if you wanted to read over my manuscript and you jumped at the chance. I'm so grateful for your time and your suggestions. I can't wait to see you thrive next!

Kirsty, thank you for your incredible skills in editing! This book definitely needed your magical touch. Thank you for believing in me.

Trinah, thank you for this beautiful cover. To this day I still cannot stop staring at it.

And lastly, thank you to all of my readers. I wouldn't be here without you and I owe it all to you. I can't believe I can finally say I'm a published author. Eek.

ABOUT THE AUTHOR

Savanna Rose is a paranormal romance author from London, England, who loves to write about strong women and swoony men.

When she's not creating one hundred new book ideas, she is either enjoying life with her boyfriend, reading anything with spice, hitting the dance floor with her friends, or sipping on a well deserved Aperol Spritz.

Instagram/Tik Tok: savannaroseauthor
Goodreads: Savanna Rose

Printed in Great Britain
by Amazon